LAND

MW00882631

Book Two of

IMMORTALITY AND CHAOS
(epic fantasy series)
Wreckers Gate: Book One
Landsend Plateau: Book Two
Guardians Watch: Book Three
Hunger's Reach: Book Four
Oblivion's Grasp: Book Five

ALSO BY ERIC T KNIGHT

CHAOS AND RETRIBUTION
(sequel to Immortality and Chaos)
Stone Bound: Book One
Sky Touched: Book Two
Sea Born: Book Three
(BOOK 4 SPRING OF 2018)

THE ACTION-ADVENTURE-COMEDY SERIES
Lone Wolf Howls

THE ACTION THRILLER
WATCHING THE END OF THE WORLD

All books available at Amazon.com

Follow me at:
ericTknight.com

LANDSEND PLATEAU
Book Two of
Immortality and Chaos
by
Eric T Knight

ISBN-13: 978-1985754164
ISBN-10: 1985754169

Author's Note:
To aid in pronunciation, important names and terms in this story are spelled
phonetically in the glossary at the end of the story.

FOR MOM
MY FIRST FAN

PROLOGUE

The Guardian known as Kasai stood waiting at the mouth of the cave. It was night and the moon hung bright in the sky, showing the sharp gash of the thing's mouth and the faint slits of its nose.

A figure came walking up the trail that led to the cave. It was a sharp blade of a man, with a hatchet face and cold eyes.

The man walked up to Kasai without hesitation and bowed before the Guardian. "I am Achsiel," he said. "I have answered the call."

Kasai took Achsiel's face in its hands and turned it upwards. Its fingers gripped the sides of his head, while its thumbs hung poised inches from his eyes.

Then a single, red-rimmed eye opened in the center of its forehead.

At the same instant, gray flames burst from its thumbs.

"Are you afraid?" it asked him in a voice that sounded like it came from the bottom of a deep pit.

"For a hundred and fifty-four generations my line has been faithful," he answered. "I do not waver now."

"Are you *afraid*?"

The gray flames were reflected in the man's eyes. He blinked. Finally, he said, "Yes."

"Good," Kasai said, and pressed its thumbs to his eyes.

Achsiel screamed and writhed in its grasp but it did not let him go. Then the flames flickered and died out and it released him.

Achsiel staggered backward. Where his eyes had been were only ruined, blackened holes. The skin around the empty sockets was blistered.

"The pain will never leave," Kasai said.

Shaking, Achsiel stood upright and faced Kasai.

"I have blinded you to mortal sight. Now you see as I do and I see through you," Kasai said, placing one hand on the man's head for a

1

moment, then releasing him. "Thus do I name you the first of my blinded ones."

Achsiel raised his head. "Twenty times this would I endure for my faith."

"Come." Kasai led the way into the cave and Achsiel followed.

The cave became a tunnel that led down at a steep angle. The tunnel was not natural. It had been Shaped eons before by two of those humans called gods, at the height of yet another of the seemingly-endless wars waged between those beings. They sought greater power. They found it and attempted to Shape it.

One was destroyed, the other nearly so.

None had entered this tunnel since then.

The blackness was absolute but neither Guardian nor follower wavered or stumbled. At one point the tunnel was choked with fallen stone. Kasai placed its hands on the stone. The stone glowed, then melted like wax, clearing the way. They continued on.

Straight as an arrow in flight the tunnel continued down and down, the hours broken only by those times when the tunnel had to be cleared in order to continue on.

Finally, a purplish glow in the distance.

The tunnel ended at a translucent wall. The purple light flickered from beyond it, casting grotesque shadows behind them.

As if it were no more than soft clay, Kasai scooped a double-handful of stone from the wall of the tunnel, then formed it into a crude pot and set it aside.

"Come here," it said to Achsiel. With a clawed finger it opened a deep cut on the man's forehead. The man did not flinch. Blood welled forth.

Kasai closed one long-fingered hand on the back of the man's head and then pressed his face against the translucent wall. When the man's blood contacted the wall it was immediately absorbed.

The area that had absorbed the blood began to soften.

"They come," Kasai said.

On the other side darting silvery shapes appeared, all voracious mouths and sharp teeth, each about the size of a man's hand.

Blood was still flowing down Achsiel's face. Kasai held the mouth of the stone pot to his face, catching some of the blood in it. Then it held the pot up against the softened area of the wall.

Drawn by the blood, the silvery creatures clustered up against the wall, trying to get through. After a minute the wall had weakened enough that one was able to slip through. In rapid succession a half dozen more followed.

Quickly, Kasai pinched the mouth of the stone pot shut, sealing them inside. Then it wiped away the remaining blood from the wall and scooped up more stone from the tunnel wall to seal over the weak spot.

Guardian and follower returned the way they had come. When they were once again outside, Kasai handed the stone pot to Achsiel.

"Take the *ingerlings* to the Plateau, to the place known as the Godstooth, and release them there."

"What shall I do with those I encounter on the way?"

"Give them the choice to follow as you do. If they choose correctly, mark them that I may know them."

"And those who choose incorrectly?"

"Burn them."

Achsiel bowed and disappeared into the coming dawn.

CHAPTER 1

Shortly after leaving the Haven, Netra stopped by a mesquite tree. Tied up in the lower branches was a small bundle of clothes, the ones she wore when she went on her forays. She ducked out of her bulky robe and pulled on the sturdy pants and the shirt. Behind the mesquite tree was a short cliff that dropped into a narrow slot canyon. She walked to the edge and threw her robe into its depths.

West of the Haven a long, tall ridge reached out from the mountains, its sides steep and dotted with cholla cactus and loose rock. She followed a game trail up its face, walking hard, feeling the sweat start under her shirt, the straps of the pack digging into her shoulders. She saw a gray fox slip across the trail on its way home for the daylight hours. Birds flitted amongst the naked green limbs of the palo verde trees and gradually a line of light appeared far in the east.

At the top she stopped and looked back. The Haven was just visible, nestled between two hills. From here it was beautiful and perfect. There were no cracks in the stone walls, no broken windows replaced with wood planks. No troubles, no fears, no worries. By now they would be up and all of them would know she was gone. The unsteadiness came on her again and she swallowed hard against the sudden doubts that flitted inside her like the morning birds in the trees.

Did my mother stand in this very place? she wondered. Did she stand here and look back on the life she had lost, the child she had left behind? Did she cry for me?

She turned away and plunged down the other side.

She walked hard that day and was glad she had broken her fast the night before and eaten her fill, glad she had filled her pack with as much food as she could carry. She kept an eye out for anything she could scrounge as she walked, but the pickings were sparse, as she had known they would be. Still, she managed to find a few handfuls

of jojoba nuts which
the night there was
of the fruit were re
with her knife and
over a small fire,
staring at the sky.
day long she'd s
homes, nothing
person in the w

When she
clattering nois
down at the r
and wondere
She'd meant

She used
sign from Xochitl. But
that happened. Wasn't it far more likely

In the afternoon she felt a faint un
of some far-off scent just barely the
several times and looked into
causing it, hoping that it was n
creature. It returned again a
tried to take hold of it and
her *sonkrill* she would
take the *sonkrill* from
things were for Ten
Mostly she tri
breaking into
she was ru
didn't kn
things
mindl
ate

She was no longer a Tender. She had broken
sacred vow. She had killed a person, another Tender even. How
times had she relived that moment in Nelton? Shoving Tara in front of
Gulagh's attack, the black, toothy thing striking her in the back, the
veins in her neck and face turning black as she fell dead.

Whatever her *sonkrill* had symbolized no longer applied to her.

She started to throw it into the darkness, but found she couldn't
and grudgingly slipped it back into her pack. Some ties were too
strong.

The elevation began to increase the next day as she walked, the
land gradually rising, the sharp ridges and narrow washes flattening
out at the same time. The creosote bushes faded and disappeared
altogether and sagebrush began to appear, along with increasing
numbers of a type of agave she had never seen before. Some of the
agave plants were as tall as she was, no leaves, no limbs, no trunk,
only a bristle of stout, waxy green shoots stretching out from a
common center. Each shoot ended in a sharp spike as long as her
hand, and the sides were lined with hard, curved thorns. She saw one
lying on its side, dead, a long shoot like a lance grown up from the
center in a single slender trunk that ended in a burst of tiny limbs and
seed pods. The plants bloomed once and then died, apparently. She
looked at it and felt her sadness grow stronger.

...ease stir within her, like a whiff
...re. It bothered her and she stopped
...the distance, wondering what was
...ot a Guardian or some other monstrous
...d again but always faded away when she
...she thought more than once that if she held
...be able to trace it. But she made no move to
...her pack, nor did she try to go *beyond.* Such
...ders, and she was no longer one.
...ed to just keep walking as quickly as she could, even
...trot a few times when the going was easy. Whether
...ning away from something or towards something she
...w and didn't speculate on. Her thoughts were dangerous
...nd she avoided them as much as she could, preferring the
...essness of action. She did not even stop completely when she
...some food around midday, but simply ate as she walked. When
...e did stop she could feel the ghosts catching up to her, asking her
with their hollow voices where she was going, what she was doing, if
she wasn't afraid.

She *was* afraid. She couldn't deny that, not even to herself. Every
step took her further from everything she had ever known. Ahead
were only strangers. Even the land, the plants and the animals were
changing. She walked into the unknown and she did not even know
who she was. The terrain inside her was more alien than the land
around her. But if she kept moving, if she didn't slow down for too
long, she could manage it; it wouldn't control her or make her turn
back. When the clamor inside her seemed too much she thought of her
mother, Shakre, and imagined her walking this same route twenty
years before. Did she stop under this very tree? she wondered. Did
she lean against this rock and wipe the sweat from her forehead?
Almost she felt she could see her with her mind's eye, an older
version of herself, maybe chased by the same demons.

And she imagined finding her, walking into some nameless
village and seeing her coming out of a home. Or in some tiny
farmhouse tucked back in the hills. She imagined her mother looking
up, catching her eye and seeing the spark of sudden recognition. But
she did not try to imagine further than that. Too much uncertainty
waited there as well. It was enough that she was moving closer to her
with every step. She would have to wait and let the rest of it work
itself out.

The nights were the hardest, when it grew too dark to continue on, when she had to give in to her body's demands for rest. Then the shadows crowded close to her and she shrank until she was so small she could not be seen. Sleep was poor or nonexistent and she tossed and turned, unable to find a quiet space. More than once she started up from a fitful sleep and called out to Xochitl before she remembered herself and bit off her pleas. Why call out to what might not even be there at all, when any answer might only be her own need surfacing, tricking her into believing? And if Xochitl was there, would she not just turn away in anger from this fallen daughter of hers? Either way, Netra vowed not to pray to her.

For hours she lay in the darkness wondering what she still believed in. Was Xochitl really what she'd been raised to believe, the creator of life, first among the gods? Was she a god at all? Was there even such a thing as a god? According to Dorn, *god* was only a word trying to capture something people didn't understand. He'd told her to forget about them.

But without a god to turn to, what did she have left? Where would she draw strength and hope?

Several days after leaving the Haven she came across a wide swath of dead and dying plants. She had circled around the west end of the Firkath Mountains by then and climbed even higher, so that they did not loom nearly as large as they did at home. She seemed to be on the edge of a high, flat valley that stretched off to the north and the west. Sagebrush had given way to knee-high grasses and small thickets of mountain lilac, short, bushy trees with thick, dark green leaves and smooth branches. Far to the west was a faint purple line of hump-backed mountains, like nameless behemoths heaving themselves up from the depths of the earth. In the north, not as far but still some days away, was a vast mountain range whose top was wreathed in clouds.

She stopped at the edge of the dead swath and looked at it, confused. It was about fifty yards long and perhaps ten wide, an irregular slash, as if a huge hand had reached down out of the sky and dragged a finger across the land. All the grasses within it had turned gray. What could cause such a thing?

Netra concentrated, listening for the Song radiated by the plants. It wasn't easy for her. PlantSong was different than the Song from animals and people. It was much subtler, much slower.

There it was. She closed her eyes, listening deeper. It was faint and fading fast, but she could just make out a dull buzzing sound mixed in with the normal melody.

She backed away quickly, her eyes going wide. She'd heard that sound before, when she and Siena and Dorn were standing outside the doomed town of Critnell.

This had been caused by one of those diseased yellow flows of Song. The spot on her arm where she'd been touched by one of those yellow flows—the night Jolene used the dream powder—throbbed suddenly, and her hand went to it.

She turned away from the dead swath and continued on, troubled. It struck her then that nothing that happened to her mattered. For the past few days she had been completely caught up in her own fears and hurts, had forgotten the hurts in the larger world around her. But just because she lost her faith and left her family did not mean that the Circle ceased to turn. Melekath was still freeing himself. His Guardians were still killing people. The poison that infected the flows of LifeSong was still spreading.

She felt very selfish and small then, so lost in her own troubles that she had lost sight of suffering that dwarfed hers. How did what she had been through compare to any of this? She was still alive; she had not been struck dead by a plague that appeared from the very ground and killed the entire village. She wondered what her mother would say about the spreading poison. Would Shakre, too, think it was Melekath, or would she have another explanation? Was she trying to do anything to stop it? Was there anything that could be done?

Several days later she came upon a farm. It was late afternoon. She was still crossing the long, grassy valley, but she was in an area of low hills covered with cedar and scrub pine. Lost somewhere inside herself, she didn't notice the farmhouse until she was right on top of it. She looked up and there it was, a squat thing made of gnarled cedar logs and packed earth. A simple barn stood awkwardly nearby.

A woman stood out front, washing clothes in a tub, and she looked up and called out a greeting. Netra lifted her hand in response, surprised, not ready for this. Not ready either for the wave of loneliness that struck her low down and hard. She would just fill her water skins, she told herself. That was all. Then she would move on.

The woman was already approaching, her gait determined, a smile lighting her face. She was nearly as tall as Netra, but older and thicker. A few strands of brown hair had escaped from under the scarf tied around her head and her hands and forearms were red from the wash water.

"Could I trouble you for some water?" Netra asked.

"Of course you may," she said, taking hold of Netra's arm and drawing her towards the house. Her hands were roughened by work, but their touch was soft. "We are always happy to help a traveler in need."

A rough well had been dug behind the house and the woman drew a bucket from its depths then watched as Netra filled her water skins, her eyes traveling over her closely. Netra was suddenly aware of how she must look. She was dressed in what were, essentially, men's clothes. The few times she had come across other people while wearing them she had hidden until they went by, not wanting anyone to see her this way. On top of that she had not washed her hands or her face since she left the Haven, hadn't thought to so much as brush her hair and when she reached for her braid self-consciously it seemed as lank and dirty as an old rope, leaves and twigs stuck in it.

All that she felt must have been written on her face because the woman smiled again and said, "A day with my three boys and the farm chores and I feel the same, believe me. Help yourself to more water if you're of a mind to do some scrubbing. There's something that passes for soap on that flat stone there."

Just then the back door of the house opened and three boys tumbled out, all yelling at once. They saw Netra and skidded to a halt, all going quiet, staring at her with round eyes. The oldest was probably ten, the youngest little more than a toddler.

"Don't just stand there with your lip brushing the ground, Jahn," the woman said. "We've got a guest for dinner. Get the axe and butcher me that old rooster." Then she assigned the middle one to bring in wood for the stove and picked up the littlest one, pulling back his diaper and peering in.

"Oh, no," Netra said, suddenly realizing what was happening. "I couldn't...I mean, I have to be—"

"It's too late," a voice said from behind her.

Netra spun around. A man stood there. He was slim and wiry, his forearms corded with muscle from years of hard work, a shapeless hat on his head. He held up his hands. One of his fingers was missing.

9

"Didn't mean to startle you, miss. I just meant to say that once Grila makes up her mind about something, it's too late for the rest of us to do anything about it. Best to just go along. Unless there was somewhere else you had to be tonight?"

"No," Netra stammered, feeling a flush rising in her cheeks. She suddenly didn't know what to say or do. Embarrassment and gratitude tangled up inside her. "I would be glad to stay, I really would." She wondered when she had last meant anything so fervently as she did those words. The world seemed very big and empty.

"Good, then." He came forward and stuck out a work-scarred hand. "I'm Ilan. The trembling beauty over there is my wife, Grila, and standing there waiting for extra chores are the boys." At these words the boys' paralysis broke and with a communal whoop they burst into action once again, the oldest heading for the barn, the middle around the edge of the house, while the youngest struggled in his mother's arms until she let him down and he ran after the others.

"I'm Netra."

"Well met, Netra." He turned to his wife. "I may be a bit late for dinner. There's one of the spring shatren calves down by the drop off. I'm going to put it on a travois and bring it back to the barn, see if I can't do something for it."

Grila's eyebrows drew together in a worried frown and Netra suddenly realized how poor these people were, what a sacrifice killing a chicken was. And she didn't even eat meat. Then Grila caught her looking at her and the woman's smile returned. "Don't be too late, then, or the bird will be naught but bones when you return. The boys eat like wild dogs and this poor thing looks a mite hungry herself."

Ilan gave a shrill whistle and a horse stuck its head up from where it had been grazing behind a dilapidated wagon. Ilan whistled again and it trotted over to him, nuzzling at his shoulder. He led it into the barn and Netra turned to Grila, not sure how to say what she needed to say. She had never dealt with people outside the Haven much.

"There's no need, about the chicken, I mean," she said. She wanted to tell her she didn't eat meat, that she couldn't, then realized that she didn't want to explain why, didn't want to seem different. For once she wanted to just be an ordinary person like everyone else. She didn't want to be a woman from an order that no one liked, even if she wasn't really one anymore. "I'm really not that hungry," she said lamely.

Grila pulled off her scarf and shook out her hair. "Well, whether you're not that hungry or just being polite we'll still go ahead with it. We've been needing a reason to eat that tough old rooster anyway. He's mean as a skunk with a bad tooth and too slow to catch the hens anymore." She gestured towards the well again. "Go ahead and clean up. I'll be inside chopping when you're finished. You can give me a hand."

Netra stood outside after she'd finished washing up and looked at the sky. The sun was setting in a blaze of reds and oranges. All of a sudden she was nervous about going inside, facing the inevitable questions that she didn't know how to answer. She needed something to tell people, a story they would believe. She couldn't avoid them, not if she wanted to find her mother, and she would need to work for meals soon. She was almost completely out of food. For the first time she considered what people would think when they saw her. She didn't know all that much about the world and the ways of people, but she did know that women, young or old, didn't travel alone in it. She held her braid in her hand and looked at it, thinking. If she cut it off, kept her head down and didn't talk much, she might be able to pass herself off as a man, especially if she could get a hat. She looked back at the house. It was too late to do anything like that now. If Grila asked, she would tell her that she was heading north, to her uncle's farm. Her father was sick and she had no brothers to go with her, but someone had to go. It wasn't much of a story, but it would have to do.

Grila was sitting at the table in the cramped little home plucking the rooster and humming. She looked up when Netra came in and smiled at her again, a smile that took away much of Netra's uneasiness. "Feels better, doesn't it? There's nothing like some splashing water to give the world a new look." Netra murmured something and took a seat across the table from her. The chairs and the table were rough-hewn wood and clearly handmade. At one end of the room was an open fireplace with a cook kettle hanging in it. At the other end were some simple straw-filled mattresses leaning up against the wall. Grila saw her looking and said brightly, "The luxuries of life on the frontier, right? The good china is in the other room." There clearly was no other room. Grila laughed at her own joke and handed Netra a knife and a pile of vegetables.

When they were finished they sat there in companionable silence while the stew on the fire started to come to a slow boil. It was growing dark in the little house. From outside sounded the whoops and hollers of the boys, now and then punctuated by some tears from the little one, though that didn't seem to slow any of them down much. Grila turned to her, much of her face in shadow, and gave her a slow, sad, knowing look. "Did you lose your home, then?"

Netra stared at her, her mouth working, her prepared story fluttering away like torn rags in the wind. She tried to get hold of herself, to say something casual or offhand, but when she finally could speak all that came out was, "I did." Just like that the tears burst loose and she was wiping at her face, trying to hold back the hurt that was too much for her.

Grila moved around the table and held her to her breast. "There, there," she whispered, stroking Netra's hair. She didn't say anything else, didn't try to offer any words of condolence, just held her.

When she could slow the tears Netra said, "I'm sorry. I didn't mean to do that."

"It's okay," Grila said, and from the warmth in her eyes Netra could see that it truly was. She swallowed against a fresh onslaught of tears. "We've a few moments before the menfolk storm in," Grila said. "If you'll sit down here on the floor before me, and if you don't mind, I'll brush some of the tangles out of your hair."

Netra said yes before she could think about it and was immediately surprised at herself. She felt herself flush again and then bent over her pack to look for her brush. She couldn't find it and had to tug out her traveling cloak and when she did the *sonkrill* came with it.

"Oh," Grila said, picking it up, "that's lovely. It's from a rock lion, isn't it?"

"It is," Netra admitted, catching herself as she started to reach for it, not wanting to give away anything. "My, uh, mother gave it to me."

"That's not something you find every day. Best be careful with it. You don't want to lose it now." Grila held it out and Netra moved to put it away, glad that the woman had not recognized it for what it was, even though anyone other than a Tender would have been unlikely to do so. She brushed against the claw with her hand as she did so and there was a sudden lurch inside her that made her pause. For a moment something flared in her heart and then she pushed it away and dropped the *sonkrill* in her pack.

Then she sat at Grila's feet while she lit a candle and by the warm light untied her braid and began to work the brush through her hair with slow, patient strokes.

"I had a daughter once," Grila said after a time. "She died when she was but a baby, but she would have been about your age had she lived."

Netra didn't know what to say. Feelings she didn't understand ebbed and flowed within her. She looked around the little house; her eyes blurred with fresh tears and saw it in a new way. It was not just a poor shack with a dirt floor. It was a home. She heard the boys outside and wondered what it would have been like to be born here, to have brothers to play with, a mother who brushed her hair. A father who came home at the end of the day.

"I'm looking for my mother," she said abruptly, again surprised at her words. "I think she's somewhere to the north of here. She...she left when I was a baby and I..." For a long minute she was unable to go on, as she wrestled to control feelings she had never spoken of. "I don't know if she even wants to see me. I don't know if I'll even know it's her."

"Hush, child," Grila remonstrated her gently. "Of course you'll know it's her, and she'll know it's you." Her fingers worked at the knots gently. "When she sees you, she won't be able to help but be happy."

"But how do you know?" Netra said brokenly. "She left me. Maybe she didn't want me." At last the terrible words that had festered inside her were out. They came with a gasp, like a thorn pulled from deep in her heart.

"Every woman wants her baby," Grila said with absolute certainty.

"Then why would she leave me?" Now that the wound was open she could not leave it alone.

"Only she knows that, child, but I will tell you this: things happen to us in this world. We get pushed into corners or let ourselves get pushed there and we get stuck making decisions that maybe aren't so good, but maybe they're all we can see at the time. Maybe they seem like the only way out of a bad mess. I don't know where she was or why she did it, but I do know we can't judge her from where we stand." She laid her cheek on top of Netra's head. "I have a feeling though, that she looks at the stars at night sometimes and can't sleep for wondering of you, what became of the child she left behind."

Netra trembled under her words, wanting, needing to believe her, but too hurt to be sure. "I hope you're right," she said at last. "More than anything in the world."

X X X

The boys were complaining for dinner when Ilan stuck his head in the door. "The calf's worse," he said, his face clouded. "Eat without me. I'm going to do what I can."

He started to back out when Netra jumped up. "Let me come. I have some small skill with healing and I may be able to help." The first thing she'd put in her pack were the pouches that held her herbs and ointments, all carefully prepared under Karyn's tutelage. If there was one part of her studies that she had never neglected it was the healing lore that Karyn taught. She might no longer be a Tender, but she would still help wherever she could.

Some of the worried look left Ilan and he nodded. "You're welcome to do what you can. I'm afraid I've no real hope for myself."

Grila served the boys bowls of stew and, after warning them sternly not to get into what was left until she returned, she followed Netra and her husband out into the night.

The calf lay on its side in the barn, dimly lit by the flickering of a lone candle. It had its mouth open and was gasping for air, its tongue distended, eyes bulging. It looked to be four or five months old, a sturdy young beast, but it was clearly dying. Netra could hear its Song fading, weakening. Underneath its Song was a buzzing, whining sound.

Was the calf's illness caused by one of the diseased yellow flows?

If she wanted to know more, she needed to touch the animal. Listening to Song only revealed so much. Touch went deeper.

Netra knelt beside the animal. Even as she reached out her hands to touch the calf she felt the wrongness, like a snake coiled in the darkness. She wanted to pull her hands back, but she had to know more, not just for herself, but to repay the kindness these people had shown her.

She laid both hands on the calf's side. Almost instantly she felt nauseated and a cold sweat broke out on her forehead. Her hands began to tremble.

"What is it?" Grila asked. "What's wrong?"

"I'm not sure." Netra bit her lip. If this calf was infected the same way that the people of Critnell had been infected—the whole town died in less than a day—then she needed to tell Ilan that the calf had to die. Right now.

But if she was wrong... These people were poor. Losing an animal like this could really hurt them.

She needed to be sure, and there was only one way to be sure.

Slowing her breathing, she concentrated on her breath, in, out, then caught an outgoing breath and let it pull her out of herself. The day changed and she was *beyond*.

She *saw* the glow of her hands against the glow of the calf's *akirma*. Its *akirma* was not the healthy golden brown that an animal's *akirma* should be. There were streaks of cancerous yellow within it.

She'd learned what she needed to know. It was time to pull back—

Something stirred inside the calf's *akirma*, a wormlike, parasitical thing, coiled around its Heartglow.

It was aware of her.

It surged towards her—

Netra fell back, gasping and leaving *beyond*. Ilan and Grila stared at her in alarm, but neither reached out to help her up.

"You have to kill the calf at once!" she cried. "Before it's too late!"

"Now, hold on," Ilan said. "Let's not be hasty. It looks grim, but the calf may still live."

"What do you mean, 'Before it's too late'?" Grila asked her.

Netra looked up at her, beseeching. She could feel the thing moving inside the calf. What if it was strong enough to break free of its host, to live on its own? Would it attack them?

"There's something living inside the calf! I think it's trying to break free! Please! You have to believe me. Kill it now!"

Grila and Ilan exchanged looks. They looked at the calf. It began to thrash about.

Grila reacted first. "You heard her, Ilan."

"But—"

"Kill the calf. Now."

Kneeling, Ilan drew a knife from a belt sheath and held it to the creature's throat. He hesitated, then slit its throat.

Its blood was spilling over the hard earth when Netra said, "We have to take it outside and burn it. It's the only way to be sure."

Ilan looked at her like she was mad but when Grila spoke to him he took hold of the calf's back legs and, with a sigh, dragged it outside.

It wasn't easy to get the animal to burn. It took most of the family's supply of firewood and by then the boys were outside too, wide-eyed with excitement, wanting to know what was going on. But neither Ilan nor his wife answered them and Netra stood apart, her arms wrapped about herself. She knew the bizarre rhythm of its Song now and she could hear it inside the calf. It was weaker, but it was not dead.

She kept her eyes fixed on the animal as the flames rose into the night, afraid to meet Ilan's unhappy gaze or see the wariness that had replaced the earlier compassion in Grila's eyes.

When the flames were at their highest one of the boys suddenly shouted, "Look, Da! There, in the flames! What's that?"

The skin over the calf's ribs tore suddenly and the ribs were forced apart with a sound of cracking bone. Something like a blunt, pink face came free, amid rubbery limbs that writhed in the flames. Netra fell back from it, her hand to her mouth. Then a burning log snapped and fell on it and it was buried in flame. A minute later she knew it was dead.

"What was it? What was it?" the kids were clamoring.

"I don't know," Ilan snapped at them. "Get back in the house now. Go with them, Grila."

When they were gone he looked at Netra and she drew back from what she saw in his face. "I know I should be grateful to you for warning us about that thing. I know it's not your fault it was in there. That's what I keep telling myself." He looked very thin in the firelight. The shadows gathered under his cheekbones. His hands clutched helplessly at the air. They were strong hands that could handle the myriad problems of a rock-hard farm beyond the edges, but had no idea how to grapple with something like this. "How did you know that thing was in there?" he croaked. "What are you?" He didn't wait for Netra's answer but turned away with shuffling steps and went to the house.

"I don't know," Netra said after him, too softly for him to hear. The night pressed down on her from all sides. She wanted to run away but all her things were still inside. She was an outsider. She would never belong.

She was still standing out there some time later when Grila came out. "Come in, come in. I won't have my guest standing out here."

"I should go."

Grila came closer and Netra could almost see her face in the dying flames. "I've spoken with Ilan. I know what he said. I have to ask you to forgive him. He's afraid. It had to come out of him somehow. This isn't the first…thing we've seen in the past weeks. It's like there's a curse on the whole land. All the farmers around here are afraid. I can't make you come inside, but I'd like you to if you will. You're still welcome in our home."

And though Netra could not see her face she knew the woman was afraid too. She could hear it. There was a distance between them now that was there for good. Whatever connection they'd had was gone now and it would never return. But she could not bear to be alone tonight so she followed her in.

CHAPTER 2

Netra woke up early the next day, planning to leave before the others got up, but Ilan and Grila were already up. She stuffed her cloak into her pack and said, "Thank you again for having me. I'm...sorry about what happened."

Ilan stood with his head down as Grila gave him a meaningful look. Then he raised his eyes to Netra's. "We're going into town today. It's north of here. Grila says you're going that way. Why don't you ride with us?"

"I'm glad that's settled," Grila said, before Netra could reply. "The land's not safe these days, what with all these strange happenings about. You'll be safer with us and maybe someone in town will be going your way and you can go with them."

So it was that Netra found herself a short while later sitting in the back of their old wagon with the boys as it creaked along a faint road towards a town she had never heard of.

It was a bad idea. She knew it was a bad idea. She told herself so over and over, but she went along with them anyway. They were going the direction she needed to go and she was tired of walking. She was tired of being alone. Any company, however uncomfortable, was better than none. So she sat in the back of the wagon and tried to ignore the round-eyed stares and whispers of the boys. Finally, the oldest one, after much rib-jabbing from his younger brother, got up the courage and asked her:

"Are you a witch?"

Grila spun around and grabbed his ear so fast he didn't have time to duck. "You tell her you're sorry, right now!" she snapped, giving his ear a good twist.

"But Da said—" She twisted his ear harder and he babbled out a quick apology. Grila added an apologetic look which Netra acknowledged with a nod, but after that she sank even lower into herself. Grila was trying to be as polite and hospitable as she could, but Netra could sense her unease. Ilan was even easier to read. He was more ashamed than anything, though there was a strong current of fear in his Song too. They weren't just afraid of her, she realized. It was everything that was going on. She wanted to ask them what they'd seen, what they'd heard recently, but she couldn't break the thickness that hung over the wagon and she realized that she didn't really want to know.

The road grew a little wider and better used. A couple of other farmhouses appeared, set back from the road, but Netra didn't see any people. She wondered if the inhabitants were working or hiding. Occasionally there were small herds of quickbuck and deer as well as shatren and a few sheep.

Late that morning Ilan spoke to his wife and pointed to something ahead. Buzzards were circling something beside the road. They saw them on the ground too, as they drew closer, waddling around with their heavy, ungainly gaits, tearing at whatever it was they had found. Netra felt her stomach tighten when she saw them. Of all the Mother's creations, the ones she liked the least were buzzards. They were only birds, she knew, and they served a necessary purpose, but she disliked them all the same. To her they were the servants of death, the harbingers of the silence that comes when Song has fled.

It was a horse. That was all they could see under the blanket of birds, for there were crows as well as buzzards feeding on the carcass. Jahn jumped down, quick, before his mother could speak to him, and grabbing up a rock, flung it into their midst. A number of them flew away and that was when they saw the body, a man perhaps, with one leg trapped beneath the fallen horse. What the birds had done to him was not pleasant to look at. Grila gave a little gasp and grabbed her husband's arm. He snapped the reins and they moved on, while she took the youngest boy into her lap and held him close, whispering to him.

Netra stared at the carcasses as they dwindled in the distance, wondering if they had died naturally. She felt very melancholy and caught herself thinking that the dead man was perhaps the best off of all of them. It was over for him now, while the rest of them still had to face who knew what horrors still to come. Again and again she looked at the cloud-wreathed mountain to the north, slowly growing closer, and felt herself wanting to jump out of the slow-moving wagon and run there as fast as she could. It was massive, unassailable, a refuge. If anywhere was safe, it would be there. All at once she was sure that was where her mother had gone, all those years ago. She had come through this same valley, filled with sorrows and fears, and she had seen it as a refuge too, an island high above the scratches and bites of the ordinary world. Netra pictured her living in a tiny village in a home she had built with her own hands, caring for the sick, and the wounded. Up there it didn't matter whether Xochitl was really watching or not. Up there a woman could live according to her own vows. Even the horrors that Melekath brought would not come up there, for still she could not make herself believe that he would really seek to destroy all life everywhere. Such a thing was unimaginable, impossible. He would take his vengeance down here and then he would be satisfied. She could avoid it all.

A lone rider caught up with them some time later and rode alongside for a time, talking in low tones with Ilan. He seemed surprised to see them out there alone and he spoke the whole time about wild happenings in the region, monsters rising out of the ground, lightning striking out of the clear sky, sudden, unexplainable fires, and of a plague of some kind of bug that no one had ever seen before. People were fleeing to the towns and cities, he said. It wasn't safe out here alone. They'd be crazy to go back to their farm.

He rode away then and though the day was hot a chill settled on them so that even the boys were quiet and subdued. Netra was thinking about what he'd said, wondering how much of it was true, when she felt eyes on her and looked up to see Grila staring at her. The last traces of kindness were gone from those eyes and Netra couldn't help but feel as if somehow the woman blamed her for all this. Grila tried to smile but they both knew it was false and they both looked away at the same time. Netra almost got out right then, but one of the boys stood up and yelled that he could see the town and she decided to wait it out.

✗ ✗ ✗

The town stood in a hollow alongside a shallow stream that was lined with willows and aspens. There was a low mud and stone wall around it and some heavy wooden gates. The gates stood open, nobody watching them, no one visible inside either. Netra sat in the wagon, remembering Nelton, how close she and Sienna had come to falling under Gulagh's sway. If she hadn't *seen* the truth that day, would she and Siena still be trapped there?

"I wonder where everybody is," Grila said.

20

Once Ilan stopped the wagon they could hear shouting. Netra listened and then she could hear the waves of anger and fear in the Song emanating from the town, the two emotions feeding off each other, building toward some kind of release. She could smell smoke. She crouched in the back of the wagon, trembling, wanting to run away, but afraid to be alone.

Then all at once she heard something else and her eyes widened.

It was a Song unlike anything she had ever experienced. It was different in a fundamental way; within its rhythms was a sense of great age.

There was also confusion, pain, and fear.

So much fear.

She stood up, feeling it calling to her, drawing her, and almost fell out of the wagon when it lurched forward again and passed through the gates. She knelt in the back of the wagon, oblivious to the stares of Grila and the boys, oblivious to everything but the alien Song.

The wagon rolled up to a plaza in the center of town and then it could go no further, because the street was jammed with people, all staring and pointing at the tree in the middle of the plaza. It was a huge tree, its trunk as big around as a small house, its limbs broad enough to walk on. Its limbs were thrashing and tossing as if caught in a great storm, though the day was calm. Leaves fell in a green shower and now and then one of the smaller limbs snapped and plunged to the ground. An eerie moaning arose from it.

"What is going on?" Ilan asked. Grila took his arm.

Netra got down out of the wagon and walked toward the tree, drawn by the raw need of its suffering. Grila called after her, but she couldn't hear her. She couldn't hear anything but the tree's unusual Song. She pushed through the crowd of people. They paid no attention to her.

Then she was through them, standing inside the ring of people, staring up at the tree.

All at once she was *beyond*, pushed there by the sheer force of the tree's Song. What she *saw* there stunned her. Its *akirma* was like a bonfire, containing so much Song it was almost painful to observe. It was clear then that the tree was so much more than a mere plant.

Suddenly, she realized that it was aware of her. She could feel its attention turn on her.

Help me! it cried.

She *saw* it then, what she'd missed. A thick flow of Song, far bigger than normal, was attached to the tree's *akirma*, sustaining it. But the flow was yellow, gnarled, diseased. She realized that there were blotches of sickly yellow scattered across the tree's *akirma*, contrasting sharply with the golden green of the healthy areas.

Help me!

I don't know how! she replied.

Help me...I'm dying...

She had to do something. She couldn't just stand here and not even try. Even if it was futile, even if she was injured in the attempt, she had to try.

She was not aware that she had walked forward until she was directly beneath the tree, not aware that the crowd of townspeople had gone silent, everyone watching her.

An idea came to her. Could she do it? Could she rip away the poisoned flow the same way she pulled away the flow attached to her when Tharn came after her in Treeside, after killing Gerath?

But this flow was so much bigger. Did she have the strength to move it? And what would happen to her if she touched it? Would the disease spread to her?

While she hesitated, a pulse of foulness rippled down the flow and into the tree and in the depths of *beyond*, the tree *screamed*.

Netra reached up—

And the tree grabbed her. A limb snapped down, wrapped around her, and lifted her into the air, screaming for help all the while.

Netra cried out in pain. She couldn't breathe. The limb was too tight. She might already have broken ribs. Desperately, she cried—

You're killing me!

Somehow her cry penetrated the tree's fear and pain and it set her down. The limb loosened and pulled back.

Netra gasped and drew breath. Her chest hurt terribly. *You have to stop thrashing around or I can't help you!*

The tree began to settle down. Its limbs stopped moving and hung limply. *Hurry*, it told her.

Netra started to move forward again, her gaze fixed on the poisonous flow. It was too big. The flow attached to a person was generally about the size of little finger; this was as big around as her waist. But she had to try.

Suddenly a wave of new energy coruscated across the tree's *akirma*, a blaze of red and orange. The tree went instantly berserk. A flailing limb struck Netra on the side and she was knocked sprawling.

She sat up. The impact had knocked her out of *beyond* and she could see now what had happened. Some of the townspeople had taken advantage of the lull and thrown buckets of lamp oil on the tree and lit it.

She leapt to her feet with an inarticulate cry and threw herself at the tree, meaning to put the fire out with her own body if she had to.

But hands grabbed her and pulled her back. She fought to get free and found herself staring into Ilan's face. Grila was beside him. "There's nothing you can do, miss," he said. "The fire's got too far."

Netra looked up at the tree and saw that his words were true. The flames were spreading with breathtaking speed and already much of the tree was wreathed in flame.

"You don't understand," she said brokenly. "It was more than just a tree."

"You did all you could," Grila said.

"It wasn't enough," Netra replied fiercely, wiping angrily at the tears in her eyes.

"We need to go now," Grila said. "We have to get you out of here before it's too late."

Netra blinked and stared at her, confused. "What are you talking about?"

"Them."

People were surging towards her. Some had their hands out, their faces supplicating. "She saved us!" she heard some of these cry, and, "Help us, help us!"

But there were others who shook fists and clubs, whose faces were twisted with fear and hate. They were yelling, "She's one of them!" and "She spoke with the thing! She would have turned it loose on us!"

Netra fell back away from them, shaken by the intensity of their emotions, overwhelmed by too much happening too fast. She looked around. They were all around her. There was nowhere to run.

The burning tree shook violently then, and a couple of the biggest limbs snapped off. They landed on the roofs of nearby buildings, setting them ablaze.

Immediately the crowd stopped advancing on Netra, and a new cry arose, as the age-old fear of fire took over. They began to run here and there, some for water buckets, some just away.

"Let's go," Grila said, taking her hand. She and Ilan hurried her back the way she'd come, to where the boys were waiting on the wagon. The oldest held her pack out to her and Netra took it numbly.

Grila touched her hair and gave her a kind smile. "This street will lead you right back to the gates. If you're quick, you'll be gone before they remember you."

"I'm sorry—" Netra began, but Grila put a finger over her lips.

"No, it's us who should be sorry. I don't know who or what you are, really, but I should have listened to my heart all along. It told me you were good, but I couldn't seem to hear over my own fear."

"Thank you," Netra said, her eyes filling with new tears. Grila gave her a quick hug and Ilan patted her on the shoulder. She pulled away from them and stumbled down the street, hardly aware of where she was going, surprised that her legs still supported her.

She was almost to the city gates when she heard tree's Song fade to nothing. She stopped and looked back. It was dead. Who knew what it was or how old it was? Gone, just like that. It hurt her to think of it. She wished she could have saved it. She wished she could have had time to communicate with it. What might she have learned?

And now it was all gone. The shocking finality of death, the waste, the pain—she hated it. If she could end death forever, she would.

Why, Xochitl? Why did you create us only to let us die?

But there were no answers. Not now, not ever.

She turned away and trudged through the gates, out into the countryside. The sun was still shining. Birds chirped in trees and a rabbit ran across the road. There were hours left before nighttime. Did all that just happen? she wondered. It seemed impossible, as so much of her life recently was impossible. She felt caught up, swept along by events she could not understand or control. The world no longer seemed to bear any resemblance to the place she had grown up in. There were ancient, powerful creatures living in trees, godlike beings in the clouds, poison in the flow of LifeSong. It was an alien world she found herself in and she had no idea which way to turn or what to do.

She took one last look at the town—she didn't even know its name—and turned away. Then she started north once again, heading for the cloud-wreathed mountains.

CHAPTER 3

Lying on her blanket that first night after the death of the strange tree, Netra stared up at the stars, her thoughts so full she couldn't sleep. Mostly her thoughts were about the tree. It was clearly much more than a simple plant.

It *spoke* to her. It asked her for *help*.

Things like that were supposed to be impossible. Trees weren't aware. They couldn't think, or speak.

Just as unbelievable was the fact that it had grabbed her, nearly crushed her. How could that happen? Plants didn't move. They didn't grab people.

What was that thing? How did it get that way?

She thought of the poisoned flow attached to the tree and shuddered. What a horrible way to die. There was no way to defend against something like that. The poison could show up anywhere, strike anyone and anything. It might be seeping into her right that moment and she wouldn't know until it was too late.

Even if she did know it was coming, she was helpless against it. She might be able to pull the flow away from her *akirma*—like she did when Tharn came after her—before the poison got to her, but what then? She'd die without LifeSong to sustain her.

This made three times since she'd left the Haven that she'd encountered the poison. Clearly it was spreading, and fast. Did this mean Melekath was almost free? How bad would it get then?

"Where are you, Xochitl?" she asked the sky. "Why don't you help us?"

But there was nothing. She wished there was someone, anyone, she could turn to for answers. So much was happening, so fast, and she felt so lost.

She wished she could talk to Dorn...her father. Was he really her father? Siena thought he was, but even she wasn't sure, since she'd never actually met him.

Netra had a feeling that Dorn would have answers. He would at least have an idea. Asking him would be more helpful than praying to a god who never answered. What was it he'd said about the gods? Something about how 'god' was only a restrictive word for something beyond our understanding. Was he saying that there were no gods then?

The thought made her feel sick and afraid. If there were no gods, then how could they fight Melekath? How could mere people possibly fight something with the power to poison the River itself?

She stared up at the sky and felt impossibly tiny and insignificant. There was nothing she could do. Nothing anyone could do. She might as well give up.

X X X

Netra awakened in the morning feeling cold and stiff and hopeless. She stuffed her blanket into her pack and shouldered it. She was hungry but there were too many ghosts crowding her mind and she needed to get moving or she had no chance.

Walking helped her feel somewhat better, more like herself. Around midmorning she stopped to drink some water and as she did so her gaze traveled towards the cloud-wreathed mountains to the north and she received a surprise. The clouds had shifted for the first time and she was able to see that they were not mountains at all, but a huge plateau, rising thousands of feet above the surrounding terrain.

She stared at the plateau. How could she have been so wrong about it? This whole time she'd thought it was something it wasn't. What else was she wrong about? What made her think her mother was there anyway? The weight of what she was doing settled heavily on her and she wanted to just lie down and curl up in a ball. She should never have left the Haven. She was an idiot.

But when she continued walking a few minutes later she kept going north. It felt like she had no choice.

Later that day she passed a farm. She saw no one in the fields around it and no smoke rose from the chimney. Were the inhabitants in the nameless town? Were they dead? She shuddered and continued on without going closer.

Over the next few days she passed a handful of other farms. She saw no one at any of them except one where she thought she saw

27

someone duck behind the farmhouse, but it might have been her imagination.

The next morning she came upon a farm that looked abandoned. The door was open. There were shatren in a pen beside the barn bawling miserably. It had clearly been days since they were let out to graze.

She stood there and stared at them, uncertain. She was afraid of what she might find here, but at the same time the animals' plight moved her. If the farmer didn't return in the next couple of days, they would most likely die. She could hear no Song other than that of the animals. There was no sign of disease that she could see.

Finally, she worked up her nerve and approached the pen. The shatren crowded up against the gate, bawling. When she opened the gate, they rushed out and began grazing immediately.

She eyed the farmhouse. She was almost out of food. There could be some in there. She didn't like the idea of stealing, but there was every chance the farmer wasn't coming back.

She approached the building cautiously, listening for Song, trying to sense if there was anything wrong. She stood in the doorway staring into the dimness until her eyes adjusted. Everything looked normal. There was no sign of violence. It looked like the farmer had just walked out the door and never returned. She wondered what had happened to him and his family.

A few minutes later she was back on the road, hurrying away. She'd found one rock-hard loaf of bread and some potatoes. It wasn't much, but it would get her through the next couple of days if she was careful.

The next few days brought more of the same. The farms she saw all seemed to be deserted. The only time she saw anyone was late one afternoon when she heard a horse approaching on the road. Quickly she got off the road and hid in some bushes.

There was a young woman on the horse, only a few years older than Netra. She had a small boy sitting before her, her arms wrapped protectively around him. Netra could see from her face that she'd been crying. She kept looking over her shoulder as if she feared pursuit and kicking the horse to go faster, but the animal was old, unable to manage more than a walk.

Netra thought about calling out to her. She didn't look dangerous. But she couldn't seem to make herself do it. It was almost as if she was afraid of the answers she might receive. So she crouched there and watched until the two of them were out of sight.

Around sunset she came on another farm, but this one had been burned. There was nothing left except for a few charred timbers. People had died here, she was sure of it. She hurried on and walked for some time after dark before stopping to sleep, wanting to be as far from the place as possible.

The next afternoon she crested a hill and looked down upon another town. Since leaving the last town, the road had been climbing steadily. She'd left behind the broad valley and the land had become hilly, much of it covered in forest. There seemed to be water everywhere, swift little streams with mossy rocks and fern-covered banks. To someone raised in the desert it was truly awe-inspiring. In the desert streams only ran after a hard rain, and then they filled with frothing brown water that lasted for just a few hours or a couple days at most, receding to scattered murky puddles that melted away before the desert sun. But here they ran nonstop, a seemingly endless supply of water. She'd never imagined there was this much water in the whole world.

There was no sign of life in the town, nor could she hear the Songs of any people. It looked like a few of the homes had burned down, but most of the town was intact.

She wanted to circle around the town, but she was completely out of food and she'd had nothing to eat since the night before. She was going to have to go in and scavenge for food.

Reluctantly, she made her way down the slope, every sense alert, listening closely for anything wrong in the flows of LifeSong. When she was a stone's throw from the open gates she stopped, slowed her breathing, and went *beyond*. She could *see* no poisonous yellow flows.

Gathering her courage, she entered the town. It looked like a fairly prosperous place. Many of the buildings were stone and most were neatly painted. The main street was paved with cobblestones. There were quite a few flowerboxes in the windows, though the flowers were wilted and in need of watering.

She walked down the main street, staying in the center, trying to look every direction at once, not liking how loud her footsteps sounded in the quiet. It felt like people were watching her, but she could hear no Selfsong at all, not even from birds or animals. The place seemed utterly deserted.

She chose a large, two-story house, with green shutters and clay tiles on the roof. The shutters were all closed. The door's hinges were well-oiled and it opened silently when she turned the knob. She stood there on the threshold, peering into the gloom, listening hard, searching for any danger.

But there was nothing. The house was quiet. The room she looked into was neat, with sturdy wooden furniture and rugs on the polished wooden floors. The fireplace was cold, wood stacked neatly beside it, a brass fire poker leaning against the wall.

As quietly as she could, she passed through that room and looked through the doorway on the far side. It opened onto a large kitchen. Pots and pans hung neatly on hooks set in the wall. There was an iron stove in one corner. A pantry at the far end of the room stood open, a lone carrot lying on the floor in front of it.

The owners had taken their food with them, then, she thought with a sinking heart. She hated the thought of having to search through multiple houses to find what she needed. The silence, the emptiness, in this town was unnerving. Why would everyone just leave like that? What had happened here?

She walked over to the panty and looked inside. The room was dim and cool and at first it looked empty. But when she looked closer, she saw a welcome sight. Not all the food had been taken. There were more carrots, several onions and potatoes.

She was hurriedly stuffing the food into her pack when she heard something, a Selfsong, definitely human. She paused, inner senses alert.

It was gone.

Her pulse speeding up, she shouldered her pack. Then she heard it again, faint, but unmistakably there.

But there was something wrong with it, a cold hatred that made her blood run cold. It was as if another Song was intertwined with it.

She ran out of the house, stopping in the yard, scanning her surroundings, her heart pounding.

The Selfsong was gone again. Had she imagined it?

She decided then that it was time to get out of this town. Doubtless there was more food to be found, but she didn't want to be here a single minute longer. The blank windows and doorways seemed to be hiding something, something that leered at her and hated her.

She began jogging back toward the gate. As she neared it, she passed one of the burned-out houses and she saw something out of the corner of her eye. It was a girl, probably around twelve years old. When she turned to look, the girl ducked back into the ruins of the house.

Netra stopped, unsure what to do. All she wanted was to get out of the town as fast as she could, but she couldn't just leave the child here.

Netra looked around. There was no sign of anyone else. She could hear no Songs other than the girl's and it sounded normal, though clearly frightened.

The house was fairly large, a sprawling one-story building of stone and wood, plastered on the outside, with a large, fenced-in garden out front. The fire had caused part of the roof to collapse, but the rest was intact. There were large black smudges above the windows from the flames and the front door was completely gone.

Netra opened the swinging gate and walked the flagstone path that led up to the front door, looking around as she went. It occurred to her that this could be a trap, but she could pick up nothing from the girl's Song but genuine fear.

At the doorway she stopped. Poking her head in, she called out in a low voice. "It's okay. You don't need to be afraid of me. I won't hurt you."

There was no answer. There were no sounds. Probably she was hiding in some corner.

Netra looked over her shoulder. The town was still quiet, empty. She couldn't hear a thing except the blood pounding in her ears. She stepped tentatively into the house. There were large holes in the ceiling from the fire and whole sections of interior walls had burned away. She eyed the ceiling nervously, hoping the place wouldn't collapse on her. She would have to be careful.

She walked down a short hallway, picking her way around fallen chunks of burned timber. Through the remains of the wall on her right she could see a sitting room, the furniture all reduced to ashes. The door itself lay in charred fragments. She could tell the girl wasn't in there and didn't enter.

On her left was a room with the remains of a long table in the middle, along with the burned scraps of chairs. A large mirror on the wall had melted partway. The heat must have been incredible. Why did some houses burn in this town, yet the houses on either side were untouched? It didn't make any sense.

At the end of the hall was another room with a large fireplace. Several rooms adjoined it. Through the burned remains of a wall was what looked like a kitchen, though it was hard to tell because most of the ceiling had collapsed.

The girl's Selfsong was coming from a room to the left. Most of the wall separating the rooms had burned away. It looked like all that was holding up that part of the roof was an iron support column. She walked a few steps that way and then stopped. "My name is Netra," she said softly. "I'm not going to hurt you. I just want to help."

No answer.

She went to the edge of the room and peered in. Some attempt had been made to clean this room. The worst of the ashes and charred wood had been swept up against one wall. There was a large, four-poster bed against one wall, only burned on one corner.

The girl was crouched on the other side of the bed, peering over it. The whites of her eyes were in stark contrast to the soot smeared all over her face. Her brown hair was tangled and dirty.

"It's okay, it's okay," Netra murmured over and over as she stepped into the room and moved slowly toward the girl.

Suddenly the girl's eyes went very wide and she pointed at something over Netra's shoulder.

CHAPTER 4

Netra was just starting to turn when a loop of rope flew through the air and dropped over her head.

She grabbed at the rope but it was yanked tight around her neck. There was a hard jerk on the rope and she fell backwards.

Choking, she tried to get her fingers under the rope, but it was too tight. She was dragged backwards across the floor until she struck the iron support column.

She tried to stand, to scream, to do anything, but the rope was too tight and then the other end was looped around her neck and the column once, twice, three times and quickly tied off.

A woman walked around and crouched in front of her. She was old, her hair gray and cut short, her face seamed with deep wrinkles. There was a black mark on her forehead. The finger she pointed at Netra was bent with arthritis.

"I got you!" the woman cackled. She had only two teeth left and they were blackened. Her breath was sour and fetid. "I was the best at roping the shatren calves and I ain't lost the skill, old as I am. You won't get away, oh no."

"Please," Netra moaned. "I can't breathe." The rope was cutting cruelly into her neck and each breath was a chore.

"Oh, you can breathe, all right. If you couldn't breathe, you wouldn't be able to talk. Don't I know it." The woman tapped her temple with her gnarled finger.

It was true. As much as the rope hurt, Netra could still breathe, though not very well. She looked past the woman, noticing that the girl was gone. At least she had escaped. That was something.

The old woman saw her look and glanced over her shoulder. "It's just little Alissa. The blinded man will do for her when he returns. She won't get away again, the little rat." She sat back on her haunches and regarded Netra balefully. "He'll see for you too. Then you'll get one

33

of these." She pointed to the black mark on her forehead. It looked like a burned thumbprint. "Or you'll get this." She gestured at the destruction around her. "Makes no difference to me."

Netra was pulling futilely at the rope knotted around her neck but she couldn't loosen it, not even slightly. The old woman saw what she was doing and shook her head.

"You won't get anywhere with that. The knots Edna ties stay tied, that's a fact." She smiled, supremely proud of herself, and stood up. She was wearing trousers and a man's shirt that hung almost to her knees. The clothes were badly stained.

"They wouldn't take me, you know, with all the rest, off to Fanethrin. They said I was too old." She jabbed a thumb at herself. "Me! Too old!" She shook her head, scowling. "They took Maybeth and she's two winters past me, but somehow I'm no good to them. Well, I showed them. When the blinded man returns and sees what I've caught, then we'll see who's useless and I'll go to Fanethrin too."

Netra struggled to make sense of what the woman said. She'd heard the name Fanethrin before in one of Brelisha's lessons. It was a city, but that was all she remembered. Who was this blinded man? He must have been the one who burned this house.

Then, out of nowhere, the girl returned.

She burst into the room with a scream, firing rocks at the old woman. The first one missed, but the second one struck the old woman squarely in the face, knocking her back. Blood flew and she screamed.

The girl snatched up a stick that was lying on the floor and threw herself at the old woman, swinging wildly, hitting her over and over.

The old woman caved before the onslaught, shrieking as the girl landed blow after blow. The girl hit her on the head, on the shoulders, on the ribs, and finally she broke and fled, the girl chasing after her.

"He'll find you anyway!" she yelled as she left the room.

Netra was left in the room alone, tugging uselessly at the rope.

After a minute, the girl returned. She was panting, the stick held down by her side. It had broken in half.

"We'll have you out," she said, crouching beside Netra. She produced an old knife from the pocket of her dress and started sawing at the rope.

Soon Netra was free and she stood up, touching her throat gingerly. The skin was sore and abraded. It hurt when she swallowed.

"Thank you, Alissa," she gasped.

The girl shrugged, her face impassive. "I wouldn't let her have you. She's always been a hateful old thing, even before the blinded man showed up with his followers and started with their questions. I'm not afraid of her."

Netra put her hand on the girl's shoulder. She felt painfully thin. The dress she was wearing had once been yellow but it was badly stained with soot and dirt. "What happened here?"

All at once the girl's tough façade disappeared. Her lips trembled, her shoulders shook, and she looked down. Netra reached for her but she jerked away.

"It was the blinded man. He did this. When my mam told him no he burned her. He burned her and my two little brothers." Her shoulders shook as she fought tears she wouldn't let out. "I was hiding in the garden. I saw it all. I couldn't do anything." She spun on Netra, her eyes blazing. "You hear me? I couldn't do anything!"

"I believe you," Netra said.

"Then they took them, those that said yes. They took them away and that's why there's no one here."

"When they said yes to what?"

"To the question. They ask everybody it. Then when you don't…" She broke off and tilted her head to the side. "She's coming back. She'll have Lisbeth with her." She took hold of Netra's arm and started pushing her toward the back of the house. "You have to leave now. I can't take them both. I have to run. You should too."

They fled through the back of the house. By then Netra could hear the Songs of two people approaching. Within their Songs was the same cold hatred that she'd felt earlier, when scavenging for food.

"Come with me," she told the girl. "It's not safe here for you."

"I can't. I have to stay here. It's Da. He'll come back. I know he will. He's just waiting for the right time. I have to be here or he won't be able to find me." She pushed Netra toward the back of the property. "You have to go. I don't know if I can save you again."

"But you can't…you shouldn't…"

"I can take care of myself. Da taught me. He'll be proud. He'll show the blinded man what's all about. Now go. There's no more time."

The girl ran off into the bushes and disappeared. Netra stared after her for a second, then turned and ran as well.

CHAPTER 5

On the day the wind drove her north, Shakre awoke from bad dreams once again and for a while she could only lie there, feeling too weak to get up. She no longer had to try to hear the dissonance in LifeSong, the energy that sustains all living things. It had been there for months and then a few weeks ago it suddenly got worse.

She whispered a brief prayer to Xochitl, the Mother of Life, but it was a reflex, devoid of any real feeling or hope. Xochitl never answered. Had never answered in her entire life.

Why did she still pray, then?

Too many questions with no answers. Or rather, one answer, but one she fervently hoped was not the right one.

She rose and dressed, pulling on the tanned-leather trousers and shirt that was all the Takare wore. She had not worn cotton or wool in nearly twenty years. The Landsend Plateau was too cold, the summers too short, for growing crops, and sheep could not have survived the numerous predators that roamed that harsh land. She hadn't worn a dress in all her time here either. Dresses were not something the Takare women had ever worn, even before they emigrated to the Plateau. Before coming to the Plateau the Takare were a race of warriors, men and women alike, and fighting in a dress was too cumbersome. Now they fought a different foe, the weather and the denizens of the Plateau, and neither of those were conducive to dresses either.

She pulled on a short, fur-lined jacket and went outside. The sky was gray, the wind sharp and cold, although it was nearly summer so perhaps it was not so sharp and cold as it had been a few days earlier. It was hard to tell.

Shakre stood there for a moment, telling herself that it really was warmer, then she went back inside and took her heavy bearskin cloak from a peg hammered into the stone wall. Summer might be coming, but to her it was still cold. The Plateau was never warm, just varying degrees of cold. The Takare would tease her good-naturedly about wearing the cloak. Most had already shed even their short jackets. All the years she had spent up here and still she had not gotten the desert completely out of her blood.

Bent Tree Shelter was a tight grouping of simple stone and earth houses clustered in a clearing in the dense surrounding forest. The clearing the village stood in was natural. No trees had been felled to build homes and none would be. It was part of the oath that the Takare had made to Tu Sinar, the god of Landsend Plateau. They were allowed to stay, but their mark on the land must be minimal. Though the surrounding forest was home to many dangerous animals, there was no wall around Bent Tree or any of the other Shelters on the Plateau. It was not the way of the Takare to hide from their fears, but to face them proudly. Warriors no longer, they were yet fierce in their own way.

She made her way to the center of the village where most of the rest of the residents of Bent Tree Shelter stood in loose groups around the fire pit, where all food was prepared. Soft words and the occasional burst of laughter rose from the gathered people. The fire was already burning and the clay pots that were hung over it gave off the smell of breakfast cooking.

A hush fell over the people as Rekus, Pastwalker for the village, emerged from his hut. He had blackened the skin around his eyes with soot. He went to a spot near the fire pit and stood with his head down, his long hair falling loose around his face. The Takare stopped what they were doing, gathered around him and sat on the ground. They joined hands and closed their eyes. When a vision of the past came on the Pastwalker, all joined him to share in it. It was how they remembered who they were. The past was their anchor that held them safe as they moved into the future.

"The past beckons," he said. Then he began to chant. There was power in his voice, deep and strong. Shakre felt it wrap around her, thrumming deep in her bones. She felt as if she were falling backwards but she made no effort to catch herself. After so many years, the feeling was a familiar one, though it was still disorienting.

When the feeling of falling passed, she opened her eyes, as did everyone else.

The world had changed.

The light was different. There was smoke in the air and hoarse shouts. She was dressed in light armor and standing on a battlefield, a sword in one hand, blood dripping from it.

But this was no battlefield.

It was a slaughter.

On the ground before her lay a dead child, no more than ten. Around her lay numerous other bodies, children, the elderly, and the crippled mostly. Only a few were of fighting age.

None of them had weapons.

Around her were other warriors, men and women alike, most of them with sick expressions on their faces, horror mixed with confusion.

What have we done?

One of the warriors began to scream. It was a terrible sound, full of animal pain. There was no answer to it, no understanding.

"What have I done!" he screamed.

Two of the warriors seemed to be trying to reason with him, but he would not listen. He raised his sword and smashed it on a stone wall. The weapon broke.

"Never again!" he screamed, over and over.

All around other warriors took up the cry and began breaking their weapons. Shakre did the same, though much of her wanted to turn the weapon on herself.

The image blurred and broke up.

Shakre was once again sitting on the ground in the center of the village. Tears were streaming down her face and she felt a sick horror that made her want to bash her head against the ground.

She wiped her tears and gave thanks to be back in her own body, back in her own time.

What she had just witnessed was the aftermath of the battle at Wreckers Gate.

Where the Takare warriors slaughtered their own people.

Shakre got shakily to her feet. Why that vision today, of all days? But she knew better than to ask. The tall, bent-shouldered man was slumped on the ground, his face buried in his hands. He paid a heavy price for his visions.

All around her the others were getting to their feet, all shaken by what they had just experienced. Many were weeping openly. The memory of Wreckers Gate was the most painful of their history.

After that, the surviving Takare turned their backs on the Empire and fled here, to the Landsend Plateau. Bereft of its deadliest warriors, the Empire fell soon after and centuries of darkness fell on Atria. The Takare swore never again to take up arms against other humans, a vow they had kept for nearly a thousand years. Amongst the Takare, the taking of another's life was so abhorrent that no other crime even came close. The Plateau was the perfect place for them. No other people lived here and so they could not be tempted to falter in their vow.

The fact that the Plateau was such a deadly place made it the perfect place for them to live out their penance.

Shakre felt a touch on her shoulder and turned around. Standing there was her old friend Elihu, Plantwalker for Bent Tree Shelter. He opened his mouth to speak but all of a sudden the wind shrieked around her, snatching his words away. The wind struck her in the back, hard, so that she had to take Elihu's arm for balance.

A moment later, it died off to a murmur that swirled around her and in that murmur she heard a sudden babble of words. Most of it made no sense, but near the end it sounded like the wind said, "...*he carries fear...*"

Shakre straightened up, pushing her hair out of her eyes. The worn edges of Elihu's face radiated with concern and his dark eyes were fixed on her. "The wind calls once again," he said softly. "Will you answer right away, or will you stay until after you have the morning meal?"

"I would like to eat first," she began, but already the wind was tugging at her again, lifting her heavy cloak around her ankles, snarling her hair, "but I think it won't wait this time."

"Then I will walk with you to your home if you like. A hand to steady you should the wind grow foolish once again."

Shakre smiled slightly at that. Many times she had spoken to Elihu of this strange relationship she had with the wind. He was the only one she had ever told about the wind, that there were creatures living in it, creatures known as *aranti*. It was one of the *aranti* that was pushing her now, most likely the same one that had marked her so many years before.

Together they began walking towards her hut. Others who had seen the way the wind pulled at her spoke to her as she passed, offering small gestures of humor and sympathy for what lay ahead of her. All knew that the wind was strangely attracted to her and that periodically it drove her off on yet another of its strange whims.

And they were strange. One time she ended up nearly on the east end of the Plateau, ragged with hunger, to look over a cliff at nothing more than a herd of what she thought were grazing deer far down in the valley below. Another time it pushed her clear to the edge of the open plain where the Godstooth stood and then uttered something very like a cry of fear and fled.

"The *aranti* spoke this time, didn't it?" Elihu asked, still holding onto her arm, as if to keep the wind from blowing her completely away. Usually there were no words, just an insistent pushing and nagging.

"It did." As always, Shakre was surprised at how perceptive Elihu was. Very little escaped his attention.

"Did you understand it?"

She shrugged. "Not really. It sounded like it said, 'he carries fear.' But I might have misunderstood."

Her hut stood at the edge of the village, almost within reach of the dark boughs of the waiting forest. No other huts stood this far from the safety of the group. None of the Takare would willingly expose themselves to the extra danger. There were too many creatures lurking out there for which a human being was simply another meal. But it had never bothered Shakre. Though she had cast off her brown robe many years before, in her heart she was still a Tender of the Arc of Animals. She did not fear any animal. She felt their rhythms, knew their movements. Almost knew their thoughts.

"Maybe it said, 'he carries a gift,'" Elihu replied, as they stopped before her hut, his long, loose-lipped face cracking into a smile. "Some new token of affection from Tu Sinar to his Chosen." The Takare often referred to themselves as the Chosen of Tu Sinar. And always with a smile. It was a standing joke among them, for Tu Sinar had not chosen them so much as they had chosen him, all those years ago, when they fled the murder at Ankha del'Ath—their homeland— and came to this harsh place to live. As the "Chosen" of Tu Sinar, they suffered a great deal in this land with its venom and claws, its brutal weather. They could have complained about it; they could have left. Instead they chose to mock it, to hurl a laugh into the teeth of the storm.

How little she really understood these people, despite all her years among them, Shakre thought. She loved them fiercely; they were more her family than the women at Rane Haven had ever been. Almost they were family enough to cover the hurt for the daughter she had given up so long ago. It was surprising how it still hurt, how much she still missed Netra, even after all these years. Why had she never gone back to see her, even once? Would the wind have allowed it?

"Perhaps that is what it said," Shakre replied, trying to match his lightheartedness and failing. Despite her long experience with the wind and its foolishness she felt a sudden foreboding, a sense that she and her adopted people were about to pass a threshold that they could never go back across.

The wind whistled and slapped her again, impatient for her to be moving.

"Your guide grows restless," Elihu said.

Shakre hurried into her hut, quickly gathering the herbs and ointments she used for healing and putting them into her pack. She never went anywhere without them. Being a healer was who she was. To the pack she added food and a water skin, then went back outside. Elihu was still standing there, unspoken words on his face.

"What is it?" she asked him.

"Perhaps you will bring me answers." He turned to look out into the forest and his face grew troubled.

"Answers?"

"To what is troubling the plants. They are frightened and cry out in their sleep. Even the *elanti* trembles. I fear…" His words trailed off and a tightness settled on his features. For a long moment he said nothing, as he visibly struggled to control something in himself. Then he shook himself and turned back to her. "Answers would be good," he said gravely.

"I will do what I can," she told him. "But you know the wind…"

"No," he said, and laughed, his laughter doing much to lift the darkness that kept trying to gain footing in her heart. Always it was this way with these people. In the midst of their greatest troubles they still retained a seemingly limitless capacity to burst into laughter. "No, I don't know the wind. And I am thinking that neither do you. Not really."

Shakre hitched her pack into place and took up her walking stick from where it leaned against the hut.

"It will be good to know what it is the plants are trying to tell me, since I am so old and deaf that I cannot hear anymore," Elihu said.

That brought another smile from Shakre. Elihu might be old, but he was one of the most vital people in the village. Since his mate passed away several years before he had offered more than once to take her as his wife, and prove that vitality. Always his offer was accompanied by a smile and a wink, so that she had never been entirely sure if he was serious or not. She wasn't even sure how she felt about it. There had been no other man for her since Netra's father, all those years ago.

She thought on all these things and more as she looked at Elihu's lopsided grin now. "I believe you were serious with your offers," she said.

"Always," he said, knowing exactly what she was talking about. His hair was gray moving to white, tossing around his head in the rising wind. She was almost out of time. She touched his arm, then drew her cloak close and walked away.

No one bade her goodbye or followed her for a parting word as she left. They did not because among the Takare it was considered a bad idea to watch a traveler leave, or wish her well. Such actions might draw the attention of Azrael, she whom they called the Mistress. They might joke about Tu Sinar. They might joke about the lethal tani, with its hooked claws and bad temper, or the poisonous trehal mushroom, whose spores caused madness and death. But they did not joke about the Mistress. Tu Sinar was their acknowledged god, and to him they made the annual journey to renew the Oath, but he might be asleep. He might even be dead. Azrael was neither, and what she did to those who stirred her ire, or even caught her attention at the wrong time, was nothing to joke about, even for the Takare.

Still, Shakre's departure was not entirely solitary. As she entered the forest that crept up to the edges of the village, she caught a movement from the corner of her eye. Little Micah stood there in a tangle of catsfoot, her large eyes turned down to the ground. She was turned half away, studiously ignoring Shakre, but she was there.

"I will return, little one," Shakre called softly, barely a whisper. "I promise that." Micah gave no sign of having heard, but Shakre felt the faintest bit of tension leave her tiny body and she whispered a prayer for the little girl. She and the little girl had been close ever since she'd healed Micah from a fever that nearly killed her two years before. Micah often followed Shakre as she went about her day, handing her things when she tended to the sick or the wounded. At night as they sat around the fire pit, Micah liked to crawl into Shakre's lap and wrap her little arms around her neck. At times like that Shakre had to fight back the tears as she thought of the daughter she had lost and wondered what it would have been like to hold her as she was growing up.

But the wind was pushing harder, impatient for her departure and Shakre slipped into the trees and was gone.

CHAPTER 6

In a way, Shakre's whole life's journey began with the wind. For it was a Windcaller that first led her down the short path that ended with her exile from the Tenders.

She was a young woman when she met Dorn. She remembered being so full of energy and life, so full of the future and what she would make of it. So naïve, so headstrong. So foolish. From a perspective of almost two decades she looked back in sadness at how much of her youth was spent chafing against the restrictions of the Haven, quarreling with the other sisters, wanting nothing more than to change the boring pace of her life. She'd had no idea how painful change could be, how fast it could happen. She'd had no understanding that today's careless decision could change every tomorrow.

From the first moment she laid eyes on Dorn she loved him. He was handsome in a remote, wild sort of way, burning quietly within from a fire he kept carefully hidden from the world. He was mysterious, different, flavored with the intoxicating allure of the forbidden. Her life was confined by rules at every turn and he lived by no rules but his own.

One night he Called the wind for her and showed her the strange creatures dwelling within it. It was still one of the most incredible experiences of her life, one of those defining moments that comes so rarely. She was utterly entranced by what she saw and knew her life would never be the same again. The sedate, musty doors that enclosed her Tender upbringing had been blasted off their hinges and the wilderness roamed free within her.

She remembered how special she'd felt when one of the *aranti* stuck around, long after the others had blown away, cavorting and playing around her. She hadn't understood the worried look that Dorn got on his face when that happened.

It wasn't until later that she realized the gravity of what had happened, what it meant to be marked by one of the *aranti*.

When she got back to the Haven she could barely make herself go inside. The air was so stale that she thought she might not be able to breathe. What had previously been safe and familiar was now crushingly dull and disappointing. The narrow confines of Tender dogma infuriated her. She argued with the other Tenders, baited them at mealtimes, felt superior to all of them. They lived in a bland little lie and she had seen the vastness of the sky. She was convinced that she alone knew the truth.

Even now she winced at the memory of her arrogance.

In the days that followed she slipped away from the Haven every chance she got. She made every excuse to get away and when no excuse would work she simply left, telling her peers bluntly that they had no right to rule her life. Her best friend, Siena, begged Shakre every day to break it off, to quit before it was too late, but she ignored her. She was wrapped up in an intoxicating mix of love and mystery. She could imagine no life without her Windcaller. She ran with him, searched with him, laughed and talked and shared with him.

In time, she lay with him.

It was around that time that everything began to go bad. Her behavior had deteriorated to the point that no one at the Haven could overlook the fact that something was going on. There were accusations—hotly denied by Shakre—though even the most strident of her critics had no idea how far she had actually fallen. But the stress of her double life was tearing her apart even then. She began to quarrel with her lover and one morning she awakened sick to her stomach and burdened with the terrible sureness that she was pregnant. She sat on her bed crying, suddenly aware of just how thick the strands of the web she had woven really were.

That night she slipped out again to see him, to tell him it was the last time. She didn't let him touch her, didn't even want him to talk to her. She did not tell him of the child she carried. She told him only to leave, never to try and see her again, and then she ran back to the Haven crying the whole way.

Ivorie, the Haven Mother, was waiting for her when she got in. Shakre could see in her face that she knew. She saw also that she had gone too far, that there would be no second chances.

In a flash it all hit her and she saw the enormity of what she had done. The pain of what she had lost—not lost, but thrown away—hit her and she fell to her knees. Her life, her home, her future. All gone, just like that. But it was worse than that, for she had condemned not just herself to exile, but her unborn daughter.

On her knees she begged them then, not for her own future, but for her daughter's. She told them she would not leave the Haven during the time of her pregnancy, would submit to every demand they made of her, would leave quietly when her time was up—if only they would let her daughter stay and have the life she had squandered.

Though there were a number of dark looks, Ivorie agreed. Shakre was stripped of her *sonkrill* and sent alone to her room.

That night the *aranti* that had marked her returned. At least she thought it was the same one. Formless, ethereal beings that they were, there was no way to tell them apart.

She was lying in her bed, half-asleep, and all at once she heard something that made her bolt upright in bed, her heart racing.

It sounded like the wind called her name.

It was not repeated that night and at last she fell asleep. But it happened again and again during the months of her pregnancy and it seemed to her that on those rare occasions when she was allowed outside the Haven that the wind was always there. Even if the day was perfectly still, as soon as she went outside it would spring up and snatch at her. Finally, she grew frightened and left off going outside altogether. She lay in her room and listened to it worrying at the shingles on the roof, rattling the glass in the window. In the last month of her pregnancy the wind became constant and it filled her thoughts and dreams. She lived in fear of the day when she had to leave the Haven and was stuck alone outside with it.

Handing Netra over to her sisters and leaving her behind was the most painful thing she had ever experienced. But with the *aranti* gnawing at the front door in its eagerness to get at her, there was no chance she could take the baby with her.

Shakre left the Haven almost running. Her original plan was to follow the front range of the Firkath Mountains east, perhaps to travel to Qarath and lose herself in its masses. But the *aranti* did not want her to go that way. It screamed in her face and threw dirt in her eyes the whole day. She spent a miserable night huddled under her cloak and the next morning when the wind still had not abated she finally lost it. Raw and brittle with fear that had been building for months, she screamed at the sky, threw rocks and sticks at nothing, pounded on the trunk of a mesquite tree until her hands bled. When the spasm passed she slumped to the ground, exhausted and hopeless. There was nothing she could do, so she simply gave up. When next she stood she was bereft of will. She lifted her feet and put them down, but the rest she left up to the wind, letting it drive her wherever it wanted to.

The wind drove her west, around the bulk of the Firkath Mountains, then north. Those first days after leaving the Haven were a painful, frightening blur. The wind was always there, prodding, harassing, screaming unintelligible things at her. At times she roused herself to scream back at it, asking what it wanted with her, begging it to leave her alone. At times she prayed, though it was difficult and there was no answer from Xochitl. She walked late into the nights, collapsing when she could go no further, rising early to stumble on.

She had heard stories of the Landsend Plateau, and when she saw it looming in the distance she knew all at once that was where the wind was pushing her. Some of her stubbornness reasserted itself then and she made more than one effort to veer off in one direction or another, but it was no use. The wind simply would not let her be and ultimately she had no choice but to abandon herself to whatever fate it had in store for her. By then she was so tired, so raw and drained from the constant stress, that nothing seemed real. People she encountered had no more substance than ghosts. The trees and the plants were smoke and mirage. She drank from streams when she encountered them and ate what she came across, but it was a mechanical thing, her body seeking to stay alive when she no longer cared. She grew very weak and fell often, each time driven again to her feet by the wind.

She climbed the rugged face of the Plateau in the dark, part of her hoping she would fall and end the nightmare. But she didn't, and when day dawned she found herself at the top, the land of mystery lying open before her.

If she'd thought the wind was bad down below, she had no idea what bad really was. The minute she arrived on the top it pounced on her like an angry cat, hissing around her, clawing at her clothes and hair. She stumbled through a bizarre world of forests filled with trees that were bent sideways like old men and weird rock formations that seemed carved by the wind. There were plants in the forest that she had never seen before, many of them clearly poisonous, and animals slipping away in the shadows for which she had no names.

Then one day she walked into a simple village of earth and stone huts. In her dazed state she nearly walked right through the village without noticing it. All at once she stopped, an amazing reality dawning on her.

The wind had stopped.

She stood there, almost dead from fatigue and fear, and knew this was it. This was where the wind wanted her to go. She looked at the people approaching her cautiously and felt like laughing hysterically. This was the most beautiful place she had ever been and they were the most beautiful people she had ever seen.

There was only one problem.

They wouldn't let her stay. They were difficult to understand, their speech filled with unfamiliar words, but their message was clear. She was an outsider. She could stay the night and eat their food, but in the morning she must go. To have come so far and gone through so much, only to be told she could not stay, was too much for her. She swayed as she stood there among them, terrified at the thought of going back out into the wind, and suddenly the dam just broke. The story poured out of her, her illicit affair with the Windcaller, her exile, and how the wind had driven her here.

They looked at her as though she were mad—all except one man with a kind, wise face and steady dark eyes. He alone met her eyes as she tried desperately to convince them. He alone seemed to seriously consider what she was saying even as the others took a half-step back from her. His gaze swung to the forest where she had come from, to the sky, then back to her. He seemed puzzled. But he did not speak up on her behalf and left before she was done talking.

She wilted then, her last hope gone, and allowed herself to be led to her temporary quarters. Exhaustion overcame her fear and she collapsed onto a pile of furs and fell into a black sleep.

That night the man with the dark eyes came to her hut. She woke from troubling dreams to see a shape silhouetted in the doorway. He stood there for a long moment; she could feel his eyes on her. Then he turned and strode away.

Dragging herself from her bed, she followed. She didn't know why, only that she felt something deep within tugging at her and she had nothing left to lose anymore. He led her out of the village and into the darkness of the surrounding forest. They walked for hours in silence. The whole time the wind followed her, but now it seemed only to be following, not pushing or forcing. Its cries were excited in a way she had not heard before.

It was past midnight when her silent guide led her out onto a long, bare stretch of rock. In the starlight she could see pools dotting the surface of the rock, bubbling, giving off heat and a stench of sulfur. One erupted in the distance, flinging steaming water into the sky, but he paid it no heed. He led her across the rock to a thick, dark patch of plant growth. Even from a distance, something about it did not look right. As she drew nearer she could feel the poison seething from it, scraping across her inner senses in the moment before she could erect her defenses and block it out, and each step grew more difficult to take. It was a malignant tumor growing out of the land's heart. Cold foreboding grew and took shape in the pit of her stomach.

He paused at the edge of the growth and looked back at her for just a moment—the starlight shining in his eyes—then, like a puff of smoke, he slipped into its depths. It was like watching a man dive into water. It was graceful, quick, and then he was just gone. She could see no sign of him, no movement, nothing.

Shakre looked up at the looming growth and all she wanted to do was get away from it. The Song emanating from it resembled no PlantSong she had ever encountered. But she sensed a test here, something she must pass if she was to have any hope of remaining at her newfound sanctuary. Gingerly she extended her hands, palms outward, close to the growth but not touching it, and lowered her inner walls just a fraction. A moment later she drew back hastily, rubbing her hands nervously. Her palms burned and it felt like a rash was crawling up her forearms. She backed away. She could no more go in there than she could swim to the bottom of the sea.

She began to circle along the edge of the growth, looking for a path or a break of some kind. But there was nothing. It was a seamless, tangled knot of heavy, rubbery leaves and thick stalks covered with hooked thorns. Its depths crawled with unseen things. Heavy, colorless flowers turned as she passed, their blank faces tracing her movements. They seemed to be waiting. She shivered in the night air and resisted the impulse to flee. She became aware that the wind was growing increasingly impatient. It tugged at her clothes and shoved at her from behind, trying to push her into the growth. She paced back and forth, trying desperately to figure out what to do. She had to find a way to follow that man in there. If she didn't, she would not pass his test, she would be turned out of the village and the wind would resume hounding her. Eventually she would collapse from sheer exhaustion, or throw herself off a cliff or into a swift river. She could not run from the wind forever, could not escape it no matter how she tried.

Then, out of the *aranti*'s babble a single word emerged:

Spirit-walking.

She stopped and stared into the darkness. Spirit-walking was an ability that the Tenders of old had, a way of separating the spirit from the body, the spirit then leaving the body behind to travel on without it. It might work. Except that spirit-walking required a large, initial jolt of power to separate the spirit from the body and she didn't have that kind of strength. During the days of the Empire the Tenders kept stables of slaves and used their Songs. And those slaves often died.

But still the *aranti* kept repeating the word. Exhausted and out of options, Shakre finally just gave in.

She took a deep breath, calmed herself, and slipped *beyond*, to that ethereal place where LifeSong became visible. What she *saw* when she looked at the unnatural growth surprised her. Its *akirma*— the glowing shell that contained its Selfsong—was not the gold-tinged green of a normal plant. Instead it was a bright, harsh green color, and laid over it was a fine lattice of red lines, like nothing she had ever *seen* before. What had done that to it? And why?

But she did not have time to ponder it because she was struck from behind by the *aranti*, as if a huge hand slapped her on the back. When she recovered, she was surprised to discover that she was looking at her own *akirma* from outside it.

She was in her spirit-body. The *aranti* had supplied the necessary power.

Around her *akirma* a cloud of glowing light was dancing. Within the light a strange face appeared and disappeared at intervals. It was the first time she had *seen* the *aranti* from *beyond*.

It rushed at her and she was knocked backward, into the unnatural growth. Instantly dozens of plant stalks wrapped around her spirit-body, binding her tightly. A blackness opened up beneath her and she was dragged toward it. Something shifted and coiled within its depths and she knew with a fatal certainty that if she was pulled down there she would never emerge.

She tried to fight back, but there was nothing she could do. Nothing she'd ever learned had prepared her for this. She knew that movement within a spirit-body required an effort of will, rather than muscle, but she was so frightened she couldn't concentrate. Nothing made any sense. In her spirit-body she should have been completely untouchable. This shouldn't be happening.

Just as she was dragged into the blackness the *aranti* acted.

It flashed toward her with breathtaking speed. Something like blades of blue ice flashed from it and the stalks wrapped around her were severed. She drifted up and away from the blackness.

Shakre wanted nothing more than to flee as fast as she could, but instead she forced herself to turn toward the center of the unnatural growth and willed herself forward. The stalks made no further attack on her and after a time she *saw* the Takare's *akirma* ahead of her, motionless. She made an effort, and then her vision flickered and she was able to see him in both mindviews, from *beyond* and in normal sight.

He knelt in a small clearing before what looked like a giant, gnarled tree. Its limbs were huge, knotted things that spread out in all directions. Its roots thrust deep into the earth, into the same darkness which had tried to swallow her.

The Takare seemed almost to be praying to the gnarled tree, his hands thrown up in the pose of a supplicant. Then he lowered his arms, stood and backed away from the tree. The soil at its base roiled and something that looked like a glowing mushroom appeared. He drew a square of cloth from his belt, dropped it over the mushroom and picked it up carefully. He bowed once to the tree then turned to leave. As he passed by her he turned his head and Shakre had the feeling that he looked straight at her, though he should not have been able to see her in her spirit-body.

Looking behind her, she saw what looked like a slender silver thread running from her back through the growth. It was her life line, her connection to her physical body. A number of stalks were curled around it, like rats trying to gnaw their way through it. She was running out of time. She latched onto it and pulled, hard. A moment later her *akirma* loomed before her. She slammed into it and all at once found herself back in her body, sitting on the ground, blinking at the sky.

At that moment her silent guide came walking out of the unnatural growth. He gave her a strange look and walked by her without pausing. All the way back to the Takare village the wind was silent and so was he. Shakre followed, wondering if she would ever make sense out of this night.

In the village, he led her to an unfamiliar hut. By then morning was approaching. He drew back the door and entered. She followed. By the dim light of a bed of coals laid on stone she saw a woman lying on a pile of skins, her face bathed in sweat, her body racked with shivers. A man sat nearby, his head bowed, whispering a soft prayer. Her silent companion drew back the woman's blanket. An angry red lesion covered much of her upper torso, weeping a clear fluid.

Her guide loosened the thong holding the square of cloth closed and held it out to Shakre, careful not to touch the contents. His gaze was questioning, and she realized all at once that he didn't know what to do with it.

By this time Shakre was so tired that clear thought was impossible. She thought back through her training in the art of healing, trying to remember if she'd learned anything even remotely similar to the situation she now faced. But her thoughts kept piling up on themselves and she could find nothing. All at once she just gave up and acted. How she managed to do the right thing she couldn't have said. Perhaps the *aranti* whispered the answer to her. Perhaps she received divine guidance. Perhaps it was just dumb luck.

Shakre picked up the mushroom. As she did so, she realized that, although it had the shape of a mushroom, it definitely was not. It twitched slightly in her hand. Quickly she dropped it on the coals. It writhed once and then went still. An odd, orange smoke rose from it and Shakre wafted it into the sick woman's face. Then she pulled the thing from the coals and rubbed it over the lesion, one time, with a circular motion. It did not move again. She dropped it onto the ground and sat back on her heels. Nothing to do now but wait.

As the sun rose and the light grew brighter in the home all could see that the lesion was beginning to shrink. The woman's features had softened and her breathing was deeper, gentler.

Shakre's midnight guide looked at her and bowed his head. "Indeed, you are she. The one the Watcher Tree told me about." He took her hand, the one she had held the odd mushroom-thing with, turned it over and examined it closely. "Even from this you are untouched." He looked back into her eyes. "I am sorry, but I had to be sure. The Watcher Tree is not always so clear in its meaning. Letting an outsider join us—this is a very great risk. The Mistress may be very angry."

He gathered up the shriveled thing with the square of cloth, careful not to touch it with his bare skin, and left the home. Shakre followed him as he walked out into the forest a short way until he came to a steep, rocky crevasse, a swift stream racing in its depths. At the edge of it he knelt, turned up some soil with a stick and buried the thing and the cloth. "Even now, after it is dead, just the touch of this is enough to sicken or even kill almost anyone."

He looked up at her. His face was long, with piercing, soulful eyes and loose features. "For Meera—the sick woman—for the people of Bent Tree Shelter, and for myself, I thank you for what you have done tonight. I wasn't sure what I would do when the *elanti* refused my request."

"The *elanti*?"

"The...tree. In the clearing."

"But it gave you the cure."

He smiled for the first time, and his whole appearance changed. His smile was deep and warm, emanating from the depths of his heart. His eyes sparkled. Shakre felt herself smile in response. "Not until you showed up. With the wind. Then it gave me permission." He patted the disturbed earth where he had placed the mushroom-thing and spoke to it in a low voice. He craned his head to the side, as if listening, then nodded and stood.

"Do the plants talk to you?" she asked suddenly.

He gave her an odd look. "Does the wind talk to you?"

"I don't know. Sometimes. It's not like what you think though."

He gave her an enigmatic smile and winked, as if they shared a secret. "My answer is the same." Then he held out both hands, palms up. She hesitated, unsure what he was doing, then placed her fingertips lightly on his palms. His smile widened. "I am Elihu, Plantwalker for Bent Tree Shelter. Welcome to our home." She opened her mouth to speak and he added, "The plants will sometimes tell me—not like you think though—" he added quickly, teasing gently. "They will sometimes tell me where to find a cure, and there are times when the *elanti* will allow me to walk through the poisonwood to beseech it for what I need—that is most surely not like you think—but neither plants nor *elanti* speak of how to use the cure. I suppose we are so different from them that they simply have no way to grasp our needs, even if they cared much."

Her curiosity overcame her then. "What is the *elanti*? Is it actually a plant?"

"I don't know," he said carefully, looking off over her shoulder into a distance only he could see. "It shares some of the same traits as plants, but it is far more than that. There are ten *elanti* on the Plateau, each one living in a barren. They are, I think, tied to the god of this place, Tu Sinar. Perhaps they are even guardians of a sort." He shrugged. "I try not to think of these things too much as they only entangle what needs to be done." He drew close to her and spoke in a lower voice. "This much I can say for sure. Most plants are indifferent to us, but the *elanti* actively dislike us. They tolerate us because Tu Sinar accepted the Oath from Taka-slin, long ago. Sometimes they help us, though I do not think—ah, there I go, thinking again—I do not think that it is their choice to do so. It is in my heart that they would turn on us if they could."

He stood there then, watching her, waiting to see if she had any more questions. She had many, but she was too tired to think of them then.

"More than a moon ago our healer and her apprentice both died," he said. "As you have seen, our cures are often more deadly than the disease. They made a mistake and it cost them. Since then we have been a shelter unprotected. Perhaps even doomed. The Plateau is not a good place to be without a healer. You will see. Life up here bites in many ways. And every bite leaves its mark. Without a healer, many of us will die, perhaps all of us."

Shakre suddenly knew what his test had been about and she opened her mouth to forestall him. She had learned the ways of healing from the Tenders, it was true, and she had a certain gift for it, but she had not studied it deeply. There was so much she didn't know, even of the plants and herbs of the desert. Up here, she was as lost as a child.

"It's all right," he said, reading her thoughts easily. "Nothing could prepare you for what life is like up here."

"But I don't—" she began.

"The wind follows you."

"It drives me."

He smiled again, the joy that was such a part of him rising to blaze from his face, warming her. "At least you see that it is so. That is the true beginning of wisdom." He put his hands together. "It is done. It requires the acceptance of neither of us to make it so. The Watcher Tree spoke of your coming." At that he pointed to the small rocky knoll that stood at the edge of the village. On top of it stood a bent, withered tree. "The wind brought you here. Welcome to our world, Windfollower."

She followed him back into the village then, dazed and awed by the direction her life was taking. Most of the villagers were gathered around a large fire pit in the center of the village. They all looked at her as she approached and a stern-looking man she remembered from the day before stepped forward.

"Why is she still here, Elihu? You know the law as well as any, you who are also Oathspeaker."

"She is staying. This is her home."

"But Tu Sinar—"

"The *elanti* accepted her," he said simply. "It had already refused me, until she intervened. Then she knew how to work the healing. She is the one we have been waiting for."

"But how could she know how to work the healing? She is an outsider. She could not possibly know our ways."

Elihu looked up. A stiff breeze blew through the village at that moment. "The wind walks with her. It was the wind that brought her here. It was the wind that gained her access to the *elanti*, the wind that told her how to work the healing."

At this there was a spatter of murmurs and people cast glances at the sky and each other.

The stern-looking man's demeanor changed completely. There was something like awe on his face when he said, "Who can understand the ways of the gods?" With a humbleness Shakre found touching, he came forward, his head lowered, and held out both hands, palms up. Shakre took hold of them gently and he said, "I, Peltyr, Dreamwalker of Bent Tree Shelter, welcome you."

Then, one after another, every person in the village came to her to repeat the ritual. She lost track of the names and faces after a while, but she never forgot the last one. It was the man who she'd seen sitting beside his dying wife. "Pleer," he managed to whisper, before his tears got the better of him. He pressed his forehead to her hands, then hurried away.

CHAPTER 7

The clouds over the Godstooth hung low and thick that morning, the wind uncharacteristically subdued. Steam spouted from vents in the sides of the spire. The surface of the small lake was placid. The clouds parted and in a sudden ray of sunshine the Godstooth burned white, a stone finger hundreds of feet tall pointed at the heavens.

Suddenly there was a loud shriek and a flaming sphere punched through the clouds and plunged into the lake. Water spewed outward from the impact, slapping the edges of the rock walls that surrounded the lake. The sudden waves were beginning to subside when the water was churned from beneath and a figure broke the surface. He howled and lashed at the air with thick, powerful arms, before the lake drew him back under. Blood floated on the surface of the water.

A moment later the figure reappeared, thrashing wildly, as if he fought a living foe that sought to hold him fast. More blood marked the water. Again he went under, and was down for a long time, so that it seemed the lake would win. But at last he surfaced a final time and began to swim towards the shore.

He dragged himself onto the black sand, his great body heaving. Free of the lake, he collapsed and lay still, fingers dug into the sand as if clinging to the face of a cliff. He was shaped like a man, but he was far too large to be human, with skin the color of burnt copper. His arms and legs were thick with muscle. Deep wounds crisscrossed his chest and shoulders and one side was badly burned. Blood leaked from his mouth, tracing the lines of scars old and new on his cheeks.

But he still breathed, and he would not die so easily.

Shakre's head snapped up as the fireball burst through the clouds, her eyes tracing the distant streak in the sky. She stood motionless, staring at the fading streak in the sky. A chill went through her that had nothing to do with the cold wind or the gray sky.

So this is it, she thought. *This is what the wind brought me here to see.*

In the two days since she'd left the village she'd suspected that the wind was driving her toward the tall spire of white rock known as the Godstooth. Now there could be no doubt. Though she couldn't yet see the Godstooth, the fireball must have struck near it.

Which meant that whatever was happening involved Tu Sinar.

For the Godstooth was more than simple stone. According to legend, it marked the dwelling place of Tu Sinar.

CHAPTER 8

Meholah had four learners with him on the day the fireball burst out of the sky. They had been away from the Shelter for four days already, and two more to go before any would actually draw arrow or release a spear against prey. This was their final time in the field, the last test to determine who would be allowed to join the hunters when next they ventured out to find game for Bent Tree Shelter.

Meholah had been Huntwalker for Bent Tree Shelter for twenty winters. As Huntwalker it was his task to teach his students how to still the heart and mind as they stalked their prey, then to stop the world completely in that last fateful moment when they bent the bowstring, or drew back the spear for the throw. It was his task to make sure they did not stumble, or hesitate, at that crucial moment, for on the Plateau, hunter could become prey all too easily. He had seen his hunters die, had nearly been killed himself several times, as he dealt the killing stroke that they had missed. He had seen men and women torn open from chin to navel by the lightning-fast claws of the tani, legs and ribs crushed when the normally placid lumberbeest charged with sudden speed, swinging its massive tail. Anything could, and did, strike back if given the chance. Even the fleet-footed splinterhorn buck might turn on its attacker when wounded, and gore him with its twisted horns, horns that shattered easily inside the body, causing infections and terrible fevers and usually death.

But, as terrible as those things were, they were not the worst danger that could face a Takare hunter when he did not make a clean kill. With the Oath, they had made peace with one god on the Plateau. But Tu Sinar was not the only god who lived there.

The five Takare were crouched under the spreading limbs of a yewl tree, Meholah showing them the faint marks of a lish badger's passing, when the boom stopped him in mid-sentence and made all of

58

them look up. They stepped out under the open sky, and stared to the north at the trail of smoke leading down to the place all of them knew by heart, but only Meholah had seen.

"What is that?" Hazael asked. Her braid was dyed gray, as was right for any who aspired to hunter status, her face as wide and open as her nature.

Meholah waited a moment before answering. He was not a man to rush his words, to say or do anything without careful consideration. It was part of why he was such a good Huntwalker. On the Plateau, all too often he who hurried, died. The Takare had a saying: All men go to the same place at the end — and those who hurry get there faster.

"A sign," he said at last, turning away.

"But a sign of what?" Libnah asked. She was tall and thin. She seemed to wince as she spoke, as if regretting her words as soon as they were out.

"I do not know. Nor do I care. It is for the Dreamwalker to make sense of such things. You may ask him when we return to the village. For now there is only one thing to focus on. Come." He motioned to them to follow and strode away, not once looking back at the fading streak in the sky. A hunter who allowed himself to be distracted did not live long. As he walked away his ears told him that two pairs of feet followed him immediately, without hesitation. From the sound of their passing, he knew who they were: Libnah and Hazael. Libnah almost gingerly, as if afraid she was stepping on something about to break. Hazael solid and methodical. It was as Meholah expected. He had trained hunters for many years and while the men were stronger and faster, it was the women who often made the better hunters. They did not let their pride get in the way. They knew how to listen, how to follow commands without question, and they knew how to work together as a team, which was the most important ability for a successful hunter. Humans were so much slower and weaker and frailer than virtually everything they hunted. Only their ability to plan and work together gave them a chance.

A moment later his ears picked up the swift, confident stride of Rehobim, then the reluctant, dragging steps of Jehu, who was no doubt glancing back over his shoulder, wanting to know more about the strange phenomenon. Jehu would not be a hunter. He belonged with those who sought the world in a different, less substantial way, always watching the clouds, gazing into the fire while others spoke around him.

Another sense, call it intuition, told him that Rehobim was shaking his head as he followed, mentally adding one more deficiency to the list which he ascribed to his teacher. Rehobim thought Meholah dull, lifeless, bereft of imagination. And perhaps he was. But he didn't care. He wished only to know what the animals and birds he hunted were thinking, to sense what they would do before they themselves knew they would do it. He wished to sense the safest path through the knotted forests and across the barren, windswept rock plains. He wished to know his students' hearts and minds, to guide and shape those who would follow his path, and gently turn aside those who did not belong out here, where the hand of Azrael, Mistress of the Plateau, waited always to slap down those who incurred her disfavor. These things were his life, his calling. They were enough for him. Leave the rest of the world's mysteries to those better suited for understanding them.

"Twice I have seen kelen spoor," Rehobim said, after they had been walking for some time. He had passed the two women and walked directly behind Meholah. "Only recently passed."

His tone clearly said that he thought Meholah had simply missed the signs. Meholah knew Rehobim thought him senile, past the time when he could competently teach the hunt. "I should be back at the shelter, nodding off around the embers of the fire, smoking the trevin bark and reliving old memories, shouldn't I?" Meholah said, stopping and turning around. "Is that what you meant to say?"

Rehobim looked down on him, almost smiling. He was broad in the chest, his muscles flat and taut. His gray-dyed braid was bound tightly behind his head in a long tail. The tanned hides that wrapped his frame were dyed in stripes of gray and black and faded green, similar to the clothes that all the hunters wore. Meholah sighed, and felt the sadness inside him. There was no questioning Rehobim's courage. Or his ability. Rehobim never faltered, never flinched. He was possibly the best with a bow or a spear Meholah had ever trained. If only his attributes were tempered by just a little common sense.

"You have seen many winters, revered elder," Rehobim said.

"Indeed, I have." Meholah could feel them pressing on him at that moment, the ache in his back that never seemed to go away anymore, the tiniest tremor in his hands. Soon he would have to cease, settle himself by the coals. But not yet. Not today. Today he was still Walker for the hunt. "Enough to see the marks of the tani that shadowed the kelen. Perhaps that is what you wished to hunt?"

Rehobim's confidence wavered slightly, as his eyes narrowed and he thought back, trying to recall the signs that he had missed. No one with any sense came between a tani and its prey. They were all teeth and claws and lethal speed, with a bad temper to boot, and one of them could kill an entire hunting party, if it was angered. At last Rehobim dipped his head slightly in a sign of acquiescence. But he did not admit his mistake aloud and it was another mark against him. He would not take the refusal easily, Meholah knew. This one would hate for many years. Meholah made a decision then. Another chance. He would give Rehobim one more. He stepped aside and motioned forward.

"Just there. Beyond the rise. A yulin feeds. Show me your skill."

Rehobim's jaw set and he gave Meholah a suspicious look. "You mock me. There is no way you could know." His eyes darted over the ground. "There is no sign."

"Does the old woman by the fire know when the fever gnat sets its feet on the back of her neck, though she cannot see it?" Meholah asked. "So a true Huntwalker can feel what walks on the land—his other skin—though he cannot see it."

Rehobim brushed past him, anger and aggression and doubt coming strong from him. Even so, he did not move rashly, but with the soft precision of an accomplished stalker. Meholah could not deny that he was impressed with the young man's talent and the thought deep within him was that perhaps Rehobim could still acquire what he lacked, perhaps if he would submit to one more season of training.

Rehobim moved through the foliage like smoke, his feet instinctively avoiding the twigs and leaves that would give away his position, half-stepping to the left around a patch of rashweed, whose touch caused painful, suppurating lesions. Meholah followed closely, noting everything. They skirted a swatch of sawtooth ribbon grass, its inviting green color a mask for stalks so sharp they could cut to the bone, and crested the rise. Meholah heard the sharp intake of Rehobim's breath when he saw the grazing yulin right where the older man had known it would be. But the animal was still too far away, a good hundred paces or more, and limbs crowded down from overhead to make the shot more difficult. Rehobim tensed to move closer and the grazing animal raised its head. It took a step away, then another, heading for deeper undergrowth where it would be lost to the bow. Just before it would have been lost to sight it paused and turned back to look again.

Already crouching, Rehobim raised his bow and drew the string back. There was no arrow nocked to the string. This was practice. The arrows would come later.

In two quick steps Meholah was beside him, slapping the bow aside.

Rehobim shot to his feet and spun on his teacher. The yulin bounded away into the trees. Rehobim's face was red, his words choked. "*I...I* am denied?" Meholah could not have said whether he was more angry or incredulous. The young man clearly did not understand anything he had been trying to teach him. "You would deny *me* the right to wear the bones? I am the best shot in the shelter. I could strike at two times the distance."

Meholah stood his ground, though the younger man was a hand taller and substantially broader than he was. Bones from his first kill hung around Meholah's neck. "And if you carried the arrow, would you have taken that shot?" He did not need an answer, and to Rehobim's credit he did not try a false one. "You are too proud of your own skill," the older man said roughly. "Too eager to boast at the fire."

"I am only sure of what I know I can do," Rehobim said angrily. "Can any of them say the same?" He gestured at the other three learners.

"A hunter must know his limitations—"

"A hunter must take chances sometimes, unless he wants his people to go hungry."

"Going hungry is part of the price we pay for our place here. You know this as well as I," Meholah said, gentler now, his annoyance gone as soon as it came. Rehobim was not alone in his impatience with the old ways. Anger would not reach him.

"I can make that shot. You know I can. You've seen me do it many times in practice."

"You are right. I know you can." The rest of the learners came up then, watching. "But it was still too long. It is one thing to shoot that long in practice, where there are no risks, but out here..." Meholah turned to look at the others. "If the prey does not die quickly, if it has time, it may call. You know what that means."

Rehobim looked away, his face tight as he struggled to contain himself.

"Speak the words," Meholah said, turning back to him. "Tell me what it means if the prey sends out the call."

"It means that they call out to their mother, Azrael, the Mistress of the Plateau, and if she hears, she may join the hunt—against us."

"Do not forget that all animals on the Plateau are children of Azrael," Meholah said. "If she comes to the aid of her own, woe to you, to your entire shelter, if she deems the insult grave enough."

"So we have always been told," Rehobim said, his strangely dark eyes flashing. They were the eyes of the ice wolf, depthless and cold. "Over and over since our days still on the milk. But it hasn't happened in a hundred winters. No one living has ever seen this Mistress. How do we know she is not asleep, as Tu Sinar is? Maybe she has gone west like the others and we fear only shadows and ghosts, while our people go hungry as often as not?"

Meholah regarded him sadly, knowing in that moment that Rehobim would never be allowed to hunt again. His willfulness could endanger them all. "I am sorry," he said.

"You should be." Rehobim threw his bow on the ground with a sound of disgust. "Your time has passed, old man. The world has changed and you cannot see it."

Meholah opened his mouth to answer when all at once something twisted inside him and a shadow fell over his vision. He latched onto Rehobim's arm in a fierce grip, but his eyes did not see the young man. He saw instead a lean, hungry thing of claws and teeth, wrapped about with a slash of gray flame. Its head twisted up and its eyes fixed on him.

Meholah cried out and pressed his fingers into his eyes, trying to dispel the darkness. The vision slowly faded, and when he took his fingers from his eyes, he again stood in sunshine. Libnah and Hazael were at his sides, their hands holding him up.

"What is it, teacher?" Hazael asked.

In a voice that was not his own, Meholah answered. "Death comes."

The four young Takare started and looked around them in every direction, their faces taut. Rehobim dropped into a half crouch. "Which way?" he whispered, drawing the long knife from his belt.

"There," Meholah said, and pointed to the south. A few moments later the bushes at the far edge of a small clearing rustled and a line of men came into view. The one who led them was skeletally lean, and sharp, as if his whole body was a blade and indeed, he carried himself like a weapon. The leader raised his head and Meholah saw the blackened holes where the man's eyes had been.

The Takare stood frozen in place as the men approached them. At the last, Meholah made himself step towards the men and hold up his hand. He had no choice. It was the Oath of Taka-slin that compelled him.

"There is no place for you here, outsider," Meholah said, trying to keep his voice steady. "None may walk the Plateau but the Takare."

The bladed man stopped and surveyed Meholah with his eyeless gaze. Something had burned his eyes completely away, but Meholah knew he was not blind. He moved with confident assurance. His gaze probed deep into the Huntwalker. The man was dressed all in gray. A cloth sling was looped over his shoulder, and in it was what looked like a stone pot. Something knocked against the inside of the stone pot, as if it was trying to escape. Whatever it was, Meholah was sure he never wanted to see it.

Suddenly Meholah felt out of place, unsure upon the land he had walked confidently for so many years. "I am Meholah of Bent Tree Shelter, of the Takare, walkers of the Landsend Plateau," he said, his words coming too fast. "I honor the Oath made by Taka-slin centuries ago to Tu Sinar, Lord of the Plateau, that none may set foot upon his land but the Takare."

The bladed man's face remained impassive. There was an odd black mark on his forehead. The silence dragged out while he stared at Meholah. At last he spoke. "I am Achsiel. It is for Tu Sinar that we have come."

Meholah struggled to understand the words. Finally, he said, "I do not understand. You seek our god? Why?"

"It is the will of Kasai. Tu Sinar has much to answer for," replied the stranger. It was then that Meholah realized that the odd mark on his forehead was a fingerprint, burned into the skin. The others all carried the same mark.

"It is the mark of our faith," the bladed man said, raising a finger to touch the burn. "The mark of our choice. The same choice you will have. It is the only real choice you will ever make." His voice sounded subtly different suddenly, with an echo to it that it had not had before. Meholah felt death's coils slip tighter around him and he thought to turn and send the learners away, back to the shelter, to warn them. But he could not seem to move and now the stranger was pressing closer. Heat radiated from him, a fire strong enough that it would blister Meholah's skin if he could not find the strength to move, but still he was held thus, motionless, while his death came closer.

"Now you will hear the past you have forgotten," the bladed man commanded, in a voice that boomed and echoed off the stones. And he was no longer a man, but a vessel for a thing of vast age and hatred. Meholah fell to his knees and heard three of his pupils do the same. He heard harsh breathing, one man's inner struggle with himself and knew that Rehobim, of all of them, still stood. "Now you will remember your crimes."

Then he spoke of a time beyond the memory of Meholah's people. He spoke of an ancient god betrayed by his brethren, betrayed, worst of all, by his own children. Then millennia of black suffering, while the betrayers ran free under the sun. He spoke of an opportunity finally come, a time when wrongs would at last be righted, and old evils avenged.

At last he asked a question. Just one question, with only one correct answer, only one answer that could lead to life. Meholah wanted to give it to him. From the depths of his fear he desired it, but the Oath was too strong in him. He could not turn away from it now, even to save his life.

He closed his eyes and lowered his head, not wanting the sky to see his tears.

Then the world exploded in fire and searing pain.

As the last of the three corpses slumped to the ground, smoking, Achsiel motioned for the young man to come to him. The youth shuffled before him, his lowered head not completely hiding the tears streaming down his face. He was a soft-looking youth with the eyes of a deer. The back of his neck was white, the stem of a flower too thin for support.

"Look at me," Achsiel said. When the young man raised his trembling face, Achsiel pressed his thumb to his forehead. There was a sound of grease sizzling in a hot pan and the young man screamed and fell to the ground, clutching his face.

"It is rebirth," Achsiel told him. "Rebirth hurts. The sins of the past do not leave the body easily. You are reborn now," Achsiel said, raising him to his feet. "Whoever you were is gone from you. You are one of the faithful now. Prove your devotion, or you will suffer what they did and more." He gestured at the three bodies. The young man nodded numbly. "Go now, back to your people. He will let you know when he needs you. Until then you will be his eyes here." The young man stumbled away just as the rest of Achsiel's men emerged from the undergrowth.

"He got away," said the one in front, a low-slung man whose face looked pushed in on itself. "Like chasing a deer." Behind him a balding man was fumbling at a long tear in the sleeve of his shirt. The arm underneath was scored with swollen red pustules. He turned imploring eyes to his leader, sweat already gathering on his face. The low-slung man turned back and gave his companion an incurious look. "Ramos ran into something."

A third man came out of the bushes. He had a shock of red hair over a nose that had broken badly and never been set. "You want us to track him down?" he asked eagerly. Of all of them, Trachsel was the most eager to prove his devotion.

"No."

"I don't understand. They challenged us, but they made no move to defend themselves, though they carried weapons," Trachsel said. "What kind of people are these?"

"They are the Takare," Achsiel said. The clouds had broken somewhat and thin sunlight filtered through. The wind snapped the hem of his gray cloak as if trying to take it from him. "They have sworn not to strike another again. It is their vow. It is why Kasai did not send more of us for this task."

"Achsiel," the balding man whined. "My arm." Several of the pustules had already broken open and an angry white fluid was leaking from them. Dark red streaks reached up the man's arm nearly to his shoulder.

Achsiel turned toward him and the balding man shrank back. "Poison." He raised his right hand and held it over the wound. "It will hurt."

The balding man quivered but said nothing.

"Speak the words," Achsiel commanded. "And Kasai will heal you."

"No sacrifice too great for my repentance." The balding man's words were strained, his whole body shaking.

Achsiel's hand began to burn with a gray flame. The other men shifted back, away from him, but he motioned to two of them. "Hold him." When he brought the flame against the balding man's arm he began to scream. His flesh smoked and in the gray flame flared gouts of black as the poison burned away. A minute later it was done.

Achsiel lifted his hand, and the flame went out. The men holding the balding man let go and he slumped to the ground, moaning, cradling what was left of his arm. The flesh was withered and blackened, the bone no longer straight, like metal left in the fire too long.

"The poison was bad," Achsiel said. To the other men he said, "Kasai does not easily let those who follow him die."

"Praise him," they mumbled in ragged unison, all of them trying to avoid looking at the man kneeling on the ground in their midst.

They continued on a few minutes later, seven men bundled tightly against the wind. The balding man came last, his face ghost-pale, his steps stumbling.

The day passed and they made their way steadily north, crossing barren expanses of twisted gray and white rock, circling around the frequent crevasses when they could not jump across them.

Achsiel led them, striding purposefully, tirelessly, in as direct a line as the landscape would allow, drawn forward by something only he could hear. As he walked he cradled the stone pot in his left arm, now and then inclining his head down towards it, as if listening to something inside.

It was late afternoon, the sun only a gray glow far in the west, when they broke through a thin line of trees and there it was. Godstooth, two hundred, three hundred feet tall at least. A needle of old white stone piercing the clouds. At its base, the solid, rippling mass of stone that surrounded it was unbroken except for a cleft where a river issued forth in a puff of steam and sulfur. The men stood and stared, all of them feeling it now. They did not move except to flinch when their leader cracked the whip of his voice over them.

"Our prey waits in there." He led them forward and into the cleft.

CHAPTER 9

When Shakre picked her way up over the top of a ridge and saw the white spire of the Godstooth piercing the sky in the distance she stopped, struck by a renewed sense of foreboding. What lay ahead would change her and the Takare's lives forever. Once she went down there, there would be no turning back.

The wind's desperation grew. It slapped at her with its many hands, babbling voicelessly and fearfully. Shakre started down the long slope, her steps heavy. She mouthed a prayer to Xochitl then, though it was devoid of belief. Too many years yawned between her and the past. The wind had scoured too many of her old beliefs away.

She had never been to the Godstooth before. It was forbidden to all Takare except for the Oathspeakers, and they only traveled there once a year, to lay hands on the stone and speak once again the ancient oath of Taka-slin, reaffirming the pact that allowed them to dwell on the Landsend Plateau in relative peace.

The Godstooth was ringed by a tangled mass of cliffs, like castle walls around a tower. From a notch in the cliffs issued the river known as the Cleaver. That notch marked the only way in to the Godstooth. Surrounding the whole area was a large barren.

Barrens dotted the face of the Plateau like old scars, but none were as large as this one. It was a lifeless area of bare rock, crisscrossed with fissures and pocked with pools of oily, sulfurous water. Steam hissed from the fissures and sudden geysers burst from the pools at irregular intervals. A dense, low-lying fog clung to the area.

The Takare avoided the barrens as much as possible, for there was a malevolence about them that was undeniable. It was as if some other power ruled the barrens and that power resented the intrusion of living things.

Shakre peered down at the barren as she approached, knowing there had to be a path that the Oathspeakers took. A moment later she saw it, at least the beginning of it, marked by a white blaze chipped on a lone boulder that sat at the edge of the barren. She crossed to the edge of the barren and then stopped, sensing something.

Men had passed this way recently, perhaps a half-dozen of them. Violence and pain clung to them, reflected in the ripples of Song caused by their passage. Death too, and she knew intuitively that the dead were Takare. So the changes had come already.

But there was something even more frightening, something that made her hands grow clammy and her heart speed up.

The men were carrying something, something inimical to all life. *What was it?*

This, then, must be what the *aranti* was afraid of. But it made no sense. The *aranti* cared nothing for living things. It was not hostile to them; it simply didn't care. So why would it fear this thing they carried?

Unless the thing was a threat to the *aranti* as well…

If she was going in there, she needed to know more. There was one option open to her, but it was not one she would lightly take, for it was dangerous.

In order to do it she would first have to let the *aranti* inside her, something she was always careful not to let happen. The danger was that once it was inside her it would run wild, careening through every nook and cranny of her being. If it got too deep, if she could not drive it from her, she would lose her mind.

But that was only the beginning of what she was considering. Assuming she did not immediately lose herself to the *aranti*, she would then have to bend it to her will, make it take her where she wanted to go. It was something Dorn had showed her, all those years ago. Somewhat similar to what the Tenders called spirit-walking. But far more dangerous. She had only done it once before, under Dorn's supervision.

The wind shrieked around her, pushing her so hard she nearly stumbled forward onto the barren.

Hurry, hurry, hurry…

Shakre made up her mind. She wasn't going in without more information.

She sat down and crossed her legs. The wind batted and howled at her, but she ignored it, taking a deep breath and readying herself.

Then she lowered the barriers she kept in place always. Just a fraction, the tiniest keyhole of an opening, but the *aranti* seized it instantly and raced into her.

She was tossed about wildly, like a leaf caught in a windstorm, and for a moment she could do nothing. The thought came to her that she had badly miscalculated. The *aranti* was far too strong and she had nothing to hold onto.

But the moment passed. She was not one to give in so easily. She fought back, wrestling with the creature for control of her own perception. Dorn's words from so long ago came back to her:

The aranti *are strong, but erratic. Stay calm. Stay focused. Exert the force of your will steadily and wait for the opening...*

There it was. Like a momentary lull in the midst of the storm.

She pushed into the opening with everything she had...

And all at once she was on top. She was riding the *aranti*, not the other way around.

Her control was tenuous. She had at best only seconds before she lost her hold. The *aranti* was too strong, too panicky.

Exerting her will, she pushed the *aranti* upwards, into the sky. Eager for a direction, any direction, the *aranti* raced upwards, carrying her with it.

Shakre looked around. It was difficult to make sense of what she saw, everything distorted by the creature's perception, laid over hers.

There. Just entering a cleft in the cliffs. A line of men. One of them was carrying something, some kind of stone container. Whatever was in that container was the source of the *aranti*'s fear because when she tried to force it closer it bolted wildly and she felt her grip slipping. She had to let go, to get back to her body before it was too late.

She pushed away from the *aranti*, willing herself back down the silver thread that connected her to her body. Just as she did so, she heard the leader of the men speak a name:

Kasai.

Shakre fell back into her body, the impact painful. She opened her eyes, realized she was lying on the ground. With an effort she sat up.

Why did the man say that name? What did Kasai have to do with this?

What was the thing he was carrying?

Something occurred to her, pieces of the puzzle falling into place. Kasai was the most feared of Melekath's Guardians. Also known as the Eye, Kasai was Melekath's enforcer, the one responsible for meting out punishment. Tu Sinar was one of the Eight, those gods who created the prison, sealing Melekath and his Children away.

Was it possible Kasai had sent those men here, that what they carried was meant to destroy Tu Sinar?

But Kasai was sealed away in the Gur al Krin, along with the other Guardians.

Unless the prison was breaking...

With a sick feeling Shakre suddenly realized where the dissonance she'd been hearing in LifeSong was coming from. It all made sense.

She scrambled to her feet. Whatever was happening here was far too big for her. She needed to get away.

Instantly the wind slammed into her with renewed force. Shakre staggered backward onto the barren.

"Okay, okay!" she yelled. "I'm going!" Clearly there was no way she was leaving before she'd witnessed whatever it was the *aranti* wanted her to witness.

She turned around.

Near her was a small pool, its edges crusted thick with residual minerals. A small geyser erupted from it, shooting a column of steaming, sulfurous water twenty feet into the air. It subsided into its oily pool after a few seconds. The pool continued to bubble uneasily.

She circled the pool and made her way across the bare rock, peering through the fog. More geysers erupted around her, each one causing her to flinch. She was starting to feel sick. There was something hostile in the very air of the place. She spent a few moments setting up barriers, sealing off her inner senses—during which time the wind slapped and whined at her—then continued on.

Shattered boulders littered the ground, which rumbled and groaned under her feet. Steam hissed from unseen vents. Fifty yards onto the barren and she no longer knew which way to go. The steam was too thick. She couldn't even tell if the sun was still shining.

She stopped, unsure which way to go, then breathed a sigh of relief as she saw a white blaze on a rock just ahead of her. The path. She walked to it, then saw another ahead in the gloom. How long she walked she didn't know, but eventually she heard a dull roaring ahead of her. That would be the Cleaver.

She hurried on and all at once through the fog she could see the river and the narrow defile in the cliffs that it exited from.

Just disappearing into the defile was a line of men.

Shakre stopped. The wind roared and pushed her so hard she almost fell down.

"What am I supposed to do?" she yelled. "What do you want from me?"

But the *aranti* had no answer. It just kept shoving and growling. Shakre pulled her cloak close around her and continued on. In a few minutes she had crossed the intervening ground and stood before cliffs that were the color of old ice, dirty from too many years. The river hissed and boiled, smoking hot and stinking of sulfur. The passage it had carved through the cliffs was narrow and twisted, so that Shakre could not see more than a few feet into it. Hot air wafted out of the defile, damp and filled with madness that clung to her like cobwebs. As she stood there she thought she heard a scream come from its depths. Perhaps there was now one less armed man to worry about.

Alongside the river was a narrow, barely-defined path, hardly wide enough for a child. If the wind pushed her while she was on that…

"Stop pushing!" she yelled. "I'll go in, but if you push me I'll fall, and then I can't help you at all!"

She had no way of knowing if the *aranti* understood her, but it did seem to ease up somewhat. She put one foot on the path.

Something in the water caught her eye. It was a man. There was no way to tell if he was still alive, and nothing she could do anyway. The river's edge was sheer stone, wet and slippery.

She edged forward another step and as she did so she put one hand on the wall of the defile to steady herself.

As she touched the stone, she was assaulted by a sense of fear so strong she gasped. It pounded against her inner walls like storm-driven waves on a breakwater, slamming over and over, a scream that had no end.

She jerked her hand away and the fear receded, though not completely. Where did that come from? Clearly not from the men who preceded her. They were too small, too brief, for fear this immense.

She wondered at this even as she knotted her fists, lowered her head, and pushed forward. Later, if there was a later, she would puzzle over this. For now, she must act, before the wind grew impatient and she was shoved into the river.

The defile closed in about her. Its walls soared far overhead, leaving only a thin, cloudy ribbon of sky. The river was a thrashing, hissing beast that snarled its way through the tumbled boulders it had chewed from the walls, slowly digesting them. The path was a mere scar on the rock beside the river, slick as new ice. It was overwhelming, sound and smell and fear all snarled together into an indistinguishable mass.

Shakre focused on the placement of each step, trying to block everything else from her mind. As she rounded a sharp corner something loomed up before her suddenly, a huge indistinct shape in the gloom. She flinched back, realizing a moment later that it was only a rock formation jutting out from the wall. But for just a moment it had been a hunched creature waiting there, stubby wings protruding from its back. There was a flash from one of the hollows where an eye should be, but she told herself it was only the trick of a stray beam of sunlight. She hurried past it, careful not to touch it.

After that she saw them everywhere. Some were only dark eyes and mouths in the walls above her. Others were like the first, predatory things that crouched on stone outcroppings or lurked in shallow caves. But all of them were stone. Whatever they had once been, Shakre told herself, they were only stone now. They could not move. They were not watching her. But her steps grew faster and she tried to avoid looking at them.

She came to a place where the defile opened up slightly and the river settled into a large, somewhat circular pool. The only way forward was a tiny ledge that circled the pool on one side, only a hand's width above the water. She looked down at the river, up at the looming walls. No way but forward. Taking a deep breath, she stepped out on the ledge. She was halfway around the pool when she became aware of another presence, there in the defile with her. It probed along her inner barriers with cold tentacles. It was alien, unlike anything she had ever encountered. She gasped and came to a stop.

Frantically, she scanned the dim walls around her, looking for any hint of movement. Only at the last moment did she look down.

A dark shape was rising up out of the water.

Shakre ran, her heart pounding in her chest. As she hit the far side of the pool, she slipped and fell hard on the rock. Behind her she heard a single splash. She clambered to her feet and ran without looking back.

Only after she felt the strange presence recede did she slow to catch her breath. Her ankle throbbed and there was a pain in her chest. *What was that thing?*

The realization came to her all at once, as something clicked open inside her and jumbled pieces fell into place. She knew where the fear came from now:

Tu Sinar.

A god whose fear was so strong it poisoned the very air. A god who feared so much that he built a fortress around his dwelling place, and filled it with guards to protect him.

Shakre stared around her in awe. The hunched, frozen shapes, the twisted faces gaping from the stone walls, they were Tu Sinar's guards. Tu Sinar had fled to this place, hidden himself in a fortress, all because he feared Melekath, and what would happen if Melekath ever freed himself from his prison.

But his guards had fallen asleep at their posts. Only now were they beginning to rouse themselves, alerted finally by a closing danger. But it was not she who was the danger. It was the men she followed and the thing they carried.

Shakre hurried on, around another bend, then another, and all at once the defile opened up. Before her was a large bowl, the ground covered in black sand, glowering cliffs looming on all sides. Filling most of the bowl was a murky lake, fed by the river as it surged from the base of the Godstooth, standing on the far side.

Sprawled beside the lake was a motionless copper-skinned figure. The line of men she'd been following was approaching it. The first man jabbed the still figure with the tip of his sword. When it didn't move, he turned his head back toward his leader, and asked him something, the words lost in the roar of water. The leader nodded and the first man turned back, raising his sword. One of the men in the rear sensed her presence and turned to look at Shakre.

What happened next was unbelievable. Something from a legend, or a nightmare.

The copper-skinned figure moved, the motion blurred by distance and moisture in the air. A huge hand closed over the first man's wrist and he was yanked down so hard Shakre clearly heard the pop as his shoulder violently dislocated.

The copper-skinned figure's other hand closed on the man's throat, stifling his startled yelp. A twist of the wrist and the man's neck broke; his body flopped lifelessly on the sand.

Then the copper-skinned figure came to his feet and threw himself at the other men. They had no chance.

Startled, they fell back as he broke over them with the brutal power of an avalanche. There was no finesse, no attempt to evade the blows aimed at him. He simply charged into them.

The two closest men were still fighting to get their swords unsheathed when he got to them. He grabbed them around their necks and smashed their heads together. When he dropped them, they didn't move.

He punched the next man in the torso, so hard that his rib cage simply collapsed. Shattered bones suddenly sprouted from several places in his chest and side and he fell screaming.

The next man had his weapon free when the copper-skinned figure reached him. He struck once, a glancing blow that opened a wound in his attacker's forearm but did nothing to slow him down. Before he could swing again, the copper-skinned figure grabbed his sword and ripped it out of his hands. As he turned to run, he was felled by a blow to the back of the neck.

The next man threw his weapon down and put his hands in the air, but it made no difference. The copper-skinned figure punched him in the face. His head snapped back, blood spraying everywhere, and he flew backwards, ending up in a motionless tangle of limbs on the ground.

That left only the gray-cloaked leader. He did not draw a weapon or try to run away when the fighting started. Instead, he took off running for the Godstooth. Once the others were dispatched, the copper-skinned figure turned toward him, as if to pursue him.

He began to sway. He bared his teeth and snarled.

He tried to take a step, then slumped to his knees on the black sand, and slowly toppled backwards.

The leader reached the base of the Godstooth. Where the river issued forth from the base of the spire was a dark opening. He ran inside and disappeared from sight.

Shakre stood frozen, wounded to the core of her being. She was a natural empath. She could literally *feel* the pain of her patients; it was what made her such a good healer. And it was why she hurt so much now. She'd felt each man's pain as if it were her own. It was almost too much to bear.

But she had no time for weakness right now. She sensed that one of the men still lived. She might be able to help him.

She hurried around the edge of the lake and knelt by the man who'd been punched in the face. She realized quickly that there was nothing she could do for him. His face was a ruined mess, most of his teeth knocked out or splintered, his nose a pulpy mass, the bones around his eye sockets broken. He was only moments from death.

She closed his eyes and said a quiet prayer for him as he died.

She stood and looked toward the Godstooth. There was no sign of the gray-cloaked leader.

She walked slowly toward the copper-skinned figure, half hoping that he was dead. The wind was silent. She wanted nothing to do with a creature of such brute violence and rage. She wanted nothing but to leave this place as quickly as she could.

She stood looking down at him. He was bare-chested, wearing only shoes and pants, both completely unlike anything she had ever seen, made of materials the origin of which she couldn't even guess at. He was a mass of wounds. Blood ran from his mouth and deep wounds on his chest and shoulders. There was a puncture wound in his abdomen. His broad, blunt face was covered with a latticework of fine scars, some fairly recent, others gone gray with age. They were clearly too regular to be caused by accidents or fighting.

For a long moment she paused there, conflicted. Her gut told her this creature, whatever he was, would bring only suffering to her people. The best thing would be to simply let him die, leave his body here to the elements.

But then she knelt beside him. She was a healer. It was what she was. Healing was not something she could choose to withhold, however much she might want to.

She placed her hands on his chest and opened herself to his Selfsong.

She frowned. His Selfsong—what LifeSong became when it passed into a person's *akirma*—was unusual, with a rhythm and melody unlike any she had ever heard.

Where did he come from?

She remembered the fireball and looked over her shoulder at the lake. From the marks in the sand it was clear that he had crawled out of the lake.

She dismissed her thoughts and turned back to him. There would be time for answers later.

Probing with her inner senses, unraveling the information she gleaned from his Selfsong, she assessed his wounds. The deep wounds on his chest and shoulders, while bloody and garish, were not life-threatening. She placed her hands beside the puncture wound in his abdomen. She could find no damage to his internal organs. She ran her fingers lightly across his torso. There was no sign of internal bleeding at all.

She pulled back. That was surprising. She took off her pack and began digging around in it, looking for the dried moss that she used to pack wounds to staunch the bleeding. But when she went to apply them, she received a bigger surprise. The flow of blood from the wounds had already slowed to a mere trickle. She could almost see the clots forming.

She dug out a needle and catgut and in a few minutes had stitched up his wounds. He didn't move a single time.

She stood. It was getting dark, and with the darkness came the cold and he was barely clothed. She could gather the cloaks from the fallen and speak a prayer for them at the same time.

The first man she came to was short, balding, his eyes and mouth still wide with fear. But what drew her attention was his left arm. It was blackened and burned and it looked like it had happened recently. Then she saw the black mark on his forehead. It was a thumbprint and it was also recent. She wondered what it meant.

Careful not to touch him, she untied his cloak and pulled it off him, then whispered a short prayer for him.

She gathered the rest of the cloaks and covered the copper-skinned stranger with them then walked over to the Godstooth. It looked old and brittle in the weak light, as if it would fall from the first sharp blow. She peered into the dark opening where the leader had gone. It turned into a shaft that led steeply downward. There was no sign of the leader or what he had been carrying.

What was he doing there? What was he carrying?

She should leave. She didn't want to be there if he emerged during the night. But then she thought of the copper-skinned stranger and she had a feeling that if the man came out of there he would probably give them a wide berth. Nor would she be able to make it through the defile before it was dark and she was afraid she would make a mistake and fall into the river. Finally, she had to admit to herself that she was intrigued by the copper-skinned stranger. She wanted to be there when he woke up.

She made up her mind then to stay the night. As she turned away from the Godstooth she saw something and paused. Carved into the base of the spire was the Oath that secured the Takare's right to live on the Plateau. One sentence in particular leapt out at her:

We will keep this land inviolate for you, though it cost us our very lives.

What else might it cost them? she wondered. What was coming for them?

CHAPTER 10

In the morning when she sat up and brushed her hair from her eyes, Shakre saw that the stranger was awake, lying on his side, watching her. She saw that his wounds looked good and there was no sign of inflammation.

In the morning light his facial scars were more prominent. He looked much like a human, though his face was coarser in its features, his nose broad and flat, his eyes deep set below a thick brow. He was hairless, his scalp smooth except for some old scars. His ears were tiny, pressed into his head almost like an afterthought. His neck was as big around as his head, solid muscle joined to massive shoulders and a chest that bulged with more muscle. There didn't look to be any fat on him, just layer after layer of muscle all the way down to the bone. Mindful of the violence which crouched within him, she made no move to approach him, only sat there with her hands in her lap and returned his gaze.

The clouds were thin and shredded by a brisk wind. The lake grumbled to itself. The Godstooth loomed over them like an aged grandfather about to fall. After a few minutes he sat up, then pushed himself to his feet, though it was with some difficulty. She wanted to help, but she sensed that he did not accept help easily, that it was likely only to enrage him, and she sat without moving while he grunted and levered himself upright. He looked down at her, his eyes almond-shaped and yellow-gold in color, like a cat's.

"I am Shakre. Who are you?"

There was no sign of recognition on his face, so probably he did not understand her. He turned away from her and looked at the fallen bodies of his foes, then over to the Godstooth.

Shakre stood and walked over to where she could look at the tracks, careful to stay well away from the stranger. "I don't see any new tracks. I think he's still in there."

He turned a flat gaze on her, but made no reply.

She gave him a smile. "I guess I don't have to worry about you talking the whole time, do I?" Still he showed no expression.

He picked up the largest of the cloaks and tied it around his neck. It was ridiculously small on him, not even reaching his waist. He took the rest of them and slung them over his shoulder. Then he picked up one of the dead men's swords and stuck it in his belt. It looked like a dagger next to his huge frame. He scanned his surroundings, staring into the depths for a moment, then he headed for the defile. He completely ignored Shakre, as if, having determined that she was no threat to him, she did not exist.

Shakre followed him. At the mouth of the defile, when he saw how narrow and treacherous the path was, he hesitated for a moment, then plunged ahead. He had trouble keeping his footing on the path, and slipped right away, grabbing at the slick wall to stabilize himself. He was clearly still very weak. A short while later he slipped again and this time he fell, one foot going into the river, smacking his knee hard on the stone. He growled and hissed to himself as he jerked back to his feet. He was forced to go even slower after that, sometimes leaning against the cliff wall while he inched forward through a particularly bad spot.

Shakre longed to help him but knew that to do so would be a mistake. He seethed with barely-contained rage, and it boiled over at the smallest opportunity. After yet another slip, he punched the rock several times and pieces of it broke away. She was beginning to think that staying with him had been a bad idea. She knew all too well what he was capable of. Once they were free of the defile it would be best if she slipped away.

By the time they emerged from the defile the day had changed. The wind was stronger and the sky was a tattered gray that promised snow. Early flakes already swirled. The stranger looked this way and that, clearly unsure which way to go. Now was her chance to rid herself of him.

But even as she thought that, Shakre knew she wouldn't do it. As powerful as he was, he was virtually helpless up here. If the flora and fauna didn't kill him, a night in the snow would. She stepped up beside him and touched him lightly on the forearm.

"That way," she said, motioning to the south. "My village." She mimed a roof overhead and then brought her hand to her mouth several times. "Shelter. Food."

Frowning, he shook her hand off and stalked off in the opposite direction. Shakre looked at the sky, tugged her cloak closer about her, and followed him, shaking her head.

After leaving the barren, the land climbed steeply in the direction he chose, heading up to a rocky escarpment that faced the Godstooth from the north. The slope was covered with loose slate. He slipped again and again, finally falling to his knees. With a growl, he lurched to his feet and forged on. A tree limb that he slapped out of his way snapped back and struck him in the face and he ripped the limb off and tossed it aside. Sullenly, he forged on, but by then he was panting hard, his steps starting to waver. Snarling at his own weakness, he forced himself onwards, but it was clear his wounds were taking a toll on him. Finally, he leaned against a boulder, his chest heaving. He stood there for long minutes, catching his breath, while the wind gusted around him. He shivered and tried to pull his cloak closer about him but it was too small to even go all the way around him.

Shakre followed and waited. The snow grew thicker. It was getting colder. Summer was coming, but that didn't mean the Plateau was warm.

At last he turned around and looked down on her. He made a contemptuous gesture with one clawed hand and grunted something in a guttural tongue.

Without a word, Shakre turned and started for home and the stranger followed.

She did not try and take him far that day, mindful of his wounds. She was careful to choose the easiest path and, disguising her actions as bending to check her moccasin, or looking back at the terrain, kept a close eye on him to see how well he was holding up. She paused for a long time at midday, sharing her meager rations with him. What little she had was quickly gone, far too soon to satisfy his hunger. By then the snow had tapered off and even the wind was calm, as if satisfied with her actions.

By late afternoon he had had enough. He walked with his head down, and his breathing was ragged. She kept her eyes open and a short while later she found the spot she was looking for. Some tall stones had fallen against each other and in the shadow of their embrace was a bit of shelter from the wind, enough to keep the worst of it off, even enough overhang to get back out of the snow. The stones stood amongst a copse of scraggly trees that had somehow clawed out a life in the midst of a long open stretch of bare rock.

Shakre rooted around the base of the stones and found some fairly dry grasses and bits of bark. From the underside of one of the trees she snapped off a couple handfuls of small, dead limbs. A few thin sticks gleaned from under the trees and she was ready to build a fire. In a few minutes she had a small, tidy blaze burning up against the base of one of the stones. It was not much, but properly tended it would give off enough heat to get them through the coming night. She cast an appraising glance at the stranger, wondering if she could get him to accept her cloak. Even without it she was better equipped to survive the night than he was. Over the years she had learned some of the Takare methods for mastering breath and body, techniques used to keep the cold at bay.

The stranger looked from her to the fire and back again, an expectant look on his broad face.

"Go ahead," Shakre told him gently, motioning towards the tiny blaze.

He frowned, his heavy brows drawing together in a thundercloud. He made a sharp, disgusted noise in his throat and turned away. "Wait—" Shakre started, then broke off when she saw what he was doing.

The trees standing around the stones were ancient things, survivors of many winters, bent over by the ceaseless winds, their limbs skeletal, grasping. But for the scattering of tiny leaves bursting from the limbs, they might have been dead. The stranger went to the closest, grabbed the trunk as high up as he could reach and bent it over, almost to the ground. The trunk snapped. He quickly broke the trunk in several more places, grabbed a huge armload of wood in his arms, turned and flung it onto the fire. The dead limbs on the tree began to catch almost immediately. He stepped up to it, putting his hands out over the growing blaze, and grunted with satisfaction.

Shakre just stared, sick inside. That tree was centuries old. All that time, through the most brutal weather, it had eked out a living. And he was burning it. He was burning a thousand years of gentle, patient growth for a few minutes of warmth. She could hear, even now, the tree's Song fading, dying away to nothing in the wind. The waste was heartbreaking.

"You," she said, pointing an accusing finger at him, "are a killer. Nothing more."

Then she stalked away into the growing darkness. Let him die, she thought. Nothing good could come from a beast such as him. He would only kill and kill until he himself was dead. Why should she help such a thing to live?

Yet she could not walk all the way away. She spent the night crouched among some boulders a few hundred feet away, wincing inside every time the fire died down and the stranger broke off another tree to feed it.

In the morning she returned to him. Each shattered tree trunk was a painful wound bleeding into her inner senses. She avoided looking at them, avoided looking at him. "Come on," she told him hoarsely. "We have a long way to go."

He stared at her with his yellow eyes. Then he said a word and mimed bringing food to his mouth.

Shakre pointed to the south. "There. In my village. I don't have any more with me. You ate it all yesterday."

His eyes went to the small pouch she carried, then back to her, his expression flat, unreadable.

"You don't believe me, here, look for yourself!" she burst out. She tore open the pouch and brought out a fistful of herb packets. "They're only for healing and you...you don't even need that!" She thrust them back into the pouch and spun away from him.

For a time she walked quickly through the rugged terrain, not trying to make it easier on him, wanting him to hurt, to fall behind, to be sorry for what he had done. She took grim satisfaction from his grunts of pain when he fell or slammed into something. Wherever he was from, he was clearly not used to the outdoors.

Gradually, the sound of his heavy footsteps and ragged breathing fell further and further behind her. The turning point came at a sharp gulch that crossed their path. Its sides were steep, loose rock, the bottom covered with boulders. She moved lithely down into it and was already up the other side before he reached its edge. He fell while descending into it, as she had known he would, his fall accompanied by the grate of sliding rock and crashing stone. But the echoes died away and he did not get up and immediately she regretted her actions. What kind of healer was she anyway?

She looked over the edge of the gulch just as he was hoisting himself painfully to his feet. One of his wounds had reopened and was seeping blood. Once on his feet he looked up at her, his gaze measuring the distance between them, calculating whether she was ally or enemy. She unhooked her water skin from her belt and threw it to him. He caught it easily and then held it in one hand while his eyes continued to weigh her.

"It's okay," she told him. "It's only water."

His face showed no response, its broad expanse unmoving, but after a moment he raised it to his lips and drank. Then he threw it back up to her and began picking his way up the slope. The first time he only got halfway up when a rock came loose in his hand and he slipped back down to the bottom.

"Come up over here," Shakre said, pointing. "Use that rock there, and that one. They're solid."

The line between his heavy brows deepened for a moment, but he did as she said. When he neared the top she reached down and held out her hand to him. He looked at it as if unsure what it was, then closed his hand over hers.

It felt like a stone had taken hold of her. She leaned back and pulled as hard as she could, but it didn't seem like she could budge him at all. Still, a moment later his other hand found the lip of the gulch, he pulled and then he was up, looming over her. She looked up at him. "I'm sorry," she said. When he showed no response she gestured down into the gulch. "About that. I'm sorry." Was his face flesh and blood or carved stone? His mouth was set in a flat line; his eyes stared unblinking into her. Then he made a dismissive noise and motioned for her to lead on.

By the time they entered the shelter late that afternoon, everyone was lined up watching them. All of them, from tottering oldster to small child. They stood silently and they stared. Shakre had to admit that they probably made a pretty spectacular entrance, beyond anything seen by the people of the Plateau before. The stranger—she still did not know his name—strode into the village like a force of nature, as fierce and implacable as a coming storm, his massive head swiveling side to side as his flat eyes took in the people who stared at him. He stood head and shoulders above the biggest man in the Shelter. His skin was a burned, coppery brown, his eyes pale brown in some light, almost yellow at other times. His body showed no change in stride or bearing, but she sensed that he was coiled and ready, measuring those who surrounded him, prepared to spring into action, to kill any who appeared to be a threat. He was a warrior, a killer. Violence was the only response he knew.

She shook her head. She'd spent the last two days trying to figure him out. Hour after hour she'd combed through the strange Song coming off him, trying to read him, to learn anything she could of him. And after all that time, all she could feel was waiting violence and rage. It was maddening and it was frightening. Was she making a terrible mistake, bringing this killer in amongst her people? Would he eventually attack them with the same viciousness he'd attacked the others?

She led him to the fire pit in the center of the village. All important business, almost all social life, was conducted there. It was the way of the Takare. What was important was brought before the group, taken out into the open and passed around to be understood. It was there she would explain, or try to explain, who he was, and why she had broken their oath to bring him among them. One outsider explaining the presence of another. This was probably not going to go well.

Making it worse was the fact that even she wasn't sure why she had brought him.

All at once she noticed a different air to the village. She'd been too preoccupied to notice it at first. With her eyes she searched faces, while with her inner senses she searched through their Songs. Something had happened while she was gone. Something that had upset her adopted people very much. Slipping *beyond*, she searched around the fabric of the village as a whole. Like people, communities, especially small, tight-knit ones like Bent Tree Shelter, had a sort of *akirma* of their own. Within the fabric of that *akirma* could be *seen* evidence of the underlying emotions, tensions and feelings of those within it.

She *saw* the holes right away. Ragged tears in the shell of the community, empty places where before had been lives. Death came easily and often on the Plateau. That it should lay its hand on several Takare at once was not such an unusual occurrence. But clearly this went beyond any normal loss. Something about the way these had died had rocked the village to its core. She knew in a heartbeat who it was the emissaries of Kasai had killed.

Her inner gaze fell on Jehu and she received a shock when she *saw* the black smudge on his *akirma*. The Selfsong radiating from him felt *scorched* somehow.

The young man's eyes were downcast, his face twisted in on itself, his shoulders bowed. On his forehead was the same burn mark she had seen on the outsiders. He opened his mouth as if to cry out and then his face dissolved into silent tears. Her heart cried out for him. *Oh Jehu, what have you done?* She longed to run after him, to comfort him, to try and heal him.

She felt something else then, a streak of anger as loud as a shout, and turned her eyes to one who stood on the opposite side of her path, staring at the fleeing young man with narrowed eyes. Rehobim. His heart burned with rage and...something else. Self-loathing?

Elihu fell into step beside her. His fingertips brushed the back of her hand softly, so much passing between them in that moment.

"What happened?" she asked him softly.

"Change, my old friend," he returned, and there was sadness in his voice. "Change has happened. It has come for us while we lay sleeping, thinking our remoteness from the world would keep us safe from it. We forgot." He shook his head. "We forgot that simple distance is not enough to break us from our place in the world."

Set in an arc, off to one side of the fire pit, were five large, flat stones. It was on these stones that the Walkers stood when addressing the village. The Walkers—Dreamwalker, Pastwalker, Huntwalker, Plantwalker and Firewalker—were the leaders of the village, in that it was their wisdom which collectively guided the villagers through the dangers of the Plateau, but they did not tell the villagers what to do. When faced with a decision which affected all of them, the residents of the village gathered by the fire pit to discuss it, often at some length. Only after a compromise had been reached that all could live with were decisions arrived at. In this, the Walkers were more mediators than leaders, though each Walker's word was absolute in his or her area of expertise.

Rekus, the Pastwalker, was already there when Shakre arrived, his chin thrust forward as if expecting a fight. Beside him stood Intyr, the Dreamwalker, a thin, mousy woman with clouds in her eyes. Her long hair was dyed a vivid blue. Often she never spoke at all, just stood there staring off into realms only she could see. Elihu, the Plantwalker, left Shakre's side and stepped to his spot in the line with the other two. Slowly the whole village gathered around while Asoken, the Firewalker, knelt and brought the sleeping coals back to life in the fire pit, though darkness was still some ways away. Fire was always present for the important meetings.

When the fire was burning, Asoken stood and took his spot. That left one stone empty, the place where Meholah, Huntwalker, had long stood. The sight of his empty space left a dull ache in Shakre's heart. She had greatly respected and loved the simple, plainspoken man.

Rekus stared at Shakre as she approached, his mouth drawn in a tight line. He said nothing. There was no need to ask the question when all knew what it was.

"I found him at the Godstooth," she said, as if he was a stray dog that she had brought home.

The hush deepened. Rekus's eyes widened and even Intyr came back to earth with a startled look, as if just noticing the stranger for the first time. The flames danced in Asoken's eyes as he looked at her, his expression unreadable. Elihu alone was unsurprised. Not for the first time, Shakre wondered just how much the Plantwalker really knew. Rarely did anything really catch him off balance.

"You went to the *Godstooth*?" Rekus said, his tone incredulous. "You went to the forbidden place?"

"The wind drove me there," she said simply. Around her there were nods from the other villagers. All had seen the wind seize on her and drive her from the village. Even on the Plateau, where the unusual was almost ordinary, Shakre's relationship with the wind was odd. Most of the Takare seemed to regard her with a certain amount of awe. She dismissed the crime of her trespass on forbidden ground with a sharp gesture and returned to what was most important. "He fell from the sky in a streak of fire and landed in the lake there."

"So that's where he came from," Rehobim said. "I knew the fireball was an omen." The stranger was standing off to one side. No one stood near him except for Rehobim. As Rehobim spoke he looked at the stranger as if searching for something.

"He killed the outsiders," Shakre said, more to Rehobim than to the others.

Rehobim tensed at her words and turned back to her. "All of them?" he asked, and there was an odd hunger blazing in his eyes.

"All but one of them, their leader, who fled into the crack in the Godstooth."

"An outsider went *there*?" Rekus looked pale. The other Walkers looked alarmed also.

"He was carrying something," Shakre said. "I believe it was meant to harm Tu Sinar."

Rekus looked like he was having trouble comprehending such a thing. Intyr had her hand to her mouth. Asoken looked grim.

"What do you think it was?" Elihu asked, staring very intently at her.

"I have no idea," she admitted. "But it was the reason the wind drove me there. The wind was frightened of it and while I never got close to it, I sensed its malevolence."

"This makes no sense," Rekus blurted out suddenly. "Tu Sinar is a god. No human could pose a threat to him. You must be mistaken."

Shakre didn't look at him. Her eyes were fixed on Elihu, much that was unspoken passing between them.

"She is not mistaken," Elihu said. "I have felt this thing's approach for the last few days. The plants cry out in fear of it."

Rekus looked like he wanted to argue with him, but he knew also that he dared not challenge the Plantwalker when it came to his realm. He turned on Shakre, his eyes flashing, as if he blamed her for this. "That still does not explain why men would dare attack a god."

"I think the men were sent by Kasai. Through the wind I heard one of them say his name." She decided not to tell him how she'd actually heard the name. It was doubtful he would believe it and thus it would weaken her credibility.

"And who is this Kasai?"

"One of the chief lieutenants of the banished god, Melekath."

Rekus pounced on her words as if she'd made a critical mistake. "Now I know you are mistaken." He said the last word as if he'd caught her in a lie. "Melekath is imprisoned, never to return."

"Unless the prison is broken," Elihu said mildly.

Concerned voices rose up from the watching villagers. Rekus was shaking his head violently. The other two Walkers looked stunned. Only Shakre and Elihu remained calm. Both of them had feared this very thing, though neither had spoken of it to the other, as if afraid that saying it aloud would lend the idea strength they did not want it to have.

Finally, Rekus shouted for everyone to be quiet and the babble subsided. "For now I will not address the possibility of what we have all known to be impossible. We can take that up later. For now, I want to focus on what is important." He pointed one long finger at Shakre. "You have not explained the one thing that we are really here for."

Now he pointed the finger at the stranger. "You know outsiders are forbidden. Why is *he* here?"

Why indeed? Shakre wanted to admit that she didn't know, but she knew Rekus would not take that well. So she went with what she did know. "He does not understand our world up here. I could not just leave him there to die."

That got through to Rekus somewhat. She was their healer, after all. But it did not placate him. "He cannot stay here. He must go. He must leave the Plateau immediately."

"Okay," Shakre said simply. "I agree with you." Rekus looked startled. He hadn't expected acquiescence. "Are you going to be the one to tell him? What if he says no?"

All eyes went to the stranger. He stood with his arms crossed over his chest, his eyes—turned almost brown in the late afternoon sunlight—fierce and forbidding. He looked as immovable as a boulder.

"We must stand together in this," Rekus choked out. "He must leave here."

Then Rehobim spoke again. "I say we let him stay."

A murmur of voices arose at his words and once again Rekus had to call for quiet. "How can you say this? You know the oath we took."

Rehobim shrugged. "Of course I do. Everyone does. You never let us forget it." Rekus began to rebuke him, but before he could speak Rehobim continued, only this time he spoke not to Rekus or the Walkers, but to the other Takare.

"There has been no sign of Tu Sinar since we came to this place. He may be asleep, or dead." He curled his lip as he said the words, showing how little respect he had for their chosen god. "But these outsiders, these soldiers of Kasai, they are here and they are real. They have already killed some of our people and they will kill more." He turned and pointed at the stranger, whose scowl deepened. "Right there stands one who knows how to fight. Windfollower said he killed all but one of them by himself. I say we welcome him. I say we need him here."

This time Rekus had to shout several times to get silence to return. "How dare you challenge the sacred oath that is the basis for our lives here?" His voice had risen and there was color in his cheeks.

"How dare you chain us to the distant past and so condemn us to die in the present?" Rehobim shot back. "War is coming. Are we to stand by and let ourselves be slaughtered because of an oath sworn centuries ago to a god who cares nothing for us?"

Rekus opened his mouth to reply, but Elihu stayed him with a hand on his arm. The villagers went quiet and every eye turned to him.

"And what of our other vow?" Elihu said softly. When speaking to the village, he never raised his voice, but lowered it. His authority was such that people went still, straining to hear what he had to say. "When we swore never to raise a weapon against our brothers and sisters again. Are you suggesting we discard that one as well?"

Even Rehobim had no easy answer to that. He lowered his head, his face darkening. But he did not give up so easily for a moment later he raised his head and looked at Elihu. "This is different. I saw the black marks on their foreheads. They have sworn themselves to evil. They have no claim to our vow."

At this many people turned to look at Jehu, standing off on the edge, alone. The black mark stood out strongly on his skin.

"Are you saying that Jehu is no longer your brother either?" Elihu asked.

Rehobim didn't answer, but just glared at Jehu. Jehu seemed to crumple then. His face contorted with grief and misery and he turned and fled.

Elihu spoke then, his voice as smooth and calm as if they discussed the morrow's weather. "No river can be crossed until you stand on its banks," he said. "Until you can see with your eyes if its waters flood or run calm. I suggest we have our evening meal. We have a guest who has not fed, and an honored member of our community who looks badly in need of food herself." He smiled at the gathered villagers as if they were his children. "We will eat. We will talk. Tomorrow will look different when we are there."

Soon the communal cook pot was over the coals, the smell of food was in the air and the children were taking turns daring each other, vying to see who would venture closest to the stranger, before shrieking and running away.

Though a number of the villagers were trying to carry on as if it were a normal evening, most were clearly divided into one of two camps. The larger group, consisting mostly of those villagers middle-aged and older, was gathered loosely around Rekus, who was talking to them, his expression serious.

The smaller group, consisting mainly of the younger adults, was gathered around Rehobim, whose face was dark as he spoke to them.

"The rifts have begun already," Shakre said gloomily. She and Elihu were standing by themselves watching what was happening.

Elihu nodded. "We stand on the edge of a difficult time, faced with a difficult choice."

"I fear it's going to tear us apart," Shakre said.

"It might."

"We either stay true to our vows, in which case the outsiders will kill us. Or we break our deepest vow and return to violence. Either way the Takare will never be the same."

"There is a third choice," Elihu said mildly. "The one Jehu made."

"I don't know how you can sound so calm about it. No matter how we choose, we can't win." Shakre knew she sounded peevish, but she couldn't help herself.

Elihu sighed softly and squeezed her arm. "Would it help if I got upset? Would it change anything?"

Shakre leaned her head on his shoulder. "You're right, of course. It's just that I feel so helpless. I can see the danger we're heading toward and there doesn't seem to be anything I can do about it."

"That's how it looks now. But you may be surprised. There are undoubtedly choices ahead of us that we have no idea of yet."

Shakre had spent enough time around Elihu to know where he was going next. "And if I get too worked up, I'll have a harder time seeing them, right?"

He smiled gently at her. "I could not have said it so well myself."

Their conversation broke off as the big stranger suddenly moved towards the cook pot. Olera, who handled most of the cooking, moved back as he approached, but he paid no attention to her. Beside the pot was a stack of wooden eating bowls. He took one, dipped it into the stew and gulped it down noisily. He ate several more in quick succession, while Olera and the rest of Bent Tree Shelter watched wide-eyed. Then he tossed the bowl in the dirt, wiped his mouth with the back of his hand and walked over to the stones that the Walkers used for addressing the village.

He stopped at the one Rekus used and crouched down. Everyone seemed to hold their breath. It was a large stone and had taken five men using stout sticks as levers to move it into place.

The stranger's muscles flexed and he lifted the stone. Then he carried it over next to the fire and dropped it. He arranged it to his liking, then sat down on it and stared into the fire.

The Takare looked at each other in awe. Rekus looked stunned. He turned and walked away, heading for his hut.

"I don't think it was a coincidence that he chose the Pastwalker's stone, do you?" Elihu asked Shakre.

Dinner was finished and the Takare were starting to drift away to their beds when Rekus returned to the fire pit. His eyes had been blackened with soot and his gray hair hung loose. He walked up and stood on the opposite side of the fire pit from where the stranger was sitting.

"Summon everyone to gather," he said in a loud voice. "The past beckons."

"Pastwalker," one man said. It was Pinlir, a stout, middle-aged man with graying hair and a long, braided beard. He was the son of Asoken, the Firewalker. "Is this wise?" He gestured at the stranger. "With him right there?"

"Do you question my realm?" Rekus barked. "Am I not the Pastwalker here?"

"No, of course not," Pinlir said. "My deepest apologies."

Those who had left returned and all the people of the village sat down on the ground and joined hands. Rekus loomed over them. There was a look in his eyes that chilled Shakre and she and Elihu exchanged glances. She had always found Rekus to be a hard, unyielding man, perhaps a little too proud of his position as Pastwalker and arrogant because of it. But she bore him no ill will and it was hard to see the effect this was already having on him.

"Life was hard for us when we came here," Rekus said. "Tu Sinar did not want us here and all the land turned against us. The ground shook. Cracks split the stone and fire spewed forth. The denizens of the Plateau threw themselves at us. Not just the tani and the ice wolf, but even the kelen and the splinterhorn buck. Many of us died." He grimaced, baring his teeth.

"But the worst was still to come. For then the Mistress vented her wrath on us."

He began to chant. The power of his voice swept over them, carrying them back into the past...

Only a ragged band of survivors remained, no more than a few score. Ice screamed from the black sky in sheets. The children huddled around a dying fire as the adults tried to shield them with their bodies.

Suddenly, out of the darkness came a thing of nightmare, the claws of a tani, the fangs of the ice wolf, the horns of the kelen. Azrael, the Mistress of the Plateau. She screamed with rage and fell on them like a storm.

Their meager hunting weapons were no match for this thing and the most feared warriors in the world fell like wheat before the scythe.

Then, out of their midst their greatest warrior, the untouchable Taka-slin, flew at Azrael, his spear flashing like lightning. A cry of hope went up from the survivors—a cry that quickly turned to dismay as his spear was broken and he was slapped aside like a child, to lie bleeding and senseless in the snow.

The final extinction of the Takare loomed over them. The desperate defense of the few remaining warriors was quickly broken and all that remained upright were the very young and the very old. Between the beast and them stood one woman.

The woman was Erined, mate of Taka-slin, and in her hand was her famed bow. Before Azrael could move, Erined put three arrows into her eye.

Azrael screamed her rage and pain, her advance halted. But they were the last of Erined's arrows and even as she looked down for another weapon the beast ripped the arrows free then flew at her and tore her to shreds.

When she was done venting her rage, Azrael stood and stalked towards the pitiful survivors, blood dripping from her smile.

But the cries of his dying mate had brought Taka-slin back to his senses. He came to his feet and from his throat came a fell cry that made all who still stood fall to the ground holding their ears, that made even Azrael, Mistress of the Plateau, freeze in her tracks and turn.

In that instant of hesitation, Taka-slin acted. A dead tree lay at his feet and with the strength of ten he wrenched it from the ground and flung it at the Mistress. Like a spear it shot through the night. Azrael started to twist away, but her own amazement slowed her and the tree caught her in the side and pierced her through. She fell, screaming and spitting. Even she, with all her power, could not withstand such a wound. She turned her one good eye on Taka-slin, cursed him, and then the body she wore slumped and was still.

Moments later her body tore completely in half and a thing of patchy darkness and sparks flew forth and disappeared to the north.

On this night the Mistress was beaten, but she was not destroyed.

Taka-slin did not need to look on his mate's body to know she was dead. Without a word he turned and left his people, following the direction of the Mistress's flight. The survivors cried out to him but he was maddened by his despair and he heard them not.

The vision relented and Shakre shuddered and drew a deep breath. Around her the others stirred. Many were shaking and tears ran down faces. Shakre was surprised. Rekus had never summoned the past with such intensity before. This was the first time she had ever completely lost her sense of self in the vision.

"But Taka-slin was not mad," Rekus said, pacing back and forth before them, his power still radiating from him. "He was not abandoning us. He went to secure our future.

"Drawn by an inner vision none of the rest of us could see, he went north, traveling through the wind and ice until he saw the Godstooth, shining against the sky. He followed the Cleaver through its lair in the stone, but it did not let him pass easily. Things rose up out of the water and wrapped themselves around him, trying to drag him into the river's maw. Creatures came to life in the stone and fell on him from above. But he was Taka-slin, champion from a race of champions, and one by one he overcame them all until he emerged from the defile and stood at the foot of the towering spire of white stone that is Tu Sinar's dwelling place.

"Three times he challenged the god, saying, 'I have defeated all your minions. There is only you now. Come out and answer for your crimes.' And three times the god refused, while the ground shook and stone cracked." Rekus's eyes glowed with fierce pride as he spoke. "Finally, Taka-slin spoke again. 'Since you will not come forth, I will set the terms of our pact and bind you with them. Hear my words: You will call off your creatures and let my people dwell on this land in peace. In return we will walk quietly across the face of your home. We will respect your denizens, taking only what we need to live. We will build no cities. We will start no wars. We will allow no others to dwell here. We will keep this land inviolate for you, though it cost us our very lives.'

"Then Taka-slin took a stone and carved the words of his oath into the Godstooth. When he was done, he placed his hands on the stone and spoke the words aloud, binding himself and all his ancestors to it."

No one spoke. Even Rehobim seemed subdued.

"This is the past you would turn your back on," Rekus said, fixing them all with his gimlet stare. "This is the oath you would break. Think on this before you rush off into the darkness."

With that he turned and stalked away, back to his hut.

"I think our Pastwalker will not give up so easily," Elihu said.

"I don't think Rehobim will either," she replied. Rehobim was walking away from the fire, three companions with him. He was speaking to them in a low voice.

"I believe I will go and see if there is anything the plants will share with me," Elihu said. He patted her arm and walked off into the darkness, leaving Shakre there alone with her thoughts.

Her eyes went to the hulking figure seated by the fire. His presence pulled at her. If she closed her eyes and tuned into her inner senses she could locate any member of Bent Tree Shelter by concentrating on them. But she had to make an effort to do so. With him it was different. His alien Song, so unlike any she had ever encountered, growled and roared inside her mind. He was like a rock lion among rabbits, so fierce and implacable was his presence.

She was struck by a sudden feeling that it was no coincidence, him arriving there at the Godstooth, at that precise point in time. She could almost say he had been sent by the gods, except that she was no longer sure what that particular appellation meant.

He was a pivot point. On him the fate of thousands, maybe tens of thousands, hinged. She sensed that it went beyond his formidable fighting skills, to something inherent in who and what he was. He was like a boulder dropped into a stream. Whether the stream flowed around him or smashed into him, it could not ignore his presence and must, inevitably, alter its flow.

And, like it or not, she was tied to that boulder. It seemed she would not be free of him so easily.

Wearily, she stood and walked after two old women who were walking slowly away, soft words passing between them, their heads tilted towards each other. "Pardons, Lize and Ekna," she said as she caught up to them. They paused and looked back at her. Both had lost their life mates in the past winter. They had become inseparable since then, to the point where Ekna had moved into Lize's hut. "The stranger. He will need warmer clothing. I thought…" She broke off purposefully. None were as adept at sewing as these two women. Their fingers knew things they did not.

Their heads moving as one, the two women looked from her to the massive stranger sitting beside the fire, then back to her. They exchanged looks then, holding a moment beyond words—Shakre caught a glimpse of it but turned her attention away, as she always did, out of respect for the privacy of others—then they nodded at her. Lize, whose voice was high, with some of a bird's shrillness, said, "By morning. But you must give it to him. He scares me."

"He scares me too," Shakre said. Then she sighed. It got worse. She never liked this part, always asking. The wind had brought her things she did not want to know, brought her responsibilities she did not want to bear. "I ask too much, I fear, but he will need shelter as well." Then she waited. It took a bit longer for an answer this time, but Ekna answered as she had known, or at least hoped, she would. This simple generosity of the Takare was one of the things she cherished most about them. Would that too, come to an end?

"With Elath gone, it is no more than a shell now," Ekna said. "I no longer think of it as mine." The frail, yet solid, woman reached out to pat Shakre on the arm. It seemed like every day at least one of the Takare patted her on the arm, as if she were a child who needed comforting. "Do not let tomorrow squeeze you in its cold hands, child. What will come, will come." Then the two women turned and shuffled away and Shakre was left fighting sudden tears.

When she had mastered herself, she returned to the fire. Everyone else had gone. It was only the two of them. For a time, she just stood there, looking at the stranger. He did not bother to acknowledge her presence, but sat staring into the embers as if he would never move again.

"I don't even know your name," she said finally. "But then, you don't seem to know mine either, though I already told you once." Still he did not stir. "I am Shakre," she said, then repeated it louder. No response. Aggravated, she took her walking staff and poked him in the foot. Like that her staff was ripped out of her hand and he was on his feet. He stared down at her from his height, his eyes narrowed to slits. He did not hold himself or the staff in a threatening manner, but nonetheless his anger was undeniable and she found her heart beating faster.

"At least I got your attention," she managed after a moment. He reached toward her. She stiffened. His hand opened and the staff clattered to the ground between them. She bent and retrieved it, feeling awkward and vulnerable. When she straightened, she made herself look him in the eye. She found herself wondering about the scars that covered his face. They were not all the same age. Some were almost pink, others long since turned brown. They were clearly done deliberately, but why? Were his people so brutal, so savage, that they marked their own kind this way?

"I just want to show you your shelter," she said, and mimed a roof over her head. She pointed at a bank of clouds scudding down from the north. "It will snow again tonight." She knew because the wind told her so; the wind ran before the storm, frolicking like a puppy running before its master. "If you don't want to sit out here and freeze, you can follow me." Right then she didn't care if he did or not. She was beginning to heartily dislike this cold savage.

But when she walked away she heard his heavy steps behind her. She showed him Ekna's shelter, a simple structure like all the rest in Bent Tree. It was circular, stacked rock chinked with dried mud and layers of dirt on the top. Small shrubs and hardy grasses grew from it at all angles. The door was hide stretched over a simple wooden frame. There were no windows. The hut was small. He would barely be able to lie down. She pulled the door aside and motioned to him to enter.

He bent his head and looked into the hut. Then he walked away.

Shakre took a deep breath and tried hard not to really loathe him. Then she sighed and walked alone to her hut. She had done what she could. There was no need to let his arrogance upset her. She knew before she reached the door that her home was not empty. For a moment, while her thoughts jumped ahead of her inner senses, she thought it was Elihu. Now and then he came to her hut late at night, and they sat for long hours, sometimes speaking in low voices, usually just sitting, sharing silently the things that they could share with no one else. But she knew a moment later that it was not him, and then she knew it was Micah and she smiled in spite of her weariness.

Shakre stepped inside and sat down. She uncovered the bowl of glow moss that sat on the small shelf above her sleeping furs and in the steady orange light she saw Micah staring at her. She was smiling, her eyes shining. The child was small for her age, her blue-gray eyes huge in her tiny, alabaster face. She was like a doll, thin and petite, set down amongst a people who tended toward broad and tall.

"He comes from up there, doesn't he?" Micah pointed skyward. "From the sky, sent by the stars."

Shakre shrugged. "I don't know for sure." But she had at least considered the point. Perhaps there were beings beyond the confines of this world and its petty gods, beings who, for whatever reason, took interest in the events here.

In a very serious tone Micah added, "I knew he was coming." She folded her small arms around her knees and drew them up to her chest. She smiled, a child's confident smile. "We're going to be friends, you know."

CHAPTER 11

The next morning the stranger was sitting on his rock when Asoken came forth to light the fire. All through the morning sun-greeting and first meal he sat there, scowling at the ground, thunderclouds over his head. The Takare tripped over themselves to stay away from him, but he had evidently decided they were no threat to him for not once did he deign to look at any of them. The morning was strained, the conversations subdued, as the Takare stepped gingerly around the rift which had opened in their village the night before. Even Birna's impending childbirth did little to lift their spirits. The meal was finished and most of the village had drifted away, when Micah began to make good on her words.

She bounced up to the hulking stranger, gave him a big smile which he ignored, then sat cross legged on the ground right next to him. She had a smudge of dirt on one cheek and her hair was tangled with leaves and twigs.

Shakre drifted closer, wanting to hear what went on. She heard someone call Micah's name and turned to see her mother almost at a run, her eyes big, her arms out. Shakre intercepted her. "It's okay," she said.

"My daughter..." the woman managed, trying to see over Shakre's shoulder.

"It's going to be okay," Shakre repeated. "Trust me."

"But you said...blood stains him. He kills."

"I did," she replied. "But I don't in my heart believe he would harm your daughter."

The woman gave her a long, searching look.

"Stand here with me," Shakre said. "We can watch together. I think...I have a feeling that she may be able to do something none of the rest of us can."

99

Micah's mother shuddered, then drew herself up resolutely and planted herself beside Shakre.

"I'm Micah," the little girl was saying cheerfully to the glowering stranger. "Why are you so mad?"

No response.

The little girl waited, absently pulling some leaves out of her hair. Then she laughed. "Sure. That's silly of me. You don't even speak our tongue, do you? No wonder you're so mad." She clapped her hands together with childish delight. "I'll teach you our words. Then we can be friends."

Very slowly, she said, "My name is Micah. Your name is…?" She pointed at herself as she said her name, then pointed at him. He ignored her. After a long moment where he did nothing, she went on. She pointed at the rock the stranger sat on. "Rock," she said slowly, then repeated it. She waited, and when he still did not respond she went on to the next thing. "Tree. Sky. Bird." On and on she went, while the sun climbed in the sky and the stranger pointedly ignored her.

Finally, after more than an hour, he looked at her, bared his teeth and growled. Micah just sat there and smiled up at him. He shook his head, stood up and stalked away.

Micah got up and bounced happily over to Shakre. The little girl's mother had left some time before, to aid in Birna's childbirth, after first securing Shakre's promise that she would not move from the spot. "He likes me," Micah bubbled. "We're going to be friends."

Shakre watched her run off, feeling a ray of hope pierce the gloom that she couldn't seem to shake off. Where a child could be that cheerful, things could not be all that gray. A moment later she heard the excited cries echoing from across the village and started that way. Apparently Birna had delivered her child. As she walked she wondered who it would be that the Dreamwalker would declare reborn this time. The Takare believed that eventually all who died were reborn to them in another form, and there was always great excitement at each new birth as people gathered to see which loved one had returned to them.

Intyr was already there when Shakre arrived, her gangly form bent over the newborn, her long blue hair falling around the infant like a shroud. Birna squatted on the birthing mat beside her, a large, joyful smile on her face, and the people of Bent Tree Shelter were gathering around. Like virtually everything else they did, the Takare gave birth outside. As she had so many times before, Shakre marveled at the ease with which these women gave birth. Rarely was there any need for her to use her healing skills to help. It was all very different from the pain and suffering she remembered from birthing Netra. A sudden pang struck her then and she could not help but envy Birna the joy she felt at this moment. How she longed to share the same with her daughter.

Intyr's low chanting faded away and she stood, lifting the infant in her arms, a smile on her face. It was a girl. "The spirit of Lionil has returned to us," she proclaimed in her soft voice. "He is much refreshed from his time in the soothing waters of the River, and ready to be a part of us once again." A cheer broke out. Lionil had been a much respected Huntwalker for the village, gone from them for nearly twenty winters. His reappearance now, so soon after the death of Meholah, was a good sign, though there was no guarantee he would resume the same duties in this life. That Lionil had been born female this time around was of no concern to the Takare. Male and female were simply two sides of the same tree and the undying spirit knew no gender.

Already Lionel's two surviving grandchildren—grown men now—were coming forward to hold the baby, smiles wreathing their faces. As the child grew up she would be told much of her former life and would be considered as closely related to the two men holding her now as to her own birth parents. This belief in reincarnation was part of what made the Takare close knit, Shakre reflected. With the constant rebirth of past loved ones into new families, everyone here was related in ways that were so complex and varied as to make anyone's head spin. More than once she had listened to Takare detail their family tree and ended up with a headache. And Takare weren't always born into the Shelter in which they'd lived before either. As often as not it was a member from another Shelter and word would have to be sent off soon after the birth so that surviving family members could gather to pay respects.

As she walked back to her home, Shakre thought about the Takare belief in reincarnation. Even after all these years she wasn't sure what she herself believed. Were loved ones really reborn into new bodies? She had seen people demonstrate knowledge of their past lives—both in skills and memories—that went beyond normal explanation. Reincarnation definitely clashed with the Tender belief that humans received only one life, then moved on to live in eternal bliss with the

Mother—or eternal torment with Melekath. Perhaps this belief was just a way to help them cope with the harshness of life up here. Certainly the knowledge that a loved one who had just died would return to them someday made it easier to handle the losses suffered by all.

CHAPTER 12

Netra was a day past the town when she found the corpses.

There were two of them. They had been tied to wooden stakes that were driven into the ground, then set on fire. Their corpses were charred beyond recognition, bodies twisted, heads thrown back, mouths open, gaping holes from which incongruously white teeth protruded.

But this was no ordinary fire. There was no pile of ashes and half-burned logs around their feet. Nor could any normal fire have been hot enough to burn these bodies as they had been burned, until there was little of them left beyond bone and scraps of blackened tissue. Nor was that all that was unusual. The wooden stakes they were tied to were not even blackened. The ropes which had tied them in place were untouched as well, as was the grass they stood on. Only their bodies had burned.

Around the neck of one hung a crude sign, lettered in dried blood. It had one word on it: Choose.

Netra stared at them, sick at heart. What did it mean, "choose"? What choice had they been given?

She'd spent the last day trying to figure it all out. Who was the blinded man the old lady and the girl had spoken of? Why was he taking people to Fanethrin? Was there a Guardian at Fanethrin? What did all this have to do with Melekath?

And the question she couldn't get out of her mind: Why was she still out here, chasing the slim hope of finding a mother who might not even be alive—who might not even want to see her—when she should be heading back to the Haven?

Strangely, part of her wanted to see this blinded man and his followers, see for herself if they were monsters or only men. Was the choice whether to follow Melekath or not? And if so, what would make someone choose to follow evil? What drove any of them? What could Melekath possibly offer them?

She told herself she would hear the blinded man's Selfsong if she got near him. She would have enough time to hide. She would not be one of his victims.

Late that afternoon she found more of his victims.

The terrain was getting progressively steeper as she approached the foothills of the huge, cloud-swathed plateau. The road had narrowed to a barely-visible track. The trees were thicker, taller, the air cooler.

Smoke still curled from blackened timbers of the house. The barn was ashes. A dog lay in the middle of the road, cut nearly in half.

Before the house stood three stakes, a charred body tied to each one. The one in the middle was small, a child, probably not more than six or seven. Something tore inside Netra when she saw the child and without thinking she ran forward. This child could not be left here like this. Such a horror could not be tolerated. She tore the sign from around the child's neck and threw it.

She took her knife out of her pack and sawed at the bonds until they parted. When she took hold of the child's body to lower it to the ground, she received a shock, so strong that she yelped and dropped the body.

She stood there staring at the child's remains, shaking all over. When she touched the body she felt like she was on fire. The pain was so intense, so real. With the pain came a surge of terror.

Somehow, when she touched the child's body, she picked up residual emotions left over from her last minutes of life, like an echo of the child's Selfsong. It was horrifying, what that poor child went through. She found herself suddenly enraged. What kind of monster would do such a thing to a child? Right then she wanted nothing more than to stab the ones responsible for this, stab them over and over until they could never hurt anyone else again.

She knelt beside the body and touched it with one finger, but this time there was nothing. Whatever leftover Song there was had dissipated.

She realized then that she was going to bury these bodies. She was not going to leave them here, like this. It was little enough, but she could deny the blinded man this one victory.

When she got up to see if she could find a shovel or some other digging implement, she saw the trail of blood leading back into the trees.

XXX

The blood wasn't that old. Whoever it came from might still be alive.

She took off at a run, following the trail. It wasn't difficult. There was quite a lot of blood, more spatters every few feet. She read the signs as she ran. The injured person was staggering, weakening fast.

She saw also that someone had pursued the injured person, a man by the size of his tracks. He hadn't been hurrying. He'd been confident that the injured person couldn't get away.

There was a hillside behind the burned farmhouse. Netra found her partway up it, lying at the base of a tree, two arrows sticking out of her. From the tracks, her pursuer hadn't even bothered to make sure she was dead. He'd simply shot another arrow into her and then left.

Netra ran to her. Both arrows were sticking out of her back. Shockingly, she was still alive, though she was pale and still. She looked to be about Netra's age.

Netra threw herself down beside her, her mind racing, trying to figure out what the best thing to do was. She wished Karyn were here. She knew more about healing than anyone else at Rane Haven. Should she leave the arrows in, or pull them out? If she pulled them out, she might make the bleeding worse.

She tore pieces from the girl's skirt and pressed them against the wounds, trying to staunch the bleeding. It helped, but not much.

Unsure what else to do, she put one hand on the girl's forehead and closed her eyes, concentrating, trying to learn more.

She could feel the girl's Selfsong fading quickly. She would be dead soon.

Netra bit her lip and forced herself to calm down. After a few deep breaths, she was able to go *beyond*. What she *saw* there filled her with despair.

The girl's *akirma* was torn in two places, where the arrows had struck. Song was pouring out of both wounds. Looking deeper inside the girl, she could *see* the brighter patch that was the girl's Heartglow. It was flickering, getting weaker. Once it went out, the girl would die.

"No," Netra growled. "You're not going to die. I won't let you."

As she'd done when Tharn was coming after her, she focused her Selfsong in her hands. The *akirma* around them began to glow brighter. Then she pressed her hands to the girl's wounds and began to will her Selfsong to flow into the girl.

She wasn't quite sure how to do it, only that she had to do it or the girl would die. So she gritted her teeth and somehow, through sheer force of will, she did it.

Selfsong began to flow from her into the girl. The girl's Heartglow slowed its flickering and grew marginally brighter. The rips on her *akirma* closed partway.

Netra allowed herself a ray of hope.

It was working!

Then she felt herself falter. The flow of Song from her slowed. The rips in the girl's *akirma* began to grow wider; her Heartglow resumed its wild flickering.

No!

Netra dug deep, pouring out everything she had, paying no regard to the cost to herself. She would give everything she had and more, if only she could save this one—

There was a sudden flash. The girl's *akirma* disintegrated. Her Heartglow flickered one last time and then fled.

Netra collapsed across her, unconscious.

The next thing she knew there were voices and someone was kicking her in the side. Waking up was like digging her way out of a deep, dark hole. She rolled away from the foot, disoriented, no memory of where she was.

"Get up, get up," a voice said angrily, grabbing her upper arm and yanking her to her feet.

Awareness returned all at once and Netra suddenly realized what was happening. It was dark, and she could not see more than dim shapes, but she knew with awful certainty who they were. She fought to free herself but she was tired, so tired, and the one who had hauled her to her feet tightened his grip and swung her around to face him.

"This one smells funny," he said, thrusting his face into hers and snuffling. Netra tried to push him away and when she did so her fingers brushed his face. As his skin met hers she felt his Selfsong. It felt burned and it hurt. She jerked her hands back.

"Bring her here, Bloodhound," a voice ordered from down the hill. "Where I can see her."

The one called Bloodhound pinned her arms behind her back and hustled her down the hill and around to the front of the burned-down farmhouse, where a dozen or so men stood in a loose group. Several held torches. In the weak light she saw the black marks on every forehead. Behind them were the other two burned bodies, still tied to their stakes.

Then they parted and their leader emerged and her heart turned to ice.

He wore a gray cloak, the hood thrown back. He was completely hairless, his skin gleaming like polished bone. He had no eyes. Where his eyes had been were only blackened sockets. Burn scars covered the entire upper half of his face. His nose was mostly gone, his lips twisted in a perpetual snarl.

"There's something different about this one," Bloodhound whined. He had long, shaggy red hair and very white, prominent teeth. "It hurts when I touch her."

The blinded man ignored him. As he walked up to her, Netra panicked and fought wildly to get free, but others took hold of her and forced her to hold still. She could not even look away as he put his face up close to hers.

Though he had no eyes, still she could feel the awful weight of his terrible scrutiny. This was not just a man here. There was something else, something old and fiercely malevolent that looked through those burned sockets, that gazed down into the depths of her being. She shrank before that scrutiny, feeling tiny and helpless.

"She is one of Xochitl's," the burned man said. His voice was different than it had been when he ordered Bloodhound to bring her down the hill. It was no longer his own. It came from far away and it was cold and inhuman. "One of her Tenders."

Then he smiled, an awful expression that pulled his twisted lips back to expose yellow teeth.

Netra almost screamed then. Facing Tharn had been terrifying, but Tharn's hatred had an almost animal mindlessness to it. This was a hatred that was cold and calculating, that had pondered long on its revenge.

And it hated her most of all because she was a Tender.

"Let me go. Let me go. Please. I promise, I'll do anything. Just let me go." Dimly she realized she was babbling, but she felt helpless to stop it.

"It's too late for that," the inhuman voice said. "Much too late. From the moment Xochitl chose to imprison me it was too late."

"I don't...that wasn't me. I didn't have anything to do with that."

One hand rose and the fingers touched her cheek, almost gently. When they did, Netra suddenly felt the terrible pain that the blinded man lived with every moment of his existence. Then it was as if a doorway opened in the middle of his face and she no longer saw him but found herself staring at a white-skinned face with a lipless mouth and a single, red-rimmed eye that burned into her.

"I don't care," the thing said.

"Please," Netra moaned, trying feebly to turn away.

"There is one chance."

The tiniest hope flared in her. "Anything…anything."

"I do not yet possess one of her followers. I think I would like this. One small measure of vengeance for what she did." The red-rimmed eye drew very close, until it filled all of her vision.

"So I will allow you to make your choice."

"What…what choice is that?"

"Me. Renounce her. Swear your deathless loyalty to me."

"Anything," Netra whispered.

CHAPTER 13

The red-rimmed eye drew back. There was a smile on the white-skinned face. The vision broke up and once again Netra was staring at the burned man, his smile mirroring his master's.

"It is the only real choice," he told her.

He held up one hand. Gray flame flickered around his thumb. "Let go of her," he told the men holding her. "She is ours now."

The hands released her. He reached out with his thumb.

Netra took an involuntary step back and when she did so, she stepped on something and almost lost her balance. She glanced down.

It was the burned body of the child she had cut down from the stake.

Suddenly she realized what she was about to do.

"No!" she shouted.

The blinded man froze.

"I reject you and that thing you follow," she told him.

The men seized her once again. Oddly, the blinded man did not look upset. In fact, his smile seemed to grow larger. "I prefer this choice. My master does too. We would rather see you suffer."

Netra was dragged over to the middle stake and shoved up against it. Her wrists were bound roughly behind her back.

"This will hurt more than you can imagine," the blinded man told her.

"I don't care. Anything is better than what you have all become." Though she tried to sound brave, she could not keep the tremor out of her voice. She seemed to have lost all strength in her limbs. What would it be like, as the flames engulfed her? Would anyone find her and cut her down, or would she stand here as mute warning to others? It struck her that no one she loved would ever know what happened to her. She would simply be gone, from their lives and eventually from their memories.

The blinded man raised both hands. Gray flames leapt up to engulf them.

Netra began to pray.

As she prayed, her vision altered, and she realized that she was slipping *beyond*. She embraced the change. In here, perhaps the pain would not be so bad. Perhaps she would be able to distance herself from what was happening to her body.

The blinded man's *akirma* was almost completely covered with what looked like a gray cobweb. Now and then the web shifted and something like red sparks erupted from inside him. The other men all had black smudges on their *akirmas*. From each smudge a network of black lines branched out, crisscrossing the interior of the *akirma* like a spider web.

Netra could feel the heat from the flames on her face and she tensed. It would not be long now.

But then she noticed something in the corner of her vision and turned her head to look.

There was a nebulous creature there, in the form of a rock lion with glowing eyes. She knew instantly what it was.

Her spirit guide.

It seemed she could hear it speak in her mind.

You know what to do. Simply let go and do it.

An ethereal calm came over her. Time seemed to slow down. Perception expanded, everything available to her at once. She could see the blinded man reaching, his hands about to cup her face. She could see the other men, leaning forward, hungry expressions on their faces.

And she knew what to do.

Song was all around her. And what was Song, but pure power, just waiting to be used? Once the Tenders of old had wielded Song as naturally as they wielded simple tools. She could do the same. It was all so clear.

The easiest source to use was Selfsong. Not hers, which was already depleted from trying to heal the injured girl, but that which was contained within the *akirmas* of the men around her.

If she wanted it, all she had to do was take it. It mattered not at all that her hands were bound; she didn't need hands to do this.

She gave a mighty push outward. Glowing tendrils emerged from her *akirma* and stabbed into the *akirmas* of three of the men nearest her.

Instantly, Song rushed into her. It was foul with the taint of Kasai, but to her it was unbelievably sweet.

The three men closest to her suddenly staggered, one going to his knees. The blinded man hesitated, confused.

Then she blew the power outward.

There was a flash of light and a shockwave of power burst outwards from her. The men were knocked sprawling, cries of pain coming from them. The torches went out.

The blinded man was knocked backwards and fell down. The flame around his hands went out. There was a fell cry as the ancient presence within him was banished.

Laughing from the sheer ecstasy of all the Song booming within her—she had held some back for herself—Netra easily snapped the bonds on her wrists.

She snatched up her pack and ran into the forest. Though it was pitch black under the trees she could see easily. She dodged limbs, leapt over fallen logs, and soon left her blundering, cursing pursuers far behind.

CHAPTER 14

It grew light as Netra ran and finally she had to stop. The burst of energy and strength she had gotten from siphoning off the men's Songs was gone and weariness once again laid its clinging touch on her. She also felt faintly sick to her stomach; despite her efforts she must have absorbed some of the taint from the men's black marks. She stood under a soaring fir tree and listened for her pursuers, but she heard nothing.

She resumed walking, taking her time. She allowed herself to bask then in what had happened.

She had done something no Tender had done since the time of the Kaetrian Empire. She had taken Selfsong from others and used it to make herself stronger.

She was not blind to the fact that the Tenders of old had badly misused that ability. Brelisha—the old Tender responsible for much of her and Cara's education—had been brutally persistent in teaching them everything she knew about the errors those Tenders made. According to her, there were powerful Tenders who kept dozens or even hundreds of slaves like cattle, using them for the sole purpose of making themselves stronger. It had completely corrupted them all in the end, Brelisha maintained.

But this was different. Netra had taken from those men only to save herself from a terrible fate. She felt quite certain that the Mother would not judge her harshly for her actions.

Had Xochitl heard her prayers? Was it she who sent the spirit guide to save her?

"Thank you, Xochitl," she said. "Thank you for saving me." All her earlier doubts and fears were gone, blown away like smoke in the wind. Xochitl was listening. She did care. Melekath had not already triumphed. There was hope and light in the world.

Deeper within her was the thought that she was frightened to examine too closely, the thought that she truly *was* the one chosen by Xochitl to play a vital role in the salvation of the world. It seemed almost heretical to consider it, but look at all she had already been through.

She had faced Tharn and survived. That time, like this time, her spirit guide appeared and helped her. She faced Gulagh in the city of Nelton and when she saw through the Guardian's illusion—with the help of her *sonkrill*—she saved both herself and Siena.

And now this had happened. Whatever the foul creature with the red-rimmed eye was, she would be willing to bet it was the third Guardian, Kasai.

How else could she have possibly faced all three of Melekath's most powerful minions and survived? What other explanation was there?

A new thought occurred to her. What if the reason the Mother hadn't shown herself yet to fight Melekath was because she couldn't? What if Melekath, or his Guardians, had somehow managed to imprison her? It would explain so much.

If that was true, and it was a big if, then might it not be possible that Xochitl was trying to find that one woman among her Tenders who could free her? And might not that one woman be Netra?

The thought was staggering in its implications and Netra felt faintly guilty for even considering it, but it was certainly possible. After all, why else would Xochitl not have shown up to fight Melekath? However angry she was with the Tenders, surely she still cared about the rest of her creation. She wouldn't just sit by and let Melekath destroy it all.

Unless there was nothing she could do. Unless she was waiting for that one Tender who would answer her call for help.

Why not me? Netra thought. *Are any of the other Tenders even doing anything at all, or are they just hiding like the women at Rane Haven?*

"Guide me, Mother," she prayed. "If this is true, send me a sign. I promise that I will do anything, sacrifice anything, to do as you command."

She paused to take her *sonkrill* out of her pack and hang it around her neck. She looked up and there was the plateau, closer than ever, though still a couple days away through increasingly rough terrain. She saw no sign of a road or any houses, but she didn't need them.

The gnawing fear which had driven her for so many days was gone. She could take her time, forage from the land, think about what she would say to her mother when she found her.

Then she heard something in the distance behind her and she froze, a cold tendril of fear tickling her belly.

A lone cry, a triumphant keening. It was distant still, but she knew it was Bloodhound, that he was on her trail.

She was not free yet.

She moved all day long, jogging when she could, walking hard the rest of the time, never stopping to rest. She pushed as hard as she could, but still they closed the gap, drawing closer with every hour.

She tried every trick she could think of, walking in icy streams until her feet were numb, doubling back, walking only on rock, but it did no good. The man's cry was like the baying of a hound behind her. Sometimes he lost the trail for a bit and she would widen the distance between them, but always he found it and came on again with renewed vigor.

Time and again she looked up at the cloud-topped plateau, willing it to be closer, because she felt sure if she could get onto it she would be safe, that somehow they would not follow her there. But always it stayed just out of reach, taunting her with its illusion of closeness.

And with every step her muscles weakened. She was hungry, but there was little food left in her pack. She began to stumble now and then, tripping over roots that seemed to rise up and grab at her ankles. The terrain grew ever steeper and more difficult as she entered the foothills of the great plateau and there were times when she crested a sharp ridge and had to slump against a rock or a tree for precious minutes until she regained the strength to go on.

By the next morning Netra walked in a gray haze of exhaustion. Ghosts seemed to rise up from the ground and trip her. Her left palm was gashed and bleeding from where she had cut it during one of the countless falls she had suffered during the night. There was another cut across her cheek and bruises all over her, too numerous to count. Her ankle throbbed and she wondered if she had sprained it but there was nothing she could do about it. She didn't even have time to bind it.

The men were close. She could hear their hated voices now and then, mixed with Bloodhound's eerie cry, carried to her on stray breezes. She wondered dimly how it was that they were not tired as well, if Kasai somehow fed them strength to continue on, and why Xochitl could not bless her so as well. She heard them congratulating each other, yelling of what they would do to her when they caught her, before they dragged her back to face the blinded man. If only she had taken more Song from them. They would not be so energetic and she would have the extra strength she needed to outdistance them. If only she had drained them to unconsciousness.

During the night she had come to hate them as she had never imagined she could hate other human beings. She hated them all, but most of all she hated Bloodhound. He was the one who could not lose her trail, who always led the pack as they yelped at her heels. In the worst hours of the early morning as she stumbled through a waking nightmare of falling, getting up and falling yet again, she had dark, vivid fantasies of plunging her knife into his throat, of stabbing him again and again until he was nothing but a bloody, lifeless mess.

Either they would die, or she would die. She saw that now. There were no other alternatives. She wished for a miracle, a tree to fall on them, a pack of wolves to attack them, but of course no such thing happened. She prayed often to Xochitl, but there was no answer and her earlier certainty that the Mother was looking out for her now seemed distant and absurd. Who knew what was real and what was in her mind? Maybe she had imagined it all.

She started down yet another steep hillside, the ground covered in loose pine needles that slipped with every step. She lost her footing and fell awkwardly, rolling and sliding down the hill out of control. She banged into some rocks, bounced, and for a moment there was only air underneath her. Then she hit hard and lay there trying to force breath back into her lungs.

By some miracle she seemed to have broken nothing. She tried to stand but lost her balance and fell. For a moment she just gave up. Let them have her. There was no escape.

She heard the voices drawing ever closer and knew she was not yet ready to die. She got to her knees and that was when she saw the cave nearby. It was mostly screened by bushes and hard to see; she just happened to be in the right spot. Most people would pass right by it.

She got up and stumbled toward it. A voice in her head was telling her this was a mistake, that the men would find her and then she'd be trapped, but she ignored it. She could go no further right now. She must rest for a little while.

She forced her way through the bushes. The entrance was low and she had to drop to her hands and knees to enter. She stopped when she was inside and looked around. What she saw then had to be an apparition. She stared in amazement.

It was her spirit guide.

She blinked and realized that this was no apparition. It was a real rock lion. A female.

Rock lions were very rare. They were secretive, solitary animals that generally only came out at night and they were careful to avoid humans. Even in all the years Netra had been prowling the foothills of the Firkath Mountains she had never seen one. She'd only ever even seen their tracks twice, and she'd never been able to follow the animals for long, they were so elusive. There were people in Tornith who didn't even believe they existed. But here was one right before her, close enough almost to reach out and touch. She could smell its muskiness, see the white-tipped, silver fur.

"Please," she said, reaching out with one hand, acting on impulse or desperation. "Help me."

The big cat growled softly at her.

Then the lion slipped by her and went outside.

Netra simply lay down on the spot and closed her eyes. In the moments before sleep claimed her she heard a coughing roar, followed by surprised shouting, and then the sound of running feet.

When she awakened it was early afternoon. She sat up and saw the lioness lying off to the side, calmly licking her paw and washing herself. There was blood on her muzzle. The cat seemed supremely pleased with herself.

"Thank you," Netra said. Then she turned away and crawled out of the cave.

Netra stood up outside and stretched. She felt better. Not good, but better. The plateau loomed over her, one hard dash away. She might be able to make it by dark.

She started picking her way down the hillside. She hurt everywhere and her stomach was pinched and empty, but she was alive. For now, that was enough. She crossed the small icy stream at the bottom of the gulch and started up the other side. She was just nearing the top when she heard a familiar, hateful voice shout in the distance.

"There she is!"

Netra groaned and started running.

By nightfall she was on the side of the great plateau, inching her way up the steep side. But if she had thought that merely setting foot on those slopes would mean safety, she was badly mistaken, for her pursuers had not given up.

At least, one of them had not.

Bloodhound still followed her. As she searched for another handhold and wearily pulled herself up, she heard him behind her, less than a hundred feet away. The others might be back there somewhere too, but she had not heard them in hours and had not seen them since before sunset, when she had glimpsed them standing on top of a ridge staring up at her, their weariness evident in the slumped way they held themselves. They were men then, not demons, and she believed that their strength had finally failed them. All of them, that is, but Bloodhound.

The mountainside was nearly sheer. Climbing had replaced walking. She clutched tufts of grass, tree roots and jutting rocks to pull herself up one painful foot at a time. A weariness such as she had never known enclosed her. It went beyond simple physical exhaustion, permeating her heart, her spirit. It seemed she had been on the run forever, never stopping, always in fear. She knew with utter black certainty that it would never end either, not as long as Bloodhound lived, for he would never stop, never lose her trail. Why couldn't the rock lion have killed him? she asked herself for the hundredth time. One swipe of its powerful claws and she would be free right now.

A short while ago she had lost control of herself, exhaustion and fear overwhelming her temporarily. She had stood on a tiny ledge and screamed at the black shape which dogged her every move. She had cursed him with a ferocity that she'd never suspected existed inside her. And all he had done was laugh. She had nearly flung herself down the slope and attacked him physically.

Netra came to what amounted to a crease in the side of the plateau, where she could stand and walk for a short distance. It led to the left and up and she followed it, grateful for the respite for her arms, which ached terribly, though the walk made her injured ankle throb once again. But all too soon the crease ended and she was faced with yet another steep rock face, barely visible in the light of the just-rising moon.

She craned her head back and looked up, and up. The mountainside seemed to go on forever, the clouds that wreathed the top blotting out the stars. It was too far. She could not make it to the top before he caught her. And even if she did by some miracle make it there, what would that gain her? He would still chase her, and eventually he would catch her. She could hear the rasp of his breathing behind her, getting closer.

She felt her knees start to buckle and forced herself to move forward. She had to move or lie down and die. There was nothing else left for her. She took hold of a spindly tree that grew out of the rock face and pulled herself up, one foot, then two. Grimly she fought her way onwards, her mind disappearing into some nether region, leaving her body alone to move one hand, then one foot, woodenly, ceaselessly.

Sometime later she grabbed a protruding rock with her left hand. It shifted and she lost her grip, started to fall back and out. She hung there for a long moment, balanced between falling backwards and regaining her hold. She clawed at the rock face, trying to find anything to grab onto. Then her fingers found faint purchase and she pulled herself forward. The awful feeling subsided and she clung there with her cheek pressed to the rock, breathing hard.

When she had calmed enough to assess her situation, she realized that the mountainside had gotten dramatically steeper without her even noticing it, that she was clinging to a cliff. It fell away below her, almost sheer, for a good twenty feet, and stretched above for a great deal further than that. This was crazy. There was no way she could climb this, even if she wasn't exhausted. She needed to go down, find another way.

She looked down and her heart fell when she saw Bloodhound below her, too close. She couldn't climb back down; he would catch her. There was no other way but up. She reached up, found another handhold, and another, forcing her weary body onwards. She reached again and her arm hooked over a ledge. Gasping with relief, she pulled herself up onto the ledge and lay there for a moment, catching her breath.

But when she got to her knees and looked up to see where she would go from here, she nearly cried out. Above her loomed an unbroken cliff for as far as she could see. The ledge did not extend in either direction. She was out of options.

She peered over the edge and saw Bloodhound down at the foot of the cliff she was on. She held her breath, daring to hope that he would pass by, that he might lose her trail just long enough to give her another chance.

When he looked up at her and took hold of the first handhold, she would have wept with frustration had she not been too weary to do so. Frustration gave way to fear as he made his slow, inexorable way towards her. As she watched him, listened to the rasp of his breathing, the scratching of his hands and feet on the rock, her fear gave way to anger. Abruptly she felt a surge of hatred engulf her. This was no human being which pursued her, but a monster straight out of Melekath's pit. He was a worm, a thing, a cancer to be cut out and stomped on.

If only he were dead, she thought. If the rock lion had killed him. If he would slip and fall. If a boulder would just come loose and roll down on top of him.

She shifted her position and felt a rock under her right hand move slightly. Disbelieving, she tugged on it. It was larger than a man's head, and definitely loose. He was directly below her, not a dozen feet away. It would be so easy to push the rock onto him. At the very least he would be badly wounded, both from the rock striking him and the ensuing fall. With one action she could solve all her problems, remove this hated man from her life forever. Her heart leaped at the thought of him lying dead below her, unable to ever follow her again.

Excited now, she moved to where she could brace herself, get a good hold on it. Her hands were slick with sweat, her movements abrupt, almost frenzied. She had to push it over now before his path took him to one side or the other and she couldn't hit him with the rock.

All at once the enormity of what she was about to do struck her. She froze and stared down at him. She had told Kasai no. She had refused to swear herself to Melekath, to take his brand on her forehead, even when doing so would have saved her life. She had stood up to a Guardian and refused him because she would not be a murderer.

Yet here she was, less than two days later, preparing to kill a man to save her life.

I vow never to kill, never to take the life of another…

It was hard, clear, unequivocal. It was the basic lesson that the Tenders of the Empire had forgotten, that Netra and every other Tender swore never to forget. She saw very clearly then that if she went through with this deed it wouldn't matter if she wore Melekath's brand or not, because she would wear it on her heart and that was all that mattered. She would become his as surely as if she knelt before him and took his vow.

Trembling over what she had almost done, Netra moved away from the rock. She knelt on the ledge, held her *sonkrill* in both hands, looked up at the sky and prayed for forgiveness.

How could she almost have done such a thing? she wondered. Especially after the Mother had so clearly acted not once, but *twice*, in the last two days to save her? Was her faith so fragile, so useless, that as soon as she was in danger she would just throw it away?

She moved to the edge and settled herself where she could see Bloodhound. If it was the will of Xochitl that she die here, then so be it, she decided. If she was to die, then she would die, but at least she would go without more blood on her hands.

She felt strangely calm and peaceful as she sat there, watching the man who would kill her draw ever closer. Maybe it was the combination of exhaustion and hunger and fear that had brought her to this point, but she no longer felt afraid. Her fate was in the hands of the Mother. There was nothing else she could do, so therefore there was no reason left to fear. It was completely out of her hands.

Bloodhound came closer. He was right where she was when she nearly fell. He stopped and looked up at her. His teeth glinted in the moonlight. There was blood on his cheek.

"Now I have you," he said, and reached for a protruding rock—

The rock came loose in his hand. For a moment he hung there, staring up at her, horrible realization in his eyes. His fingers clawed uselessly at the cliff face.

Then he fell backwards and down.

He hit, bounced high, hit again and then struck the ground at the base of the cliff. He lay there bent at an awkward angle, his body a dark blotch in the moonlight, while Netra tried not to hope that he was dead.

Then he moaned and moved his head, his arms and legs. He rolled onto his side and got to his hands and knees. When he tried to get to his feet his leg buckled and he went down hard. The next time he stayed on his hands and knees.

Without looking up at her he started crawling back down the mountain.

The blinded man stood in the morning light and watched the tiny figure of his prey move slowly up the side of the mountain. They had lost her this time. But they had come very close. Well he knew how close they had come to having her last night. He had seen her poised over the loose rock, so close to hurling it down on Bloodhound and killing him. Yes, he saw many things with this vision given to him by Kasai. He saw the cracks in her faith, cracks she did not even realize were there. He saw where she would break and he knew that next time it would be different.

Bloodhound crawled out of the trees. Blood had soaked through his shirt and one leg was bent badly. His face was gray, lined with exhaustion and pain, but his eyes glittered brightly. "Once my leg heals," he said. "I will go after her again."

"Yes," the blinded man replied.

Bloodhound sniffed. "I can still smell her. There's nowhere she can go I can't find her."

CHAPTER 15

The brief warmth of summer was at its peak. With each passing day that the strangers didn't return to the Plateau, the rift that had formed between the Takare closed somewhat. Perhaps the outsiders would never return. Perhaps Melekath had given up his revenge on Tu Sinar. Perhaps it was all a mistake.

Rehobim still tried to goad the few who listened to him into preparing to fight, but their numbers dwindled and his outbursts grew shorter and shorter until finally he spent his evenings around the fire sulking silently. There was the troubling presence of Jehu and the reality he represented, but he kept to himself and so could be overlooked.

Even the big stranger in their midst wasn't so noticeable anymore. He never spoke. Every morning he sat on his stone by the fire pit, scowling at nothing. Every morning Micah sat at his feet, chattering on and on, pointing things out to him, telling him stories. At some point he would grow tired of her constant noise and stalk off into the woods, not to be seen again until nightfall.

But, ever so slowly, Micah *was* wearing down his barriers, Shakre was sure of it. To the casual observer the big warrior paid no attention to the small form that crouched beside him. Yet, Shakre had watched the two of them enough to know that wasn't completely true. She saw it in the way he cocked his head to the side now and then, the way he sometimes forgot himself and followed the motion of Micah's arm as she pointed out something she found fascinating in the world around her. Even a soft rain could, given enough time, wear down a stone.

This day started out just like the others. After the morning meal, as soon as Micah had completed the small tasks her mother had for her, she came running to the fire pit where the stranger sat on his stone.

"Hi, friend!" she called as she got close. "It's me, Micah, again!" She slowed as she reached him, her little face solemn. She knelt down before him and said, very slowly, and very clearly, "My name is Micah. What is your name?"

She waited, as she always did, and received only silence. But it didn't bother her. After a bit, she simply filled in the gaps herself.

"Oh, I thought I'd never get away this morning. Mam had so many chores for me to do. Clean this, sweep out the home, shake out the blankets. I kept trying to tell her she was making me late for your language lesson, but I don't think she paid any mind to me at all!" Her voice rose on the last words, as if she had just made some marvelous discovery that was sure to amaze her listener.

The copper-skinned warrior didn't move, but Shakre thought she saw his eyes flick in the little girl's direction and she smiled to herself.

"Today I want to show you something, my friend," the little girl chattered on, oblivious to his silence. "Something really special. Something you just *have* to see." She explained to him in detail how she had gone to a copse of holdcherry bushes out at the edge of the village to shake out her blankets and how she'd found the most amazing thing there. Shakre smiled as she listened. Everything Micah saw was "amazing." The little girl's enthusiasm for life was infectious, irresistible.

Unable to contain herself any longer, Micah jumped up and grabbed hold of his hand. "Come!" she cried. "See what I found!"

Shakre held her breath as the big head turned down to look at the small hand, lost against the vastness of his own large one. Micah tugged again, harder. "Come *on!* Get up! You can't just sit there like a lump every day."

For a moment Shakre thought he would pull his hand back, but then slowly, as if unsure of what he did, he stood. His head swiveled towards her, as if suddenly feeling Shakre's eyes on him. When he saw her watching he carefully removed Micah's hand from his own.

Micah clapped her hands, not the least bit bothered. "Hurry!" she cried. "Or they'll be gone when we get there." She raced off a way, then looked back. The stranger was still standing there, showing no signs of following.

On a whim, Shakre said, "Show me, Micah. I'd like to see."

The little girl lit up. "Great!" She ran over, and Shakre felt herself being tugged along in her wake. "We won't worry about old cranky," she said over her shoulder. "He'll come when he feels like it." Then, as if she couldn't be held back by Shakre's sedate pace any longer, she dropped her hand and darted on ahead. Shakre wondered what she'd found. Was it a fallen birds' nest, a bit of tattered spider web, an interesting mushroom?

"I found them under the fallen tree, over by the holdcherry bushes. Oh, I can't wait to show you!" They were just approaching the edge of the village now and Micah darted on ahead, still bubbling with enthusiasm.

Shakre had only a heartbeat of realization, a sudden clenched warning that gripped her heart, when it happened—

A flash of yellow fur and claws burst from the bushes, so fast that it took Shakre a moment to realize what it was. Then it was on the little girl. She had time only for a startled squeak, and its jaws closed on her and it was dragging her back into the forest.

Shakre ran forward, yelling, heedless of her own safety, knowing in her heart that it was already too late. No way could she catch a tani, no way could she do anything to stop it.

There was a sudden roar behind her and the big stranger burst past her at a dead run. Without slowing he snatched up a stone the size of a man's head, curling his huge hand around it. In the next instant he flung the stone, so hard it whistled.

It struck the fleeing tani on the hip. The predator spun, looked back at the mountain bearing down on it, then dropped its prey and ran.

The stranger was bent over Micah when Shakre got there. He looked up at her as she got there, and there was something in his eyes she'd never seen before. But she had no time for it now. She threw herself down beside the small, still form, her heart recoiling at what she saw. There was too much blood, the wounds were too deep.

She looked up and back into his eyes. He jerked back as if she'd struck him and his mouth opened. Then he leaped to his feet and took off running after the tani.

✗ ✗ ✗

Rehobim was sitting by himself under a tree when he heard Shakre's shouts and the word tani. He reacted at once, snatching up the spear that leaned against the tree beside him and running. He got there just as the big stranger took off into the forest. Without hesitating, he went after him.

The stranger was fast, faster than Rehobim would have guessed, but he did not know the ways of the Plateau and he crashed through the forest like a mad bull, tearing vines from trees, plowing through bushes. Nor did he know how to track, and already he was veering away from the path the tani had taken. Without stopping to think, Rehobim caught up to him and grabbed his arm. The stranger turned on him with a snarl, fists raised and Rehobim was suddenly afraid he had made a very big mistake.

"No! That's not the way the tani went!" he cried. He pointed back the way the stranger had come. "It turned there at the stone. It's heading for the crevasse. Follow me. I can track it for you."

The stranger hesitated, then slowly lowered his fists and nodded.

Rehobim and the stranger ran after the tani and Rehobim knew they were on their own. No one else from the village would be coming. It was suicide to track a tani. It would be even worse if the animal made it to its lair before they caught up to it.

But that wasn't the only reason no one else would follow the tani. They would not follow because of the unspoken parts of the Oath. Even after hundreds of years they were mere visitors on the Plateau, here only by the tolerance of its true lord and master. As visitors they had no true status. They could defend themselves against attack, and they could hunt what they needed to live—only as long as they were careful and didn't anger the Mistress—but they could not retaliate after an attack. They could not hunt down and kill those creatures which threatened them. They were not even visitors here, in their own home. To Rehobim they were no more than rodents, allowed to scurry about the edges, suffered to live so long as they did not squeak too loudly.

Rehobim burned with the shame and outrage of it. Sometimes he could not believe that they were his people. How long would they stand meekly and let themselves be preyed on? How long would they deny their true heritage? They were the Takare, the most feared warriors in all of Atria. Yet they huddled up here like children, afraid of their own shadows. The big stranger looked on them with scorn because that was all they were deserving of. Well, today he would learn differently. Today he would learn that the old blood ran true in the veins of at least one Takare. *I am not afraid,* Rehobim told himself as he ran. *I am not afraid of the tani, and I am not afraid of the outsiders.*

No matter what happened before.

Unwillingly his mind returned to that day, he saw again the gray fire, and he heard the screams of the dying. He fought it with everything he had, but he could not stop his mind from relentlessly playing back the events of that fateful day.

Once again he was lying in the crookthorn thicket, his heart caught in his throat. Slowly, a hand that could not be his own—that shook as if with a fever—reached out and parted the gray-green leaves. His eyes looked out on something he would never be free of, that would play over and over again in his heart no matter how long he lived…

X X X

"Only one question. Only one answer." Gray fire wreathed the man's hands, licked out for Meholah. The Huntwalker's face ran with sweat and muscles moved under his skin. But he stood straight and tall. He did not back down.

"No," he said, his voice shaken but clear.

"So you have chosen," the gray-clad one said, and lowered his hands.

Now! *Rehobim screamed at himself.* Now is your chance! Raise your bow. Fire!

He still had his bow. He had not dropped it during his flight. He ran like a yulin and he evaded his pursuers easily. He circled back. He had the cover. He had the weapon. All he had to do was use it.

But he could not make himself move. He lay there with muscles of water and when Meholah began to scream he buried his face in the dirt and wet himself.

He did not move until hours after the outsiders were gone, hours after the screaming stopped. Then he lurched to his feet, and ran for the Shelter like a child.

X X X

Rehobim gritted his teeth as the shame washed over him once again. He fought back with anger, lashing himself with it over and over, forcing himself forward. Let the tani kill him. He no longer had anything left to lose. Part of him hoped it would kill him.

But…if it did not, if he faced it and survived…perhaps he could learn from the stranger. Perhaps the stranger would teach him courage so that next time it would be different. Next time he would kill many of the outsiders, with his bow and his spear and his teeth if he could. Kill them until the shame went away.

At the edge of the barren Rehobim's anger failed him. Across that open expanse was the tani's lair. He could see the tangle of boulders rising from the blank stone like a malignant growth. Tani lived a long time. This one had preyed on the members of Bent Tree since his grandfather's time. That it was the same one he was sure. Before him in the dirt was a single track as big as his head. One toe was missing.

When he hesitated, the stranger pushed by him, heading straight for the boulders. A moment longer and then Rehobim ran after him. He caught up to him and muttered, "I am not afraid," to the broad back.

But his knees shook and his spear felt like a twig in his hand. It would snap if he threw it. Tani were huge, near-mythical creatures. The best one could hope for was to stay out of a tani's way. No Takare since Taka-slin had ever killed a tani. He wanted to run and hide. But he forced himself to keep going, to look only at the ground in front of each step.

The stranger strode to the base of the boulder pile and stood looking up. The mouth of the tani's lair was clearly visible, a gaping darkness about halfway up. A broad ledge ran along the front of the lair, and numerous bones were scattered across it.

In a voice loud enough to shake the rocks, the stranger bellowed something that was clearly a challenge. Rehobim crouched behind a stone, struggling to control his trembling. This was madness. No matter how good he was, the stranger could not defeat a tani. He didn't even have a weapon with him. His great size would do him no good against the tani's teeth or its claws.

Rehobim sensed movement from above and looked up, his heart stopping. The tani emerged onto the ledge and looked down on them. At its shoulder it was nearly as tall as a grown man, covered in thick yellow fur with one black stripe extending down each side. Its incisors curved out of its mouth and down to its chin. Slowly, majestically, it drew itself up to its full height, balancing on its hind legs as a bear would. It raised its front legs, extending claws as long as Rehobim's hand. It growled, low and deep, and then it came. The first leap carried it halfway down the boulder pile. With the second it would land on the stranger, who stood motionless.

The world slowed down as the drama unfolded. Rehobim saw the muscles bunching under the creature's hide as it gathered itself, saw it launch and fly through the air, teeth gleaming, claws reaching—

In the split second before the tani reached him the stranger acted. He leapt forward, inside the extended claws, and struck the beast with a vicious left hook to the side of its head.

The blow knocked the tani onto its side, temporarily stunning it, and as it fell the stranger jumped on it. One powerful arm encircled the tani's thick neck. Before the stunned beast could recover, he joined his hands and twisted his whole body violently to the side.

There was a loud crack and the tani abruptly went still.

The stranger unlocked his hands and stood. Without looking down at the creature, without looking at Rehobim, he walked away.

Rehobim crouched behind the rock, frozen. His gaze flitted from the tani's lair, to the stranger's retreating back, to the broken form of the tani. Over and over. Nothing happened. The tani was still dead. After a few minutes he straightened up and moved toward the still form, one slow step at a time.

He nudged the thing with his foot, then spun in a crouch to scan the horizon. Still nothing happened, and something like a sneer twisted his lip. All at once he leaped on the creature, his knife in his hand, sinking the blade into the dead flesh over and over. His teeth stood out behind bared lips and his eyes went dark as he grunted with the exertion of each blow.

His passion spent, he sank back and again looked around. The rocks watched impassively. Even the bubbling sulfurous pools were quiet. His eyes roamed the ground until he found a broken chunk of rock the size of both fists. With several hard blows he smashed out one of the long canine teeth. Then he stood, holding the tooth over his head, and screamed at the emptiness:

"Azrael! Azrael!"

Shakre felt the stranger's presence long before he stepped into the circle of firelight. As he came into sight she met his almond gaze. For one brief, fleeting moment his carefully maintained shields lowered, and she saw clearly the depths of his pain, pain that went to the heart of his being. She longed to give him the answer he sought, just as she longed to give Micah's parents the answer they sought. But she could not. She had tended Micah all day, sewing the ragged slashes together, treating her as best she knew how. Somehow, when she should already be dead, Micah was still alive. She might live to morning. She might die tonight. But Shakre was sure she would die. Her wounds were too great.

The stranger saw the answer in her eyes and he sagged perceptibly. Then his shields rose back into place and he retreated behind them, the cold mask once again dropping. He turned and moved back into the darkness of the forest.

A while later there was another movement in the shadows and Shakre turned to see Rehobim stride up to the fire circle, carrying something large in his arms, wrapped in a bloody piece of hide. Around his neck a large tooth dangled on a leather thong. He threw the bundle on the ground. There was a thump and a fanged face rolled out of the hide. Everyone grew very quiet.

"Justice," Rehobim said, his voice thick with animal emotion. "For the first time since we came to this place, we have justice. The tani attacked us, and the stranger killed it. It will never feed on us again."

The people went very still, everyone pondering the awesomeness of what had happened. Suddenly Rekus cried out. "What have you done?" His voice was shrill, the whites of his eyes showing. "What has that monster done?"

Rehobim's reply was low and frightening in its intensity. "He has showed us how to fight back. After too many years of living like cowards, he has showed us courage."

"The tani is the favorite child of the Mistress!" Rekus cried, his horror echoed by many of the villagers. "You have brought her wrath down on all of us!"

"I knew you would say that, old man," Rehobim sneered. "I knew you would quiver and try to cut the heart from our victory."

"And if the price of your victory is the Mistress killing us all?" Rekus quavered. "What then? Will you still crow when she comes for you?"

"But she won't," Rehobim replied, turning so that he spoke to all of them, not just Rekus. "You wait. You'll see. Nothing will happen, because Azrael is *gone*. Gone like the rest of them."

As he said these words Shakre's eyes shot to Elihu and they shared unspoken thoughts. *The gods gone!* It explained so much, the restlessness in the wind, the uneasiness in the plants. Gone, while the taint in the flows of LifeSong spread and pooled. The Eight and the lesser gods who stood with them made the war that sealed Melekath and his followers away. Now Melekath was returning and the gods had fled and left the world to its doom. It was so much worse than she had dreamed. In that moment she realized how much she still did believe in the old gods, how much she had believed they would return to help when the need was great. Despair gripped Shakre's heart. What hope did they have now?

"Let me tell you a new truth," Rehobim continued, unaware of the effect of his words. "A new way, brought to us by the outsiders. The only power left is the one they call Father. *He* is the truth. *He* is the reality we have to deal with. The only thing we have left is one question: Will we crawl before him and become his slaves? Or will we stand up and fight?"

Excited voices rose and the firelight glimmered on Rehobim's face. He seemed taller then, Rekus little more than a shadow beside him, the old man's hands flashing, his worried voice skittering of the past, of what they had always been.

"You speak of fighting a god," someone cried out. "How can we do this?"

"Look at him," Rehobim replied, pointing at Jehu off to the side, his misery as plain as a shout. "And ask yourself instead how you can *not* fight."

Rehobim did not wait for an answer, but continued. "Consider this: once before all was lost for our people. We came here to find refuge and the very land turned against us. Then, as now, a god struck at us, and sought to destroy us." He waited, let the silence build.

"But were we destroyed?" he cried, raising his fist.

A low murmur, almost a growl, came from the villagers.

Rehobim put one foot on the tani's head. "No, we were not destroyed. We were delivered. A hero saved us."

Every eye fixed on him, every breath caught.

"Taka-slin."

He began to chant it. *"Taka-slin. Taka-slin. Taka-slin."* One by one a number of Takare, mostly the young, took up his chant.

Rekus at last managed to find his voice. "That has nothing to do with now," he croaked, his voice wavering. "Taka-slin has never been reborn among us. His oath to Tu Sinar went beyond death. It binds him still. Tu Sinar will never release him." The chant died away, those who raised it lowering sheepish eyes.

"Tu Sinar is gone. Or asleep—it makes no difference," Rehobim said, advancing on the old man, his eyes glittering. "The oath no longer holds."

"Then you're saying...but you're saying..." the old man said helplessly.

"There stands Taka-slin!" Rehobim cried, pointing off beyond the crowd. As one, the villagers' heads turned. Standing at the edge of the trees was the stranger, the firelight turning his skin gold.

"No," Rekus said weakly. "He is not Takare, not even human."

"Yet he appeared where Taka-slin disappeared—at the Godstooth. He killed all the outsiders. By himself. He killed a tani. By himself. Who since Taka-slin could do such a thing?"

Rehobim paced the edge of the fire, his gaze holding them one at a time. "Pastwalker," he said, without turning towards Rekus. "What were Taka-slin's last words before he entered the mouth of Tu Sinar's demesne for the last time?"

Rekus was stricken. His mouth moved, but no words came out. He looked like he wanted to crawl away and hide. But Rehobim had asked him a direct question about the past. As Pastwalker, he had an obligation to reply. He tried again and this time he found the words.

"I will return. When next I am needed. You will not expect me. You will not know me. But it will be me." His voice faded off into nothing as he backed away from the fire and his face became a pale smear in the darkness.

Rehobim looked over them, his face triumphant. Shakre could not deny the power of his words, though deep down she did not think it was as he said. But right now he had them, he held them all. The people of Bent Tree Shelter were his.

"For me, there is only one choice." So saying, Rehobim dropped his spear. He drew his knife and made his way through the gathered people. They parted, then flowed after him. The stranger watched as he approached, eyes flat, expressionless.

Rehobim stopped before the stranger and stared up at him for a long moment. Then he went to his knees. He thrust his knife into the dirt and bared the back of his neck. "Taka-slin," he said clearly. "Where you lead, I will follow."

The stranger stared down at him for a long moment, then he said his first word since arriving among them:

"No."

Shakre crouched beside Micah later that night, holding the small wrist in her hand. Micah still clung to life, though she wasn't sure how. The wounds on the small body were terrible, grisly red in the light of the glow moss. Across from her knelt Micah's mother, her voice hoarse as she whispered prayers nonstop. The young woman was the only one in the village unaware of the drama that had taken place that night at the fire.

Taka-slin. Such an outrageous claim Rehobim made, but was it any more outrageous than anything else that was happening? The gods fled or hiding. Melekath loose, or nearly so. If the old demons were returning, why not the old heroes? She saw again Rehobim's face when the stranger refused him, and stalked off into the darkness. The young man seemed to collapse in on himself and she found herself wondering just what had happened to him that day when the outsiders appeared. In a way he was just as wounded as Jehu. But, unlike Jehu, he'd seen his salvation.

Only to have it ripped from him. What would such rejection do to him?

She felt the stranger's presence before he thrust the door aside and stepped into the doorway of the home. For a moment she just looked up at him, then she moved back and gestured him forward.

Micah's mother looked up as the stranger bent to enter the home, but she did not protest, though her prayers seemed to become more fervent.

He knelt beside Micah, his huge form filling the small dwelling, dwarfing the rest of them into insignificance. Slowly, as if afraid of his own movement, he reached out one gnarled hand and touched the little girl's hair. Shakre, watching closely, saw his rough face twist into a grimace of pain, just for a moment, before he mastered himself once again. Softly, almost gently, he spoke to the little girl in his own tongue. Then, quite clearly, he whispered:

"My name is…Shorn."

He closed his eyes for a long moment, then backed out of the hut and was gone.

CHAPTER 16

The day was overcast and chill with a stiff north wind blowing when Shakre made her way up the rocky knoll that jutted up above Bent Tree Shelter like an ancient tower. Except for the lone pine tree at the top—the Watcher Tree—the hill was barren of vegetation, a stony fist overlooking a harsh land. The sides were steep and the going was difficult. More than once she slipped and nearly fell. There was no true path. Halfway up she stopped to catch her breath and look around. Already she was high enough that she could see the whole village laid out below her.

Automatically her eyes went to one hut, not far from the fire pit in the center of the village. Olera's home. Shakre frowned. The woman had contracted a strange malady, one she had never seen before. Several days before she had left her place by the communal cook pot and gone to her home to lie down. When Shakre went to her, the woman complained of fever and weakness. Shakre treated her with a feverbark tea and told her to sleep. It didn't seem too serious.

But the next morning Olera's face was taut with pain and there was a strange bluish mark on her upper chest that looked like a deep bruise. She winced when Shakre touched it. The morning after that there were three more bruises and Olera moaned with the pain. Yesterday the bruises started to turn yellow and suppurate. Nothing Shakre did seemed to help.

And today the hallucinations started.

Shakre was preparing another poultice when Olera suddenly bolted upright on her bed and screamed.

"They're all over me! Get them off me! *Get them off!*"

She tried to stand, lost her balance and fell. She shrieked and rolled around on the ground and Shakre had to get two people to help her put her back into her bed and hold her down. Finally, her struggles weakened. Just before she lapsed into unconsciousness she looked at

133

Shakre and said, "He's afraid, terribly afraid. He hates us. He blames *us*."

In the silence that followed, Shakre sent the two villagers out of the hut and sat looking at the woman for a long time. She knew what she needed to do but she was loath to do so, fearing what she would encounter. Finally, she laid her hands on the woman and went *beyond*. What she *saw* there shocked her.

The flow of LifeSong that was connected to Olera was tainted with a cancerous yellow. The same yellow color infused her *akirma*, and was darker where the strange bruises were.

Nor was Olera's strange illness the only one. Last night two other Takare had become ill with symptoms Shakre had never seen before. Though they were not bedridden or near death like Olera, they were far from well. Both looked drained, listless. Their skin had turned very pale, while the flesh around their eyes was dark and bruised.

The flows supporting both of them showed the same cancerous yellow color.

The land itself seemed ill. Takare hunters returned from their forays to report finding dead and dying kelen, splinterhorn buck and yulin. All seemed to have contracted a strange madness, the ground around them torn up by their death throes, bodies twisted at unnatural angles.

Elihu spoke daily of a growing poison in the plants around the village. Trees had split and fallen over for no reason. The copse of holdcherry that stood just beyond the edge of the village had yellowed and died in one night, its leaves falling to cover the small, still-fresh grave at its foot.

Whatever was happening, it was getting worse fast. Shakre no longer lowered her inner walls unless she had to for healing. The pain and the fear that assaulted her inner senses were constant. Making it worse was the wind. It whined and moaned to her whenever she left her hut, following her everywhere, making it hard to think.

That was why she was climbing up here. She needed to get away from the miasma of anger and fear that enveloped Bent Tree Shelter these days. She needed to find some small place of calm to gather herself and try to think clearly.

After a moment she resumed her climb. All the years she had lived in Bent Tree and she'd never climbed up here. She saw a track and stopped to look at it. Someone else had been up here recently. She raised her head to look at the peak, not that far away now. Could it be

Rehobim? she wondered. No one had seen him since the night Shorn rejected him. Shorn himself was nearly invisible, appearing only occasionally for a meal. Not once did he speak again.

Shakre sighed and continued on. Ahead loomed the rough pile of boulders that marked the top of the knoll. When she reached the edge of them she had to stop and lean against one of them, letting her breathing return to normal. She found a gap in the rocks and squirmed through it. To her surprise, in the midst of the tumbled boulders was a sizable, natural clearing, in the middle of which stood the Watcher Tree. It looked like something was hanging from one of the limbs of the Watcher Tree, but just then the setting sun broke through the clouds and with it shining in her eyes she couldn't see what it was. She moved closer, putting up her hand to shield her eyes from the sun.

That's odd, she thought. The thing hanging from the tree limb appeared to be pieces of raw hide, crudely sewn together in the shape of a man. Charcoal had been used to make a face on it and it was stuffed with leaves and grasses. Then she saw the arrow sticking out of its chest, and she knew suddenly what it was and who had made it.

The wind shifted and a powerful stench of death wafted over her. Turning, she put her hand over her mouth and that was when she saw where the smell came from.

Dead, sunken eyes stared at her from every side.

Staggered, the walls she had erected around her inner senses slipped and she heard the rawness in LifeSong that spoke of violent death, a wound she would have heard sooner, had she not been closed off.

Shakre gathered herself, tightened her walls, and looked around. All around the clearing the hides of dead animals lay stretched over the rocks, the heads still attached. Each was placed so that the dead animal faced toward the center. There were more than a dozen of them, and none of them were animals the Takare typically hunted for food. She identified sharp paw, cave wolf, tunnel bear and spike-tail badger. Every one was a dangerous denizen of the Plateau. Looming over them all, impaled on a sharpened stick stuck into the ground, was the rotting head of the tani Shorn had killed.

"Meholah said I didn't have what it took to be a hunter," Rehobim said suddenly, from right behind her.

Shakre whirled, her heart racing.

The tall young man had the wet, bloody hide of a night cat draped over his shoulder. He held a spear in his hand and there was a bow

135

and a quiver of arrows slung across his back. His tanned leather shirt and breeches were stained dark with blood. Around his neck was a leather thong from which hung a number of sharp teeth. Prominent in the center of them was a curved canine from the tani. "It was one of the last things he ever said. Before the outsiders burned him." He dumped the cat on the ground, drew a long-bladed flint knife from his belt and gestured at the hides. "He was wrong." He pulled the cat's mouth open and with a sharp blow from the butt of his knife knocked one of its teeth out. This he set aside. There was blood at the corners of his mouth. He saw Shakre looking at it and wiped it away. "Heart's blood. It mixes with my blood. They have all become part of me." He touched the necklace around his throat gently, almost reverently.

"Rehobim," Shakre said, finally finding her voice. "What have you done?" To the Takare, the animals of the Plateau were sacred. They were not killed for no reason. They were not displayed as grisly trophies.

"Done? It's not what I've done; it's what I'm *doing*. I'm making myself strong. I am preparing for the war."

"Rehobim, listen to me. This is…wrong. You know that."

His eyes flattened and he rose in one fluid movement. He stepped towards her, the knife still clutched in his hand, though he did not raise it. "What's wrong is to stand by and wait for them to come again and kill more of our people. Or worse, turn them into something like Jehu."

Shakre stared at him, feeling the anger and hurt flow off him, wanting desperately to reach out, to help him in some way. But she could think of nothing. She could help him no more than she could help Olera. Suddenly she felt old and useless. What kind of healer was she anyway, standing helplessly aside while her people died?

"Rehobim, let me help you," she stammered, raising her hands without knowing where she would put them. A hunted, feral look gleamed in his eyes as she approached and he backed away.

"Get away from me!" he hissed. "There is nothing you can do for me." With that he whirled and ran across the clearing, vaulted up onto the rocks and disappeared.

CHAPTER 17

Shakre bolted upright on the pile of furs that served as her bed, the echoes of a scream ringing in her mind. Heart pounding, she cast out with her inner senses, but already he had faded away.

Elihu.

The poisonwood had him.

It took only a moment to pull the bearskin cloak on, snatch up her medicine bag and hurry out into the night. By the stars it was close to midnight. The woods were dark and close. The wind howled around her, full of inarticulate cries. There were no answers there, no help at all. She set off at a run, hoping she was not too late to help her old friend.

Elihu had come to her that afternoon and she'd known by the look in his eyes where he was going. Again. His face was set and grim, the face of one who mounts the stand for his own execution. The past moon had carved lines around his eyes and into his forehead. For the first time since she'd known him, he seemed old, unsure. Somehow, that upset her more than anything else. Elihu had always been her rock. If even he was falling victim to despair…

"You're going back in there?" It wasn't really a question, but she needed to say something.

"What else can I do?" he whispered. "My people need answers. So far I have only failure for them." They both knew that what was happening was caused by whatever the gray-cloaked outsider had carried into the base of the Godstooth. Tu Sinar was poisoned; the entire Plateau was poisoned. But what they could do about it, neither one knew. More than once they had spoken of urging the Takare to flee the Plateau, but to go where? It was not so easy to give up one's entire life and run away.

"It's not your fault. You're doing everything you can." The words were dry in her mouth. She'd said them to herself too many times already and they helped him no more than they helped her. The tainted, yellow flow that had killed Olera had killed others. Were killing two Takare right now. Every day Elihu left the village, alone, entering that special communion that only Plantwalkers could attain. Searching for answers, the same answers that eluded Shakre, though she had gone so far as to open herself completely to the wind.

The wind had not helped. It simply swept through her, gathering her up with the force of its fear and blowing her over the cliff and down into the bottomless chasms within herself. She would still be there, lost within her own mind, lost *beyond*, if Elihu had not been there to help her find her way back. Since then she'd had to redouble her inner walls as the wind clawed desperately at her without respite.

Nor could any of the other Walkers help. Meholah, the Huntwalker, was dead, and there was still no replacement for him. Rekus, the Pastwalker, could find nothing in the past to shed any light on what was going on. Asoken, the Firewalker, spent most of his days at the fire pit, staring into the flames. Two days earlier Intyr, the Dreamwalker, went into a trance and she hadn't come out. They'd met with Walkers from other Shelters and none of them had any answers.

The poisonwood had been closed to Elihu since the troubles started, but a few days earlier he'd tried to enter anyway. The cuts on his face and arms were still livid and there was a large purple bruise on his cheek.

"I must try again."

Shakre knew she could not dissuade him. In his place, she would do the same. The memory of the wind sweeping unchecked through her inner self still frightened her deeply but she would try it again if she thought it would help. "I'll come with you."

In answer he just looked at her. Both knew she had too many patients. There was nothing she could really do for them, but neither could she leave them.

"If there is trouble, I will come anyway," she said.

"I know," he replied, and smiled. "I'm counting on it." Years seemed to melt away with his smile and Shakre wanted nothing more than to just hold him tight.

He started to walk away, then turned back at the edge of the forest. "Tell me again why we never brought our homes together," he asked, with just a hint of his former playfulness.

"Maybe you were never firm enough with your offers," she said, feeling a smile rise up inside her that could not get by the shadow of her heart.

"Perhaps when I get back we will have to fix that."

"I would like that," she replied, and meant it. Maybe it was time to take another look at old oaths.

Maybe it was too late.

Now she was running through the forest night, hoping desperately that she still had some chance of saving the only man she had come close to loving since Dorn. She could not move this fast, in the dark, without her inner senses and so she cracked her inner defenses just enough. Even so, it was painful. The trees whispered and swayed around her. They were hostile, hating her for reasons that had no words. The forest felt empty, the wildlife fearful and distant. Only the wind accompanied her, shrieking around her, slapping at her back with its myriad hands. Never had she felt so alone, so frightened and lost. She pushed herself harder, knowing if she paused, if she gave her fears a chance to catch up to her, she would become paralyzed and Elihu would die.

At last she broke out of the forest and onto the barren where the poisonwood stood. The pools that dotted the bare stone glowed like animal eyes with a viscous, yellow light. They bubbled and seethed, periodically spouting geysers of smoking water. As she ran by one of the glowing pools she thought she saw something surface from its depths, a pale visage with milky eyes that fixed on her, but she did not slow.

She circled around a jumble of boulders and there was the poisonwood. The unnatural growth crouched like a malignant thing. She felt its hatred and its fear. It seemed to be pulsing. It would tear her apart if it could. She came to a stop, breathing hard. Every instinct shouted at her to run away. But then she saw a familiar form on the ground, lying half in the poisonwood's clutches, and her concern for him overcame her fear. She ran towards him.

Elihu was lying on his face, only his head and arms sticking out of the poisonous growth. He was not moving. Shakre knelt by him and touched his face. His skin was cold, but she could feel the Life-energy still pulsing through him and she mentally whispered a short prayer to Xochitl.

She cast a nervous glance at the looming plant life overhead. Its malice was like a low growl in the breast of a predator. Blood streamed from Elihu's face and head. His breathing was shallow and fast. She sensed a great pain in his back. If she moved him before ascertaining the extent of his injuries she could permanently injure him.

Then a movement in the dimness caught her eye. A vine was wrapped around Elihu's chest. As she stared at it, it tightened visibly and began to draw him back into the poisonwood.

There was no time. Shakre grabbed Elihu's arms and tried to pull him free. The vine held him fast. She was losing him. Crying wordlessly, she dropped him and grabbed the vine, thinking to pull it away from him.

Pain lanced up her arms, nearly stopping her heart. She felt an alien presence like thousands of tiny, spreading rootlets boring into her, spreading quickly. She tried to stop them with her inner defenses, but it was too late and they were too numerous. They were inside her, as they were inside Elihu. She could never push them out. Her walls were collapsing faster than she could build them. She lost her hold on the vine, her body no longer responding to her commands.

Then into the breach came the *aranti*, blowing into her and through her. Its rush was mindless and headlong and the rootlets withered away before it. She was free and in control of herself once again.

But still she was in danger, as the *aranti* picked her spirit-body up and carried her before it, through lost caverns *beyond*. It had no sense of her frailties, could not conceive of death and so she would be blown over the edge and lost to her body forever.

Mustering her will, she grabbed onto the thin tether that connected her to her physical body. She managed to slow and then stop herself. Then, like a woman fighting to make it back to her home in the teeth of a mighty storm, she fought her way back, step by step.

At last she made it back to her body. All she needed to do now was to break the *aranti*'s hold on her.

But she knew that the rootlets still writhed within Elihu. Even if she dragged him free, he would never return to her. The poisonwood owned him and it would consume him.

Now it was she who would not let go of the *aranti*. With a strength she did not know she possessed, she forced it toward Elihu. In the still clarity of *beyond* she could *see* his *akirma* before her, the clean white glow shot through with the writhing rootlets. The *aranti* was a racing blue light that jerked like a wild thing as she bore it steadily down on him. The two touched and for a moment, before she lost her hold on it, the *aranti* was inside Elihu. Only for a moment, but it was enough. The blue light raced through Elihu and out, but when it was gone, the rootlets were too.

Shuddering, her whole body aching, Shakre returned from *beyond*. With hands that were as stiff as blocks of wood, she pulled Elihu away from the poisonwood and the vine did not resist. When he was free and they were out of reach of the malignant growth, she fell over him, breast to breast, gasping. She felt the wild thundering of her heart and, underneath, so quiet it was almost not there, the faint flutter of his heart, slowing, weakening. She didn't have much time. She took deep breaths, slowing her heart, regaining her energy.

When she was recovered somewhat, she put her mouth over his and blew, releasing her Selfsong into her breath and into him.

Her Selfsong flowed into him, bolstering his, and gradually his heart returned to its normal beat. Utterly spent, Shakre lay across him. All at once the sobs broke from her in a flood. He was alive. *He was alive.* There was still hope. It was all she could think. Right then she almost felt peaceful. Elihu was alive and there was nothing they could not face together.

Slowly, his arms came up and wrapped around her. Shakre pulled back so that she could look at his face. Through eyes still blurred with tears she saw him looking at her, the ghost of a smile on his face. "It is good to see you," he said, stroking the hair back from her face.

At that the tears resumed and she pressed herself to him again. "I thought you were gone," she cried. "I thought I'd lost you."

"Not this time."

"Can you stand if I help you?" she asked him. By now she knew his spine was not injured, that the pain was bad but it was only from a broken rib. "We need to get off this barren and I can't carry you by myself."

Elihu closed his eyes and then she saw his head nod imperceptibly. He grunted with pain as she got his arm over her shoulders and dragged him to his feet. Then the two of them made their slow, tortuous way off the rock and toward the dubious safety of the forest beyond.

CHAPTER 18

Shakre sat near the fire pit, her head in her hands. She was alone in the chill grayness of predawn. She was brittle, worn thin by too little sleep and too many fears she couldn't get away from. She huddled deeper into her cloak when the wind blew past her ear, muttering in its disconnected way. She shrugged it away without raising her head. She didn't have time for the wind's foolishness. Not now. Not today. Not with Elihu's words echoing through her.

Physically, Elihu had improved since she'd brought him back from the poisonwood. He could now sit up and he was no longer sleeping all the time. But his mental state was what worried her. If anything, he seemed to be getting worse by the day. His eyes were sunken, and when he was awake he looked inward on things he could not share with anyone—not even her. He didn't speak unless he was spoken to, and then his replies were monosyllabic. The man she'd known for so long seemed to be gone—and it frightened her. Knowing that whatever he'd experienced was undoubtedly traumatic, she'd waited for him to tell her what happened to him in the poisonwood. But this morning she finally couldn't take it anymore and she asked him outright.

For a long time he said nothing, didn't turn his head toward her, didn't react, and she wondered if he'd even heard her. He just lay there on his blankets with his eyes closed. The waiting dragged on. The air in his hut seemed very close, though the hide door was thrown open. She noticed that his hands were trembling slightly and impulsively she took one and put it in her lap.

"What happened?" she asked him again. "What did you see?"

His eyes opened and he turned his head to look at her. What she saw there chilled her. His voice, when it came, was a hoarse rasp.

"The end."

Now it was Shakre's turn to freeze. For a long time it seemed she could not make her mouth work. "What do you mean?" she asked finally.

"The *elanti* at the heart of the poisonwood is afraid. *Afraid.* It...asked me for help. *Me.* A thing millennia old, powerful beyond dreams, and it asked me. For help." His voice conveyed the disbelief he still carried. "What could I *do?* I didn't even know what it was afraid of." He turned his face away from her and squeezed his eyes shut. "Then it *showed* me."

Shakre realized she was squeezing his hand too tightly, but she couldn't seem to loosen her grip. "What?" she nearly cried. "*What did you see?*"

Elihu moved his other hand to grip hers, pulled her hands to his chest. She could feel his heart beating fast. The silence dragged on longer this time. Finally, he whispered, "The stone pot."

Shakre's breath caught. "The...stone pot?"

"You said the gray-cloaked man carried a stone pot."

Shakre's heart ran cold. She nodded.

"The *elanti*," Elihu continued, "all the plants—they don't talk to me in words. It is like an image that appears in my mind's eye, but that is not right either. More that as Plantwalker I can go to a place where I can perceive the world as they do, and then I can share in that awareness they are willing to give up to me. It is not something that roots in words. They are terribly different from us, plants are, and the *elanti* are vastly different from ordinary plants. This *elanti* I journey to has never shared awareness with me, never with any Plantwalker before me. It will hear my pleas sometimes, and it may give a response, but that is all. All I know of it is that it loathes all warm-blooded life."

Elihu sighed and shifted himself on his bedding. Slowly his head turned so that he was looking at Shakre again. She saw too much there and found her own vision blurred with tears.

"The *elanti* is afraid of the things that man carried."

"What are they?"

"The *elanti* thought of them as...*ingerlings*. They are things from the abyss."

"The abyss? Can that be true?" Shakre sat back on her heels. The Book of Xochitl spoke of the abyss. It was the place the Eight reached into to create the prison. The Book claimed the abyss was the complete antithesis of the normal world.

"I do not know," he replied. "I know only that it is what the *elanti* believes. It doesn't matter where they came from or what they are. Not really. What matters is that they have *bitten* Tu Sinar. Our god cannot get free." He was shaking. "All the Plateau feels their master's fear. They run. Some escape. Some succumb to the poison that seeps up from below."

The wind broke into Shakre's memories, slapping her back to the present, snapping her hair around her face.

"Go away!" she said sharply. She was tired of the *aranti*'s fear. She had enough of her own.

In response it increased its intensity, strong enough that she was almost pushed off the stone she sat on. She stood up, started to yell— when all at once she realized that there were voices on the wind that she had never heard before. They were human voices. And they did not belong to anyone in the village.

Outsiders.

"Outsiders!" she yelled. "The outsiders have returned!"

The Takare began to emerge from their homes, gathering around Shakre, peppering her with questions. Should they run? Prepare to fight? The divisions among them, the toll from the strange illnesses and bizarre happenings, had left them disoriented. They were shaken, unsure, too slow to move. Shakre cursed herself. If only she'd known sooner. If only she'd listened the first time the *aranti* tried to catch her attention. They might have gotten away. They might still. "Help me!" she cried. "Get the sick out of their homes. Follow me. We have to move!" Then she ran for Elihu's home. She would carry him if she had to.

Elihu's hut was on the edge of the village, not far from the forest canopy. Shakre flung his door wide. "Elihu!" she hissed. "Get up! We have to go!"

He was already on his knees, one hand reaching out to her for help. She got him to his feet and pulled him outside just as the first outsider emerged from the forest, his weapon in his hand.

"Move," he said gruffly, brandishing his sword. He seemed very young. The black mark on his forehead stood out against his pale skin. His upper lip was hairless and beaded with sweat. He pointed his sword at her and the tip trembled ever so slightly. Shakre hesitated and another man stepped out of the forest and came up beside him.

"You heard him! Go before I stick you!" His hair was black and unwashed. There was a glint in his eyes and his sword trembled too, but his was excitement. This was a man glad to have his darkness set free.

With Elihu's arm around her shoulders for support, Shakre backed away, then turned toward the center of the village, a cold hand clenching in her guts. Now they would face the same choice as Jehu. Now they would know what he knew.

At the next hut they passed Shakre paused to pull the door back. This was the home that Lize and Ekna shared. The two old women emerged, blinking in the morning light. Shakre started to reassure them, realized that her words would be only lies, and kept her mouth shut. Besides, both looked a lot calmer than she felt.

"It's okay," Lize said in her curiously high voice. "We're coming." She drew Shakre close for a moment and whispered in her ear. "Whatever happens, you are Takare, the soul of Merat reborn. You will be reborn to us yet again. We will care for you."

Shakre felt something loosen fractionally within her. "She is right," Elihu said, as the old women shuffled off towards the fire circle. Now that death had come for them, the lines around his eyes and mouth had lessened. Now that the worst was here, her old friend seemed to have finally reached acceptance. Shakre opened her mouth to reply, when she was shoved by the black-haired man.

Just then a commotion broke out nearby. It was Birna, her baby daughter clutched in her arms. She stood outside Asoken's hut facing one of the outsiders. "He's very sick," she cried. "He can't be moved." Suddenly Shakre felt guilty. She'd been so worried about Elihu that she'd forgotten about her patients. Asoken had been bedridden for two days now, and just last night he'd slipped into unconsciousness. Elihu released her and gave her a gentle shove, his eyes telling her he could walk on his own. She hurried over. The outsider was the same pale-faced young man she'd seen first.

"She's telling the truth," Shakre said to him. "I am the healer here."

The young man looked to a hulking man with red hair and a bristling beard for guidance. "Is he awake?" the bearded man growled impatiently. "Sick or no, if his eyes can open, he can answer the question."

The pale-faced young man pushed Birna aside and stuck his head in the door. With his sword point he poked the still form within the blankets. Shakre took hold of his arm. "Let me in," she pleaded. "I will bring him."

The young man turned back to his leader and shook his head.

"Kill him," the red-haired man said. Raising his voice, he said, "Kill any who cannot answer the question or who will not come to hear of it."

"No!" Shakre cried. "I'm a healer—let me help!" She grabbed at the young man's arm, but he shook her off and then other hands grabbed her from behind and pulled her back.

The young man disappeared into Asoken's home and Shakre ceased her struggles, a sick helplessness settling over her. All of a sudden it was all terribly real. She had listened to Rehobim, she had argued with him, she had seen proof of his words in the blackened forms of the hunting party—but until this moment she had not really believed that the same could, and would, happen to them.

The young man emerged from Asoken's hut, his sword dripping. The black mark on his forehead was a bruise that went clear through to his soul. His eyes were very wide as he stared down at the blood that dripped to the cold ground.

"First time," the red-haired man said, slapping the young man on the back. "You'll come to like it." He raised his sword and turned on Shakre. "I won't speak to you again." Just then Pinlir came at a run. Birna leaned up against him, sobbing. In a moment he took it all in, his mate's tears, the outsider by the door of his father's home, his sword dripping blood, and he growled, raising his fists and starting towards the killer. Two steps later he was brought up short by the point of the red-haired man's sword.

"Keep coming. You can answer the question right here, right now."

Pinlir's hands came up and closed into empty fists. He looked on them and saw that they were empty and despair fluttered through his eyes. Birna was pulling on him, saying his name, and all at once he sagged visibly and let her draw him away, though his eyes lingered long on his father's final resting place.

Shakre stumbled toward the center of the village in a daze, barely seeing the people around her. The ground under her was rotten ice and in a moment it would give way. Why had she not listened to the wind?

Soon all the Takare of Bent Tree Shelter were gathered at the fire circle. Shakre stood with the others in a loose group and when she raised her head to look on her fate she saw Jehu, standing outside the ring of armed men who surrounded them. His face was twisted with horror. His mouth worked soundlessly. Then he turned and ran away, disappearing into the village.

How many of us will join you? Shakre wondered. She heard a baby cry and looked down at the infant in Birna's arms. *What will you decide for your daughter?* Her thoughts went to her own daughter, left behind so many years before. For the first time she was glad Netra was not there with her. With every fiber of her being she prayed her daughter was safe, that the Haven was somehow spared the madness—even as she knew it wasn't.

Rehobim crouched behind some stones at the base of the rocky knoll as his people were gathered like sheep for the slaughter. His hands were shaking so badly he could barely string his bow and twice already he had dropped his spear. The past and the present were overlapping each other. His ears rang with the screams of the dying, and the odor of burning flesh filled his nostrils. That fateful day with the hunting party replayed itself over and over in his mind.

They are my people, he told himself over and over. *I must save them. They have no one else.*

But however he tried, he could not make his limbs move. His fear was strangling him. Tears blurred his vision.

I have to go to them. I have to save them. I'm not afraid. I'm not afraid.

But he was. He was terribly, desperately afraid. His muscles had turned to water and every part of him trembled.

At last the Takare were all gathered. The outsiders stood in a loose ring around them, perhaps two score of them, their weapons at the ready, though clearly they did not expect trouble. All knew that the Takare no longer fought. On the faces of his people Rehobim saw grim determination, resignation, acceptance and even peace. The only thing he did not see was fear.

They were not afraid!

His shame grew into a vast thing that took him in its teeth and shook him like a doll. They were going to die while he watched from safety. It was going to happen again. But still he could not make himself move. The memory of Meholah and the other learners burning was too strong. It overwhelmed him. He could not free himself from it.

Then a new outsider entered the picture, walking in from the forest mist, seemingly appearing out of thin air. Tall and angular, his face sharp like a blade, ruined hole where his eyes had been. This time he carried no stone pot. Rehobim knew him instantly, his face forever imprinted on his mind.

Achsiel.

Achsiel stopped then, and his head swiveled as if seeking something. Rehobim shrank lower. The eyeless gaze came to rest on the spot where Rehobim hid and Achsiel nodded ever so slightly. At that, Rehobim wet himself. Just like last time.

As Achsiel approached the villagers, Rekus broke from them and intercepted him. "I am Pastwalker. You will ask me first." His voice trembled, but he held himself straight and tall.

Achsiel looked Rekus over and nodded. Rehobim pressed his hands over his ears, but it did no good. Through his hands, over the hammering of his heart, Rehobim heard Achsiel's words. He could not help but hear them. They were burned into his heart. They were with him always.

At last the question came, followed by silence. Rekus took a deep breath and drew himself up, forcing himself to look into that awful gaze. The wind whipped his cloak about his skinny form and tangled the gray shards of his hair.

"No. Never."

Achsiel held up his hands and the flame began to rise. Rekus flinched, but he did not back away.

And Rehobim could no longer watch. He buried his face in the dirt and cried out as the first scream went through him like a knife...

It took a moment for realization to bloom inside Rehobim.

That was not Rekus who screamed!

Then he raised his face and looked on in a daze at the scene he saw before him.

A copper-skinned tornado had erupted seemingly from within the ranks of the outsiders. It was Shorn. He held a massive knot of wood in each fist, and was wielding them like clubs. Three men were already down and before Rehobim's stunned eyes several more followed, screaming.

All at once his paralysis broke and Rehobim lurched to his feet like a man returned from the dead. He screamed with rage and terror and hatred and ran at the invaders. Such was his state that he completely forgot his bow, leaving it on the ground where he had been hiding, and it was only at the last moment that he thought to use his spear as a piercing weapon instead of a club. Then he struck with it far too hard, driving it into the back of an outsider who didn't even see him coming, as all his attention was fixed on the monster rampaging in their midst. The spear went clear through him and came out through his chest. As he slumped to the ground he took Rehobim's spear with him and the young man suddenly found himself without a weapon.

But the first blow had steadied him, and enough of the madness was past that he had the sense to snatch up the fallen man's sword and awkwardly parry the axe-blow that the next invader aimed at him.

His attacker's face twisted as he sought to recover his balance and bring the axe back around. Too late, Rehobim saw another outsider close on him from his left, sword slashing down and across...

As if with a will of its own, Rehobim's blade flashed up, slapped the attacker's blade aside, and then flicked out to slash across the man's throat, deep enough to sever arteries, shallow enough that it came through freely and on the continuation of the stroke he swiped across the first attacker's face, who dropped his axe and fell back with a scream, both hands futilely trying to staunch the flow of blood.

For a moment Rehobim could only stand there gaping. *What just happened?* He had not consciously meant to do those things.

Another man lunged at him and almost effortlessly Rehobim stepped inside his attack, struck him in the face with the hilt of his sword, and killed him as he fell. Just like that the battle raging around him was no longer frightening chaos but a deadly, high-stakes game played at high speed. A game which he knew intimately. His eyes took in the minor shifts of weight of the men around him, the tensing of muscles that told him what they were going to do almost before they knew themselves. Even as he saw these things his body was already reacting, moving through them with the grace and speed of a tani, the sword in his hand a living extension of his arm, a flashing tooth that stole life each time it bit.

Rehobim heard himself laughing and he welcomed it.

As quickly as the battle began, it was over. Shorn dropped the last man standing, then turned around. The clubs in his hands dripped ruin and death. He had no wounds. He didn't even seem to be breathing hard. Men moaned and stirred weakly at his feet, but none of them would stand again. From the forest came crashing sounds as the remaining survivors fled wildly. Shorn's face was dispassionate as his eyes took in the destruction that surrounded him.

Rehobim had the feeling that even in the midst of battle Shorn had seen each man fall, that he knew exactly who had gone down and who had run away. This was a seasoned veteran who knew what went on around him in battle at every moment, even when it was distant from him.

Then the amber gaze fell on Rehobim and the young man saw something there that he would cling to for a very long time, when things were darker than he'd ever imagined they could be. Not quite respect. Perhaps...*acknowledgement.*

Shorn had seen what he'd done.

Rehobim raised his blade to the strange warrior in a bloody salute and Shorn stared at him for a moment longer. Then he dropped his clubs and began to walk away. He was at the edge of the surrounding forest when Rehobim raised his cry:

"Taka-slin!"

But now it did not sound to Rehobim like the idle bleating of a foolish youth. Now his voice boomed across the battlefield and he was at last a warrior as his ancestors had been. He was a man and he was no longer afraid.

One by one the watching Takare took up Rehobim's cry.

"Taka-slin! Taka-slin! Taka-slin!"

The sound went on and on, reverberating through the forest. Shorn backed away, an unreadable emotion twisting his face. With each repetition he flinched slightly; then all at once he spun and dove into the forest.

"He will return," Rehobim said over and over, in the muted glow of the aftermath. "Not to worry, Taka-slin will return." Most of the others took up his words, repeating it to each other like a mantra.

"What do you think?" Elihu asked Shakre as she helped him walk back to his hut.

"The truth?" she said, looking deep into Elihu's eyes as they paused at the doorway to his home. "I was certain we were all going to die. Right now I feel like chanting his name too."

"And what of the outsiders who died here?" he asked softly.

It took her longer to answer this time. "I grieve for them," she said at last. "They are people like us, people who made a choice." As she said this, she saw Pinlir make his way to the hut where his father lay in his own blood. The son's face was contorted, tears and rage fighting for dominance. In his hand was an axe taken from one of the

151

dead. His shoulders shook as he bent to enter the simple home. A moment later his cries rose into the sky and they were incoherent cries of rage. "But I must confess, I would grieve more to lose all of you."

What now? Shakre wondered as she emerged from Elihu's home. She had seen firsthand the true face of the enemy. There would be no quarter, no mercy, there. She thought of gentle Asoken, his sly sense of humor, his concern for his fellow Takare. Asoken who now lay dead because he could not answer a question to suit a god's hatred. *Why should we not fight as they do? Why should I fight the hatred I feel rising within me? What do I truly believe?*

Rehobim approached, dragging by the heels a dead man whose head bounced over the rocks and exposed roots. It was the pale-faced young man. This was the one who killed Asoken, killed him as he lay unconscious and helpless. This was her enemy.

She followed Rehobim. When he was far enough from the village, Rehobim dropped the body and went back for another, not even sparing Shakre a glance as he went by. Shakre squatted beside the body and stared at the still face, the pale skin. There was still sweat gathered on his upper lip. He looked so young. He couldn't have been more than sixteen.

Was he really any different than Jehu? How many others had made the same choice, their only real crime their own fear? If she hated them all, would she also have to hate those she loved, if they could not overcome their own fear? Of its own accord her hand came up and closed the staring eyes and all at once she found she could not hate him. Ever so softly she started to chant, closing her eyes and letting the words fill her.

"What are you doing?" Rehobim's voice was filled with disbelief that was quickly turning to anger. He held the heels of yet another body and behind him other Takare were dragging more of their fallen foe.

Shakre stopped and looked up at him. "How else will he find his way through the void to his next body?" The Takare believed that without the chants to guide them, the spirits of the newly dead would drift off into the darkness and be swallowed by the *nadu*, ravenous shades that waited beyond the edges of the light.

"He is not one of us! He is our enemy!"

Pinlir came up then. In his eyes Shakre did not see the man she knew. In his hands he gripped the axe. She remembered those hands only yesterday carving a knot of wood into a child's toy for his infant daughter. "He killed my father," he spat. "I hope the shades devour him forever."

Slowly Shakre stood. The villagers were gathering about her. On their faces she saw the same shock and outrage. How could she, who had been accepted as one of them, profane their beliefs this way? The guidance chants were for Takare only, not for outsiders. And especially not for those who brought death with them.

Shakre drew a deep breath, finally seeing in that moment the true shape of the burden she would carry. In her heart she cried out against it. Why must this burden be hers? It would make her a pariah among her own people. They would turn on her and she would be alone. She didn't want to go there again. She had already lost one family; must she now lose another?

But she could not do otherwise. Not and remain true to her heart. Because this body on the ground before her was much more than just a dead enemy. The truth was that he was a person just like she was, just like they all were. Takare, outsider, enemy—they were only words stuck onto another, while the truth was that they were all cut from the same cloth. Because of this, she would have to make a stand, not for herself, not for any lofty ideals, but for the Takare. For her people. However much it hurt, however much her mind rebelled against it, she knew she must keep this one small flame burning. She must be the light to shine for her people when the night was darkest, so that when they were ready, they could find their way back to the truth. For if they lost themselves to their hatred, it was they who would be devoured.

"I am sorry," she told them at last. "But I see more than enemies lying here. I see the lost and the frightened, and I may not turn my back on them."

"Then you are no longer one of us," Rehobim said roughly. "We turn our backs on you."

Their faces closed to her then and Shakre felt as if she had been punched in the stomach. She lowered her head so they could not see her tears. Then she knelt once again by the growing pile of bodies.

Rehobim stood near the fire pit, by the pile of weapons stripped from the dead. He was very conscious of the heavy blade hanging at his hip, how it changed everything for him. He was weak and afraid no longer. As the last of the dead were dragged away, the villagers gathered around him and waited. He touched the sword at his side reverently. "It is time for you to choose your weapons as well," he told them. "Our spears and our bows will still serve, but there will be times when we need blades to meet our enemies, to match the weapons they carry."

One by one they came forward, all but the old and the very young, and picked up the unfamiliar blades. The weapons were poor quality, rusted, dinged and notched, but they would have to serve for now. Werthin hesitated as he picked up a short sword, holding it like a dead snake that might still bite him. He was a young man, hardly past his middle teens, and much slenderer than most of the Takare, who tended to be broad. His long hair was blond, also unusual among them.

"It feels dead in my hand," he said, turning his serious eyes on Rehobim. He was a youth who thought things through. "I do not think I can fight with this thing."

Rehobim put his hand on the younger man's shoulder and raised his voice so the others could hear. "Yet once you did. Once we all did. In a time when we were the most feared warriors in the land. We are those warriors, reborn. When the time comes, your memories of how to fight will return to you, just as they did for me."

He spoke confidently, but he could not completely deny that his sword felt strange to him too. He had nearly cut himself while sheathing it. The perfect clarity of battle had faded and there was only an emptiness inside where it had once been. He shook his head, trying to drive it away. The past would return when he needed it. He had to believe that.

"I need the fleet and the strong to join me. We will pursue the survivors and make sure that none of them leave the Plateau alive. We will make sure that none ever come here again." Every eye was fixed on him. "The rest will stay here, to protect the very young and the very old. Now go and get what you need. Hurry. We leave before the sun climbs another hand span into the sky."

Shakre sat in Elihu's hut next to him, gripping his hand fiercely, trying to control the sobs that kept trying to break free, as she told him what had happened.

"You are doing the right thing," he told her softly when she was finished. "Without someone to remind us of the truth, we will once again lose ourselves until one day we turn on our own, as we did at Wreckers Gate. But you do not need me to tell you this."

They sat for a time in silence, then Shakre said, "I have to gather my things. Rehobim and his followers will leave soon."

"I am sorry I cannot come with you." Elihu's eyes were on her in the dimness. He was far from healed from his ordeal in the poisonwood.

At the door, Shakre turned back. "I think…I think it is time for the Takare to leave the Plateau." Though she had been thinking of the words for some days, still they were hard to say.

He nodded grimly. "I have been thinking the same thing."

"You will prepare them?" Shakre asked.

"I will. And I will talk to the other Walkers. When you return, we will leave."

Shakre hurried to her hut, relieved that Elihu agreed with her. The Plateau was no longer safe. They should have left already. It took her only moments to pack what she needed for healing and the few things she needed for her own survival. Even so, she was barely in time to join the group as they headed out of the village.

"You will not come with us," Rehobim said. Next to him, Pinlir looked like he wanted to strike her with the axe he still gripped in both hands.

"After the battle, you will need a healer," Shakre said simply, trying to stand straight and tall before his disdain.

"She's right," Werthin said. Others murmured their assent.

Rehobim looked uncertain. Clearly he did not want her along, but he was not so far gone that he couldn't recognize the truth of what she offered. "You will not hinder us in any way. You will not speak. We will not wait for you if you cannot keep up."

Shakre lowered her head in assent.

CHAPTER 19

The trail led them southeast, instead of south, as they had expected. Clearly the outsiders had more in mind than simply fleeing the Plateau as quickly as they could. The outsiders were traveling fast, obviously expecting pursuit. They found discarded blankets, food, even weapons along the way, sacrifices to the need for speed. There were other sacrifices as well, for to travel heedlessly on the Plateau invariably exacted a toll.

In the early afternoon they came upon a copse of trelnit trees, each trailing their many fingers of slowcaught vines. Not realizing what they were, the invaders had tried to pass straight through the deadly vines. A patch of vines at the edge were badly torn up, showing where some of the invaders had tangled with them and had managed to fight their way free, probably with help from their fellows. But deeper into the tangle of vines it was a different story. Something was caught there, something the size of a man. As they watched, the figure squirmed weakly.

There was no hope of rescuing whoever it was, even if they were so inclined. All had seen what even brief contact with a slowcaught vine did to bare skin. The vine was saturated with harsh acids that began eating through skin immediately. The person's face would be gone by now, only dripping flesh where skin had been.

"Even the Plateau strikes for us," Rehobim said harshly. "That is one outsider who will not prey on us again." And with that he turned and continued on, circling around the tangle of slowcaught vines.

Soon only Shakre and Werthin were still there, looking at the struggling figure. A low moan came from it. Werthin started to turn away and follow the rest, then hesitated. In one swift movement he drew an arrow from his quiver and loosed it into the struggling shape. There was a final quiver, and then it was still.

"Thank you," Shakre said, touching Werthin on the shoulder, but he quickly turned away and hurried after the others without saying anything. Shakre whispered a brief prayer for the deceased and followed.

The trail they followed veered suddenly eastward in the early afternoon and Rehobim paused to study it. The outsiders' tracks led straight towards a pile of jumbled boulders at the top of a low, steep ridge. It would be an excellent place for an ambush, if that was the outsiders' plan. He spoke briefly with Pinlir and Trelka, a tall, strongly-built woman who carried her captured sword strapped across her back, then they split off to the right with half of the Takare, while Rehobim went left with the others.

Shakre stood there for a moment, listening to her inner senses, then she called out to Rehobim softly. "I do not think—" she began, but was cut off.

"I don't want to hear what you think," he said sharply. "Be quiet, or go home."

Shakre shrugged and followed him. She had been about to tell him that she heard no Song in the boulder pile, that she thought this was a ruse by the outsiders to slow them down, but she kept quiet. Rehobim was on edge. She could feel it. They all were. The excitement of the morning battle had worn off and the fear of the coming one was sinking in. They carried unfamiliar weapons and they journeyed to do something that none of them except Rehobim had ever done. Shakre saw as, again and again, one of the Takare touched the unfamiliar weapon he or she carried, gingerly, as if it were an alien plant that might bite back. Only Pinlir seemed unaffected. He charged ahead on limbs powered by hatred and a fierce desire to strike back. Among the others Shakre often saw one of them scanning the skyline and knew they hoped to see the hulking shape of Shorn there. Him they could trust. They did not trust themselves. Not yet.

A half hour later the two groups reunited in the midst of the boulders. "They are not here," Pinlir growled. "I told you we were wasting our time. Now they are farther ahead and we will not catch them before dark."

"And if they had been here," Rehobim countered, "and we rushed in as you wanted, many of us would be dead."

Pinlir did not answer, merely headed east, out of the boulders and onto the wide barren just beyond. Tracking was much more difficult on the barren and most of the time they had to simply guess the route their prey had taken across the bare rock, though now and then they were rewarded with a dislodged stone or a scuff mark where a hobnailed boot heel had scratched. To Shakre's mind the telltale signs were just a little too obvious, a little too regular. She began to get the feeling that their quarry wanted them to follow and found herself thinking of the blinded man who led them. What powers, what knowledge, did he gain from Kasai? It frightened her to think of it.

They had been on the barren for some time when Ictirin, the sharp-eyed young woman who was leading them, hissed out a warning and pointed.

Near the edge of one of the bubbling pools the rock was scarred. Someone had been dragged toward the pool and they had been fighting it.

After the rest had passed, Shakre stood for a few moments staring into the pool's murky depths. Did the denizens of the Plateau aid them in their quest? Or were they simply striking out blindly? She felt a tremor deep in the earth and then a low rumbling sound which seemed to come from the north. When she turned and looked, she thought she saw a thin tendril of smoke rising into the sky—right about where the Godstooth was. Her unease increasing, she hurried after the others.

In the late afternoon the small band of Takare came at last to the Cleaver, the river that emerged from the Godstooth and cut the Plateau in half as it raced south. This was one of the few easy crossings of the river, a place where giant boulders stuck out of it like broken teeth, where the nimble could leap from one to the other and thus avoid touching the snarling waters.

It was on the other side that they had their first realization of real trouble. New tracks came in from the northeast and joined the ones they were following, at least two score of them.

"There are too many of them," Ictirin said.

"This just means there are more of them for us to kill," Pinlir said grimly.

Shakre noticed that no one echoed his sentiment and more than a few exchanged worried looks.

The sun had fallen from the sky and darkness loomed when Rehobim called a halt. "We'll stop here. Catch them in the morning."

"How is it that we have not yet caught up to them?" Werthin asked Rehobim. "We have traveled fast all day and still they are ahead of us. What power aids them?"

"It doesn't matter," Rehobim growled. "We will catch them tomorrow. And when we do, we'll break them. They will not stand before us."

His words were hard, but the concern amongst the Takare was growing. Shakre could hear it in their Songs. She could see it in their shifting, downcast gazes, in the way they touched their weapons when they thought no one was watching. There were only eighteen of them and they carried weapons they did not know, and could not remember. What if the memories Rehobim promised them did not come?

It had grown dark and the Takare were huddled around a small fire when a voice called out from the darkness and the two young Takare on watch, Nilus and Hone, stiffened and raised their swords suddenly. Rehobim looked up from where he had been staring morosely into the fire and got to his feet. Around him the rest of his band did the same, picking up swords and axes as they did so.

"Who comes?" Hone called out. She was a young woman with long hair tied back in a single blond braid.

"Friends from Mad River Shelter," the voice replied.

Hone shot a look back over her shoulder towards the fire, looking for direction. "Let them come," Rehobim called out.

There were only two of them, a young man and a young woman. After glancing at her, he spoke first.

"I am Tren. With me is Youlin, she who trains to be next Pastwalker for our village." He choked on the last words and Shakre saw that there was blood on the young man's face and a crude bandage on one arm.

"To all that we have, you are welcome," Rehobim said, motioning them to approach the fire.

Water skins were offered to the two and Tren accepted his gratefully. With a curt nod, Youlin refused. All the Takare watched as Tren finished his drink, then returned the skin and began to speak. "They surrounded us this morning at dawn." His words were ragged with fatigue and loss. "At least two score of them. When they began the questioning, we tried to fight back. As far as I know, we are the only ones who escaped."

Shakre felt sick. Nearly fifty Takare had lived at Mad River Shelter. Now all were gone but these two. "Did any take the mark?"

He shook his head. He stared into the fire for a minute before speaking again. "Jiuln, our Pastwalker, took the question first. He did not scream…at first. But it was a terrible, terrible thing. It was then we knew we had to fight. Before they could ask the next, we ran at them. It was little we could do, without weapons. But it was better than *that.*" He took a deep breath and rubbed at his eyes, then turned a haunted gaze on Rehobim. "I apologize, Rehobim. For—all of us. We should have paid more heed to your warnings."

Shakre shot Rehobim a look. So that explained some of his absences from the shelter. How many other shelters did he make it to? she wondered. Were they all attacked this day?

Just then there was a cracking, grinding noise in the distance, loud enough that most of the Takare leapt to their feet and stared out into the darkness.

"What was that?" Rehobim demanded, whirling on Shakre as if it were her fault.

"The attack on Tu Sinar intensifies," she replied. "I don't know how much longer it will be." *Did you hear it, Elihu? Do you ready our people to flee?*

"How much longer *what* will be?"

"Before Tu Sinar dies."

That shocked them. They looked at her with wide eyes.

"He's a god," Rehobim said coldly. "He can't die."

"Are you sure of that?"

Rehobim turned away and sat down without answering her. The rest gradually resumed what they had been doing. Werthin sidled up close to Shakre.

"How much longer do you think?" he asked softly. "Before…?"

"I don't know. But the sooner we finish this and return to our home, the better."

Food was brought out for the two refugees and Tren took his eagerly, while Youlin refused. While he ate, he took questions from the others. Where the others asked for information about family and friends, Rehobim focused on the number of attackers, their weapons and tactics.

Youlin did not speak, did not even sit, but stood gazing over the gathered Takare as if taking their measure. She was young, just starting her third decade, but, with the exception of Pinlir and Shakre, all the people at the fire were young. She wore her dark hair cropped short—unusual among the Takare, where more hair meant more protection from the weather. Her face was sharp, almost severe and there was an old anger that glittered in her proud eyes. As she studied each one in turn, the fierceness in her eyes seemed to grow stronger.

"I see warriors who have forgotten who they are," she said at last. Rehobim started to offer explanation but she cut him off with a raised hand. "You will be cut down tomorrow like rabbits," she said harshly.

"We've been trying to remember," Rehobim snapped.

"I saw today what trying does. Trying only gets you killed."

"Do you have something better?" Rehobim asked her roughly.

"I do," she replied. "It lies in the past. *Your* past."

Rehobim looked at her uneasily. There was something in her voice, some power that could not be ignored. Even Shakre felt it. Young she might be, but Youlin was clearly one in whom the powers of the past were strong.

"You need to remember who you are. All of you need to remember."

She sat down by the fire and reached into the ashes. She blackened the skin around her eyes. The firelight reflected off the sharp planes of her face as she stared into the flames. For a long time she sat and said nothing. She seemed to glow with a cold power that drew them to her. The would-be warriors gathered around her, like children gathering at the feet of their mother.

"You were once she who was called Kirin." Youlin pointed at Hone without looking. The young woman stiffened and made as if to draw back a step. The others all looked at her. "At the battle of the Leap, in the year 298 after our people joined the Kaetrian Empire, you led a band of Takare warriors through the hidden chasm below the Leap in the middle of the night. You slew the gate watchers and opened the gates to your fellow warriors. The fortress was taken by mid-morning." She beckoned with a finger. "Come here." Hone shifted from one foot to another, looked at her companions, then moved slowly forward. Youlin took her forearm in a grip so hard that Hone winced and then Youlin turned the full force of her gaze on her.

"You *will* remember who you are!" she hissed suddenly, so fiercely that Hone flinched. "Look into my eyes! Find yourself!" Her eyes had gone milky. Hone stared into her eyes and for a long minute neither of them moved. When at last she released her, Hone sagged backwards with a sigh. After a moment she shook herself and then looked around, like one awakening from sleep.

"I *saw* it," she said with wonder. "I *saw* myself!" She raised her sword and looked at it as if she had never seen it before. "The one I used to carry was longer," she said softly. "It was of far better quality than this thing."

One by one Youlin went through them, until only Rehobim and Pinlir were left. The stocky man glared off into space when she called him, then abruptly stood up and stalked out into the surrounding darkness. Youlin turned to Rehobim. "You were once called Frint," she said. "A great warrior among our people."

Rehobim looked startled. She continued. "It is fitting that you lead us back into the world. But do not fail us," she said, pointing a long finger at him, "or the curses of every Takare will hound you beyond the grave."

CHAPTER 20

The morning came, cold and gray. They set out before dawn, not bothering with a fire. They walked hard and fast and as they went Rehobim noticed Shakre stopped now and then to look behind them, her head turned as if listening to something. But she did not volunteer information and he did not ask. Likely she listened to the wind. He had his own problems to think of anyway. Last night had been rousing—and disturbing. Listening to Youlin remind them of their past made it seem real, so alive, so possible. But her warning to him had echoed through his dreams and now in the dawn he felt lost and alone. Nor was he the only one. The little band of Takare walked without speaking, each wrapped in their own thoughts. Something palpable hung over all of them and Rehobim did not know how to fight it. Nor did Youlin help. She walked in her own world, her hood drawn up over her head to hide her face and she would not speak to any of them. How would the battle go? Would he fail his people and die in disgrace? Or would he remember himself and fight as he once had? More than once he found his gaze drawn to their back trail, looking for some sign of the huge warrior who might be Taka-slin.

It was late morning before the outsiders made their stand. The Takare were crossing a sharp, narrow gorge when Shakre suddenly sensed them. She would have sensed them sooner, but the chaos in the very air of the Plateau thwarted her. It was like trying to pick one voice out of a babble of hundreds of confused, frightened voices. Shakre's gaze lifted and in the rocks at the top of the far side of the gorge she caught the merest flicker of movement. Rehobim was pushing his way past her and she grabbed his arm. His glance was furious but she ignored it.

"Just ahead. They are waiting for us in the rocks."

163

His head swiveled to look up the slope. "Finally," he whispered. "An end to the running."

"We have to pull back," Shakre hissed. "There's still time but we have to—"

"No," he grated. "We will not begin this war by running away." He said it loud enough for the others to hear. "We are the *Takare* and we will fight *here*." He drew the awkward, heavy blade from his belt and cried out; then he charged up the hill.

The only thing that saved them was the outsiders' overconfidence. They should have stayed in the shelter of the rocks and decimated the Takare with missile fire. They could have done it. A number carried bows. But they knew from experience that the Takare were weak, ineffectual fighters. They came down from the rocks in a wave of shouting men, outnumbering the Takare more than two to one.

Rehobim barely ducked under the blow swung at him by the first opponent he encountered. He swung back with an awkward counterstroke which the man easily blocked. The man's eyes widened and then a broad grin split his face as his low estimate of his foe's skill was reinforced. He swung again and again, almost leisurely, and Rehobim was forced backward, barely keeping the blade away from himself.

Come to me, Frint! he cried again and again. But he was empty, alone. From the corner of his eye he saw Hone go down in a splash of blood and he heard others of his band crying out. They were losing. They could not beat these men. He flung himself violently to the side to dodge another wicked sword cut and slipped on a loose stone and went down hard. His opponent grinned again and drew back his sword to finish him, when all at once he stopped and looked up, dismay wiping the smile from his face in the instant before a stone as large as his head hit him in the chest, throwing him backwards.

Everything turned to chaos as the huge form of Shorn burst into the middle of the outsiders. Shorn had a sword in each hand and with every swing someone died.

"Taka-slin!" Rehobim yelled, and all at once the chains around him fell away. He shifted his grip on his blade and waded into the battle. His foe blocked his first strike, but couldn't recover for the second and went down. Smoothly, he shifted and engaged the next, everything coming naturally to him now, the past alive within him. Around him he could see the same change coming over his companions, as awkwardness gave way to a new reassurance.

Soon it was over, the surviving outsiders fleeing to the south. The Takare looked around, awestruck. "I didn't know, I didn't believe," Nilus kept saying. Several fell to their knees and were sick.

It was Rehobim who broke their paralysis. With a wild whoop he ran to Nilus and pounded him on the back. "I knew you could find it within you," he said. But Nilus was not looking at him. His head was turning, his eyes searching the battlefield. Then he saw Hone lying motionless on the ground and he tore himself away from Rehobim and ran to her.

Rehobim watched him go and then turned to Shorn, standing motionless and alone at the edge of the battlefield.

"We could not have done it without you, Taka-slin. If you had not returned to lead us, we would all be dead and our people defenseless." All at once he knew what he must do. He drew his knife from his belt and, his eyes never leaving the big warrior's, drew a deep cut down his cheek, mirroring the scars he saw on Shorn's face. "One for each battle we emerge victorious," he proclaimed. "Until our enemies are destroyed."

The look Shorn gave him made him pause, rage and...*confusion?*...showing in the almond eyes. Rehobim faltered, his gaze darting side to side, but none of the others had seen it. Then Shorn threw his swords down, spun on his heel, and stomped away.

Rehobim stared after him for a long moment, then shrugged his shoulders and turned back to the battlefield. The brooding warrior would come and go on his own. That much was clear. There was nothing he could do about that. But what was also clear was that he had followed them here, to this battle. Which meant it was likely that he would be there for the next, and the next.

Shakre was already bent over Hone. The young woman had a deep gash that ran down her side and her face was pale. She was biting her lip hard to keep from crying out as Shakre peeled back clothing and probed the wound. Nilus stroked her cheek, his face drawn.

"How is she?" Rehobim asked.

"Her insides are okay," Shakre said. "If we can keep the rot out, she'll mend." She looked into Hone's eyes as she spoke and the young woman made a ghastly attempt at a smile. Shakre took a handful of dried moss from one of her pouches, pressed it into the wound and then pulled the young woman's torn clothing over it. "Give me your hand, Nilus," she said curtly. "Press here. No, harder than that. I know it hurts. But you need to stop the bleeding." Shakre stood up.

"But...wait!" cried Nilus. "Where are you going? Aren't you going to—"

"She'll be okay," Shakre said, already hurrying away. "I need to check on the others. Those who are hurt the worst need help first. I'll be back."

Quickly she made her way through the wounded Takare. There were only three and all were in better shape than Hone. Next she turned her attention to the wounded outsiders. The first three were dead, but the next was alive, though badly hurt. Blood was pouring from a deep puncture wound in his chest. Werthin stood nearby, his face pale as snow. There was vomit on the ground near him. Feverishly, Shakre sawed at the straps of his chain mail. If she could just—

There was a flash of steel and a blade sliced across the outsider's throat. Blood started spraying everywhere and Shakre clamped her hands over the wound, even as she knew it was too late. The man twitched several times and went still.

With a hoarse, inarticulate cry, Shakre shot to her feet and turned on Rehobim. He didn't flinch, but just stood his ground, a steel knife held out to one side, dripping slowly onto the ground.

"What have you done?!" Shakre was shaking so hard she could barely get the words out. A mixed rush of feelings raced through her and she could not sort them, could not make sense of them.

In answer, Rehobim pointed at the dead man's face, at the thumbprint burned into his forehead. "He has given his soul to Kasai. He is the enemy." He raised his voice so that all on the hillside could hear him. "No mercy! All who have given themselves to evil must die!"

The others stared at him, blood-spattered, weary, confused, shocked by what he had done. But one among them grasped Rehobim's words immediately. With a cry of savage joy, Pinlir ran to the nearest fallen outsider, a black-haired man who was desperately trying to crawl from the battlefield. Growling, Pinlir brought his war axe down in a mighty two-handed blow that nearly severed the man's head.

"What have you done?" Shakre gasped.

"What I had to do. If I let them live, and if you heal them, what then? Will we take them as prisoners? Will we let them go back to the thing that made them? So that we have to fight them again?"

"It doesn't have to be like that," Shakre said, hating that he was right, but sick about it anyway. Dimly, as if from far away, she could hear Pinlir's grunts and curses as he finished off the other survivors.

"Yes, it does. Because of that mark. Kasai owns him. He could never be anything but a tool of evil."

All at once Shakre sagged and turned away, unable to look at him any longer. She avoided all their eyes and went to stitch up Hone. She would save who she could. That would have to be enough.

"You may follow us," Rehobim called after her. "We honor you for your healing. But never again will you raise a hand to help the enemy or I will drive you away myself."

They made camp early, not far from the battlefield—Hone was too weak from loss of blood to go far—but far enough that they could no longer smell the stink of blood or hear the squawks of the carrion birds as they argued over their feast. Most of them were silent, grim. They kept their eyes down and spoke little or not at all.

Shakre stared at these people she had known her whole life, searching their faces, trying to find something that she hoped wasn't gone forever. A line had been crossed, and with each battle crossing it would grow easier. Easier and harder at the same time. They would grow hard layers of scar tissue that would inure them to their actions, while under the scars the wounds would grow ever deeper.

Rehobim kept to himself, endlessly cleaning and polishing his sword. He kept his face an emotionless mask but Shakre wondered. Had he finally driven away the demons that haunted him? Was the shame that drove him so ruthlessly finally quenched? She hoped so, but she doubted it.

Pinlir sat surrounded by weapons taken from the dead. Swords and knives made a small heap before him and he went through them again and again, testing their edges, holding them up to the fire light as if looking for something only he could find. Each time he held up a weapon he said a single word and in time Shakre realized what it was. The name of his dead father, Asoken. The grim determination on his face made it clear that each time was a solemn vow.

There was another rumble, deep in the earth, and Shakre looked to the north. It was too dark to see if smoke was still coming from the

Godstooth. When she stretched out her inner senses and listened she could hear animals in the darkness around them, heading for the edge of the Plateau.

She hoped it wasn't too late for the Takare to flee too.

CHAPTER 21

Shorn watched the young Takare fool slash himself with the blade and knew it was time to leave this place and these people. Whatever debt he owed was discharged. They held no claim over him. The only ones who did were too far away—his gaze went involuntarily to the sky overhead—and he would never see them again.

He left the battlefield and that place of dying was calm compared to the storm that raged within him. He had fought for the third time since coming to this cursed place and the pain within him only raged the fiercer for it. What honor could there be in killing a foe so small and weak? They were little more than children to him. If he killed thousands of them, he would not be one step closer to redemption.

Nothing he did would ever bring that.

For the thousandth time he stood before the Grave, the council of elders who ruled his world, as they pronounced judgment on him—

For failure on the field of battle, for weakness before the blade, we sentence you to be stricken...

Angrily, he tore his thoughts away from the past. Dwelling on it would not change anything. The past was the past.

It was time to see if this world offered real foes, ones he could truly battle. Ones against whom he could gain some small measure of personal redemption, or at least a temporary reprieve from his suffering.

If he was killed in battle, so much the better.

CHAPTER 22

After Bloodhound crawled away, Netra simply collapsed on the spot and slid into a vast and dreamless sleep. She awakened in the gray light of predawn with a panicky feeling that she was falling, sliding down the mountainside. But it wasn't she who was moving, it was the plateau itself. She crouched there, her heart racing, while the ground shivered and muttered to itself, wondering if a boulder would crash down on her, if the whole mountainside might suddenly cut loose and slide into nothing.

After a few minutes the movement subsided and Netra stood. An earthquake? she wondered. She looked down at the broken hills below, watching for movement, but there was nothing. Her pursuers seemed to have finally given up. Maybe the plateau was a sanctuary after all. Or maybe the earthquake made them turn back.

Ultimately, it really didn't matter. All that mattered was that they had gone and she was safe for the moment.

She traversed along the mountainside until she found a way up she could manage, then she resumed her climb. She wasn't sure she had the strength to make it to the top. More than once her strength failed her as she tried to pull herself up and slid back in a rush of loose stones.

The sun was up when she finally reached the top. For a moment she just stood there, catching her breath. The ground trembled again.

A small, rodent-like creature came running straight towards her. It didn't notice her until it was almost on her. All its fur stood up on its tiny body and it hissed, baring its teeth at her. When she didn't move it ran around her and then down over the edge.

Netra frowned. That was odd. She'd never seen an animal do that before. It must be the earthquake that was affecting it.

She walked on. The ground shook again, harder than before. A flock of birds flew overhead, heading off the plateau. She heard the

Songs of other animals approaching, and ducked behind a boulder. It was a herd of deer-like animals but smaller, fleeter, with short, twisted horns. The animals moved at a fast trot. One paused to look back, its head swinging side to side, ears flicking, searching for the danger it could not see. Then it snorted, rolled its eyes and ran to catch up with its fellows.

What was happening?

She broke through a line of wind-bent trees and ahead of her was something new. It was a wide, flat area of nearly solid rock with a handful of rock outcroppings on it. There were no trees or grasses growing on it. Here and there were small pools of water, steam rising from them. One of them erupted suddenly in a geyser that shot many feet into the air before it settled back, grumbling, into its pool.

This was really strange.

Cautiously, she approached the barren area. Nothing moved out on its surface. She got to the edge and stopped, listening.

Even more curious. There seemed to be no LifeSong in the barren area, or at least very little. What could cause that?

The ground shook again and two more of the pools shot steaming water into the air. Netra stepped gingerly onto the rock, all her senses alert. She walked further onto it, looking around with every step. Why did this place make her so uneasy? Maybe she should go back and circle around it. She couldn't see how far it extended but surely it couldn't be all that big.

Just as she was about to turn around, she saw something up ahead. It looked like a big mound of plant growth. She squinted. She'd never seen plants grow like that before.

She looked around again. No animals to be seen. No people. No other plants. No birds flying overhead or perched on the rocks. How could a place be so empty of life and yet have something like that growing on it?

She made her way over to the mound of plant growth. It was probably fifty feet across and about twenty feet tall in the center, a huge snarl of tangled vines with narrow, pale green leaves. It was incredibly dense. Even a rabbit would have trouble getting in there.

She moved closer, stopping when she was almost close enough to touch it. She'd never seen vines like these before, but she was almost sure they were poisonous. Her skin felt hot and prickly just being this close to them. It was hard to tell for sure, but there seemed to be a tree in the center of the mound, completely draped by the thick vines.

She cocked her head to the side, listening with her inner hearing. The Song emanating from these plants had a raw edge to it that was not all that pleasant. However, she did not sense the presence of one of the diseased yellow flows. At least there was that.

She took a couple of steps back and began controlling her breathing. It was really astonishing to her how much easier it was to go *beyond* these days. It was like she was always kind of on the edge of it now, and it took very little effort to slip over.

As she'd thought, there was no sign of any diseased yellow flows. The flows of LifeSong sustaining the plants were a normal golden color. The plant mound's *akirma* was suffused with green, just like normal also.

She stiffened. There was something unusual in the middle of the mound.

She burrowed deeper *beyond*. Just visible in the center of the mound was something very, very different. She couldn't tell what it was. It had no *akirma*, no Song radiated from it.

Another tremor hit, stronger than the rest. Netra was knocked to the ground and fell out of *beyond*.

As she got to her feet, the plant mound suddenly went crazy.

The tree in the center of the mound was thrashing wildly. But it was not a mindless thrashing. It had a purpose. All of a sudden Netra realized what it was doing. With its limbs it was grabbing great handfuls of the entangling vines and ripping them away.

Netra's eyes widened. Was this another sentient tree? Would it also try to communicate with her?

When it had most of the vines ripped away, the tree started trembling madly. After a few seconds a crack formed in the center of the trunk, down low to the ground. The crack widened, spreading halfway up the trunk.

The tree bent to one side, then the other. To Netra it looked like a man stuck in deep mud, trying to pull his legs free one at a time. There was a loud crack and one side tore free, the thick roots shearing away. It leaned the other way, there was another crack, and the roots on the other side tore away as well.

The limbs bent inward and the tree began tearing away huge chunks of bark from its trunk and throwing the pieces aside. As it did so, most of the bark on its limbs—all four of them—cracked and broke off.

What was revealed was not wood, but pebbled, dark brown hide.

Netra started backing away. This was not a tree, but rather something that had been living inside a tree, motionless for so long that a tree had grown over it.

The thing turned toward Netra. It stood on two stout, short legs. Its arms were long and weirdly jointed, ending in hands with dozens of long, slender fingers that looked like twigs. Its head was just an extension of its torso, with what appeared to be eyes glittering in a half dozen random places where its face should have been. Its mouth was a rough opening.

It bellowed at her and then started wading through the remaining vines toward her.

Netra ran.

She barely made it two steps before one of its hands closed around her middle. She was lifted into the air and turned to face the monster.

It screamed in her face in a language no human had ever spoken and shook her.

Another hand wrapped around her, taking hold of her legs, and the thing began to pull. Its strength was tremendous. Netra felt her joints popping, muscles and ligaments stretching and knew that it was going to tear her in half. She yelled and then she screamed, but it didn't do any good. She was going to die here, now, without even knowing why.

There was a low, harsh growl and a copper blur at the edge of her vision. Something struck the tree-thing hard and low. It staggered, arms waving as it tried to keep its balance. Its hands opened and Netra fell to the ground, stunned.

She rolled over and made it up onto her knees. She hurt everywhere. The monster was on the ground and there was what looked like a huge, copper-skinned man attacking it.

As the monster struggled to rise, Netra's rescuer grabbed one of its limbs with both of his hands. He bent the limb and there was a loud crack as it snapped. The monster screamed in pain and rage and struck her rescuer with one of its other limbs.

Her rescuer was knocked sprawling into the patch of torn up vines. Almost as soon as he hit he was back on his feet, charging at the monster.

But the monster had regained its balance and it was ready for his attack. It grabbed him with two of its limbs and lifted him into the air.

The limbs flexed and Netra could see that it was trying to tear him in half, like it had nearly done to her.

Her rescuer grabbed at the hand wrapped around his chest. He pried one of the long fingers up and then ripped it off. He peeled back another and tore it off as well. After the third one, the monster screamed and threw him down.

There was another tremor. The ground bucked, knocking Netra down. There was the sound of tortured stone, and a huge crack opened up right behind her. The whole slab of stone she was on tilted upwards and began sliding into the crack, which was growing swiftly, widening and branching across the barren area as the ground continued to shake wildly.

Netra started sliding down toward the crack. She tried to find a hold on the slab of stone, but the rock was too smooth.

The crack widened and the stone tilted upwards at an even steeper angle as Netra slid across it, picking up speed. As she went over the edge, she somehow managed to grab onto it.

For a moment she dangled there helplessly. Looking down, she could see that lava was filling the crack, rising upwards quickly.

She pulled herself up, swinging her legs up until she could get one knee on the edge. As she reached for another hold, the slab of rock tilted further and she slipped over the edge once again. The heat from below was intense and drawing closer.

What happened next was a blur. She went kind of crazy, scrabbling and clawing at the rock for any hold she could find. Somehow she made it up and over the edge, just as the slab of rock finally slid into the lava.

She staggered away from the crack, bent over, trying to catch her breath. Her fingernails were bleeding and she'd scraped one side of her face pretty badly.

Oblivious to the destruction around them, the two combatants fought on. Her rescuer had broken another one of the monster's limbs and it was dangling uselessly, but the monster had hurt him as well. He was bleeding furiously from the side of his head and limping badly.

When the monster came at him again, the limp slowed him enough that he couldn't elude it. The thing got a hold of his bad leg with one hand and jerked him up into the air. Then it began to bash him on the ground, over and over, like a child throwing a tantrum and slamming a doll against the ground.

Netra cringed with each impact. The force he struck with was tremendous. Nothing could survive that.

And it seemed she was right, because after bashing him a couple more times, the monster threw her rescuer down and he lay there on the ground without moving.

Netra tensed to run, but the monster ignored her. It turned to the northeast, toward the center of the plateau, and it raised it limbs into the air, emitting a loud, sorrowful wail as it did so.

Netra was starting to back away, hoping the thing wouldn't notice her, when she saw her rescuer move. She turned to him in disbelief. How was he still alive?

He sat up, a harsh smile on his face.

Soundlessly, Netra implored him to stay down.

He came to his feet and charged soundlessly at the monster.

The thing heard, or sensed, him coming just before he got to it. It ceased wailing and started to turn just as he hit it, low down, and wrapped his arms around its legs.

It howled and began striking him in the back over and over, but he ignored the blows. His muscles bunched and with a mighty heave he straightened up, lifting the monster into the air.

Netra watched, awestruck, as he carried the struggling creature one step, then two, three, four—right to the edge of the crack…

And threw it in.

The thing hit the lava and began shrieking wildly. Flames raced over its body. It reached up, grabbed the edge of the crack, and tried to pull itself free.

But her rescuer was ready for that and he savagely ripped off fingers until its hold failed and it fell back into the lava.

It went under, surfaced, then went under again for a final time.

Her rescuer turned away, took two steps, then collapsed.

CHAPTER 23

Netra stumbled over to him. She was exhausted and the ground was still moving, making walking difficult. His wounds were grievous. Blood poured from a dozen different cuts, including a gash on his head. More leaked from his mouth. When she went *beyond* and laid her hands on him she gasped, for it was the wounds inside that were truly frightening. Selfsong was draining out of his *akirma* in a number of places and his Heartglow was weakening steadily.

No! She wasn't going to let him die too. She was going to save him, no matter what it took. She'd failed to save Gerath from Tharn. She'd distracted the tree so the townspeople could burn it. She'd been too weak to save the girl shot with arrows.

She wasn't going to fail again.

She knew she was too weak from her flight to save him by using her Selfsong. Even if she wasn't exhausted, she hadn't had enough Selfsong to save the girl shot with arrows and he was much more seriously wounded than she was.

She left *beyond* and sat back on her heels, thinking. She needed more Song. But from where?

Could she pull free the flow of LifeSong attached to her and attach it to his *akirma*? It was possible. From what she had learned from Brelisha a flow of LifeSong could be made to adhere to any *akirma*. The Tenders of old had done it to heal.

The problem was that she was too weak to do that. She remembered how she felt when she pulled the flow away from her *akirma* to hide from Tharn. It was like drowning in a black pool. If she left it off for too long, she would first fall unconscious, and then she would die.

She needed the flow attached to someone, or something, else.

She pushed herself to her feet and hurried as fast as she could back across the barren area. She didn't like leaving him there alone. If the crack opened wider he might just fall in. But he was far too heavy to move, so she had no choice. She would just have to hurry.

At the edge of the barren area she stopped and listened with her inner hearing. It wasn't easy. There was so much chaos that the very flows of raw LifeSong sounded fuzzy and unclear. Radiated Selfsong was even harder to pick out.

But after a minute she found what she sought. A small herd of some kind of animal was running toward her. It would pass close by her.

She hid behind some rocks and went *beyond*. From there she could *see* the *akirmas* of the approaching animals. There were five of them, larger than deer, with flat, curved horns. Their coats were black streaked with white under their bellies. One was a male, larger and stronger than the others.

As they passed by—ears flicking to pick up every sound, heads turning constantly—the flow connected to one drifted near Netra. She took a moment to focus her will, gathering Selfsong in her hands so that the *akirma* around them began to glow more brightly. Then she only had to take a single step forward.

The animals heard her immediately and bolted, but not fast enough to avoid Netra's grasp. She lunged and caught hold of the flow.

Touching it sent a tingle clear up her arms. It was a surprisingly pleasurable feeling, but she didn't have time to think about it. The animal was strong; she wouldn't be able to hang onto it for more than a couple of seconds, which was something she hadn't considered.

Reflexively, she clamped down on the flow, pinching it closed.

The doe snorted and came to a stop, then stood there, panting, trembling.

The buck stopped in mid-flight and turned back, as the others continued running. He looked at Netra and took several steps toward her, his head lowered. Then he stopped, sniffed the air, and turned and fled as well.

"It's okay," Netra said soothingly. "I won't hurt you."

But she knew that wasn't true. She was already hurting the doe and she hadn't truly started yet.

She started walking back toward her fallen rescuer. It was slow going. The doe fought every step of the way. She could stop the fighting by clamping down harder on the flow of Song, but when she did the animal became glassy-eyed and slumped to the ground. She had to allow the doe enough energy to walk, but not enough to put up a real fight.

Finally, she got the animal back to her rescuer. A quick check showed that he was still alive, but his Heartglow was dangerously dim. She was running out of time.

There was another explosion in the distance and the ground shook. Lava spewed into the air from the depths of the crack, hissing as it spattered on the rock around them.

Netra wasn't quite sure how to do this. She knew that the Tenders of old were able to siphon Selfsong from one living thing into another, but her lessons had been frustratingly vague on actual details. She was just going to have to proceed by feel.

She pulled the doe closer, where she could touch it. The animal was trembling hard and throwing her head around, one wild eye fixed on Netra. Netra clamped down harder on the flow and forced the doe first to her knees, then all the way down to lie on her side.

"It's okay," she murmured. "It will be over soon."

Still holding tightly to the flow with one hand, Netra reached out with her other hand and laid it on the doe's side. She could feel the panicky heartbeat and a sick feeling rose in her. What had she come to, that she was doing this? She had always loved animals. She had never dreamed she would be doing something like this to one.

But what choice did she have? Without the doe's Song, her rescuer would die. He'd saved her life. Would she refuse the chance to do the same for him?

Whispering a prayer for forgiveness, she concentrated, focusing her will on the hand that was resting on the doe, narrowing the gathered Selfsong there to one finger, which soon began to glow more brightly.

Then she took a deep breath and poked the finger through the doe's *akirma*.

A heart-rending squeal came from the animal and its whole body convulsed.

But she had control of it now and it could not resist. Its struggles died as soon as they started.

The doe's Selfsong began to rush into her. As it did so, Netra gasped, her eyes going wide. The feeling was electric. It was amazing. The pain and weakness of the past few days disappeared in a euphoric flood. She'd never imagined such a thing. It hadn't been the same at all when she drew in the power from the followers of the blinded man. There'd been something foul about their energy, something caused by the black marks burned not just into their skin, but deep into who and what they were.

Netra realized she was shaking. She wanted to just keep basking in the feeling, but she knew her rescuer's time was limited.

She no longer had to clamp down on the doe's flow of LifeSong. Nor did she need to keep one hand on it. The connection between them had been made; the doe's Selfsong would continue flowing into her until she stopped it.

When she turned to put her hands on her rescuer she saw with surprise that he had regained consciousness and was looking at her. She smiled at him. "It's all right now." And it *was* all right. She'd never felt so right in her whole life.

But when she leaned toward him he scowled at her and slapped her hands away.

"What's wrong with you?" she snapped, suddenly irritated. "I'm trying to help you." She reached for him again.

His scowl deepened and he slapped her hands away again. He said something to her in his own tongue and it sounded like a curse.

Irritation flared into anger. "I don't care," she told him. "I'm healing you."

She grabbed his wrists when he raised his hands again. His eyes narrowed and he tried to twist free, but she was greatly strengthened by the Song she was receiving from the doe and he was weakened by his wounds and he could not break free.

Then she released the Song she was holding, dumping it into him.

His mouth opened in shock and his lips worked, but no words came out. He looked utterly baffled by what was happening.

It was working. Netra could *see* the holes in his *akirma* beginning to seal up, his Heartglow growing brighter.

At the same time, though, she felt a curious emptiness flooding into her as the doe's Song left her. For some reason it made her desperate and afraid.

Then she realized that the Selfsong coming from the doe was tapering off. She turned her head and *saw* that the animal was dying; her *akirma* looked brittle, her Heartglow fuzzy and weak. If she didn't stop now, it would be too late.

But when she turned back to her rescuer, she knew that she couldn't stop yet. The holes in his *akirma* had not fully closed and he was too weak. He had to be strong enough to walk; she couldn't leave him up here on the plateau, not with what was going on.

Through eyes filled with sudden tears she turned back to the doe. "I'm sorry."

Then it was done. His wounds, both in his flesh and in his *akirma*, were closed, only inflamed skin remaining. Netra pulled back and left *beyond*. The doe stared up at the sky through unseeing eyes. Netra sagged there, her weariness returning all at once. He sat up and turned on her.

"Why?" he growled. "Why did you not leave me to die?"

Even through her fatigue Netra's anger flared to life. "What are you talking about? You *wanted* to die?"

"It was an..." He hesitated, searching for the word. "A good death. A death with meaning."

"That's crazy," she snapped. "There is no good death. There is only death."

He muttered something at her in his own tongue and stood up. The ground bucked again and more lava spewed into the air.

"We leave now," he said, and picked her up.

"Hey!" she cried. "Put me down! I can walk on my own!"

"Too weak," he told her roughly. "Too slow. Better this way."

Then he slung her over his shoulder and began trotting toward the edge of the plateau.

CHAPTER 24

The lands around the Godstooth were a scene from a nightmare. The ground lurched and heaved constantly, the bare rock splitting, releasing steam and gouts of molten rock that geysered into the air. The lake at the spire's base churned and foamed like a storm-tossed sea. Strange cries split the air.

Then, something new.

The ground before the Godstooth split open with a sudden, terrific crack. In the depths of the crack something huge thrashed. A deep, booming howl came from it.

Reddish, stone hands easily five feet across reached up out of the crack and grabbed onto the edge. The arms flexed and a massive, irregularly-shaped stone head appeared, deep depressions where the eyes should be, the mouth an open hole.

More of it rose up out of the crack, shoulders and a torso. It was almost clear of the crack when silvery, toothed shapes raced up its sides, at least a dozen of them. It howled and slapped at them, but they were too fast.

They reached its head and swarmed around its eyes and mouth. In seconds they had disappeared inside its head.

It screamed then, a terrible, lost sound of pain and despair, digging the thick fingers of one hand into its eye sockets.

The scream went on and on, the sound loud enough to crack stone.

Then it stopped and the stone thing went still. It fell back into the crack and disappeared from sight.

In the silence that followed, a jagged crack rippled up the side of the Godstooth. The massive white spire fractured and then collapsed. There was an explosion—rocks and dirt and ash thrown skyward—and from the depths of the crack spouted a tidal wave of molten rock, bubbling up and over the edges.

The molten stone poured into the lake, the water evaporating almost instantly in a giant cloud of steam. It flowed up and over the surrounding rock walls and then spilled out into the rest of the Plateau.

The last echoes of the unearthly scream died away and the small party of Takare stood staring to the north.

"What was that?" Rehobim asked Shakre.

Shakre held up her hand for silence, listening. With her inner senses she could still hear the echoes of Tu Sinar's pain. It faded until it was only a whisper in her mind.

But it was not gone. Not all the way. Shattered. Ruined beyond repair. But still there.

"He's still alive," she gasped, and grieved for him. Never before had she grieved for something still alive. Only death grieved her. Life meant hope. Life was always good. But this wasn't life. The vast presence was no longer alive, but neither was it dead. It was destroyed, but still it was aware.

And the things which had brought it down still clustered around it, feeding off it. "He can't die," she said, realizing the truth of the words as she spoke them. "He *can't* die."

The others stared at her in stunned disbelief. "The Plateau is doomed. We have to go back to our home, help our families escape."

Rehobim hesitated, confusion on his face.

At that moment there was a tremendous explosion to the north.

"There's no *time!*" Shakre snapped. "We have to go!" She started jogging toward home and the others followed her.

They reached the edge of the plateau and he paused, looking out over the vast sweep of land down below.

"Put me down!" Netra said. He did so and she stood there next to him, trying to recover her dignity. Being carried like a child was humiliating. Then she realized something.

The wind had stopped. Even the earth had ceased its heaving. It was as if the entire plateau held its breath, waiting. But not for long.

Netra felt the cry a moment before she heard it and she spun just as a vast, unearthly scream of pain and anguish rent the air. The scream faded and died and for long moments there was nothing.

Next was an explosion, flinging dirt and ash high into the air. A sudden rent appeared in the ground to one side.

"We go. Now," he said. He reached for her, but she pulled away.

"I won't be carried anymore," she said. He shrugged and started down the steep slope. Netra followed him.

Clouds of ash blotted out the sun and lava started to pour down the sides as the Landsend Plateau tore itself apart.

PART TWO: QARATH

CHAPTER 25

Quyloc's aide opened the door to his office and bowed. "Frink is here to see you, sir."

"Send him in." Quyloc set aside the parchment he was working on and sat back in his chair. He shifted the sheath with the bone knife in it—concealed inside his shirt—to a more comfortable position and folded his hands on the desk.

Frink entered. Quyloc gestured to the chair before his desk and the man sat. He was the head of Quyloc's fledgling spy network, an ordinary-looking man in his middle years with sharp eyes and a knack for ferreting out information. Those eyes noted the bleached skin of Quyloc's hands and wrists, along with the speckles on his neck and face, but he said nothing. Quyloc was not the sort of employer who encouraged questions.

"Your report," Quyloc said. He could see from the man's face that he wasn't going to like this report any better than the last one.

"There was another one last night."

"And still you didn't learn anything, nothing about why they are going there or what they are doing," Quyloc said flatly.

"No, sir," Frink replied tightly. He didn't like this failure any more than Quyloc did. He was a man who prided himself on his abilities. "I was in the main worship hall by mid-afternoon. My hiding place was perfect. Yet still the same thing happened."

It had been several days since Nalene FirstMother first walked alone one afternoon up to the ruined Tender temple in old Qarath. One of Frink's spies, a young woman with a real talent for tailing people, had followed her. She'd made it clear up to the entrance to the ruined Tender temple when, without warning, she lost consciousness and didn't awaken until the next morning, after the FirstMother had already left.

Since then three more Tenders had made the trek but still Quyloc knew nothing.

"Did you see anything at all?" Quyloc asked him.

"The Tender entered the worship hall just after sunset. She walked over to the big crack in the floor and looked down into it, then backed away and sat down. She was clearly nervous and appeared to have been crying."

"Is there a chance she saw you?"

Frink was offended, but he hid it well. "Impossible. There was no way she could have seen me, no way she could have known I was there."

Quyloc knew better than anyone that there were ways to know a person was nearby without actually seeing them. Right this moment he could hear Frink's Selfsong with his inner hearing. It was faint, but unmistakably there. From it he could even tell that Frink was not deceiving him.

His inner hearing, and his intuition, had both grown noticeably stronger since his last trip to the *Pente Akka*, the shadow world that Lowellin had shown him. It was the water he'd touched, of course, the water that bleached his hands and wrists, the water that nearly killed him, *would* have killed him, without Lowellin's intervention.

"It was starting to get dark when I realized that we were not alone in there," Frink continued.

Quyloc sat forward. This was something knew. The other spies hadn't said anything about another presence.

"I looked around, but I couldn't see anything. The feeling grew stronger and then out of the corner of my eye I saw a shadow."

"What did it look like?"

"I don't know. It was just a shadow. But I don't think it was cast by anything. I think…it was just a shadow. Before I could react, it was on me, wrapping around me. I fell unconscious then, but before I was completely out, I think I heard the Tender say something, a name."

"What name?" Quyloc asked, though he already knew what it would be.

"I think she said 'Protector.'"

Quyloc sat back in his chair, thinking. Of course Lowellin was involved. Who else would the Tenders be going to meet? But he'd wanted verification. He made a decision.

"Don't bother following them to the temple anymore. Confine your efforts to watching the Haven and following the women as they move around the city. I want to know everything they do. Look for anything unusual, anything at all, that might be a clue to what they are doing there."

When Frink was gone, Quyloc went into his living quarters and from there out on the balcony that overlooked the sea and stood there, thinking. Lowellin had spoken of there being weapons for the Tenders to use against Melekath. That had to be what the women were going to the temple for. But what sort of weapons were they? Were they something left over from the days of the Empire? But that didn't make sense. From everything he had learned, the Tenders' weapon was LifeSong itself. It was their ability to manipulate that power that made them so dangerous.

So what were they doing there then? Was it possible Lowellin was showing them how to enter the *Pente Akka*? But if so, why go all the way to the ruined temple to do it? The *Pente Akka* could be entered from anywhere.

Maybe he was teaching them how to regain control of LifeSong. But why only one at a time?

Not for the first time Quyloc considered going to the ruined temple himself, to see if he could learn anything. But that would mean missing one of his nightly journeys to the *Pente Akka*, and he didn't want to do that. He needed to go as often as he could. He had a feeling that time was slipping through his fingers, that the war with Melekath was closer than anyone realized and he wanted to make sure he had the weapon Lowellin had spoken of when that time came.

It was all immensely frustrating. He was on his own while Lowellin was meeting with the Tenders almost every day.

He hadn't even seen Lowellin since the night when he'd bled the chaos power out of Quyloc, after he'd poisoned himself with the water he'd found in the *Pente Akka*. According to Lowellin, he was supposed to be looking for some river, but he had no idea where to find it. He was just stumbling around in the darkness. He'd even gone looking for the cloaked figure that he'd met on the dunes outside the Veil, but he hadn't seen it either. What was he supposed to do?

"I figured I'd find you out here!" Rome boomed, startling Quyloc.

Quyloc smoothed the irritation from his face and turned to face his old friend. "Most people don't like it when you sneak up on them," he said.

"Ha! So I *did* surprise you." A huge grin split Wulf Rome's bearded face. He dropped into a chair and put his feet up on the railing that ran around the balcony. He was a big man, broad and muscular in contrast to Quyloc's lean, wiry build. He had long, curly black hair and a thick beard. More black hair sprouted from the backs of his hands, arms, neck, anywhere it could. He looked rested and fit in a nondescript military uniform of black breeches and a tunic with the wolf shield on the breast. The heroic efforts made by the servants to make his clothes presentable had helped, but they could not disguise how worn and faded they really were and Rome refused to let them discard the clothes and replace them. When he worked with the men—weapons training, drilling, marching—he dressed like them. Being king—or macht as he insisted on being called now—wasn't about to change that.

"It's not often I get to do that," Rome continued. "This is a good day."

Quyloc sighed and sat down in the other chair. It wouldn't do any good to tell Rome that he was busy, that he was doing something important. The big man would just laugh it off and tell him he worried too much, that he shouldn't work so hard.

"What do you want, Rome?"

"What makes you think I want something?" Rome spat over the railing and watched it drop toward the sea, hundreds of feet below. Rome was the only person Quyloc knew who didn't feel uncomfortable on this balcony, who didn't seem to retain any of the age-old fear of the sea.

God, how Quyloc envied him. Was the man afraid of nothing? How was that possible?

"So you just came by to make sure I didn't get any work done this morning?"

"Quyloc, you worry too much. I've always said that about you. Sometimes you just need to put your feet up and relax."

"Really, Rome? Have you forgotten about someone called Melekath? Maybe you didn't hear about the events at Lord Ergood's estate yesterday?" Out of nowhere, nearly everyone on the estate had apparently gone crazy. They turned on each other, slaughtering each other and screaming about things that weren't there. Most of them were dead now, including Ergood.

"Right. Lord Ergood. I never really liked him. What an ass." Rome frowned. "Actually, I kind of hated him. He used to have one of his servants sprinkle scented water on me whenever I went to those stuffy meetings with the king and his closest friends. He claimed I smelled like a horse."

Which was generally true. Rome wasn't big on bathing and he loved horses.

"Whether you liked him or not is not the issue here."

"No. The issue is that you're too serious. You've always been that way."

Quyloc rubbed his temples. Did he have a headache before Rome got here? He made one more attempt.

"After Lowellin showed you the memories you lost, the ones about how *we* found the axe..." Slight accent on the *we*. Quyloc could never fully shake the feeling that the axe should have been his. How different would things be if it was? Would he still be risking his life in the *Pente Akka*? "You indicated that you believed him, that the threat from Melekath is real. Or have you forgotten that?"

Rome scratched his chest. "I didn't forget." He picked at something under a fingernail.

"Well?" Quyloc asked.

"What?"

"Don't you think this is a matter of some concern? Maybe we should be, I don't know, putting some effort into making sure we're ready for this?"

Rome grinned and, despite himself, a lot of Quyloc's irritation faded when he did so. There was something infectious about the man that made it hard to stay angry at him.

"I *have* been working hard on it," Rome said. "I've got men out recruiting new soldiers everywhere in the city. They even have stalls set up in the busiest markets, the ones where boys coming in from the farms go. I've got the armories working night and day, turning out new weapons. I've got people out buying wagons to carry supplies, other people buying food, leather, whatever. Qarath's army is growing fast." He leaned back and put his hands behind his head, pleased with himself. "What do you think of that?"

Quyloc had to admit to himself that it was a lot. But then, that was Rome. It wasn't even that surprising. This was a man who could do the work of three men for hours on end.

"I just thought it was time to take a break. That's why I'm here. What do you say we ride on down into the city and get a feel for the pulse of things?"

And this was the other side of the man. Work like three men, then suddenly throw down whatever he was doing and go looking for someone to have a mug of ale with.

Though clearly not ale, not in this case. Quyloc wasn't much for drinking. He hated how it made him feel out of control.

"I have a lot to do," Quyloc protested, knowing it was futile. Rome was always bad at taking no for an answer and, since he became king—or macht—he no longer had to.

"You always have a lot to do," Rome said, standing up. "Come on. Let's go. I want you to see this new horse I just got. He's a real beauty."

And so Quyloc followed his macht out of the palace and down to the stables, to a stall that held a shining black stallion that flared his nostrils, snorted and pawed the earth when they approached.

"This is Niko," Rome said proudly.

"Want me to saddle him, Macht?" one of the stable boys asked, bowing as he did so.

"No. I got this."

The stable boy bowed again and disappeared, clearly happy to avoid that frightening chore.

"Pretty impressive, isn't he?" Rome asked.

Even Quyloc, who viewed horses as a necessary evil, had to admit that it was an impressive horse. Easily eighteen hands tall with abundant rippling muscle under a glossy black coat, Niko was basically the definition of a stallion.

The stallion rolled his eyes and lashed at Rome with one front foot when he entered the stall, but Rome dodged him and in a flash had a headstall on him. Rome didn't use a bit on his bridles, claimed he didn't need them to make a horse obey. The thing was, he didn't. Horsemanship was just one more of the many things Rome did with natural ease. Which was surprising because as common foot soldiers he and Quyloc had not been allowed near horses during their early years in the army. Horses were for the noble-born and the high ranking.

That all changed a few years back when they were out patrolling. Their squad got ambushed by a large band of highwaymen that had been terrorizing the road between Qarath and Managil. Things looked bad when Rome knocked one of their leaders out of his saddle and leaped up on the horse. He rallied the Qarathian soldiers and they routed the band.

When they got back to the barracks Rome simply kept the horse and no one tried to take it away from him. He was promoted a few months after that. Looking back, Quyloc saw that that was the first step down a long road leading to finding the black axe in the Gur al Krin desert.

The black axe.

The weapon that won Rome a kingdom. As he had so many times before, Quyloc wondered what the thing really was. Even Lowellin didn't know. How was it able to cut through stone like it did?

And, the most frightening thought of all: *Was it alive?*

Rome led the horse out of the stall, patting the animal's neck and speaking low words to it. Already the stallion was calmer. Quyloc shook his head and went outside to wait while his horse was saddled.

They rode across the palace grounds and Quyloc was struck again by how different the place was from when Rix was king. There were no opulent carriages waiting on the grand circular carriage way to carry the nobility to and fro, no dainty ladies walking the garden paths with their parasols.

Taking their place were soldiers at weapons practice, and the clang of metal on metal filled the air. Heavy supply carts rolled through heading for the granaries at the back of the palace. No one lounged around out here, especially not with Rome in sight. This was a place of activity. Rome had little use for that which did not serve a function.

They rode across the carriage way, Rome calling greetings to nearly everyone he passed, whether the person was a soldier or a servant. As he had hundreds of times before, Quyloc felt envious of the easy way Rome had with everyone. People—men and women alike—just seemed to fall all over themselves to gain his approval. And it had always been like that, ever since they were children. Quyloc couldn't understand it.

The guards at the gate called out to Rome as he approached. "An escort, sir?" Several were already moving toward horses tethered nearby.

"I've all the escort I need right here," Rome laughed, banging Quyloc on the shoulder. The guards saluted and went back to their places.

The palace sat on a hill at the rear of the city. After they passed through the gates they could see the city spread out below them. Bisecting the city was the Cron River, surging out of the Eagle

Mountains and cutting through the city before looping around to flow into the sea, outside the city walls. The main street sloped gently downwards, and the two men began to pass by the estates of the nobility. The street was mostly empty, only liveried servants and personal guards visible as they hurried about on chores given to them by their masters.

The estates were large and ostentatious, but underneath the trappings of wealth the signs of strain were showing. There were rose bushes that were untrimmed, paint that was beginning to peel in the corners, a squeak in the wheels of a passing carriage. The nobility were suffering under Rome's rule. He taxed them heavily; he called it taking back what they'd taken from the people over the years. The nobility still clung to their positions, but their manicured fingernails were cracking.

They passed a lady dressed in layers of petticoats and too much makeup being helped into an ornate carriage. Quyloc recognized her as Lady Heminwal. The apartments she'd kept inside the palace walls were now being used to store weapons and armor. She gave Rome a cold look and a stiff curtsy before getting into her carriage. Rome smiled broadly at her.

"I love when they do that," he told Quyloc.

There, Quyloc had to agree with him. As street children, stealing and begging what they needed to get by, he and Rome hadn't even been allowed to come into this part of the city. They'd found out the hard way that when the wealthy did come down into their part of town that trying to beg something off them was a sure way to earn a cuff from the guards.

They left the nobles' domain and moved down into an area whose houses which, though clearly belonging to wealthy people, were not so obviously ostentatious. Rome's reception was markedly different here. He was hailed often by well-dressed men as they climbed into their carriages. This was where the wealthy traders and merchants lived. They were doing well under the new regime. Lower taxes and tariffs, safer roads. Those things were good for trade. Business was good and as long as the macht was the one who made it so, they liked him. To Quyloc, they were snakes no less than the ones just above them. The difference was that their star was on the rise.

But it was in the lower reaches of the city, where the great masses of the population lived, that Rome really shone. People called to him constantly. Girls blew him kisses and men doffed their caps. A small crowd of children soon gathered, running behind them—though not getting too close. People were clearly awed and a little afraid of the huge stallion, though Rome had the animal well under control.

Yes, they loved him, Quyloc thought. And why not? He'd cut taxes down to a fraction of what they once were. He'd conquered their old enemies in Thrikyl. He'd brought real justice, laws that applied to rich and poor alike. And he was accessible. He was as likely to be found drinking in a tavern in the city as he was in the palace. He was never too busy or too drunk to listen to some fool's minor problem and he was prone to act right then on it too. He'd improved the lives of virtually everyone down here. He'd done everything but walk on air.

The whole time Rome grinned like a kid and waved back at them like he was in some kind of parade, his shirt open halfway down his chest, showing black tufts of hair sprouted like spring grass. He was bareheaded, his beard untrimmed. There was no doubt he was one of them.

The street they were on led them past the prison. Its grim walls and rusted gates had long inspired dread. King Rix hadn't been particular about who he threw behind its bars. Now there was a group of kids playing in the shadow of its walls. Things had definitely changed.

Rome's views of justice were distinctly military. Quick and harsh. Imprisonment was a waste of time and money. Penalties tended towards things like public lashes. For lesser crimes there were work gangs who toiled on the city walls or hauled garbage away and such. "Put them to work," was Rome's motto. "Just like a soldier, they get into less trouble that way."

For the extreme crimes there was still capital punishment. A pair of gallows stood just outside the gates of the prison. As Rome and Quyloc approached the prison two men were being dragged there. When they saw Rome one of them, a beefy man with red cheeks and a thick neck, broke free from the jailers for a moment and fell on the ground before Rome's horse. He buried his face in the dirt, bound hands held out before him.

"Macht Rome!" he cried. "Have pity on me! I didn't do it!"

Rome held out a hand to stay the jailers before they could grab the man. "Get up, man. If you're going to plead for your life, at least stand on your feet to do it."

The man hauled himself to his feet. Tears streaked the dust on his face, but he looked his macht in the eye when he spoke. "I didn't do it. Me and Lar, we're innocent." The other prisoner didn't even look up. He had clearly given up hope and was only waiting to die.

Rome looked over him to the jailers. "He had his fair trial, didn't he?" Rome was adamant that everyone accused of a crime have his chance before a judge.

"Yes, Macht," one of them said. "Same as everyone. But it wasn't necessary. A hundred people saw them kill the old Tender. And the punishment for murder's hanging, just as you said."

"But it wasn't like that!" the prisoner blurted out. When Rome gave him a sharp glance he took a step back, but then he shrugged and bulled forward. "We did it, Lord, but it wasn't us!"

"You're not making any sense," Quyloc cut in. The prisoner didn't even look at him. He knew there was no help coming from that quarter.

"Something made us do it," the man insisted stubbornly.

A crowd was gathering now. Many of them had come to watch the hanging and more were gathering to see what Rome would do. Someone yelled abuse from the crowd, and a stone bounced off the man's shoulder.

The man didn't even move, his eyes fixed on Rome like a starving dog. But Rome spun towards the source of the stone. "Who threw that?"

Hands pushed one man forward and Rome motioned to the guards at the gate of the prison. "Take him. Put him on the crew carrying stones for the wall for the rest of the day. Let him think about taunting those who can't do anything about it."

The man tried to run away but the people around him took hold of him and then the guards got hold of him and dragged him away.

"What do you mean, something made you do it?" Quyloc asked the man, his curiosity aroused. Something didn't seem right here.

For the first time he looked at Quyloc. "We were sitting by ourselves, minding nothing, not bothering anyone, and then...then it was like a shadow wrapped around me. I didn't know anything more and then I was standing over the old woman and my knife all bloody in my hand."

Quyloc felt a chill pass over him. Could it be the same shadow that his spies had encountered?

"Sounds like you had too much to drink," Rome said.

"No," the man protested. "We were drinking, sure, but no more'n usual and drink ain't never affected me in that way anyway."

Rome shook his head and the man wilted. "Carry on," he said to the jailers.

"Wait," Quyloc said. The jailers paused. The prisoner looked up hopefully. "There may be something in what he says."

"What are you talking about?" Rome asked him.

"Not right here," Quyloc replied. "There's too many people around."

Rome nodded. "Lock them up," he told the jailers. Some in the crowd complained loudly, seeing their entertainment taken from them. Rome looked over at them and they shut up. Turning back to the jailers he said, "Move these gallows inside the prison and do your hanging there from now on. There's children out here. This is no thing for them to be watching."

The jailers hustled the men away and the crowd began to disperse. Rome leaned in close to Quyloc. "You think there's something to their story?" he said in a low voice.

"I think Lowellin might have been involved."

Rome looked surprised. "But why would Lowellin have a Tender killed? I thought he was helping them."

"He is."

"Then what's going on?"

Quyloc hesitated, thinking quickly. He knew about the murder of course, through his spies. "The Tender who was murdered was the old FirstMother. She was replaced shortly after Lowellin showed up."

"That still doesn't explain why he'd want her killed."

"No. But there are hints that she was opposed to Lowellin, that she wasn't convinced he is who he says he is. He may have just wanted her out of the way."

"How do you know all this?"

"It's my job to know. I'm your advisor, remember?"

"And you think Lowellin has the power to make people do things without their knowing it?"

"I don't know. I have no real idea what he's capable of."

"And he's the one helping us against Melekath."

"I know."

"I hope you're keeping a good eye on him too."

"I'm doing what I can." It wasn't much. Lowellin seemed able to appear and disappear at will.

Rome looked past Quyloc and scowled. "Speaking of Lowellin…"

Quyloc turned. There was Lowellin, approaching through the diminishing crowd, his black walking staff in his hand. With him was a heavyset woman in a white robe. The new FirstMother.

They drew close and Quyloc's inner senses started tingling. There was something *different* about the FirstMother. He could hear it in her Song, feel it in his bones. It had to be something to do with whatever was happening in the ruined temple. She carried nothing that he could see with his eyes, but it was there all the same.

"Macht Rome," Lowellin said when he got to them. "Advisor Quyloc. May I present to you Nalene FirstMother?"

Rome and Quyloc nodded to her and she gave a tight-lipped nod in response. Her eyes were hard.

"What are you doing here, Lowellin?" Rome asked.

"We came to see justice served for the murder of Melanine, the former FirstMother of the Tenders."

"Justice that *wasn't* served," Nalene snapped.

"You will not speak to your macht this way," Quyloc said roughly. "It's not your place to question him."

"I thought things had changed under the new king, but I see I was wrong," she retorted.

"Enough," Lowellin interjected, before Quyloc could reply. "If you wish to fight, do it on your own time. Mine is too valuable to waste." He looked up at Rome. "There is another reason we are here."

"What is it, then?" Rome's face was flat, impassive, his tone cold. Quyloc didn't need his inner senses to tell him how much Rome detested Lowellin.

"It is about the Tenders. As I told you before, they are vital in the war to come."

"So?"

"They cannot help from the shadows. They need to be able to act openly."

Rome shrugged. "The law banning the Tenders was removed months ago. They have the same protections as anyone else now."

Quyloc saw the contempt on Nalene's face when Rome said this, but she kept her mouth shut.

"That is not enough."

"What is it you want?" Rome's voice had grown even colder, but Lowellin ignored it.

"Give them your official sanction."

Rome looked at Quyloc. "What does that mean?"

"It means they have your official approval."

"I don't like it," Rome told Lowellin.

"You don't have to like it." Lowellin had dropped all pretense of respectfulness. "Like has nothing to do with this. My concern is focused solely on defeating Melekath when he emerges. To have even a chance of that, we have to work together. We have to fight together. I need the Tenders for this, and I need them strong. Do you understand me?"

Quyloc could sense how still Rome had become. It was how Rome became right before a battle, when he focused all his energies on the sole task of defeating his enemy.

Right then Quyloc could not have said how this would end. He could not tell what Rome would do.

Then the moment passed and Rome exhaled. "Okay. They have my sanction."

"And the FirstMother will be included in preparations and plans for the war."

Rome nodded slowly. "Is that all?"

"No. One more thing."

Quyloc could tell that Rome was gritting his teeth.

"Their current residence is not suitable to their station. They need something larger, something closer to the palace."

"And here I thought you were going to demand the palace itself," Rome said.

"I speak of the late Lord Ergood's estate."

"I will not just seize a man's property."

"Actually…" Quyloc put in. Rome turned to him. "Ergood has no heirs. His wife has been dead for years and both of his children died of fever last year. He has no brothers or sisters."

Rome considered this. "Okay," he said at last. "But this is only temporary, until this is over. They are tenants, nothing more."

Quyloc had to admit he enjoyed the look on Nalene's face when Rome said that.

Lowellin nodded. "That is enough." He turned and walked away. After giving them a baleful look, Nalene followed.

Rome took a deep breath. "I really hate that guy."

"I could say the same for the FirstMother," Quyloc replied.

Rome gave him a look. "I get the feeling you two already know each other."

"We've met. It didn't go well."

"You really think we need the Tenders in this fight?"

"Lowellin thinks we do."

"I don't trust him even a little bit."

"Neither do I. Unfortunately, I think we need him."

"You think he had something to do with what happened to Ergood?" Rome asked him. "It's all strangely convenient."

"The thought crossed my mind."

"Let's say we win this war. What then?"

"You're saying that we should be thinking about what to do with Lowellin, in case he doesn't want to leave."

"That's what I'm saying."

CHAPTER 26

Nalene was angry as she followed the Protector away from the meeting with the macht, but she was also excited. So much was happening, so fast. It angered her that the macht had not given them the estate outright, but it was still quite a jump from their current living situation.

Her hand went to her *sulbit*, where it clung to her chest, just above her heart. She'd seen the way Quyloc looked at her as they walked up. Clearly he had sensed the creature. That surprised her. She would need to keep an eye on him. What else was he capable of? Lowellin had spoken of a weapon that he had sent Quyloc to find. Whatever it was, she doubted that it would pose a real threat to her, not once she had her own small army of Tenders all armed with *sulbits*. But still, it was best not to become complacent.

It had been difficult at first to get any of the other Tenders to go for their *sulbits*. When she returned from old Qarath she called them all together and showed them her *sulbit*. They were awed by the sight of it, but none would get too close to it and when she asked for the first volunteer, they all went silent.

She yelled at them and they scurried from the room. For the rest of the day they all but hid from her like frightened children. Finally, she cornered Velma and straight out told her that if she didn't go to meet the Protector that night, not only would she not be her second in command, but she was going to banish her from the Haven and the order completely.

It still made Nalene grit her teeth to think about it. How were they supposed to regain Xochitl's trust, how were they supposed to help defeat Melekath, if they couldn't even take this one risk? Couldn't they see what an opportunity they had? She tried to tell them what a wonderful thing her *sulbit* was, the sense of deep connection, even love, that she felt for hers, and the way it opened her to the wonder and beauty of LifeSong, but it didn't seem to make any difference.

What she wouldn't give for just one with a dram of courage in her—

"Look out where you're going!" a man's voice said harshly.

Nalene felt herself shoved and she staggered to the side, fighting to keep her balance. She recovered herself and turned to see a man glaring at her. He was a tough, wiry little man with a crooked nose that had been broken too many times and a large scar on his chin that spoke of a knife fight. His clothes were dirty, his hair unkempt and graying.

"You ran into me!"

Alarmed, Nalene took a step back and looked around for the Protector. He would take care of this vermin for her.

But, though the street she was on was not very crowded, she couldn't see the Protector anywhere. She'd been so lost in her thoughts that she'd allowed herself to become separated from her.

Abruptly the look on the wiry man's face changed, going from outrage to greed, his eyes narrowing. "What's that around your neck then? Is that a Reminder?"

Nalene looked down and was horrified to see that somehow the gold Reminder—the ancient symbol of the Tender faith—she'd gotten from Melanine was no longer hidden inside her robe.

"It *is* a Reminder." His words were loud enough that other people were slowing down and turning to look. Nalene's heart started to beat faster. She'd seen how fast a crowd could get ugly and it would be worse now, with people already afraid.

"Those are illegal, you know," he said roughly. There was a nasty glint in his eye that said he had her in a bad situation.

She tucked it quickly back into her robe and tried to gain some control over the situation. "Not anymore. Not since Macht Rome took power."

"That doesn't mean you can flash that thing wherever you want," he hissed. He drew forth a long dagger from his belt and Nalene's eyes went very wide. Where was the Protector? How could he just abandon her like this?

"I don't want any trouble," she said, trying to back away and finding it difficult. A crowd was starting to gather and those behind her weren't letting her through.

"Then don't struggle," he replied, smiling and showing a handful of missing teeth. He advanced on her, the dagger glittering in the sunlight. "Hold still and I might not cut you. That thing looks like gold to me. What say I take it off you and maybe you can go on your way without getting hurt?"

He darted forward with surprising quickness and grabbed the front of her robe in his fist, then jerked her close to him. He smelled like sour wine and filth. He held the dagger up to her eyes and his smile grew wider. "What do you say, eh?"

Nalene stared at his face, the broken blood vessels in his nose, the twitching in one eye, and she hated him with a huge, towering passion. It was scum like this that had lorded it over the Tenders for far too long.

But what she hated most was how helpless she felt. It had gone on for far too long.

"I'm getting impatient. If I have to cut it free myself, you might get hurt."

Reluctantly, Nalene reached for the Reminder. But when she did, something unexpected happened.

Her hand seemed to move with a mind of its own. Instead of taking hold of the Reminder, she put it down the front of her robe and grabbed her *sulbit* instead. She pulled it out.

"What's that?" he said, surprised.

Nalene watched, dumbfounded, as her hand shot forward—

And pressed the *sulbit* against his forehead.

The man's eyes grew very wide. "No," he gasped.

Nalene gasped as well, as some of the Song the *sulbit* drained from him poured into her. It was an incredible feeling. She felt powerful, unstoppable.

The dagger clattered to the ground. The man tried to grab onto her, but there was no strength in his hands. "I'm..." he said. With a sigh he collapsed to his knees.

"You are vermin," Nalene hissed at him. "Not fit to breathe the same air as one of the Mother's chosen. By all rights I should kill you here."

She was aware of the crowd pulling back suddenly. She could taste their fear and she loved the flavor.

He was whimpering. All the color had drained from his face. His crotch was wet where he had loosed his bladder. A trembling came over him and Nalene knew he would be dead soon.

She had to stop. As much as she hated him, she did not want to murder this man. But when she tried to pull her *sulbit* back, it refused to let go.

He fell over on his side and she lost her hold on her *sulbit*. It was stuck on his forehead. She went to one knee and grabbed onto it. It wasn't easy, but she managed to pry the creature away. It writhed in her hand.

She stood up, putting the *sulbit* back inside her robe, against her skin. The man lay on the ground before her, unmoving, but not dead. She could still hear Song within him.

She turned and saw how the crowd had pulled away from her, how they were gaping at her.

"What you have witnessed is the dawn of a new day," she told them, her voice echoing with power that they could not deny. "The Tenders of Xochitl have returned from their exile." She knew suddenly what she needed to say, the good that could come from this. She liked that they feared her, but this was not what the Mother would want. The Tenders of the Kaetrian Empire had trod that path before.

"Dark times are coming!" she boomed. They flinched slightly at her words. "You know what I speak of. You have seen the signs, the diseases, the monsters that roam the land. Melekath is freeing himself from his prison and he means to take his revenge on all of you!"

Now they were cowering. She had them right where she wanted them.

"But you are not alone. In these evil times the Tenders have returned to protect you. Our power is once again ours and with it we will defeat Melekath once and for all!"

They stared at her, enraptured. By nightfall word of what happened here would have spread throughout the entire city. This, *this*, was why Lowellin had left her alone. To give her this chance.

She started feeling dizzy then, as the stolen Song faded from her. It would not do to let them see her weakness. Giving them one, last imperious look, she passed through them and strode away.

When she was out of sight of the crowd she stopped and leaned against a building, recovering her strength. She opened the front of her robe and looked down at the *sulbit* nestled against her skin.

It was slightly bigger now, larger than her thumb. It was no longer milky-white, but yellowed like an old bone.

CHAPTER 27

"I couldn't see it clearly, sir."

"That's not good enough," Quyloc snapped. He had his hands on his desk and was leaning over it, glaring at the young woman on the other side. "I pay you, I pay you *well*, so that you *do* see clearly."

The young woman shifted from one foot to the other nervously. She shot a look at Frink, standing a few feet to her right, but he had nothing for her. She swallowed. "There's nothing else I can tell you," she said in a barely audible voice. "It was very small, less than my little finger, and white. There were too many people and she had it cupped in her hand."

With a muttered curse, Quyloc sat back down. He wished he would have followed the FirstMother himself. If only he could have been there. "You said she seemed weak afterwards?"

"Once she got around the corner, she leaned against the wall."

That was something. Whatever it was, it weakened her when she used it. But that still didn't tell him *what* it was. What had Lowellin given her? According to his spy, she'd nearly killed the man, just by touching him. What could do that?

"And then she went back to the Haven?"

"Yes, sir. I came straight here after that."

Quyloc stared at her, hoping for more, but it was clear she had nothing else. He waved her off and she left.

"My apologies, sir," Frink said, as soon as the door closed. "This is unacceptable."

Quyloc shook his head wearily. "It's not your fault. It's not hers either. What's going on here is nothing you could possibly be prepared for."

Frink hesitated, then asked, "What *is* going on, sir?"

"You heard what she said." The spy had told them about the FirstMother's pronouncement, about the prison breaking and Melekath's revenge.

"Is it true?"

Quyloc nodded. "I think so."

"There's going to be a lot of frightened people when word gets around."

"I know." What was the FirstMother thinking? Was she trying to spread panic? Rome wasn't going to like this at all.

"What do you want me to do?"

Quyloc sighed. "Keep an eye on her, on all of them. But stay well back. I don't want anyone getting hurt."

Quyloc sat there for a few minutes after Frink left, thinking. He had to find the weapon Lowellin had promised him. No matter what the risk to himself was. He had learned that when he passed through the Veil—the barrier separating the *Pente Akka* from the normal world—if he had fixed in his mind a specific place, that was where he ended up. So at least each time he returned he could pick up where he left off. Landmarks could be hard to come by there, but he was doing his best to travel in the same direction each time. Theoretically at least, if he kept doing that he would eventually hit the river.

Unless he was traveling directly away from it.

Quyloc slammed his fist on his desk. Why could he get no help from Lowellin? He'd proven he could survive in that place. What more did he want? What game was he playing?

He stood up. He needed to talk with Rome about what the FirstMother had done. It would be best if the macht heard it from him first.

"She did *what*?" Rome asked, incredulous.

"Are you sure she didn't have a blade or a club or something?" Tairus asked. "Maybe your spy saw it wrong." Quyloc had found Rome and Tairus together in Rome's favorite room in Bane's Tower, leaning over maps, discussing which of the nearby kingdoms to conquer first.

"No, she did not see it wrong. I'm sure of it."

"How is this possible?" Rome asked.

"I wish I knew. I can only speculate."

"Then speculate."

"As I told you, Lowellin has met with several of the Tenders in the ruined temple in old Qarath." Rome nodded. "My informant told me that when Nalene put her hand on the man's forehead he slumped to the ground. She said it was like his life was being drained out of him. I think Lowellin is giving the Tenders something that allows them to drain the LifeSong from people."

"LifeSong?" Tairus asked. "What's that?"

"It is the energy that keeps you alive," Quyloc told him.

"Sounds like religious nonsense to me."

"Maybe you'd like to tell that to the man she almost killed. LifeSong is real, I assure you. During the time of the Empire there were Tenders who could kill you without touching you."

"But those are just legends."

"Sure, those history books in the library are nothing but legends."

Tairus shrugged, still unconvinced.

"Is she a threat?" Rome asked.

Quyloc dropped into a chair. "Of course she's a threat." He pinched the bridge of his nose. "But I think we need her, we need all the Tenders, if we're going to have a chance against Melekath."

"You have people keeping an eye on them?"

"All the time. But no one inside, at least, not yet. That will change when they move into the estate. A place that big, they'll need servants, workers to maintain the place, and so on. I'll have people in there."

Rome nodded. "That will have to do then."

Quyloc left the room knowing he had to do something and he had to do it soon. The Tenders were getting too far ahead of him. He needed to find the river Lowellin spoke of.

An idea came to him then. He could arrive at a specific place in the *Pente Akka* by visualizing it. What if he visualized the river? Would it work? Was it possible to visualize a place he'd never been well enough to go there?

It was worth a try.

He hurried down the stairs to the bottom floor of the tower and passed through a door into a storage room. He barred the door behind him, then moved some crates, revealing a trap door set in the floor. He climbed down the iron rungs and into the passage that led to his secret chamber.

His secret chamber was a small room, with a cot and a simple table. There was a shelf with a few books on it and a window cut in the rock wall that looked out over the sea.

Quyloc always came here when he journeyed to the *Pente Akka*. He didn't like the idea of leaving his body vulnerable while he was gone in the shadow world and this was the safest place he knew.

He laid down on the cot, closed his eyes, and pictured the Veil in his mind. A moment later he was standing on the yellow sands under the purple-black sky. Before him was the Veil, like a huge, gauzy spider web, stretching out of sight in both directions and into the sky.

He stood before the Veil and concentrated, picturing a river in his mind. When he had it locked in, he stepped through the Veil…

And found himself standing in an area of low, rocky hills. He climbed up on top of one and looked around. There was no river in sight.

Frustrated, he pictured the Veil in his mind, slashed an opening with the bone knife, and left the *Pente Akka*. Outside the Veil he looked around, hoping to see the cloaked figure, but there was nothing.

A moment later he was back in his room. He lay there on his cot, thinking.

What were his options? He could go looking for Lowellin, but what were the chances he would actually find him? He could go confront the FirstMother, demand to know what she was hiding, but he couldn't see how that would help anything.

What if he was actually looking at a river when he passed over?

He left his room and climbed the tower stairs until he reached the top floor. This room was unused and covered with a thick layer of dust and cobwebs.

He walked over to the room's only window and looked out. From here he had a clear view of the Cron River. He focused on the section after it left the city, where it made its lazy loop toward the sea. He stared at it for a long time as the sun dropped toward the horizon, memorizing every facet of it, focusing his thoughts so that there was nothing there but the river.

Then he lay down on the floor, closed his eyes, and willed himself onto the yellow sands. A moment later he was before the Veil.

He stepped through and this time he appeared on the edge of a steep escarpment. Behind him was a vast grassland. Before him the land fell away to a broad valley that was shrouded in a thick fog.

It hadn't worked.

Then the fog thinned out in the middle, just for a moment, but long enough for him to glimpse a large, turgid river.

He'd done it. He'd found the river.

The ground in front of him dropped away in a long steep slope of crumbling rock. He picked his way carefully down the slope, alert for any danger. As he got near the bottom objects began to emerge from the fog. Huge trees with twisted, gnarled trunks, their limbs festooned with curtains of moss. More trees lay strewn on the ground, broken limbs reaching for the sky they'd lost. Giant orange and red mushrooms grew from the rotting trunks. Red ferns grew in clumps taller than he was. Flowers in fantastic shades of violet and yellow bloomed in profusion.

There was a quick shadow of movement as something darted through a tangle of dead limbs. He saw something that seemed to have too many legs hanging upside down amidst a shroud of moss. Something heavy crashed through the undergrowth off in the distance, snapping limbs as it went.

And the bugs. There were beetles the size of his hand scurrying through the moldering leaves that covered every bit of ground. Things like giant dragonflies hummed by, and hanging from a limb was what looked like the biggest wasp nest he had ever seen. A veritable cloud of them buzzed around it, their bodies as big as his thumb.

He stopped at the edge of the riotous growth. Going in there was suicide.

The place wants you alive.

Okay, not suicide. Something worse.

But what other choice did he have? What other choice had he ever had? It was go forward or go back—and there was nothing behind him to go back to. He had come too far to stop now. He had survived this long. If he kept the knife ready, he could summon the Veil and flee at a moment's notice.

Steeling himself, he took one step into the morass, wishing he had a sword to hack a path with. He paused, one foot in the jungle, the other still on rock. Nothing happened. Though he knew his body was not really here, he was sure he could feel fear sweat breaking out all over him.

He took several more steps. The ground felt alive, things slithering around in the murk underfoot. In front of him was a wall of ferns covered with unpleasantly large spider webs. He skirted it and found himself face to face with a flower that was bigger than his head, with wide, indigo petals and a vibrant yellow center. Carefully, Quyloc edged around it, giving it a wide berth.

It turned and followed him.

Quyloc froze, his heart beating a little faster. The plant's wide, sharp-edged leaves rustled and he thought he saw something sinewy in its depths. Backing away from it, he tried to make his way back the way he had come in, but the opening he'd passed through was gone. To his left was a huge tree that had fallen and was slowly sinking into the slushy murk that pooled at its base. He couldn't go that way.

When he moved to his right a vine snaked out and wrapped around his left arm. He tried to pull away and another came and took hold of his right leg. They tightened and began to pull him towards the flower, which was now weaving back and forth.

Quyloc began to fight, throwing everything he had into it, while trying desperately to visualize the Veil. But he was having trouble focusing. He could not picture it in his mind at all, much less with the precision that was required to summon it to him.

A vine slipped around his waist and another around his left leg. One caught his right wrist, but he yanked free before it could get a firm hold on him. Panicking now, he slashed at the nearest vine with the bone knife. The vine burst apart with a spray of sticky white fluid. Frantically, Quyloc slashed at the other vines, and looked up just in time to see the flower descending on him. It was opened wide, the petals seeming to pulsate and he got one good, close look down into the thing's maw before he plunged the knife into it.

There was something like a silent scream that resounded inside his head and the thing withdrew. Quyloc took his chance and bolted.

He ran halfway up the rocky slope before he stopped, his whole body shaking so hard he could barely hold onto the knife. His first thought was to summon the Veil and get out of the *Pente Akka* as fast as he could. But what would that get him? The jungle would still be here, still barring his path. Meanwhile, Nalene and her Tenders would only get stronger. Quyloc gripped the knife and tried to control himself. If he left now, she and all the others would only get that much further ahead of him.

Slowly, he made his way downwards once again. He noticed then that off to the side there was a lip of rock that stuck out into the jungle. No plants grew on it. It looked like a good place to wait and watch.

He crawled out onto it and knelt near the edge. The ground was a good twenty feet below. Enough of a drop to wound or kill. He gripped the bone knife tightly, alert to each tiny movement within the green blanket of vegetation.

He waited there for a while, wondering what manner of creature the bone knife was made from that it could cut both the Veil and those plants with such ease. The cloaked figure he'd seen a couple of times outside the Veil had told him the bone knife came from the *Pente Akka*, brought from there by a Tender long ago. That was why he could bring it to this place but none of the rest of his weapons.

Was he looking for another weapon made of bone, then? Something larger?

It seemed possible, but that still didn't help him find this other weapon. If only he had some idea what he was looking for.

A sudden commotion in a nearby tree drew his attention. Two large, furred creatures were fighting. They had long, pointed ears, long tails and wide mouths filled with teeth. Each was easily twice the size of a large man. The larger one, with a patch of red on its chest, lunged at the smaller with a flurry of teeth and claws. The smaller one was knocked from the limb and tumbled to the ground.

All at once there was deep grinding, rumbling sound. The trees, even the stone itself, shuddered. The creature on the ground panicked and darted for the trunk of the tree. The one that had knocked it down disappeared. The creature made it to the tree and started up, gibbering with fear. But then one foot lost purchase on the slick wood and it slipped and crashed back to the ground.

That's when something broke out of the ground right below it. A mouth big enough to swallow a horse opened up and the furred creature disappeared inside. Quyloc could only gape as the rest of the thing surfaced, moving through the heavy soil as easily as a fish through water. It was huge, with a heavy snout that tapered down a thick body to a long, finned tail. It had stumpy, powerful limbs, each of which ended in a dozen long claws. Dirt trailed down its sides. It had two large black eyes set near the top of its head. It tilted its head up and back and gave a mighty bellow that shook the trees. When it bellowed he saw rows of long, curved teeth in its mouth, each as long as his forearm.

Quyloc backed away from the edge, his heart pounding. How was he ever going to get by that thing?

CHAPTER 28

Nalene stood in the grand entrance hall of the late Lord Ergood's mansion and watched with a scowl on her face as the other Tenders ran about exploring their new home. The place was impressive; she had to admit that. Three stories of opulence and decadence. Marble floors, soaring ceilings, elaborately-carved columns, thick rugs and expensive paintings. Lord Ergood had been a very wealthy man.

What made her scowl was that they were like excited children, running from room to room, throwing open doors, calling to each other. This was no way for the chosen of Xochitl to behave.

She strode across the hall, her sandals slapping on the marble floor, and then up the curving staircase to the second floor. At the top, a long hall led in either direction, sets of double doors along both sides. As she got to the top, Lenda emerged from one of the open doors carrying a silk dress in her arms. She pressed her face into the dress and squealed with delight. Suddenly she saw the FirstMother looking at her and her smile faded. Uncertainly, she went back into the room. She did not come out again.

Nalene walked down the long hall looking into the rooms filled with wealth and comfort and she came to a decision.

She said nothing to them the rest of the day and left them to their devices. On the top floor she found Ergood's personal suite, entered, and locked the door. That night she turned in early, forgoing the huge, four-poster bed with its piles of pillows and sleeping on the floor.

In the morning she rose very early and left the mansion quietly, careful not to wake any of the sleeping women. She walked down into the lower part of the city to a square where workmen gathered every morning, waiting for someone to come hire them for the day.

She paused at the edge of the square. The sun had not yet risen. There were no other women there besides her. This was not a good part of town. The men here were rough. She needed to make sure she handled this right.

She made sure her Reminder was prominently visible around her neck, touched the slumbering shape of her *sulbit* under her robe, and walked into the square. Four men were standing in a group, all of them unshaven, the smell of the alcohol they'd drunk the night before noticeable from ten feet away. Nalene strode up to them confidently, hiding her nervousness, knowing she couldn't let these men see any fear. Two turned as she walked up and gave her appraising looks. One of them saw the Reminder and elbowed the other.

"Do you know who I am?" she asked them in a loud voice. She wanted others in the square to hear as well. They nodded. One of them, a bald man wearing a wool-lined vest, spoke up.

"You're that Tender what almost killed that man in the street."

"I am."

"She don't look all that dangerous," another one said. He had a bad squint and shaky hands.

"Shut up, Lews," the bald one said. "We don't want any trouble," he told Nalene.

Nalene tried not to let her relief show. "That's not why I'm here. I'm here to hire those who want to work."

That got their attention. A half dozen others who had been listening moved in closer. "What sort of work?" one asked.

"Now hold on," the squinty one said. "Before I work for you, I want to see the color of your coins. You don't look like the sort who can pay."

"Don't let it bother you," she told him. "You won't be working for me anyway."

The squinty man swore when she said this and took a step toward her. Out of nowhere there was a knife in his hand.

But Nalene was ready for this. She reached into her robe and pulled out her *sulbit* and thrust it at him, though she kept her hand closed around it so he couldn't see it.

"Are you sure you want to do that?" she asked him. Her *sulbit* was no longer slumbering. It was awake and hungry as always. She would have no qualms about letting it feed on him.

The rest of the men backed away when she did that. The bald one said, "You're a damn fool, Lews. You want her to do to you what she did to the other one? You know he still ain't right yet. He can barely walk."

The squinty one looked at the other men, then back at Nalene. He put the knife away and held up his hands. "I just don't like being treated disrespectful is all."

Nalene dismissed him without another look, making it clear he mattered nothing to her. To the bald one she said, "I need men to empty a house, haul everything outside."

The bald man scratched his head. "Lews is an idiot," he said apologetically, "but he had one point. *Can* you pay us?"

Nalene had been expecting this and she had an answer ready. "Do you remember Lord Ergood?" The men all nodded.

"He's the one who died a douple days ago," a man wearing a shapeless hat said. "Him and about everyone around him."

"That's him. As of yesterday, the Tenders of Xochitl are the new owners of his entire estate." They looked surprised at that. "By order of Macht Rome," she added. "Here is what I am proposing. I need men to help empty the mansion, carry everything outside, and I mean everything. In payment, at the end of the day you will be permitted to take away whatever you can carry."

That got everyone's attention. Excited voices rose on all sides and didn't settle down until the bald man yelled for quiet.

"No fooling? *Anything* we can carry? Like a painting?"

"Or silver?" another one called out.

"That's right."

"Lady, begging your pardon," the bald man said, "but *why*?"

"I will not allow my order to succumb to the wealth trap again."

Confused looks greeted her words.

"I don't pretend to understand," the bald man said, "but you can count me in."

When Nalene left the square a minute later a small army of workmen followed her. What she didn't realize is that one of the men had been following her since she left the estate. Quyloc finally had his spy on the inside.

It was near the end of the day and a huge pile of furniture, paintings, rugs, artwork, silver sets and more lay in the center of the huge carriage way outside the mansion. Only a few items had been left inside, such as pots and pans, simple chairs, some tables and desks. Things that were truly necessary.

All day long, as the work went on, the Tenders had whispered and speculated to each other. But none dared ask Nalene outright what she was doing. She had a grim look on her face that made such questions seem downright foolhardy. They'd already learned how sharp her tongue was.

Now they were all lined up, watching, as Nalene told the workers to gather up what they could and leave. As the men began to stagger away under their loads, Nalene picked up a small barrel of lamp oil sitting beside her and began to walk around the pile, dumping the oil on it as she went.

Horror dawned on the women's faces as they realized what she was doing. Lenda began to cry.

When the barrel was empty, Nalene picked up the lantern that sat on the ground and threw it on top of the pile. The fire spread quickly.

"All glory comes from the Mother," she told them. "All else is but a pale reflection. Thus were the Tenders of old led astray. They allowed themselves to stare at the reflection until they could no longer see the truth and they lost their way, just as you all lost your way yesterday. That is why I am burning these things."

The Tenders exchanged frightened looks, but none spoke up.

When the fire had died down some, Nalene led them back into the mansion. In the grand entrance hall stood a single chair, a razor and a pair of scissors sitting on it. Seating herself on the chair, she handed the scissors to Velma and told her to get started.

"On what, FirstMother? What do you mean?" The long-faced woman looked as confused as the rest of them.

She gestured at her head. "Cut it off."

"Your *hair?*"

"All of it. When you've gotten as much as you can with the scissors, use this." She held up the razor.

She sat there with her eyes closed, praying, while the deed was done. When she stood up from the chair she resisted the urge to touch her bald scalp, but she could not keep her eyes from straying to the pile of hair on the floor. "One more burden of pride cast aside. One less trap to ensnare us." She held out a hand to Velma for the scissors. "You're next."

Velma, to her credit, sat down quickly, even if she was a bit pale. From the others there were a few protests, but Nalene silenced them easily with dark looks. They needed to understand, and very clearly, that times *had* changed, and one of those changes was that Melanine was no longer FirstMother. Melanine had tolerated a great deal of dissent. Nalene tolerated none.

CHAPTER 29

Quyloc was waiting outside the ruined Tender temple, hidden in a building across the street, when the Tender showed up at dusk. He thought it was the one who'd let him into the old Haven a while back when he went there to speak to the FirstMother, but he couldn't be sure at this distance. He remembered her as being simple, but not much else about her.

He wasn't here to try and spy on whatever it was Lowellin was doing with the Tenders. Clearly that wouldn't work.

No, he was here because he needed to see Lowellin and this was the only place he could be sure he'd show up. Quyloc hadn't been back to the *Pente Akka* since finding the river. What was the point? No matter how much he thought about it, he couldn't come up with any way to get to the river. Not with the things that waited for him in the jungle that surrounded it. And even if he got there, what then?

He needed answers from Lowellin and he meant to have them.

He settled in to wait. He thought back to the report Frink had brought him the day before.

"She did *what*?" Quyloc had asked him after he finished his report.

"She burned it all," Frink replied.

"Did she say why?"

"I was getting to that. As we were leaving, I heard her tell them it was to keep them from being corrupted by wealth, like the Tenders were during the time of the Empire."

"That woman is crazy."

Frink just shrugged, not agreeing or disagreeing. His job was getting information, not making sense of it one way or another.

Quyloc was staring to think he'd underestimated Nalene. She was clearly not content to linger in the shadows. She meant to make the Tenders a force again and she meant for it to happen fast.

Which was why he was here. He *had* to find that weapon. And to do that he needed answers. He couldn't understand why Lowellin was avoiding him. The only thing he could think was that Lowellin had decided he couldn't succeed so there was no point in wasting time on him.

An hour passed and then from inside the temple he could hear a woman approaching. She was crying. It was mostly dark by then but he could see that she was stumbling as she left the temple and made her way down the street. He was briefly tempted to follow her and see what he could learn from her, but he discarded the idea. It was more important to speak with Lowellin.

He slipped into the temple, moving quickly, wanting to catch Lowellin before he left.

"I wondered when you were going to show up," Lowellin's voice said from the darkness just after he entered the building. "When you would stop sending your hirelings."

"So you've been expecting me."

"You're looking for answers."

"I found the river."

"You did?"

"I can't get to it. There's too many things living in the jungle."

"You've learned that you can appear anywhere in the *Pente Akka* just by picturing it in your mind before you enter. Why not just appear right on the river's edge next time?"

"Because I can't see the river clearly. There's too much fog, too many plants. I don't want to end up in the water."

"That would be a very bad idea."

"What am I looking for?"

"You mean your friend in the cloak hasn't told you?"

Quyloc paused, wary. "I haven't seen him in some time."

"Did you really think you could hide him from me?"

Quyloc heard the danger in Lowellin's voice and his heart began to beat faster. He took a step back.

Lowellin emerged from the shadows. His face looked like stone in the dim light, his eyes shadowed holes. His close-cropped hair was the color of old bones. "I warned you before that there are elements to this war you have no idea of. You don't trust me, but I, at least, don't actively hate you. There are others among the Nipashanti who do, I can promise you that."

"What else am I supposed to do?" Quyloc said, bitterness overcoming his fear. "You give me nothing. You leave me in the dark while you meet with the Tenders every day."

"You have no idea what I am doing. You are barely more than an ape, with only the most limited grasp of the world around you. If you had any idea, any idea at all, of what is about to happen, you would fall to your knees and beg me to help you. You would do anything I say without question."

Quyloc knew how thin the ice was that he stood on, that he would be wise to back down, to do whatever it took to keep Lowellin happy. But he also knew that he wasn't going to. All his life he had dealt with bullies and he had learned that the only way to deal with them was to show no fear. He spoke before he could consider his words.

"If Melekath himself stood here right now, his hand raised to strike me dead, still I would not beg you. I will never beg you. I would rather die standing than live for one second as a beggar."

Then he waited, surprised at his own temerity, knowing without a doubt that Lowellin could kill him without a second thought.

Lowellin strode forward and loomed over him. When he spoke, his voice was barely controlled rage. "I made a mistake when I chose you. I should kill you right now."

Quyloc closed his eyes and waited for the blow to fall.

"But it would take me too long to find another who could make it as far as you have. It seems I must keep you alive for now." His hand fell on Quyloc's shoulder and his grip, when he squeezed, was as implacable as stone. Quyloc gritted his teeth and fought to keep from crying out. Lowellin leaned very close and spoke into his ear.

"Never speak to me this way again. Do you understand?"

Quyloc managed to nod. The pain was overwhelming. He wondered if his bones were being crushed.

Lowellin let go and straightened. "Kill the biggest creature you can find. Take one of its bones and plunge it into the river. From that you will make your weapon."

"Kill the biggest creature I can find? How?"

"You will figure it out." Lowellin turned and began to walk away.

"Wait! I need to know more!"

But Lowellin was already gone, swallowed by the shadows.

CHAPTER 30

"FirstMother! FirstMother, wake up! You have to come quickly! It's Lenda!"

Nalene sat up in bed and opened her eyes. At first she was completely disoriented. Nothing she could see in the dim light looked familiar. The room was too big. Where was she?

Then it dawned on her. The mansion.

There was more banging on the door.

"Just a minute!" Nalene yelled. The banging stopped.

Nalene's *sulbit* awakened then and she felt the now-familiar enervation as it began to nurse on her Selfsong. She had to admit that she thoroughly disliked the feeling. She was always tired afterwards, tired and somehow less substantial. Even worse was that it was feeding more often than before, probably due to the fact that it had grown.

The night she received her *sulbit*, Lowellin had indicated that the creature would only be feeding off her temporarily. But since then she had only seen him one time, when they went to meet the macht to get his sanction, and he'd said nothing about it. She was frankly starting to get a little worried. Would her *sulbit* eventually demand too much?

Would it kill her?

Wearily, she got up and pulled on her robe. From the position of the moon shining in through the window, she could see that it was very late, well past midnight. Why was Lenda returning so late? She should have been back hours ago. She opened the door. Velma was standing there holding a lantern, her eyes wide, her shaven scalp shiny with sweat.

"You have to come, FirstMother. There's something wrong with Lenda."

"Did she just get back? I told you to watch for her and make sure she was okay." Velma had the room right next door to Lenda.

Velma wilted. "I'm sorry, FirstMother. I…I fell asleep and didn't wake up until a few minutes ago when she came in."

Nalene pushed past her and hurried down the stairs, thinking how she should never have let Lenda go for her *sulbit*. The woman was simple. She wasn't strong enough. She wouldn't be able to handle the responsibility.

But Lenda had come to her after breakfast the previous day and said, "I want to go to the Protector tonight. I want my *sulbit*."

Nalene shook her head. "That's not necessary, child."

"I am not a child. I'm not a servant. I am a Tender of Xochitl." Lenda held her chin up as she spoke and stared steadily at a spot beyond Nalene's shoulder. Only a tremor in her lower lip betrayed her nervousness.

At first Nalene was irritated. She opened her mouth to excoriate Lenda, teach her the folly of taking that tone with her FirstMother. But she was impressed with the courage the young woman showed. She'd never heard Lenda stand up for herself before.

"No one thinks you're a servant," she said instead.

Lenda's eyes flicked to her, then away. "Everyone treats me like one. It's always, 'Lenda, fetch tea' or 'Lenda, clean this up.'"

Nalene had to admit that she was right. They did treat her like a servant, had ever since Melanine found her on the street and brought her home, her clothes dirty and torn, her hair full of lice.

"I'm not sure you're ready…"

"I *am* ready." Now Lenda did look at her. "Everyone else has theirs already. I'm a Tender. The Protector says all Tenders need to be ready to fight Melekath."

"Maybe in a few weeks when we're all settled in here. Wouldn't that be better?"

"No!" Lenda actually stamped her foot as she said it.

"Don't speak to your FirstMother like that," Nalene snapped. Simple or not, she would only allow the girl so much latitude.

"I'm sorry, FirstMother. I didn't mean to. But I want to go. I want to do my part. Otherwise I'm not a Tender at all, can't you see?"

And the thing was, Nalene did see. How could she deny any Tender this request? Maybe Xochitl had a plan for Lenda. Was it really her place to make this decision? Besides, if Lowellin didn't think she could handle it, he would turn her down, wouldn't he?

Now Nalene stood outside Lenda's bedroom, listening to the crying coming from within, and wondered why she had ever agreed to let her go. Why didn't she listen to her instincts?

Velma, her eyes big and round in the lamplight, was staring at her and Nalene realized she'd been standing there too long, her hand on the doorknob. Other Tenders had come out of their rooms and were standing in the hallway, also staring at her. She had to go in. She had to face this.

Nalene turned the knob and opened the door. Lenda was sitting on the floor against the wall, knees drawn up to her chest. Nalene crossed over to her.

"It's late, Lenda. Where have you been?"

Lenda raised her face. Tears were flowing down her cheeks. "I don't know," she moaned. "I was walking back to the city, I remember going through the gates and then…" Fresh sobs took her and whatever she said next was unintelligible.

Nalene crouched down near her, unsure how to comfort her. Crying had always made her uncomfortable and a little angry. "I can't understand you."

Lenda rubbed the back of her forearm across her eyes in a futile effort to wipe away the tears. She swallowed a few times and tried again. "The next thing I knew I was on this street where I've never been before. It was dark and I was crouched over someone." Fresh tears came and Nalene had to wait while she fought to control herself once again.

"I think he was dead!" Lenda wailed. "I think I did it!"

"That's ridiculous," Nalene told her sternly. "I'm sure you're mistaken." But she had a sick feeling in her heart as she said the words, remembering how close she'd come to killing that man in the street. He'd be dead now if she hadn't been strong enough to pull her *sulbit* away.

"It was the *sulbits*," Lenda cried. "They made me do it!"

Nalene went cold. Suddenly she was aware of the other Tenders standing in the doorway, staring at them. "Close that door and return to your rooms right now!" she yelled at them. The door closed but she knew they were still there. She turned back to Lenda.

"Tell me everything you remember."

"That's it. I can't remember anything else. I'm afraid, FirstMother. I can't control them. I don't know what they're going to make me do."

219

Them. Was it possible she had more than one?

Her mouth dry, Nalene asked, "Can you show me your *sulbit*?"

Lenda pulled the front of her robe down. What she saw made Nalene gasp and move back.

Lenda's *sulbit* was far larger than Nalene's, easily the size of a fist. It was the yellow of old bone and it had legs, six of them, ending in claws that were dug into Lenda's flesh. It had a long, thin tail and a blunt head. The head turned and beady black eyes fixed on Nalene. A tiny mouth filled with sharp teeth opened. No sound came out, but Nalene felt sure the creature was hissing at her.

Then she realized that Lenda's mouth was open too. She was baring her teeth at Nalene, mimicking the *sulbit*.

"We'll get it off you," Nalene said. "We'll get the Protector. It will be all right. You'll see."

Then Lenda's *sulbit* began vibrating, so fast that it became blurry and hard to see. There was a wet, ripping sound—

And then there were two *sulbits* on Lenda's chest.

Nalene stood up and backed away. She looked at Lenda. The young woman's eyes had rolled back in her head and she was twitching.

Suddenly Lenda leapt to her feet, startling Nalene so badly she almost fell down. Lenda's head turned side to side as if taking in her surroundings, but still only the whites of her eyes were visible.

"Lenda, don't..." Nalene said, just as Lenda raced to the window of her room—moving with eerie, silent grace—and jumped through it.

Breakfast the next morning was utterly silent, as the Tenders grappled with what had happened. Nalene hadn't told them what Lenda's *sulbit* looked like or that there were two of them. She didn't tell them about the *sulbits* taking control of Lenda either, afraid of how they would react if they heard that. But still they knew something terrible had happened and she had no words to offer them in consolation.

How could she have consoled them anyway? She'd been awake the rest of the night, replaying the events in Lenda's room, telling herself she should have done *something*. She should have helped Lenda. She should never have let her go.

But, worst of all, were the other thoughts. *What was this thing she had on her chest? Would it take her over as well?*

Finally, she got up from the table and walked outside, needing to be alone. Randomly she chose one of the many footpaths that wound around the estate and followed it.

She hadn't gone far when she felt his presence and looked up. Lowellin was standing on the path, hands folded over the top of his walking staff.

"I know what happened," he said, before she could speak.

"It was terrible," she said. "I couldn't help her. We have to find her. We have to help her."

Lowellin shook his head. "I have more important things to do."

"What could be more—"

His face darkened. "We have a war to fight. The girl is a victim of that war. The first, but not the last. Others will die. Will you collapse each time?"

"She didn't have to be a victim," Nalene snapped suddenly, the stress of the last hours bursting out all at once. "You shouldn't have let her get a *sulbit*. You should have known what was going to happen and done something."

"I did not come here to weep for one girl," Lowellin said in a cold voice. "She doesn't matter."

But she does matter, Nalene wanted to say. Instead she clamped her mouth shut, so tightly her jaw ached.

"In this war, there is no place for weakness, no place for second thoughts. Do you understand me?"

Nalene nodded.

"I want to hear you say it."

"I understand," she choked out.

"One life counts for nothing. Ten thousand lives count for nothing. Do you understand?"

Nalene swallowed. She felt on the verge of collapse. Somehow she managed to say, "I understand."

"You took an oath to follow my orders without hesitation. Are you now doubting that oath?"

"No, Protector," she said weakly. *What have I done, Mother? Is this really the price to follow you?*

"Good, because there is much to do. What happened to the girl does serve one purpose. It demonstrates the utter importance of learning how to control the *sulbits*. Because of what happened to her, you and the others understand how vital it is that you do exactly what I tell you to." He paused, waiting.

"Yes, Protector," she said softly.

"Do the others know what happened?"

"Not really. They weren't in the room."

"When we are done here, you will tell them everything. Leave nothing out. I want them focused and the fear of what happened to her will help them with that."

Nalene blinked hard against the tears she could feel in her eyes. She hated Lowellin right then, even as she knew she and the rest were more tightly bound to him than ever.

"Do you understand?"

"Yes, Protector."

"The lessons will begin today. Send someone to purchase a cow shatren."

Nalene looked up, surprised. "A cow?"

Lowellin gave her a hard look and Nalene lowered her head. "My apologies, Protector. We will have a cow."

Telling the others what happened to Lenda hurt, more than Nalene would have ever thought possible. As she talked, she could not help but remember Melanine and the old woman's warnings about Lowellin.

Had she been right? Was it a mistake to follow him? But if so, then what else were they supposed to do? They couldn't just stand by and do nothing while Melekath destroyed Xochitl's creation. They had to fight back no matter what the cost. The Protector might be cruel, the *sulbits* might become uncontrollable and devour them all, but at least now they had a chance to do *something*.

At least that's what she told herself. It was all she had.

When she was done they stared up at her, a variety of emotions on their faces. Sorrow for Lenda. Horror at what had happened. But mostly fear. Was that going to happen to them as well? Suddenly Nalene couldn't bear looking at them anymore.

"Velma, you and Perast go buy a cow shatren."

"Why?" Velma asked.

"Because I told you to!" Nalene barked.

"Okay," Velma said. "Where do we go to buy a cow?"

"Do I have to do everything for you, Velma? Are you incapable of doing the smallest thing yourself?"

Velma gulped and hurried out of the room, Perast trailing her closely.

When they returned with the cow shatren, Nalene told the Tenders to follow her outside. The cow was tied to one of the iron hitching posts that lined the circular carriage way in front of the mansion. She gazed at them disinterestedly, slowly chewing her cud.

"Can I ask what the cow is for now?" Velma asked her.

"We're going to start training our *sulbits*, so what happened to…it's so we can control them."

A few minutes later Lowellin came walking up. He gave no greetings but simply began talking.

"The girl has provided us with our first lesson. You all see now the importance of controlling your *sulbit*, what can happen to you if you don't."

The women shifted nervously and Nalene had a terrible thought. Was that why he'd taken Lenda to get a *sulbit*? Had he known what would happen and allowed it so as to teach them all a lesson? Was he really that ruthless?

"In order to control your *sulbit*, your will must be strong. Either you control it, or it will control you. Bring your *sulbits* forth and hold them out."

The women did as they were told, plucking their *sulbits* from inside their robes and holding them out. The creatures sat there on their palms, motionless, looking like albino tadpoles.

"You took that *sulbit* from its natural home and brought it here, to a place beyond its comprehension. You took something that had no physical form and brought it into the physical world."

Along with the other Tenders, Nalene found herself looking at her *sulbit* differently. She'd never thought of that before.

"Then how is it I can touch it? Where did this form come from?" she asked.

"The *sulbits* are creatures of pure energy, Life-energy. That energy is the basic foundation of life and it is endlessly creative, always seeking form to express itself. What you see in your hand can be thought of as an idea, the creature's idea of itself. From its thought of itself that form was created."

Confused looks met his words. Nalene wasn't sure she understood it herself, but she knew better than to ask the Protector to explain further. Then Velma spoke up.

"How big are they going to get, Protector?" She put her hand over her mouth as if surprised at herself for speaking.

"The answer is, as big as they want to be. As for *what* they will become, again that is up to them. There is no way to know. Do not speak again unless I tell you to."

Velma nodded. The women exchanged nervous looks. Nalene knew how they felt. Lowellin's answer didn't make her feel any better either.

"Your *sulbit* finds itself in a world it doesn't understand, in a body it doesn't know how to use. Until recently it had no need to go here or there. At all points within the River it already had everything it could possibly need. In a way, it is like a baby. It has no way of moving itself around, yet for the first time it knows want, it knows hunger, and so must seek a way to fulfill that want.

"Because of how closely connected each of you is to your *sulbit*, when it wants something, you feel that want as your own. As it tries to fulfill that want, your muscles respond to attempt to accomplish it. In essence, it uses your body to obtain what it wants."

That explained a great deal, Nalene thought. She really hadn't meant to put her *sulbit* on that man's forehead. It had made her do it and she'd been too surprised to resist.

"Only one of you can be in control. If you are too weak, as the girl was, it will take you over and force you to do what it wants. Eventually, if you do not fight back, you will be completely enslaved by it."

There were gasps at that. Some of the Tenders were staring at their *sulbits* in horror.

"That is why you must do exactly as I say. You must learn how to control your *sulbit*. You must train it so that it does as you will, rather than the other way around."

He walked over to the cow, which looked at him placidly. "Come here, FirstMother." Nervously, Nalene walked over to him.

"Your *sulbits* have to feed. Not only are they endlessly hungry since being taken from a world where they were immersed in Song and brought to this one where Song is relatively scarce, but they need to feed if they are to grow strong enough to be useful to us. Until now, they have fed off you, as a baby nurses its mother. But they are growing fast and if you supply no other source of Song to them, they will take more than you can provide. Eventually they will kill you, probably in your sleep, when you are unable to actively oppose them."

The Tenders' eyes grew very wide as he said that. Velma looked like she would throw her *sulbit* down and run.

"That is the reason for this animal here. You will need to get more of them, because you need to feed your *sulbits* every day, and increase their food as they grow larger. Feeding them is the perfect time to train them. By only letting them feed when you say, and on what you say they can feed on, you will be teaching them that you are in control."

"Why can't they just feed directly off flows of LifeSong, Protector?" one of the women asked. "When they were in the River they fed on pure LifeSong."

Lowellin looked irritated by the question, but grudgingly he answered it. "As I said, until they were removed from the River, they had no actual physical forms. Now they do, but these forms have no *akirmas*. *Akirmas* serve to keep Selfsong within the physical body, but they also serve as a sort of filter, taking in raw LifeSong and changing it into Selfsong which the body can use. Since the *sulbits* have no *akirmas*, they have no way to filter raw LifeSong and use it to sustain their forms. So they have to feed on Selfsong from other creatures."

He motioned to Nalene. "Move closer to the cow, FirstMother. Hold your *sulbit* close to it, but do not touch the animal."

Nalene did as she was told. She noticed the way her *sulbit* suddenly grew more alert. She could feel how it strained toward the cow.

"Do you feel the way it tries to force you to move your hand closer to the cow?"

"I do." It was a strange compulsion. She experienced a strong desire to touch the cow, but the desire was not her own. Her hand trembled slightly, as she struggled with the *sulbit* for control of her own body.

"Pull it away."

It was a struggle to do so, but Nalene managed it. After her, the rest tried as well. Nalene was pleased to see that they all managed it, though Velma worried her. When it was her turn to pull away, her hand started shaking and she actually took a step closer to the cow, so that her hand almost touched it. Just when Nalene thought she was going to lose the battle, she grabbed her wrist with her other hand and wrenched it away. She was sweating when she walked back to the others and there was fear in her eyes.

"Never give in to your *sulbit*," Lowellin told them. "Even when it seems like something harmless. Make sure that whatever you do, it is you who has chosen to do it, not your *sulbit*. You must be alert at all times. They will try to manipulate you and they are sneaky and persistent."

"What happens when we're asleep?" Nalene asked him. "Won't they just take control of us then?"

He shook his head. "When you are asleep your mind is not accessible to them in the same way. They don't control your body directly; they go always through your mind. In sleep, you mind is detached from your body. That is how you can dream without actually moving in your bed. But you bring up an important point. The time right after awakening is a time when you must be extra vigilant. In those minutes when you are still returning to wakefulness your guard is down. Your *sulbits* will try to seize that opportunity."

That was some relief, at least, Nalene thought, to know that her *sulbit* could not take control of her while she slept. The idea of wandering around at night in her sleep, trying to suck the Song out of people, was a decidedly unsettling one.

"Now it is time for you to feed them. Everyone come forward and stand around the cow. Put your hands close to the animal, but don't let your *sulbits* feed until I say to do so. Again remember how vital it is that you use feeding time to train them, especially while they are still very young and weak. If you train them now, they will grow up accepting that you are in charge and not fight you as much. But if you let them start to think otherwise, they will become like spoiled children, willful and out of control. But children who can kill you."

Hesitantly, the Tenders gathered around the cow and put their hands close to it, palms down. The cow stopped chewing her cud and swung her head side to side, confused by this unusual behavior and perhaps dimly sensing the danger the *sulbits* presented.

"Before you start, know that at some point, before the animal dies, I will tell you to stop. Be ready for that. Know that they will resist you. You will need all the strength you possess. Is that clear?"

They all nodded. Most were staring at their *sulbits* fixedly, already fighting to hold them back. Nalene's was giving her more trouble than she'd expected also. The muscles in her arm kept twitching, receiving signals she hadn't intended to send. She bit her lip and fought back, determined that the creature would not get the upper hand.

"Now, place them against the cow."

When they pressed their *sulbits* against the cow she bawled loudly. She tried to kick, to run, her muscles heaving under the skin, but she was paralyzed, unable to do more than bawl and twitch.

After a minute, Lowellin said, "Stop."

At first Nalene couldn't do anything. Her *sulbit* was locked onto the animal, like a dog gripping a bone in its teeth, and she couldn't pull her hand away. She grabbed her wrist with her free hand and pulled as hard as she could.

Suddenly her *sulbit* lost its hold and she staggered back. She was breathing hard, sweat running down her back.

One by one the rest of the Tenders wrestled their *sulbits* away also, until only Velma was left. The cow made a sound like a sigh and sank to her knees; Velma was pulled down with her.

Nalene went to her side and knelt beside her. "Fight it, Velma," she said in her ear. "Fight it with everything you have.'

Velma gritted her teeth and pulled. The cow's eyes rolled back in her head and she flopped over onto her side. Velma put a foot against the cow, then the other one, and leaned back, using her legs to help her.

Just when Nalene thought she wouldn't manage, she broke free and sprawled on her back. She lay there staring at the sky, her chest heaving, tears gathering in the corners of her eyes.

"Come on," Nalene told her, bending over her and extending her hand. "Get up. You did it." Velma took her hand and she pulled her to her feet. Nalene steadied her as she got her legs back. Lowellin stared at Velma, but said nothing.

Nalene looked down at the cow. She could still hear Selfsong radiating from the animal, but it was very weak.

"Now it is time to begin learning how to use your *sulbits* as weapons," Lowellin said.

Nalene wanted to protest. The women were frightened and tired. They needed a break. But she kept her mouth shut and didn't say anything. He was the Protector. She had vowed to follow him.

"Though your *sulbits* cannot feed on raw LifeSong, they can touch it and manipulate it. They will provide the strength and you will provide the direction. In order to do this, however, you must learn to meld with your *sulbit*. When you are melded with your *sulbit*, you will see what it sees. You will feel what it feels. If your will is strong enough, you will be able to access and control its full abilities. These are elemental creatures of LifeSong. If you can gain absolute control of them, when they reach full maturity you will be more powerful even than the Tenders of Empire were."

That got everyone's attention. Excited murmurs broke out. Nalene wanted to shout for joy. All her life she had tried to touch LifeSong and she had never succeeded. She could barely muster the strength to go *beyond* and even *see* it. Touching it, controlling it—that had seemed like an impossible dream.

The Protector gave them a stern look and they all went quiet. "This step is not without risk. In order to meld with your *sulbit* you will have to lower your inner defenses and allow the creature into the deepest recesses of your being. Your will must be iron. You must cast aside fear, which will weaken you."

The women went very still, eying their *sulbits* fearfully. They had only just gotten these strange creatures, they knew hardly anything about them, and now they were being asked to allow the things inside them. Even Nalene could not deny that she found the thought disturbing at best, terrifying at worst.

"Put your hands over your *sulbits*," the Protector ordered. "Close your eyes. Feel them, not just with your hands, but inside you. Focus on their presence. Don't let any other thoughts into your mind."

He was quiet for a few minutes then. Nalene could feel her *sulbit*. It was smooth and cool. It squirmed slightly. After a couple of minutes, she realized that she could feel the creature as a deeper presence.

"Now concentrate on lowering your defenses. Let the creatures deeper and deeper into you. Wrap yourself around them. Welcome them. Let the lines between you and them blur. When you have succeeded, you will find yourself pulled *beyond*."

Nalene did as he said, pushing aside her fear and letting her *sulbit* inside her. It wasn't easy. Having another awareness move into her mind, allowing it equal space, went against all her instincts. She wanted to push the creature away, but instead she forced herself to let it come closer and closer.

Then it was as if something clicked into place. A fundamental shift occurred, a threshold crossed. The concept of "I" and "me" was pushed to the rear and in its place there was "we." It was frightening and exhilarating at the same time.

A moment later she realized that she was *beyond*. It was beautiful, wondrous. Golden flows of Song branched everywhere, gossamer in the darkness. She heard several of the women around her gasp and knew that they were *seeing* the same wonders.

"It is time to choose the flow that you will use for this next exercise. First identify the one that is attached to your own *akirma*. That should always be the one you first identify. I don't think I need to tell you that bleeding off Song from that flow would have negative repercussions for you, as you would be weakening yourself at the exact time you need your strength more than ever."

Nalene looked for, and found, the flow of Song attached to her. She looked at her *akirma* then, and *saw* her *sulbit*. It appeared as a tiny, glowing spot, from which glowing threads, like tiny roots, branched into her.

"Now, identify the flows attached to the women around you. They need to be avoided as well."

As Lowellin spoke, Nalene's attention drifted to him and she was surprised at what she *saw*. He had no *akirma*. He appeared to be covered by interlocking shapes that glowed a faint reddish color.

"Look for one of the smaller flows, one that is attached to a plant. The larger ones, those attached to animals or people, should be left alone for now until you and your *sulbit* grow stronger. The power contained in the smallest flows will be all you can manage right now."

Nalene did as she was told, locating a tiny flow that appeared to be about the thickness of a hair.

"With the strength given you by your *sulbit* reach out and take hold of it. Grasp it gently, but firmly."

Nalene did and was shocked by the sudden surge of energy that flowed through her. It almost hurt and she had to resist the urge to let go.

"While still maintaining your hold on the flow, open your eyes. Hold onto the vision of *beyond*, but reach for normal sight at the same time," Lowellin said.

Nalene made an effort and the ethereal world of *beyond* dimmed, slid into the background as the normal world re-emerged in her sight. She looked around. Only a few of the other women seemed to have been also able to follow the Protector's directions.

"Focus on that stone bench over there," Lowellin said, pointing to a bench about twenty feet away. "Feel the Song bleeding off the flow you are holding onto. Try to hold it in, rather than letting it escape. Hold it in as long as you can and when you can hold it in no longer, release it at that bench."

At first Nalene couldn't figure out how to do what he ordered, but after a minute or so she figured it out. It was just an effort of will, wrapping her mind around the extra Song instead of letting it run over her. She felt the buildup right away, like a reservoir of water collecting insider her, and her will the dam that held it back.

She held it back until she was moments from losing control of it, then she raised her other hand, the one not holding onto the flow, pointed at the stone bench and let go.

With a crackling sound, a blue-white bolt of energy shot out and struck the bench. There was a pop as it struck, a burned mark appeared on the bench and it rocked slightly.

A few seconds later a similar bolt shot out from Mulin's hand, then, almost immediately, one shot out from Perast.

The three women exchanged astonished looks. Did they really just do that? Nalene looked around. It didn't look like any of the other Tenders had managed to take hold of a flow. Nalene lowered her hand. Her head was pounding and she knew she was going to have a wicked headache soon, but she was elated also. She looked up at the Protector to see his reaction.

But if she had been expecting praise or even acknowledgement, she was disappointed. All he said was, "It is a start," and he didn't even look at her. His attention was on the other Tenders.

"Keep working on it," he told them. "You must learn to meld with your *sulbits* and you must learn soon if you are to be of use in this war. Those of you who managed it need to keep working at it. The more you try, the stronger you will become. In time you will be able to hold in Song fed to you by other Tenders and let it build to the point where it will be powerful enough to break through a stone wall."

When they were done, and the others had gone their separate ways to practice, Lowellin looked at her.

"They did not do too poorly," he said.

We did better than that! Nalene thought fiercely, but she said nothing.

"But we will need more, many more. Send messengers to every Haven and order the Tenders here."

"How will I do that? We don't have the coin to hire messengers, or to buy food for more mouths."

He brushed her concerns aside with an irritable gesture. "I will speak to the macht about funds for your order. Rome is actively recruiting men to join his army. You will do the same. You will make them *want* to join you."

"How?"

"By inspiring them, by inspiring the whole city. Starting tomorrow morning, hold your morning service in public. Warn the people of what is coming. Tell them you are their best hope in what is to come. They are frightened already and will only grow more so. The more frightened they are, the more they will flock to you."

CHAPTER 31

Rome looked up from a map he was staring at and there was Lowellin. He looked around. The door was still closed. No sign of how Lowellin had entered. He sighed.

"What is it, Lowellin? I have things to do."

"I won't take long. I want you to authorize the Tenders to draw funds from the royal treasury."

"Oh, is that all? Are you sure you don't want anything else? Maybe I could move out of the palace for them?"

"That won't be necessary," Lowellin replied, ignoring his sarcasm. "Their current residence is sufficient for now."

"Good, so glad to hear that. Now, do you want to tell me *why* I should give them my money, money I happen to need to raise an army?"

"They have no coin of their own. There numbers will soon be growing and those women will need to be fed and housed. Additional structures will have to be built. They also need to hire servants and guards as well. All these things require funds."

"I heard they had a big fire over there recently. Maybe they shouldn't have burned up all that stuff. I hear there are people who will pay for such things."

Lowellin just stared at him.

"Okay," Rome said. "I'll talk to Quyloc about it. I'm sure we can spare something." He leaned forward and pointed at Lowellin. "But you need to keep them under control. I also heard about the man the FirstMother almost killed the other day. You better make clear to her that no one in Qarath is above the law. If she, or any of her women, kill a man, they will face a judge. The punishment for murder is hanging. Women too."

Lowellin looked down at him, his face cold. "Are you finished?"

Rome shrugged. "For now, I guess."

After Lowellin left, Rome headed downstairs and walked over to the palace. Though he'd only met her the one time, he didn't like the FirstMother. His gut told him she was going to be trouble. But he also understood that wars led to unlikely allies, which meant he was stuck with her. He hoped she was smart enough not to push him too far and force his hand. He'd meant what he said about no one being above the law.

He was so lost in his thoughts that when Opus stepped out in front of him, he ran right into the little man and knocked him down. But Rome had good reflexes and he recovered quickly, grabbing him before he could hit the floor. Unfortunately, he just happened to grab the lace on the front of the chief steward's shirt and it tore.

"Sorry about that, Opus. I didn't see you there." He set Opus upright and brushed at the rip ineffectually, as if that might make it whole again.

Opus held himself very stiff, his nostrils flaring, until Rome let him go. With just the merest disapproving glance at the rip he drew himself up and said, "Macht Rome, how fortunate I found you. I wish to speak with you regarding the feast and ball at the palace this night." He was as neatly groomed as ever in black trousers that ended just below the knees, black hose and black shoes. Sewn to the breast of his white, ruffled shirt was Rome's shield, a black wolf on a white background. He'd fussed at Rome for weeks until he chose house colors and a shield, and then right away he'd complained about Rome's choice. Said the colors were gloomy, unimaginative. To which Rome replied that it wouldn't look all that good for the Black Wolf to show up wearing yellow, would it?

Rome groaned. "A feast?" This sounded bad. He scanned the hall for Tairus, Quyloc, even a servant that he could use as a diversion. But the hall was empty; Opus had planned his ambush as well as any general.

"Yes. *And* a ball," Opus replied.

"Why?" Rome sighed. He couldn't wait until he had his army mustered and marching against the enemy. At least then he wouldn't have to deal with his annoying chief steward. "Why do you do these things to me?"

Opus managed a look that was hurt and haughty at the same time. "I am not *doing* anything to you, Macht."

"Good, good," Rome said. He patted the smaller man's shoulder. "Then why can't we just let this one pass? Keep the gates locked. Let the nobles have their ball somewhere else. I'm very busy, you see." He was already trying to get by the man and down the hall.

Opus shifted to stand in front of him. "No, that won't do at all. You've been shirking your duties too much as it is."

"Shirking!" Rome bellowed. To Opus' credit, he didn't even flinch. He wore righteousness better than most soldiers wore armor, Rome thought. "I'm trying to get the whole army ready for—" He cut off. The less said about his plans the better. That he was gathering the army for something wasn't exactly a secret, but so far only a handful knew what he was going to use the army for. He didn't want talk of empire getting out, not yet. "I'm planning and doing lots of things. I'm not shirking."

Opus shook his head, then drew himself up, taking a deep breath, and now Rome really did groan. Another one was coming. Another of Opus' lectures about the duties and responsibilities of ruling. Rome hated these sermons. They made him feel like he was still a filthy urchin stealing on the streets instead of the ruler of the whole city. Why was everyone else so afraid of him, but not this man? He had a sudden vision then, of Opus lecturing his children when they misbehaved. Of them pleading, "Please, Daddy, no lecture. Just hit us, and be done with it." And then he realized he didn't even know if the man was married.

"Do you have children?" he asked abruptly.

That deflated Opus. He hadn't expected that. One immaculate hand rose to check his oiled hair. Finally, he said, "I have three, Your Gra—Macht, thank you for inquiring. But that does not change what is at hand."

"Poor things," Rome muttered, but Opus either didn't hear or he ignored him.

"There is more to ruling a kingdom than leading armies, my Lord. Much more. There are rituals to be observed, decorum to be adhered to. The ruler must fit the people's vision of what a ruler must be, lest he lose their respect and end up governing nothing more than mindless rabble.

"*One* of these things," he said, cutting Rome off before he could reply, "is presiding over the Perfection of the Few. That is what is occurring tonight and no, you cannot sidestep this one."

"What in Bereth's name is the Perfection of the Few? Is that some kind of new holiday?"

"It is not a holiday. Not for the commoners anyway. It is a reenactment of one of the greatest gifts of Protaxes to mankind." Opus followed the thin line of his mustache with one manicured fingernail, making sure every hair was still in place. "You do remember what I taught you about Protaxes, don't you? He is the three-headed god. He sprang from the fireball that was originally this world. One head, Kilon, breathed ice on the fire, putting it out, while another head, Yilon, took the raw world in his mouth and formed it into its shape. The last, Wilon, then breathed it into life.

"This ceremony is one of the most sacred to the followers of Protaxes. It occurs only once every seven years and only the ruling class are invited to witness its mysteries."

"Well, that's me, now. I'm the ruling class and I don't want to witness it." Rome sounded petulant even to himself.

"Whether you like it or not, Lord Rome, there is still a powerful nobility in this city. You have chased them out of the palace, you have taken what is theirs and you have forced them to stand even with the commoners." Opus didn't sound all that pleased with these things. "But if you deny them this, you will surely face outright rebellion."

"Okay," Rome said tiredly, though he doubted the part about rebellion. "I'll go." If he didn't agree, Opus would just dog him all day until he did. Maybe it wouldn't hurt to smooth a few feathers back into place. They should have learned who was in control by now and it would be better to have at least some of them on his side. Even a few would help; they could tell him what the others were plotting. Less trouble that way. Maybe he should try and learn some of that diplomacy that Quyloc was always going on about. It might come in handy when he had an empire to rule.

"Just tell me what it's about and what I'm supposed to do and I'll do it."

Opus gave him a look, clearly suspicious about this sudden good behavior. "I am serious here, Macht Rome."

"So am I. Look at my eyes." Rome pulled his lower lids down and loomed over him. "See?"

"It looks as though you were drinking again last night."

"Gods, man, don't you have any fun at all?"

In answer Opus picked at a piece of imaginary lint on his ruffles. "The Perfection of the Few is a celebration of the time when the great god Protaxes took pity on mankind, divided as we were by endless squabble and difficulty."

"So different from now," Rome said sarcastically.

Opus ignored him. "In his wisdom and mercy, Protaxes took a handful of humans up to the mountain with him and there undertook the awesome task of molding them into more perfect creations. When he was finished he set them back amongst their kind and gave over to them the rule of mankind. These more perfect humans are the nobility. This celebration is in gratitude to him for his benevolence."

"Cranks and culpeppers," Rome breathed. "They *believe* this garbage?" No wonder only the nobility were invited to this thing. Anyone else would be too busy laughing.

"It is not my place to judge such things," Opus said seriously. "My place is to see you ready. That I will do."

"Okay, okay." Rome held his hands out, wrists together, as if offering himself up for manacles. "Take me away, I'm yours."

The guests started arriving at sunset. Rome stood on a balcony on the top floor of the palace and watched. This was a good vantage point and as little-used as the top floor was these days he'd been able to stand here for a while without being bothered by some bowing servant or obsequious bureaucrat. The nobility came in all manner of gilded carriages, drawn by prancing horses, with liveried footmen and guards. The women wore sprays of color that would put a paradise bird to shame, while the men were laden with hose and velvet and oiled hair.

They looked stupid, every one of them. He doubted if a single one of them had an inkling of how silly they really looked. What was wrong with a simple pair of pants and a stout shirt for the men, an honest dress for the women? He couldn't even imagine spending good coin on clothing like that. Much better to buy a good horse or a well-made weapon, something useful.

He leaned over the railing to watch as an attractive young woman in a low-cut orange dress, her black hair bundled up on top of her head in what looked like some kind of elaborate knot, minced up the broad front steps of the palace to the main doors. Now a dress like *that* he approved of. He wouldn't mind getting a closer look at her later on, though probably she was better here, from a distance. In his experience, these noblewomen were about as useful as a broken belt. Nothing to them but powder and perfume. No substance, not like his

Bonnie. Now there was a woman. Too bad he couldn't get her up here. She'd show these highborn women a thing or two.

When the woman had disappeared beneath him, Rome leaned back and scratched at the stiff collar encasing his neck. This was going to be a long night. Glumly he looked down at his outfit. The shiny shoes with their narrow soles were hurting his feet already. He didn't see how he could be expected to walk in such things, much less dance in them. The pants were a deep purple—gods, but he hated purple!—skin-tight around his calves and then ballooning out from there on up until they were cinched tight with a wide, white belt. Made him feel like some kind of mushroom.

His shirt wasn't so bad, being black with slashes that were purple inside and only a few ruffles on the chest. Some kind of frills hung down from the backs of the sleeves and he had a feeling they'd be getting in the wine before the night was over. But he had to wear a voluminous purple and white jacket over the shirt, with sleeves that were big enough to stick his leg through and then only elbow-length.

Then there was the collar. It wasn't even connected to the jacket or the shirt but seemed designed strictly for the purpose of pain. It was some kind of stiff white fabric and buttoned in the back. Hanging from the front was a large red jewel cut in the shape of a heart. Opus had explained that every monarch dating back to Cletus had worn this jewel. It was to signify his place as heart of the city. Rome thought it looked ridiculous.

Rome sighed and leaned on the railing. How long before he could skip out on this thing and go see Bonnie? He missed her. With all the preparations for war he was finding it harder and harder to make time to see her.

A page appeared in the doorway behind him, slightly out of breath from running up the stairs. "There you are, Majes—Macht. Chief Steward Opus sent me to find you. He says you're to come at once. There are guests already here and they must be greeted." He waited unhappily, clearly not glad to be the bearer of this news. All the servants knew how much Rome hated anything pompous.

Rome thought about sending him away. He was the macht, by damn! He'd arrive when he felt like it. But it would only go hard on the kid when Opus heard the news and harder on him the next time Opus got within earshot. "I'm coming," he said sullenly, and followed the boy reluctantly down the stairs.

⚔ ⚔ ⚔

237

"There you are, Your Grace," Opus exclaimed as soon as he saw Rome. Rome started to correct him—what did that even mean, Your Grace?—but then gave it up. The best thing for tonight was to simply endure.

"They're all waiting for you. They're terribly annoyed."

Rome gave him a glare that Opus ignored.

"This way, this way." Opus fluttered on ahead and Rome followed. The floors seemed terribly slippery in these shoes. The soles were definitely too narrow. One wrong move and he'd topple right over on his side.

They came into what Rome thought of as the Torture Room by a side door. This was where he had to sit when he was greeting any official delegation or presiding over any royal function. It was also where he heard petitions from the wealthy and powerful—the common folk had to petition in a much smaller chamber—and he hated it. At one end of the long room sat his throne on a raised dais. It was carved from the same kind of stone the tower was built of, dark green limestone laced with veins of quartz. It was the only thing Rome liked in the whole room, mostly because he'd designed it himself. It was strong, simple, and plain. Strong enough to prop up the palace wall in a pinch. That was the sort of thing he liked.

He'd like to redo the whole palace the same way except that it would be such a nuisance and Opus would probably torment him so badly he'd end up having to kill the man. It had been enough of a fight just getting his new throne in here and getting the servants who carried the old fancy throne to "accidentally" drop it and break it on the stairs.

The rest of the throne room was way out of hand. Carvings and bas-relief filigreed with gold covered every inch of ceiling and wall space that didn't have either a tapestry or a niche with some statue in it. A massive, deep pile rug of rich purple covered the floor and more statues stood on pedestals around the room. A chandelier with about a thousand candles and twice that many cut stones hung from the ceiling. Rome thought it was too gaudy, like a bad whorehouse, but without any women.

Quyloc was already at his place beside Rome's throne, dressed all in the green that he favored, his head lowered, apparently lost in thought. His white-blond hair gleamed in the light. In contrast to Rome, his clothes were fairly simple, though there were ruffles all down his sleeves and some sort of headpiece jutted up from behind his head and spread out like a fan. Rome lit up with a wicked grin when he saw the fan. Even Quyloc hadn't escaped completely.

Other than Quyloc, some guards standing at attention around the walls, and a scattering of servants, the room was empty. Opus was nearly hyperventilating. "Please hurry. They are all waiting in the hall, my Lord. You must be seated before we can begin announcing them."

"Whatever you say, Steward," Rome said, taking his time getting there. Let them wait. Who was in charge here anyway? He sat down on the throne, brushing aside the cloth-of-gold that Opus had clearly laid over it in an attempt to cover it up as much as possible. He leaned towards Quyloc as the doors opened and the herald announced the first guests. "I like the fan. What're you supposed to be, some kind of peacock?" He chuckled.

Quyloc looked up, his eyes distant, unfamiliar. What was he seeing? Rome wondered. Did he look on other worlds even at this moment? Then Quyloc's thin lips lifted in the old sardonic grin Rome had seen so many times. "You've a lot of room for talk, puffed out like a starling rooster. I believe the heart-shaped ruby is the perfect touch."

"I know," Rome groaned. "How long do you think this thing will last?"

"Hours and hours," Quyloc said cruelly. "Most of the night anyway."

"I can't breathe in this collar."

"You should try my fan. Something pokes me in the back of my head every time I move."

Then the first guests were mounting the dais and Rome had no choice but to look at them. These people he knew, at least by name, from the affairs he had attended while still a general. Lord Atalafes and his wife. They knelt before Rome, their expressions unreadable, though Rome felt what it cost them to kneel to him and he rejoiced in it. Maybe the night wouldn't be a total loss after all. Atalafes was a stout man, what had been heavy muscles giving way to fat in his old age. There was a sharpness to his gaze and a suppleness in his movements that made Rome think he might have been a fierce opponent once. Might still be, despite his years.

"Macht Rome," they intoned in unison, bowing their heads.

Rome grinned down at them. He *was* enjoying this. "Good of you to make it," he said cheerfully. "We've missed you around here." From the corner of his eye he saw Quyloc's lips twitch in a smile.

Lady Atalafes murmured something in return, while whatever Lord Atalafes said was lost in gritted teeth.

Then a third person ascended the dais and knelt beside them.

"Macht Rome, my daughter, Marilene," Lord Atalafes said. She wasn't bad looking, Rome thought, with that raven dark hair and those doe eyes, but her chin and her nose were too sharp and her real face was lost under mounds of rouge and blush, her body impossible to see inside a dress that seemed to be all bows and ribbons. He wondered how many bows he'd have to pull to get that thing off her. She gave him a long look at her cleavage as she bent over, watching him from underneath her eyelashes. He didn't miss the coldness in her eyes. She didn't like him any better than her parents did. She was only flirting with him because they told her to, because a marriage to the macht would help their fortunes considerably, maybe even put them back in the palace. He gave her a leer and a wink and she paled slightly.

The next couple approached the dais with not one but two daughters, though from the sharpness of the taller one's features Rome had a feeling she was a shrew in the making, if not already fully accomplished, and the shorter one was as big around as she was tall.

The next nobleman after that was fat, sweating Lord Ulin Tropon with his child bride, a girl too young to show any curves yet. Tropon had made more than one joke at Rome's expense when he was still a general fumbling his way through state dinners. He was all politeness now, and careful to avoid Rome's eyes.

It was surprising how many of the nobility had daughters of marriageable age. Some of the daughters favored him with sly, seductive smiles, others blushed and turned away, but every parent watched with the same wolf eyes. Clearly they hoped to take back by marriage what they could not take by force.

The last person to approach the throne was not someone Rome had expected to see. He gave her a big grin as she reached the top step. "Welcome, FirstMother. I have to admit I had no idea you were a follower of Protaxes."

Nalene FirstMother scowled. Her white robe was new, but simple. Her only adornment was the heavy gold Reminder. Her bald pate gleamed as if oiled. "I do not find your comment amusing, Macht," she replied, her heavy jaw clenched tight.

"So you're just here for the free meal, then? Or is it the dancing?"

"I am here that they may see me. Nothing more."

And indeed she was drawing a great deal of attention, though the nobles took pains to hide it. One person in the room who wasn't hiding it was Cynar, high priest of Protaxes. He was openly glaring at her. The fact that she was ignoring him only made it worse.

As she walked away, Rome called after her, "Enjoy the party!" Turning to look at Quyloc, he said, "I don't think she likes me very much."

"I don't think she likes anyone."

Rome saw that no one else was approaching the throne and he stood up and rubbed his hands together. Finally. Time to eat. He was starving. And he'd been poking around at the back of his collar and he thought he might know how it was hooked on. With a little luck he might be able to get it to come free and look like it just fell off by accident. If he stepped on it, also accidentally, it would probably be ruined. He didn't really think he could swallow with the thing on anyway.

As if by magic, Opus materialized at his side, hissing.

"What now?" Rome grumbled. "I'm ready to eat."

"First the ritual."

"What? There's a ritual?"

"It is the point of the whole evening, Macht. Please sit down."

With another grumble, Rome sat, vowing then and there to find a way to make Opus pay for this. Maybe announce that he'd decided to have the entire palace painted orange, inside and out. The man's heart would probably give out.

Silence fell suddenly, the subdued babble of voices dying out as Cynar strode to the center of the chamber and raised his arms into the air. His robes were slashed yellow velvet with orange silk under sleeves. Around his neck hung a double strand of carved beads and a gold medallion. He had a long, gloomy face and lips that were too small to cover his horse teeth. For a long minute he simply stood and glared at the crowd. From somewhere an unseen player started up on a drum. The drumming grew louder and stronger, reverberating off the walls of the chamber. Slowly, Cynar lowered his arms and the ritual began.

Rome leaned back in the throne, crossed his ankles and closed his eyes. Somehow he just knew this was going to take forever.

CHAPTER 32

Hours dragged by. Or maybe years. Rome slumped lower in his seat. This was worse than bad. Every time he dozed off Opus hissed at him. Trying to start a conversation with Quyloc yielded nothing. His old friend seemed fixated on the FirstMother, who was studiously ignoring him.

Finally, the lights came back up and Rome stirred, thinking, thank the stars, it was finally over. But then the sermon started. At least, Rome thought it was a sermon. Since it was in some language he'd never heard before, he couldn't be sure. But it sounded like one. Cynar droned on and on, now and then reading from a large book on a podium that had been wheeled out to him, other times seeming to recite from memory, his eyes closed, head tilted back.

At some point Rome just decided that it was all too much. He no longer cared whose feathers he ruffled. He didn't care if they staged an open rebellion this very night. He simply wasn't going to take any more of this. Cynar finished a page and paused while he turned to the next. Rome saw his opportunity and acted.

He jumped out of his seat and began applauding loudly, brushing off Opus's warning hisses and ignoring the frowns of the nobility. He was the Macht and it was by god time for dinner.

"Excellent!" he bellowed. "Well done, Cynar, High Priest of Praxiles!" What was that god's name again? "You've done old Praxital proud here tonight. I'm sure he's happy with you." He kept clapping and when none of the nobles joined in he gave *them* a few murderous frowns and soon he had plenty of company. "Let's eat!" he yelled after a bit, and now the applause was more enthusiastic. Not all of them were overly pious.

Cynar gave him a look that was pure outrage, but what could he do? Rome was already leaving the dais, heading for the doors that led to the great dining hall, not waiting to see how protocol determined that this should be done. When he entered the dining hall, the servants were frantically putting the last pieces of dining ware on the table. He grinned at them and waved them off. There was too much silver and crystal on the table already. All a man really needed to eat was a big mug, a plate and his knife. Even the plate wasn't really that necessary, as long as the table wasn't too dirty.

"Bring me some wine!" he called after the last departing servant.

The wine seemed to take an awful long time to arrive and the wine glass was too small to hold even a decent swallow. "Leave the bottle here," Rome told the server, grabbing it from the startled man.

Rome drank glass after tiny glass of the wine and watched while his guests sorted themselves out and took their seats. Judging from their expressions, he had upset the order by bolting in here ahead of everyone else and now they were offended. He shrugged and made a face that said, *Oops. What did I do wrong?* He saw several of them exchange looks that weren't hard to decipher. Well, let them think he was a buffoon. They would be more likely to underestimate him that way.

Rome saw the food arriving and rubbed his hands together in anticipation. Anticipation gave way to a frown when the server set a tiny plate in front of him. On the plate was a dainty yellow thing no bigger than his thumb. He poked it with his finger and it broke in half. What *was* it? Was it some kind of potato? Was it fried? Why were there red things in it?

He gave up trying to figure it out, pinched it between his thumb and forefinger and tossed it in his mouth. Not too bad. Not too good, either, but he'd had worse many times.

He looked around and saw that most people hadn't even gotten their potato-thing yet. Those that did were sitting there politely, waiting to begin until everyone had been served. Rome shook his head. What was wrong with these people? When everyone had theirs, they took tiny little knives and carved off miniscule pieces of it, whatever it was, and daintily nibbled at them, exclaiming at how good it was.

"This is just ridiculous," he said to Quyloc, who was sitting to his right. Quyloc was the only one who hadn't touched his.

The next round was a little bigger—some kind of egg from a small bird, with a powdery dusting of some brown stuff and some green sprigs on the side—but no more satisfying. By then Rome was starting to get angry. Was this a dining room or what? When the server came with the third round—some fluffy, leafy thing—Rome growled at him. "The next thing you bring me will be meat and it will be large or tomorrow morning you'll be mucking the soldiers' latrines." The man blanched and left at a trot.

When Rome saw the huge silver platters enter the room, his good humor returned. Now they were getting somewhere. There were covers on the platters so he couldn't see what they held. Suckling pigs maybe. Or sides of shatren. Whole turkeys.

When they set one down on the table in front of him he yanked the cover off, his knife already in his hand—

And nearly drove his knife through the table in frustration. It looked like flowers. Some kind of meat sure enough, but it had been sliced so thinly that he could see through it, and then it had been folded into flower shapes.

Rome grabbed the closest server, nearly lifting the poor man off his feet. Lord Atalafes' wife stared at him openmouthed. Other nobles nearby paled and turned their eyes away. "Bring me the haunch of something," he snarled. "I don't even care if it's cooked, but it better have a bone sticking out of it and I better be able to tell what it is. And send Opus in here."

Rome was on Opus before he could even speak. Everyone was watching openly by now, but Rome didn't care. He'd never tried to be anything he was not. "I don't like this," he growled, grabbing a handful of Opus' shirt and jerking the man forward. He held up a fistful of the flowery meat. "I don't ever want to see food like this put down before me again. Am I clear?"

For once he got through the man's cultured façade. Opus swallowed and nodded and Rome let him go. Shaky hands patted his shirt back into place as he bowed and whispered, "My Lord."

Rome grinned at Lord Atalafes and winked at his daughter. "Sometimes you just have to be firm with the help," he boomed. "Don't you think so?"

Quyloc tasted none of his dinner. All of his attention was fixed on the FirstMother, specifically whatever it was that she had under her robe. Whatever it was, it was strong and growing stronger. He could sense it. It was there in his inner hearing, like a distant heartbeat. Song seemed to bend around it, as if it were a tiny vortex.

He still didn't know what it was, but Frink had earlier reported to him what happened at the Tender estate this afternoon, when the women trained with Lowellin. It still staggered Quyloc to think that already some of them were able to use these *things* as weapons. What would happen when they used them against a person?

It was more clear than ever that he was running out of time. He needed to find a way to obtain his own weapon or he would soon be irrelevant, if he was not already. It was possible that the Tenders' success with their weapons was so impressive that Lowellin was beginning to realize he didn't need Quyloc after all. It would explain why he was so conspicuously absent from Quyloc's life.

Quyloc's thoughts turned to Lowellin's words. *Kill the largest thing you can.* Initially, he had discarded the idea of going after the huge thing that came up from underground, but now he was reconsidering. If size meant power, what better choice was there?

The problem was, he just couldn't see any way that he could possibly kill something so large with such a small weapon as the bone knife.

Rome wove and stumbled his way down the dim hallway trying to find a door to outside. He'd finally managed to get a bottle of Thrikylian rum brought to him during the dance and he was feeling a whole lot better about the whole evening. He grinned as he thought about it. He'd showed those nobles a thing or two about having a good time. They'd looked pretty shocked when he got up and did the soldiers' jig for them, jumping right out in the middle of their fancy stepping around. But that was nothing compared to how they'd acted when he got the players to do a little tune that was always popular around the campfire, about the one-armed camp woman named Jill. He'd thought some of the older women were going to have a stroke. He chuckled and hummed some of the song to himself.

As Rome came around a corner he ran into a couple of guards making their rounds and had to put his hand on the wall to keep from falling down. That surprised him. Clearly Thrikylian rum was a whole lot stronger than he'd expected it to be. Rome blinked to clear his vision and bellowed a greeting at the two men, then followed the greeting with an exaggerated shushing.

"I don't want anyone to know that I snuck out of their stuffy party," he told them, racking his brain for the guards' names. He prided himself on names, but he couldn't seem to quite place these two. "Told them I was headed to the piss pot and cut out. I don't know how they stand those things. They're boring and awful." He pulled at the collar imprisoning his neck and, when he couldn't get the buttons free, settled for ripping it off and throwing it on the floor. He felt better immediately. He gave up on the soldiers' names and winked conspiratorially. "Don't say anything, especially if you see a little guy named Opus. If you see him, you should tell him..." He trailed off, wondering what they should say, then gave up. "Just don't see him. That's best."

The men laughed and continued on. Rome clapped one on the shoulder as he went by.

All those women in their fancy dresses. Rome shook his head and the motion threatened to upset his balance. Well, he'd pinched a few bottoms tonight. They wanted to flirt with the macht, that was what they got. Though it was damnable hard getting through all those clothes to find the bottom beneath. They were nothing compared to his Bonnie though. Now there was a woman. They were only girls in comparison, even the wives older than he was. He patted the flask secreted inside his coat. Bonnie'd have a nip with him.

He heard something that sounded like a strangled cry from behind him and turned, reaching for the weapon that wasn't there. There were some scuffling footsteps and then silence. He listened for a bit and when there was nothing more he shrugged and continued on. He must be drunker than he thought.

He came to a door and was grateful when it opened onto the night air. Halfway out he paused and listened, fancying he could hear Opus coming down the hall to berate him for leaving the party before the guests. But it was just a maid, giving him a little curtsy as she hurried by.

Outside, Rome leaned up against the wall and relieved himself, swearing at the clothes that were so hard to get through. Not his kind of party at all, but it did have one bright spot: the Musician. This was only the fifth time he'd ever heard one play.

There was no way to know where or when a Musician would appear and perform. They were a very secretive society, making their music when and where they decided. When they felt like it they appeared and played, popping up in a park or a plaza, in front of a merchant's stall or even on a hillside where a herder was watching his sheep.

He sighed. There was every difference in the world between players and the Musicians of Othen's Pact. Players made music that was good enough, but they might as well have been children banging on old pots compared to what the Musicians did.

What Musicians created was pure magic. There was real power in the sounds they brought forth from their instruments. Everyone felt it. When they played the world went away. They took their listeners with them to someplace else and when it was over, the world was just a little bit different.

It was Quyloc's theory that Musicians had the ability to manipulate LifeSong with their instruments, and that was where their power came from. Rome didn't know enough to say if he agreed or disagreed, but he did know if that Musician was still playing, he'd still be there at the ball. No one left when a Musician played.

Of course, he could have ordered the man to keep playing. Anyone could order a Musician to keep playing and they'd do it. It was part of the Pact that they were all sworn to. No one really knew much about Othen's Pact—other than that it was some kind of deal they'd made with their god long ago—but everyone knew they had to keep playing as long as a single member of the audience demanded it.

The thing was, no one ever did. No one wanted to risk offending them. There was a children's tale about a city called Heranor, whose citizens had actually captured a Musician, thinking to force him to play whenever they wanted. He had escaped, of course, and he and his brethren left the city, swearing never to return and cursing the city. The city fell to ruin soon after, becoming a haunted, nightmarish place.

It was only a children's tale, but no one wanted to take the risk.

Rome lurched around the edge of the palace and into the carriage way, the sudden torchlight making him blink. Carriages waited in a silent semicircle around the edge of the carriage way, grooms and drivers standing in little knots laughing and sharing tobacco and nips off bottles passed from one hand to another.

Staying to one side, keeping his head down to avoid being recognized, Rome made his way along the edge of the carriage way toward the front gates. His luck was still running good. He made it all the way there without being noticed—much. He ran into two pages who appeared out from behind one of the carriages right in his path and knocked both of them down, though he managed to stay upright.

At the gates two guards stepped out of the shadows, weapons sheathed. "Macht Rome," one of them said.

"Hari," Rome boomed, glad to see a face he recognized. Hari'd gotten that scar across his nose in the fight at Brook's Down. He was a gnarled, weather-beaten man with hair quickly turning gray and a deep, gravelly voice. "How's the night?"

"Fair enough," the man replied. "Going down to see the little lady?"

"Yes I am." Rome gave them both knowing leers. The men weren't stepping aside and he paused, puzzled. Then he heard the clatter of hooves and running, booted feet behind him and he understood.

"A horse might make it quicker, Macht," Hari said, his voice deep and solemn, but with a touch of humor under it.

"That it might. Glad you thought of it."

"Hari's too old for fighting," the other man chimed in. "Gives him lots of time to think." He had a patchy beard and perpetually bloodshot eyes that spoke of waking up on too many tavern floors.

With a quick, casual move Hari elbowed him in the stomach, bending the bigger man over. "Age and cunning," he said gravely.

It took Rome a minute to get his foot in the stirrup and heave himself in the saddle. He wasn't sure when he'd ever seen such a tall horse. He didn't notice the man holding the bridle start to step forward with a helping hand only to be stopped by Hari.

Then he was off at an easy trot into town, a born horseman for whom riding was easier than walking. No sign of drink showed in the way he handled the horse or sat it. No soldiers followed him and none offered. They all knew well enough that Rome liked to go alone to see his Bonnie.

CHAPTER 33

When Rome left the ball, Quyloc followed. He had a feeling Rome wasn't coming back, something about the furtive way he moved. What he found surprising was that when Rome got into the hallway outside the ballroom, he was actually lurching side to side as if he was about to fall down. Rome got drunk often, but he never got *that* drunk. He was just one of those men who could hold tremendous amounts of alcohol without it seeming to really impair his abilities.

Was it possible something had been done to Rome's drink? His suspicions aroused, Quyloc continued to follow, staying well back. He saw the two guardsmen appear from around a corner and bump into Rome, seemingly by accident, though how they could not have heard him coming was beyond Quyloc. Rome was humming loud and tunelessly, every now and then stepping out in something that might have passed for a dance step.

Further alerted, Quyloc huddled in the shadow of a doorway while Rome exchanged words with the men. Neither man looked familiar and Quyloc thought he recognized all the guards in the palace.

Rome continued on, while the guards appeared to do likewise. They were almost to where Quyloc was hiding when they both turned, slid swords from scabbards, and started quickly back, after Rome.

Instinctively, Quyloc reached for the dagger he always wore at his waist, only to discover that it wasn't there. He'd had it earlier, but when he arrived at the throne room Opus had badgered him about it, saying it was in poor taste, that it made it look as if he didn't trust the nobles who were guests in the palace that night, and weren't a dozen armed guards enough to make him feel safe? So he had given it to a servant to put in his office.

That left only the bone knife, in its hidden sheath inside his shirt. It was not much of a knife, no longer than his hand, and not very sharp, but it was all he had.

The would-be assassins never heard him coming. Soft-footed as a cat, Quyloc ran up behind them. One lagged a step behind his fellow. Quyloc drove the knife into the side of his neck, just below the ear. As the knife went home Quyloc felt something surge through him, a burst of electricity so strong his whole body jerked. Lights danced behind his eyes and he staggered back, his muscles unresponsive. It was only by some kind of miracle that he managed to avoid dropping the bone knife.

The moment passed and he looked up to see the other man bearing down on him, swinging his sword at Quyloc's head.

He should have died right there. There wasn't enough time to react.

Except that there was.

With a burst of speed and power that shocked him, Quyloc leapt inside the man's swing and drove his shoulder into his chest, hard enough that he knocked him across the hallway and slammed him up against the wall.

In the next instant Quyloc slashed the man across the throat, severing the artery. Blood sprayed everywhere and another jolt of power went through him.

The man's free hand went to his throat. His eyes glassed over and he slid down the wall and fell on his side.

As he died, Quyloc *felt* something leave the assassin's body. It blew across his face like a warm wind, a breath that carried with it a lifetime's worth of images and memories. Quyloc turned as it passed and saw something remarkable.

A hole opened before his eyes. Through the hole he saw a volcano set in the midst of a jungle, a plume of smoke coming from its mouth. On the rim of the volcano perched a huge, rubbery, misshapen creature. The creature roared soundlessly and its gaze fixed on Quyloc.

Then the hole closed and Quyloc was left staring at nothing.

He looked down at the two bodies and then he looked at the knife in his hand. Oddly, there was no blood on it.

Had the knife somehow absorbed some of their lives when he killed them? He still felt charged, powerful. The knife felt alive in his hand.

And what was the thing he'd seen on the volcano?

Quyloc felt a presence, looked up and Lowellin was there, scowling darkly.

"You are a fool. It would have been better by far if you had let them kill Rome, then to do what you did," Lowellin snapped.

"What just happened?" Quyloc whispered.

"You opened a doorway to the *Pente Akka* and nearly killed us all." Lowellin picked up one of the bodies as if it weighed nothing. "Get the other," he ordered, and headed off down the hall.

They threw the two men over the wall behind the palace and the sea and the blackness took them. "Hopefully, the denizens of the sea will eat them. If not, they will likely return."

"But they're dead."

"You have no idea what you are talking about. You know nothing about this world or the other."

Quyloc's anger blazed. "Then why don't you tell me? Why do you teach the Tenders and not me?"

"That thing you saw on the volcano? That was the *gromdin*. It is the lord of the *Pente Akka*. When you killed those men with the bone knife you temporarily opened a hole in the Veil that separates that world from ours. Had the *gromdin* been ready, it could have come through that hole. You'd be dead right now and by morning the rest of Qarath would be too."

"No. You're exaggerating."

"Why would I lie to you about this?" Lowellin challenged.

"I don't know. I don't know why you do anything, because you never tell me. How am I supposed to do anything when you leave me in the dark? If you'd told me not to use the bone knife—"

"How was I supposed to know that you'd be dumb enough to kill someone with it?"

"I did what I had to do."

"Yes, I know. To save your idiot friend. And this is why I don't trust you, because you still don't grasp what is at stake. That's why I spend my efforts on the FirstMother. She understands and she is willing to do whatever it takes, to make any sacrifice necessary, to defeat our common enemy. She doesn't challenge me. She accepts what I tell her to do and she does it."

Quyloc stared at Lowellin's silhouette in the darkness, knowing he would never trust him to that degree, no matter what the threat was.

"Now you have the answers you seek," Lowellin said. "See what you do with them." Then he turned and walked away.

Quyloc stared after him and knew what he had to do.

✗ ✗ ✗

Quyloc stood in his secret chamber and stared at the bone knife in the lamplight. A sea breeze blew in through the tiny window and waves boomed on the rocks far below.

The knife still thrummed with power. *He* still thrummed with power. Somehow some of the dead men's Song was still coursing through him and the knife.

It was time to act.

He lay down on the cot and closed his eyes, picturing the Veil in his mind. An instant later he opened his eyes and he was standing on the sand in the purple darkness, the Veil gleaming wetly before him.

Picturing the rock ledge in his mind, he passed through the Veil and found himself once again on the edge of the jungle, the sound of the river in the distance.

Down below was the tree the furred creature had fallen from. Already the torn ground had settled back into place, the wet morass covering any sign of the mighty, toothed thing which had risen from it.

He made his way off the rock ledge and down to the jungle floor. With the fist holding the knife he began to pound on the ground. He thumped frantically, imitating something wounded, frightened.

He did not have to wait long.

There was a rumbling from under the ground, quickly drawing closer. With two quick strides he was at the base of the rock ledge, the knife in his teeth, climbing quickly, surely to the top.

It surfaced below him, the heavy snout breaking through the soil, mouth opening to reveal its long, curved teeth. The tapered body followed, powerful limbs propelling it to the surface.

Quyloc didn't hesitate. The time for hesitation was long past.

He leapt onto the thing's back, and as he landed he drove the bone knife down into the base of the creature's skull with all his might.

The knife shattered. The creature screamed and rose into the air on its squat hind legs. Quyloc was thrown free and he rolled to avoid being crushed by it. He scurried up onto the rock ledge and turned to watch.

The creature thrashed wildly. In its death throes it clawed at the earth. Its tail swung and flattened a tree. Its screams were so loud he had to press his hands to his ears.

At last it lay still. Quyloc climbed down and walked over to it. The jungle was unnaturally silent, as if it held its breath in shock at what it had just witnessed. The thing lay on its side, its mouth open.

He walked around it, staring at it in awe. It seemed unbelievable that he had just killed such a powerful creature. He would never have managed it without the power stolen from the two assassins.

Lowellin had told him to take the biggest bone he could for his weapon, but with the bone knife shattered he could see no way that he could carve through its flesh.

He stopped by the open mouth and another idea came to him. The creature's teeth were as long as his forearm. They were slightly curved, pointed, and sharp on the leading edge.

He went to the fallen tree and broke off a long, straight limb about the size and thickness of a spear shaft. With it he banged on one of the creature's teeth until it came free. With a length of vine, he lashed the tooth to the limb. Now he had a spear.

With the spear in hand he eyed the jungle which stood between him and his goal. Even with the help of the spear, he didn't see how he could pass through it alive.

He turned and looked at the dead creature and an idea came to him. He'd read a book once by a man who claimed to have lived among the wolves by smearing their scent on him, thus passing as one of them. Would something like that work here?

Blood still leaked from the creature's death wound, pooling on the ground. He cupped his hands and let them fill with blood, then began smearing it all over his body, painting his face, arms, legs and torso.

Cautiously, he entered the jungle. With the spear he pushed plants out of the way, careful to avoid stepping in the numerous pools of water. He came to one of the large flowers that had attacked him before. Watching it closely, he circled it. It did not move.

The rest of the way was easy. In minutes he arrived at the river. It was broad, at least a hundred yards across, and slow moving. He stood at its edge for a moment, and then he plunged the spear into it.

The weapon sizzled when it contacted the water and a burning sensation went through his body, but he did not falter. The water bubbled around the spear like it was boiling.

A minute later he drew it out of the water and held it up to look at it. Tooth and shaft were now fused seamlessly together. The shaft no longer looked like wood, but almost like stone.

Quyloc raised the weapon over his head and shouted his challenge to the world. Then he summoned the Veil, slashed an opening with the spear, and walked through.

CHAPTER 34

Rome rode the darkened streets without hesitation and no thug or footpad bothered him. For one thing he rode quickly. Hard for a man on foot to bother a trotting rider. But neither did he bear that hint of weakness or fear that every predator instinctively looks for in its prey, for the truth of it is, most predators, especially human ones, are inherently cowards.

Bonnie lived down in the part of the city no guest back at the palace would have ever dreamed of going to—not publicly at least. Rome reined up in front of a two-story stone and timber building. Torches in tall bronze braziers burned out front and sounds of revelry came from within, though the hour was late. The lurid sign over the door said, "The Grinning Pig," and had a picture to prove it. Two men, clad in open leather vests, with thick muscles, cudgels and long knives hanging at their sides, stood in the doorway. One grinned and elbowed the other when he saw the fancy dress of their newest arrival. The grin disappeared when Rome slid off the horse and barked, "Don't just stand there, Arls, get my horse. Where's Tomy?"

Both men jumped forward. "Sorry, Macht Rome," Arls mumbled. "Didn't see as it was you, being dark and all." He'd fought Rome once, several years ago when Rome was still only a sergeant in the army and Rome had gotten out of hand one night after a fight with Bonnie. Rome had broken his arm and two of his ribs. Arls proudly told the story every chance he got, especially now that Rome was macht.

The other man was bellowing for Tomy and soon the boy appeared. Rome gave him the reins and a pat on the head. Tomy led the horse away and Rome stood there for a moment, breathing in the air, head thrown back, hands on his hips. It felt good to be here. This was his kind of place, his people. He didn't fit with those bowing and scraping pretty birds up there with their painted smiles and poisoned daggers. Down here if a man had a problem with you he came at you in a bull rush and you settled it tooth to tooth.

He went inside. The Grinning Pig might not be a rich man's establishment, but it wasn't a urine-soaked, dirt-floored dump either. The floor was flagstone, the tables and chairs stout wood and not too badly scarred. There were real oil lamps for light here and garish tapestries on all the walls. Rome remembered the first time he'd come here, to celebrate his promotion to sergeant. He'd spent nearly a month's pay that night, but it had been worth it. That was the night he met Bonnie.

A man approached, getting old but still thick with knotted muscle. "Your knife, sir. No weapons allowed." He stopped when Rome turned towards him. "Sorry, Macht. I didn't recognize you."

"No problem, Terk." Rome was really feeling good, though now that he was off the horse he was feeling dangerously unsteady again. What did the Thrikylians put in that rum? He dug the knife out from where it was tucked in his silly pants—it was just his dinner knife—and gave it to Terk, amazed as always how the man could spot a weapon hidden anywhere. Rome had never seen anyone get a weapon by him.

A couple dozen men were scattered about the room, some sitting at tables with women on their laps, others dancing to the music coming from the lone player on the tiny stage in the corner. Several more stood at the bar. None lay on the floor though. This was a class establishment.

Rome approached the bar. "Where's my Bonnie?" he called the fat man there.

"Where she always is, Macht Rome," the man grumbled. "In her rooms. Alone." He was wiping mugs with a towel. His bald head gleamed in the lamplight and his face drooped in a perpetual frown. Bronze bracelets encircled his arms above his elbows and a too-tight leather tunic struggled to hold in his bulk.

He put the mug down and gave Rome a pig-eyed glare. "My best woman and she don't work anymore."

"You get paid, Gelbert, more than she ever earned before." They'd been through this routine many times and Rome knew how it went.

"I'm going belly up here," the man continued, as if Rome hadn't spoken. He held thick fingers an inch apart. "This close, hear. This close to shutting my doors for good."

"No doubt," Rome agreed. Gelbert was probably richer than several of the nobility who'd been at the palace party tonight. He owned property all over the city and some outside it.

"Don't know why I don't throw her out and be done with it," Gelbert intoned.

"Because then I'd have to come in here and slit your fat belly ball sack to breastbone." Rome honestly liked Gelbert.

"Aye," Gelbert replied, looking grave. "That you would." He waved Rome away with a ponderous arm. "Go on up then. There's none here stopping you and you know the way."

Rome wove his way toward the stairs at the back of the room, exchanging greetings with several of the women and one of the men as he went. Part way up the stairs he paused and turned back. "Send up some food!" he yelled at Gelbert. "Something with some meat in it." He continued on. "I'm still hungry," he grumbled to himself.

Bonnie's rooms were at the end of the hall, in what had been the quarters for three women. Rome had had workmen come in several months ago and knock out some walls, add some paint and generally pretty the place up a bit. Gelbert had hated that but Rome wasn't having his Bonnie settle for the holes the other women got.

The door was locked and Rome had to bang several times before Bonnie answered. "That you, Rome?"

"It is," Rome replied, leaning his forehead against the door. If she opened it too fast he was going to fall down.

The door opened and there was Bonnie—red hair and dark eyes, a rich silken robe barely concealing robust breasts—and Rome loved her, loved her as hard and as fiercely as the first time he'd met her.

"Yes?" she said, not moving out of the doorway.

"Can I come in?" Rome wanted to sweep her up in his arms, carry her to her bed and ravish her. But he knew from the look in her eye that she'd slap him good if he did and he was too drunk anyway. Probably catch his feet in the thick rugs on the floor and fall flat on his face. How would that look?

"It's late," she said softly. "I was in bed."

"Good," Rome said. "Saves time." She gave him a sharp look and he stilled his tongue. She said she'd been in bed but she looked, as always, as if she'd known he was coming and had prepared for him. Just a hint of blue at the corners of her eyes to highlight their shape, a soft breath of perfume, a gold chain that disappeared tantalizingly into the darkness between her breasts. Even the slip under her robe seemed arranged, so that just enough of it showed to make Rome want to see more. Who knows? She probably did know he was coming. Women had their own magic and Bonnie had the most. It was part of what Rome loved about her.

She stepped back from the doorway, took his hand and led him in. "You'd probably pass out in the street if I sent you back, drunk as you are."

Rome stood there, swaying slightly, while she barred the door. She walked around him, hands on her waist, and gave a low whistle. "Look at you. Dressed higher than the tarts up at the Yellow Parrot. Must have had some kind of do up at the big house tonight."

Rome suddenly remembered he was wearing those stupid clothes still and he felt himself redden. Should have taken the time to change, he thought. That's why everyone was staring at him, not knowing who he was. They were probably laughing about it right now. "I don't like them," he growled, tearing clumsily at the shirt.

"Wait a minute. I didn't say I didn't like it. Kind of nice to see you trying something else for a change." Bonnie laid a soft hand on his arm. She was nearly as tall as he was, built strong, with curves and plump in just the right places. There was muscle in her too. She was not small and soft like so many women. Rome didn't like them that way.

Then she laughed and shook her head. "But this isn't you. Let me help you out." Deft fingers found his buttons and drawstrings. First the coat, then the shirt, fell away. "I can't believe they got you to put this on. Not bloody-meat Wulf Rome."

"It was Opus," he growled.

"Yes, Opus. Of course. I'll have to thank him some day when I meet him. Get him to show me what he knows that I don't."

"I nearly broke his neck at dinner. You wouldn't believe what they were calling food."

Bonnie stepped back and looked up at him. Rome was naked to the waist, all hair and muscle, only slightly smaller than a bear. "No, I probably wouldn't," she said.

Rome leaned forward, pulled her to him hard enough that she gasped, just a little. "But you would. You know that. If you'd let me—"

"Not this old argument," she said, pushing back enough so that she could look into his eyes. "Not tonight."

"Why not tonight?" Rome said, pulling away and pacing the thick rugs. "Why do you continue to refuse?"

"And can you see me, a common whore, at your side in the palace dining hall?"

"You're not common," Rome said sullenly.

"But I am a whore."

"You were. Not anymore."

"Was. Am. What are they but words? I don't take other men anymore, true. You and your money have seen to that. But if you died tomorrow, if one of those spitlickers in their shiny boots managed to finally stick a knife in your ribs and kill you, I'd be right back to what I've always been."

"That won't happen."

"Oh, it won't? And did you come down here alone tonight? Unarmed?"

"I wasn't unarmed," Rome said defensively. "I had a knife. I can take care of myself."

"Yes, you can. But drunk, against a half dozen men with swords?"

"I would find a way. Besides, it won't happen. Not down here, among my people."

"Yes, it would. They love you, most of them, and for good reason. You're the best king we've ever had."

"Macht."

"Whatever. Changing the name doesn't change anything. But there are those, give them enough gold and they'll do anything."

"I could just give the order. Have you hauled up to the palace kicking and screaming. I am the Macht. I could do it."

"Yes, you could." She faced him, fire smoldering in her dark eyes, jaw set.

"But if I did you'd make my life hell," Rome said, sounding like a little boy.

Abruptly the fire fled and she came to him with a little laugh and everything hard inside Rome melted. "It is good we understand each other."

Rome pressed his face into her hair. "That bedroom up there, the one Opus says it's my duty to sleep in as ruler. It's big as a barn, too much gilt, too much glitter. It's lonely. I hate it. If you shared it with me though…"

Bonnie led him to the bed and pushed him down on it. "Perhaps someday," she said, kneeling to unlace his shoes, unable to suppress a giggle at the sight of them. "Who knows what Hurim plans for tomorrow? But not now." She finished with the shoes and stood up. Rome was lying flat out, arms stretched wide, snoring loudly.

"You just don't understand, do you?" she said softly, moving to cradle his head in her lap. "You're just a big child still. Those nobles, the ones you treat so sneeringly, they're down but not out. Not yet. They have more poison than you imagine. You knocked them off a stool they've sat on for too many years. They won't take that so easily." She stroked the thick beard. "You need to listen to this Opus more. You bring a whore into the palace and it will inflame them more than anything else you've done."

"Gods, what do they put in that stuff?" Rome groaned and clutched his head. "I think I've been poisoned." He opened one bleary eye and regarded Bonnie, standing beside the bed, dressed and ready for the day and grinning down at him. "At least I had the good sense to make it to your place."

"It appears that's the only good sense you had," she said cheerily. She was a cheerful person by nature, but on mornings when Rome was especially hung over she was positively disgusting. She strode to the window and flung back the curtain.

Rome groaned again and rolled away from the sunlight. "You're an evil woman, Bonnie. I've always thought that and now I know it's true."

"What's wrong?" she asked, her voice dripping with false sympathy. "Big strong man have too much small brown bottle last night?"

"Come over here where I can get a hold of you and I'll show you something." His hands clutched at empty air. His eyes were shut tight.

"Get up and come get me."

"I will, then. That's it." He rolled to the edge of the bed and off but his legs betrayed him and he thumped heavily to the floor. "I'm going to outlaw that cursed stuff. Nobody should feel like this." He made it to his hands and knees. "The Thrikylians should've started exporting that stuff to us long ago. They could have conquered us with a squad of broomswipes."

Rome lay there for a minute, cursing softly. Bonnie went into the next room. When he felt up to it, Rome hauled himself to his feet. He reached for his shirt, draped over a chair by the bed, and drew his hand back, his lip curled with distaste. It was safe to say he was never putting that thing on again. He looked down at his ridiculous pants. Unless he'd left a pair here somewhere he was going to have to wear these things back to the palace. In plain daylight.

"Do I have any clothes here?" he called.

Bonnie came back into the room. "Sure. You're looking at them."

"Don't be smart, woman. You know what I mean."

Bonnie laughed. Her laughter was clear and rich. Normally Rome loved that sound. Right now it just made his head hurt.

"Here." She gave him a mug of water. "Let me see what I can find."

Rome swallowed the water in one mouthful then frowned at the mug. Silly little thing. Didn't hold nearly enough. He didn't think any of it even reached his stomach; it felt like his tongue soaked it all up before it got to his throat.

"You might still fit in these." Bonnie tossed some pants and a shirt on the bed.

"What do you mean, I might fit?" Rome grumbled.

Bonnie patted him on the stomach. "I mean, palace living has been good to you. You've put on a bit from the soft life."

"It's muscle."

"Sure it is."

Rome tugged on the pants. They were a tight fit and didn't seem to close all the way in the front. "I told you not to wash these in hot water. They shrink too much." Bonnie's only reply was another laugh. Rome pulled the shirt on and ran his fingers through his hair. "Did we…have a little fun last night?" he asked her, trying to attempt a leer. Lord, he felt bad.

Bonnie gave a derisive snort.

"Did we fight?"

Bonnie tapped her chin and appeared to think. "I don't believe so. My memory's a little vague though, so I can't be sure. Try this: any lumps or scratches on your face?"

Rome felt his face. It felt all right. He shook his head.

"Then I'd say no. Otherwise you'd feel it now, hangover or no."

Rome had to admit the truth of that. His Bonnie packed a mean wallop and she wasn't afraid to use it on him when she got mad. Bonnie came up then and gave him a hug. "How about I make you a big breakfast?" she asked. "Set you right up."

For a moment Rome just breathed in the clean scent of her. At times like this he felt all he needed to die happy was just to get old holding her like this. He pulled away reluctantly. "Can't. I'm taking the men out today on exercises. I'm probably late already."

"Go then." Bonnie turned away, dismissing him with a wave of her hand. "Don't let me keep you."

There was nothing in her tone or face…still, Rome often couldn't be sure if she was angry or not. "Hey," he said, suddenly awkward. "Maybe we could do it tomorrow—" He tried to catch hold of her but she dodged him.

"Go on, I said. There's always another time."

"You know I'd…"

"Of course, of course. I don't expect more. Being king is a full-time job. I know that."

Rome stood there, too big, too coarse. He felt like a bull in a lady's pantry. He could break a man's guard down with one blow, kill him before his arm stopped ringing, and yet he couldn't figure out how to get past this woman's defenses. Years he'd been in love with her now and she was still almost a complete mystery. Wordlessly he turned and left.

Bonnie sat down after he left, her legs suddenly too tired to hold her. "You big fool," she said softly. And then added a curse for the tear that slid unbidden down her cheek.

She touched her belly and another tear escaped her.

"You won't be part of those people up at the palace, child. I won't allow it. They won't get their hands on you."

CHAPTER 35

It was morning and Quyloc was standing out on his balcony looking at the spear. He still couldn't quite believe he finally had it. How many times had he almost died in the *Pente Akka* to get this thing? It was a tremendous relief to know he'd never have to go back to that cursed place again.

He heard Rome's voice coming from his office. A moment later the door between his quarters and his office opened and Rome came through. He walked out onto the balcony and saw the spear.

"What is that?"

"It's a spear."

"It's not like any spear I've ever seen." Rome held his hand out. "Let me look at it."

At first Quyloc was reluctant to hand it over, as if maybe Rome would take it. But that was ridiculous, wasn't it? All Rome wanted to do was take a look at it. He handed it to Rome.

"It's too light," Rome said, hefting it.

Quyloc felt a surge of irritation. Rome had no idea what he'd gone through to get this. "It's not a normal spear."

"What's it made of?" Rome asked, turning it in his hands.

"A tooth."

"You're crazy. There's not an animal in the world with teeth this big."

"Not in this world. But in the *Pente Akka* there is."

Rome gave him an incredulous look. "*This* is the weapon you've been looking for there?"

"It is."

"They have animals there with teeth this big?"

"They did." Quyloc tried to act nonchalant. "Maybe not anymore."

"Wait. You *killed* whatever had this in its mouth?"

Quyloc felt a flash of irritation. "What, you don't believe me?"

"I didn't say that."

"It's what it sounded like."

"You have to admit it's pretty incredible. Whatever this came from must have been fifty feet long."

"It was."

"How did you do it?"

"I used that bone knife, the one Lowellin gave me." Now Rome really looked skeptical. Quyloc's irritation mounted. Was he going to spend his whole life being overlooked? "You think I'm making it up, don't you?"

"No, I don't. I'm just…surprised. It's such a little knife."

"Let me tell you something, Rome. There's a lot you don't know. For instance, do you realize how close you came to being assassinated last night? Do you know who *saved* your life?"

Rome gave him a blank look. "Someone tried to assassinate me last night?"

"When you left the party. Those two guards you passed in the hall."

Rome thought about it, then nodded. "I remember them. I thought it was strange that I didn't know their names."

"Lucky for you I was there."

"I had no idea. I just came from Bonnie's. Where are they? I want to know who sent them."

"They won't talk."

"We'll see about that," Rome said grimly.

"They're in the sea."

"What?"

"I killed them…with that little bone knife we were talking about."

"Why?"

"Why did I kill them, or why did I throw them into the sea?"

"We could have learned something about who hired them."

"Lowellin seemed to think that if we didn't get rid of the bodies they might come back to life."

"I don't believe that."

"I'm not sure I do either. But then, you didn't see what I saw." Rome gave him a questioning look. Quyloc told him about the *gromdin* and the volcano.

When he was done, Rome had a sick look on his face and he sat down. "It's not bad enough we have to deal with Melekath, but now we have this?"

"I know," Quyloc said, also sitting down. "Can I have my spear back?"

"Sure." Rome gave it to him. "What are we going to do, Quyloc?" He looked as low as Quyloc had ever seen him.

"I don't know."

"At least you have that now. What's it do?"

Quyloc looked at the spear and realized he hadn't considered that. He shrugged.

"I guess killing people with it is a bad idea, huh?" Rome said with a ghost of a smile.

"It would seem so."

"You think Lowellin will help?"

"I don't know. He all but told me he was done with me because I don't follow him blindly."

"Like the FirstMother does."

"Something like that."

"I still don't get why Lowellin didn't just go get this himself," Rome said. "Seems like he hates Melekath enough to do just about anything."

"Like I told you before, I don't think Lowellin *can* go there."

"Do you think Lowellin's a god?" Rome asked.

The question startled Quyloc. "What makes you say that?"

Rome shrugged. "He has ways of moving around that seem impossible and he's very, very old. He also talks like he knows Melekath personally."

Quyloc thought about this. "Maybe he is…maybe the gods aren't what we think they are."

"Why not? It's starting to look like nothing is the way we thought it was." He snapped his fingers. "I just had an idea. Lowellin wants you to get that weapon to use against Melekath and it seems clear he's afraid to get it himself. Do you see where I'm going with this?"

Quyloc nodded, suddenly realizing what Rome was saying. There were times when Rome seemed like nothing more than muscle, but there were definitely times when he saw straight through a problem. "You're saying Lowellin might be vulnerable to this spear."

"Exactly."

"I think you're right." He realized that he was smiling.

"It seems we have a card we didn't know we had," Rome said. He stood up. "Anyway, I came by to tell you that we're moving out tomorrow."

"Already? I thought it was going to be a few more days at least."

"If it was up to Tairus it would be at least another week. Actually, if it was up to Tairus we'd never go. He thinks the whole empire idea is a bad one."

"Maybe it is."

Rome's look grew pained. "You're not going to start in on me too, are you?"

"I'm just saying I don't trust Lowellin."

"I don't either. But if Melekath really is getting free, we're going to want as big of an army as we can get to fight him."

"And if one of the battles goes against you and you lose? You know how war is. You know how anything can happen. What happens if you lose? Won't you be leaving Qarath in a worse position than before? Even if you win, you're going to lose men."

"Oh, but I have a plan for that," Rome said, holding up one finger. He proceeded to tell it to Quyloc.

When he was done, Quyloc had to admit that he was impressed. "That just might work, Rome. How come you didn't tell me this before?"

"Really? Ever since you started going to that shadow world you're harder to find than a sober soldier in a tavern."

"What does Tairus say about it?"

"It'll never work. The world is going to end. The usual."

"Then I like it. Good luck."

"I still wish you were coming with us. It doesn't seem right to go without you."

"We talked about this, Rome. Do you really want to leave the city with the FirstMother and Lowellin here? What would you return to?"

"You're right, I know. At least I can trust you." Rome gave him a sly look. "I can still trust you, right? You're not planning on taking over while I'm gone?"

Then he laughed and clapped Quyloc on the shoulder.

CHAPTER 36

"Well, there it is," Tairus said, gesturing at the city just visible across the valley. "The city of Managil. I don't think this is quite what they had in mind when they sent delegates to Qarath looking for an alliance." At that moment, some rodent darted underneath his horse. Startled, the horse shied. Tairus lost his balance and was barely able to grab the pommel of his saddle in time to keep from falling. He glared at Rome, at all the soldiers nearby, daring them to smile.

"Trouble with your horse?" Rome asked innocently, trying to hide a smile. The short, stout man had never been comfortable on horses, and only rode one now because he was a general and Rome told him he couldn't be seen walking around like the ordinary soldiers.

Tairus frowned at the horse. "There's something wrong with this animal."

"But the farmer's children said this was the gentlest horse they had. The farmer even let the baby ride him."

"I'm not going to respond to that," Tairus said sullenly. "Shouldn't we be talking about the upcoming battle instead?"

"I already told you: there's not going to be any battle."

"So you keep saying, but I'll believe it when I see it."

"Have a little faith, old friend. Managil will be ours by the end of the day."

"How do you know it will even work again?" Tairus asked, gesturing at the black axe, which was slung across Rome's back.

Rome's smile disappeared. "I don't." And that was the truth. He hadn't used the weapon since Thrikyl.

"They're not going to just let you walk up and have at it."

"We've been over this. That's what the new shields are for."

"And if they sally forth from the gates and attack? Which is what they'll do if they have any brains at all."

"That's what you and the rest of these men are for." Rome turned to his aide, waiting behind them. "Bring the shields up, Nicandro." Nicandro saluted, wheeled his horse and trotted back, calling out orders.

"You're not going to wait for the rest of the army to get here, are you?" The army was still strung out over the last couple of miles.

"No. I want to act fast. Before they really have time to think about it, I want it to already be over."

Rome stroked the axe gently, almost reverently, as he stared up at Managil's walls from just beyond bow shot. He did not notice the men nearby nudging one another and nodding towards him, those who had been at Thrikyl giving knowing looks to those who hadn't. Now they would see something.

Rome held the axe up, the light glinting off its obsidian surface, admiring the skill that had gone into its carving. The closed eye carved into each side of the blade looked so realistic, as if it might open at any moment. The cutting edge of the blade was made to look like a hooked beak. The haft was made to look like the body of the creature, its legs folded back against its body, intricately carved with scales or feathers, he was never sure which.

He hadn't forgotten what Lowellin had said about it, that it might be alive. But some things it was best not to think about too much. Like the other thing Lowellin said, that when he pulled the axe out of the wall, he cracked Melekath's prison. How many times had he pondered those words in the middle of the night? He wanted to discard them as impossible, as some ploy of Lowellin's, but he couldn't, and he couldn't shake the nagging sense of guilt that everything was happening might be his fault.

"It's time, Rome," Tairus said in a low voice, snapping him out of his thoughts.

Rome looked at him and nodded. He re-sheathed the weapon, got off his horse and started forward. As he did, a dozen men carrying huge shields came forward. The shields were so big that each one had two men to hold it and they formed up around Rome, giving him cover from above.

As Rome had expected, Managil had not put her forces into the field. Qarath's army was bigger, better trained, and better equipped, and so they'd chosen to hide behind their defensive wall.

Rome and the shield bearers approached the walls, while two armies watched them. There was none of the shouting or insults or any of the sounds that normally preceded a battle. Both armies were silent, every eye fixed on Rome.

"Stay here," Rome told the shield bearers when they got close to the wall. They stopped, though he could tell they didn't like it. They didn't understand what he was trying to do here. If he succeeded, a lot of men would live to see the end of this day, men who would otherwise have died in battle. He remembered the words of a long-dead general that Perganon had read to him from one of the old books of Empire history: *The greatest victory is the battle that was never fought.*

"I seek safe passage to come forward and treat with you!" Rome boomed. "Do you grant me this?"

After a long moment a voice called out in the affirmative. Rome started forward. His aide, Nicandro, was one of the shield bearers and as Rome walked away, he said, "Don't go! You can't trust them."

"I think I can," he replied, without looking back.

The gates were heavy oaken timbers, girded with black iron, the wall stone and thirty feet high. Twenty feet from the wall he tilted his head back to look up. Helmed heads and shadowed eyes stared back down at him. They seemed so small to him. He felt he could take them up in his free hand and set them to the side, like removing the baby birds from a nest before chopping the tree down.

He called up to them. "I have not come to fight you. I come to ask you to join me. In the war to come all men must stand together or we will die separately."

Silence greeted him, silence broken only by the sound of the grasshoppers flitting through the grass at his feet, until one man responded. He wore an elaborate helmet with glittering insignia on it.

"If you have not come to fight, then leave. We have no interest in joining you."

"Be sensible. You all know the war I am speaking of. The madness, the diseases that strike out of nowhere. The monstrous things that walk the land. You know what has happened in Nelton and the creature that now rules that place. It will only get worse. Surrender now, join me, and I will treat with you as equals."

"And if we don't surrender?"

"Then I will bring this wall down. Some of you will die." As the words passed his lips, Rome felt his hand trembling on the haft of the axe and realized that part of him hoped they would say no, that he would have an excuse to unleash the axe, to slice deep into old stone and rend it asunder.

On the wall, soldiers shifted and looked sidelong at each other, unsure what to think. It was very hot. Sweat ran through beards, down necks, under armor, and made fingers slick on the grips of weapons. He sensed how close he was to having them, how many *were* afraid of all that was happening and would welcome him as their new ruler.

But he also knew that those who ruled never gave it up easily.

"I reject your offer. Hurry back to your lines before I order my archers to fire."

Rome nodded. It was only what he had expected.

But they did not expect what he did next.

Instead of returning to his lines, he darted forward suddenly, ripping the axe free as he went. In the time it took the archers to nock arrows, he was already at the wall and swinging.

The axe sliced deep—as if it were flesh he cut into instead of solid rock—and left in its wake a smoking gash. A groan rippled through the wall, a deep sound that was felt more than heard. The wall shuddered and the first spears and arrows flew wide of their mark as the men staggered.

Even as they struggled to regain their balance, Rome struck again. This time the stone actually shrieked, a painful sound that sent men to their knees, clutching their ears. Qarathian archers surged forward, unleashing a volley of arrows as Rome struck again and again. Everywhere the axe met stone the wall smoked.

The wall began to shake violently. A network of cracks blossomed in all directions. Rome stepped back.

The entire front section of the wall collapsed. One moment it was a stone wall, and the next it was so many shards, like a clay pot dropped from a great height.

Almost a hundred yards of the wall had fallen, raising a great cloud of dust. The defenders who had been on that section were lying in the midst of the rubble, many unconscious or with broken bones. Those who were standing on undamaged sections of the wall were staring in awe. Only a handful of arrows flew out at the Qarathian army as it surged forward.

Tairus was angry when he got to Rome. "What in the name of Gorim's bloody ass did you do that for?" he growled. "You could have been killed."

"But I wasn't."

"That's not the point!" Tairus barked. He managed to get himself under control and lower his voice for his next words, but he was no less angry. "You risked yourself for no reason. Where would we be without you?"

"It wasn't for no reason. I was making a point.'

"And what point was that? That you think you're invincible?"

"Sort of. It doesn't sound as good when you say it that way. I wanted to take the fight out of them."

"You didn't think cutting down their wall would do that?"

"I wanted to be sure. And look, it worked." Though the dust hadn't even finished settling, the defenders who weren't lying on the ground were throwing their weapons down and putting their hands in the air.

While Tairus was still grumbling, Rome summoned his aide. "I want all of their soldiers gathered there." He pointed to an area outside the wall. "Send some men to go through the city and tell the citizens that their new macht would speak with them."

As the day drew to a close, Managil's army and several thousand of her citizens gathered silently. Rome climbed onto one of the largest slabs of the fallen wall and looked down on them, knowing that from here they could not look upon him without acknowledging what he had just done. Some were sullen, but many more carried the distant look of shock, and he was not surprised to see it. It sprang not just from their defeat, but the suddenness of it. They had expected to fight—and perhaps die—bravely, but had instead been defeated without the chance to do either. They had resigned themselves to rushing over the cliff of battle, only to find that it was gone when they got there.

The sun was setting off to his right. For a moment he paused, wondering what he would say. He did not know what the words were, only that he had to say something, and that what he said here would lay the foundation for all that was to come.

"Here it is, Managil. You just lost. You're not happy about this, and I don't blame you. But it's not as bad as you think. In fact, it's not bad at all. It's actually the best thing that could have happened to you."

Now many of the people were exchanging baffled looks, faces creased in frowns, mouths opening to voice questions. *What does he mean by that?*

"There is a war coming. But not just any war. If we lose, this will be the last war. There won't ever be another."

Now he had their full attention. No doubt rumors were swirling in Managil just as they were in Qarath. People were frightened and becoming more so every day. Making the fear worse was the fact that they didn't know what was happening; they only knew that it was something bad.

"Melekath is breaking free of his prison. I figure most of you don't know who he is, so I'll just say that he's powerful, so powerful it took eight gods to defeat him last time. And he's angry. He wants revenge."

The people looked pale now, but Rome thought they also looked more resolute. The unknown fear was always the worst.

"Here's the thing," he said, drawing the axe. Every eye went to it. "We're not helpless. We have weapons and we have strong hearts. When Melekath gets free, we mean to be there and we mean to hit him so hard he'll wish he never stuck his head out in the open." He lowered his voice somewhat, so they had to strain to hear him. "That's why I'm here. That's why losing is the best thing that could have happened to you today. Because if we're going to win this war, we need to all fight together."

He paused and let that sink in. Then he held the axe over his head. "Who's with me!" he yelled.

A great roar went up from them then, soldiers from both sides, and the citizens of Managil as well. He had them. They were his.

Rome climbed down off the slab of rock. Tairus was staring at him, dumbfounded. "Pretty good, eh?" Rome asked him.

"You're unbelievable."

"I know." To Nicandro, Rome said, "Give these soldiers back their weapons. Tell their commanders I want to meet with them tonight. We're marching out tomorrow at first light."

Rome added the most mobile of Managil's soldiers to his army, left some of his slower elements to take control of the city and help with rebuilding the wall, and was on the road within an hour after sunrise.

His plan was simple: Move quickly and take the smaller kingdoms as quickly as he could as he drove east to the coast. Karthije he would leave alone for now, gambling that, so long as he moved fast, he could wrap up the smaller places before Karthije reacted. He could probably take Karthije now, but it would mean a great deal of bloodshed and he wanted to keep the bloodshed as low as possible. After all, dead soldiers couldn't fight. By fall he planned to have grown his army to such an extent that he could negotiate Karthije's surrender and addition to his empire, rather than having to fight them.

However, even Rome, the eternal optimist, hadn't counted on how easy this first stage of empire would be. The first two kingdoms he marched on after Managil—Yerthin and Opulat—simply surrendered. As fast as Rome's army moved, news of him moved faster. Stories about his demolition of Managil's wall grew like wildfire until sensible people swore that he had merely pointed at the walls and they fell instantly. Those who defied him were said to simply burst into flame.

Along with the wild stories of his abilities were plenty about his mercy, how he came to save them from the coming war. The people of Atria were frightened, and Rome offered salvation. They not only surrendered, in Opulat the delirious citizens staged an impromptu parade to escort him through the streets.

The only ones not happy to see him were the rulers of each city. Power is an acquired taste that soon turns to addiction and no ruler wanted to give his up, regardless of distant dangers.

The fourth kingdom they came to was Rahn Loriten. When the Qarathian army marched up to the city they found a handful of people chained together at the foot of a hastily-erected gallows. The mob surrounding them burst into cheers when they saw Rome.

Rome rode up to them, Tairus beside him. "What's going on?" Rome called out.

A sweaty man in a blue robe ran over to them and bowed deeply. "Mighty Lord Rome!" he cried out. "Behold our humble gift to you!"

"You're giving me a hanging? Who are they?" Rome asked, though by the richness of their attire he had a good idea.

"It is the king and his advisers," the man said with a smile, rubbing his thick hands together.

"And who are you?"

"Me? I'm just a servant of the people and the people welcome Wulf Rome as our new king."

"Well," Rome said, looking at Tairus, "it is quite a gift, isn't it?"

"Not one you get every day."

"What do you think?"

"It's your gift, not mine."

Rome turned back to the sweaty man. "Bring them over here first."

The man called to some others and the king and his advisers were marched over to stand before Rome, helped along by a few well-placed kicks and punches. All of them had bruises and torn clothes. The king had blood on the side of his face.

"So you're the one they're all talking about," the king said with a sneer. One eye was blackened and rapidly swelling shut. "You look like a stable hand."

Rome looked down. His shirt was unbuttoned most of the way, freeing a fairly impressive mass of curly black hair. It wasn't a very clean shirt either. He couldn't remember if he'd changed it since leaving Qarath. He looked back at the king. "You're right."

"I demand you release me at once. In return I will invite you to a feast in the palace and we will discuss terms."

"See, here's the thing," Rome said reasonably. "I'm not a big one for demands. They're too one-sided." At his words, the king's scowl deepened. "Also, here's another thing. I'm what you might call a man of the people." Quyloc had called him that once. He thought it described him well. "And it seems to me your people have spoken, loud and clear." He gestured at the mob.

The king looked over his shoulder at the mob and paled. "I think you're done here, don't you?" Rome asked him. The king nodded slowly.

Rome looked back at the sweaty man in the blue robe. "I'll tell you what. They're looking a little rough. I can see you've worked out a bit of your frustrations on them." The man started to protest but he held up a hand. "I'm sure they deserve more, but I'm feeling generous today. You've heard that about me, right? That I'm generous?"

Beside him, Tairus whispered, "Get it over with already. You're milking it."

Rome gave him a quick smirk, then turned back to the business at hand. "I say we let them go."

"But—"

"You've already taken their power and their wealth. In my experience that's all the nobility care about anyway. Killing them now is just making it easy on them. Better to kick them out and let them live with their new stations in life. What do you say?"

The sweaty man thought this over and slowly a smile dawned on his face. "I agree!"

"Good. Then make it so. And take off the chains. There's no sense in wasting good steel."

A few minutes later the king and his advisers were limping down the road leading away from Rahn Loriten. They could be heard arguing with each other.

"You're just having way too much fun with this, you know?" Tairus said.

CHAPTER 37

Seafast Square had hundreds of people in it for the Tenders' morning services that day. The square was at the edge of the city, about halfway up the hill. On one side was a waist-high wall that overlooked the sea. The cliff there, while not nearly as high as the cliff behind the palace, was still at least forty feet high. Lining the square on the other three sides were various vendors' stalls selling mostly cloth and leather products.

Nalene didn't really like leading the morning services. Besides that, she had to admit that she wasn't very good at speaking to a crowd. She didn't really know anything about inspiring people. She didn't know how to choose just the right words or vary her tone for effect. It made her profoundly uncomfortable to stand up in front of so many people, having them looking at her, judging her. She dealt with it by trying to pretend they weren't there, the whole time staring at a spot high up on the wall of an old building on the other side of the square.

Despite this, the crowds continued to grow and on this day the square was mostly full, people arriving early to get a spot up close. They were there because they were scared. The rumors floating around the city grew wilder every day. The latest one claimed there were men in the northwest who were lighting people on fire and burning them to ashes.

Some fears struck closer to home. Only the day before a horde of rats boiled out of the sewer in the middle of the day and poured down the street, biting people, swarming over them.

Which explained why this crowd was so large, she thought. Every time some new frightening thing happened, a fresh wave of people sought out the morning services.

The Tenders weren't the only ones offering answers in this new, terrifying world they were all suddenly living in. Cynar, high priest of

Protaxes, was preaching regularly up by the palace, promising that his god would show up and save them. There was also a cult of Gorim, whose followers held midnight rituals during which they consumed some kind of drink that made them see visions and scream in unknown tongues.

In addition to them there were at least a half dozen seers, prophets and assorted charlatans, most trying to make some coin off of people's fear. Of course, the coin they made was nothing compared to those who sold the most popular fear remedy of all: alcohol. The taverns were packed every night.

The sun began to peek over the horizon and Nalene climbed up on the low wooden platform that she'd had workmen build for them some days before. Three other Tenders were already waiting up there, Velma, Mulin and Perast. The rest of the Tenders were waiting at the foot of it, clad in simple white robes, shaved heads dutifully lowered. After the service they would all walk back to the estate where they would spend most of the rest of the day training their *sulbits*.

The training was going well, though not as fast as Nalene would have liked. Other than the unfortunate Lenda—Nalene had paid a man to look for her, but so far he'd had no luck—there'd been no major incidents. They were slowly but surely learning how to control the creatures.

Looking out over the crowd, Nalene touched her *sulbit* through her robe. The daily feedings—pigs, shatren, goats—were having a big effect and it had grown quite a lot already. It was probably three times as big as when she first received it. It stirred sleepily under her touch and she felt its awareness brush up against hers.

As it did every time it awakened, it tried to nurse on her Selfsong, but Nalene was ready for it and she pushed it gently, but firmly, away.

You will feed after this, little one. I promise you.

Lowellin had been correct when he said they had to be constantly vigilant with the creatures. They were always hungry, always ready to feed. All the Tenders were getting ample practice controlling that hunger.

The hardest time to control them was at night. At least three times every night Nalene awakened to find her *sulbit* trying to nurse and she'd have to push it away. She'd gotten to the point where almost as soon as the thing stirred, she awoke. It was becoming automatic.

Not all of the Tenders had mastered this. Often women showed up for breakfast looking wan and pale, exhausted by the combination of lack of sleep and lost Song. Only yesterday Velma woke up in the middle of the night to find her *sulbit* on her face, feeding. Her screams woke up half the place.

Nalene stared at the spot on the wall and began the service. First she offered up the traditional Tender prayer of greeting for the new day, thanking the Mother for the new chance. Then she turned to the sermon.

"Most of you have heard about the rats and the people that were attacked yesterday. You are wondering what is happening. You are afraid. You are right to be afraid, for this is yet another sign that Melekath's escape is near. That is why you are here. Because you know in your hearts that it is the Tenders who are your best hope in the days to come."

She continued on in this vein for several minutes. The crowd was quiet, staring up at her with a kind of desperate intensity that seemed to grow stronger every day. If she had been honest with herself, Nalene would have admitted that sometimes they frightened her. The fear was winding them tighter and tighter and eventually something had to snap.

She broke off her sermon abruptly as she became aware of a new presence.

Something was approaching. Its Song was different, with a low, pulsing beat that Nalene had never heard before.

Nalene looked around and saw that the other Tenders had noticed it too. Since receiving their *sulbits*, they had all become much more sensitive to Song.

"What is it?" Velma asked, looking to Nalene for answers.

Perast, a thin woman with large, nervous eyes, said, "It's big."

"Where is it coming from?" Mulin asked, her head turning side to side. She was tall and graceful and very dark skinned.

Nalene reached into her robe and withdrew her *sulbit*. Whispers arose from the crowd when they saw the dull, ivory-colored creature in her palm. Rumors about the *sulbits* were everywhere, but no one had seen one since the day Nalene used hers to almost kill the man in the street.

With her *sulbit* in her hand, Nalene's inner senses became even sharper and she realized at once where the strange Song was coming from.

The sea.

Just then Perast cried out, "It's coming from the sea!" and pointed.

The crowd shifted nervously and many people turned their heads to see what she was pointing at. One man who was right next to the wall leaned over it to look.

A heartbeat later he spun back around, his face white. "There's something coming up the cliffs!" he screamed and bolted into the crowd.

Frightened cries arose from the crowd and voices were raised, asking for answers. The crowd began to draw back from the wall, fearful but not yet panicked.

Several more looked over the wall and they also turned and ran. Nervous shuffling became a retreat as the crowd started heading for the exits.

Only a handful had made it out of the square when suddenly something clambered up over the wall. It was huge, so big that the wall cracked and broke beneath it. Its body was armored by a thick shell and its two enormous forelegs ended in claws like a crab's. A dozen legs supported its mass and it had a long, segmented tail. Eyes on long stalks turned this way and that. It lunged forward, off the wall, crushing several people who were standing frozen, staring at it in terror. The crowd panicked and began fighting madly to get out of the square.

Nalene knew what she had to do. This was her moment; she could not fail.

The Tenders at the base of the platform were fleeing along with the rest of the crowd. Velma was halfway down the steps. Before they could join the exodus, Nalene grabbed onto Perast and Mulin.

"Stay here!" she yelled.

"But we'll be killed!" Perast yelped. She wasn't looking at Nalene, but over her shoulder. The clawed creature lunged at the crowd, pincers snapping. Two people were cut in half and fell in a bloody spray.

"We can fight this thing! We can kill it! But I need your help!"

Perast, still fixated on the creature, was struggling to get free of Nalene's grasp and so Nalene slapped her. Hard. Perast's hand went to her mouth and for the first time she looked at Nalene.

Nalene looked at Mulin. The tall woman was shaking, but she met Nalene's eyes and nodded.

"Get out your *sulbits*." Nalene took a quick glance over her shoulder to check the creature's location. It was about halfway across the square. It swung its tail and a row of merchants' stalls were flattened. Several more people were snatched up screaming in its claws.

She turned back to them. "If we work together, we can kill this thing. We just have to do what we've been practicing."

"But it's huge!" Perast wailed. "It will take too long to let that much Song build up."

"Not if we bleed Song off bigger flows than we have been," Nalene said.

"You're talking about flows attached to people," Mulin said.

"I don't know if I'm strong enough," Perast protested.

"You are. You *have* to be," Nalene told her fiercely, willing her to believe.

After a moment, Perast nodded. Mulin looked grim but determined.

Nalene turned around just as the creature's eye stalks swiveled toward them. It turned and began lumbering toward them. Nalene clamped one hand on Perast's arm before she could move.

"Focus your attacks on its head," she told them. "But don't release the Song until I tell you to. We need to all hit it at the same time."

It took only a heartbeat to meld with their sulbits—the act had become so natural to them—and go *beyond.* Next she located one of the larger flows and took hold of it. The jolt when she grabbed it was so strong she nearly lost her hold. It held significantly more power than she'd ever experienced before.

She began bleeding Song off it, letting it build inside her, doing her best to shut out her fear as the creature lumbered closer. The wooden platform shook underfoot. As it came it crushed an overturned cart that had been abandoned as its owner fled. Its tail swung and several people were sent flying.

"FirstMother!" Perast cried.

"Almost," Nalene whispered. She could feel how close she was to losing hold of the extra Song. She wanted to attack right then, but she knew if she did so too soon, the attack would be too weak. She had to hold on, just a few seconds longer.

The creature loomed over them. It raised its forelegs, claws clacking loudly.

"*Now!*"

Almost simultaneously three blue-white bolts of Song power burst from them.

279

The creature squealed as the Song bolts struck home, tearing jagged burned holes in its head. One of its eye stalks was torn away. It fell back, claws held up to defend its face.

But, just as Nalene was starting to think they'd done it, the creature raised its forelegs once again and came at them.

"I have nothing left," Nalene heard Mulin say. Perast staggered backward and fell down.

But Nalene's *sulbit* was bigger, stronger than theirs. It had fed on the man who attacked her while the others were still in the River. Its strength was her strength.

Desperately, she grabbed onto not one, but two fresh flows of LifeSong. Power surged through her, so strong she screamed, but she did not let go. The power built rapidly to a crescendo.

Now!

Another Song bolt shot out. This one tore away the creature's other eye stalk.

Squealing madly, the creature turned and fled, weaving as it made its way blindly across the square, leaving a trail of ichor in its wake. It smashed into the stone wall, broke through it, and fell over the cliff back into the sea.

"Blessed Mother," Mulin said. "It worked."

"Of course it did," Nalene said. "Didn't the Protector say that all we need to do is trust him and do what he says?" But she could not deny that she was shaking so badly she could hardly stand. She'd been sure she was about to die.

"I just…I had no idea." Perast, still on her knees, was looking at her *sulbit* with new respect. "It's still so small. Imagine what we will be able to do when they get bigger…"

Nalene looked around the square. There were still lots of people there. The stampede had petered out. Probably a dozen bodies lay bleeding on the ground. She sensed an opportunity here and knew she could not waste it.

She walked to the front of the platform and raised her voice. "People of Qarath!" Nalene cried out. "Listen to me!"

As one, they turned to her. Their eyes fixed on her, their faces loaded with something unspoken.

"Today you have seen the hand of the Mother, come down to save you! She comes to help her children! She will not forsake you in your time of need! In the war that is upon us, it is Xochitl and her faithful

Tenders who stand between you and the dark forces of Melekath! We alone can save you!"

They stared at her, breaths held, while this sank in. Then a low sound, almost a moan, arose from them and they began to fall to their knees, their hands stretched toward Nalene.

"I did it," Nalene kept saying fiercely. "I did it."

She was alone on the balcony outside her quarters, staring out over the estate, exulting in her victory. She had faced her first real test and she had succeeded. She had proven that the Tenders were capable of using the *sulbits'* power to fight for Xochitl.

She heard a noise behind her and turned. Lowellin stood there.

"It worked!" she told him.

"I know."

"It was close. I was lucky to have Mulin and Perast there with me, lucky that they are the strongest after me."

"Was it luck?"

She paused, thought about it. "You're right. It was the Mother's will that it happened as it did. She was testing us. She was testing *me*."

"And she is pleased."

Nalene swallowed, momentarily overcome. Was there ever anything in her life she had ever desired so strongly as Xochitl's approval? "Thank you, Protector," she said hoarsely.

"As you said, it was close. It almost went the other way."

Nalene sat down, weak suddenly. It *had* been close. A second longer and she would be lying dead in that square right now.

"You cannot falter now. You and the others must continue training your *sulbits*. They must become extensions of you, responding instantly to your will. As you saw, even the slightest hesitation can mean failure."

"Yes, Protector."

"When are you going to send more women to receive their *sulbits*? Have you no candidates yet at all?"

"It's too soon for women from the other Havens to arrive," Nalene protested. "I have sent out the word for new recruits and a few women have responded, but none of them were worthy."

His eyes glinted. "That is not for you to decide. You send them to me and I will decide which are able to handle the *sulbits* and which are not."

"I'm just worried about another incident like what happened with Lenda…" Many times Nalene had lain awake in the dark wondering what happened to the girl. She could not seem to rid herself of the guilt she felt over it.

"That will not happen again."

"That's a relief. So you'll just send them away then?"

"I will deal with them."

A chill went through her at his words. She wanted to ask what he meant by that but she was afraid she would not like the answer.

"Send me whoever you have tonight," he said.

Nalene nodded and a minute later he was gone.

Darkness had fallen and no one noticed as a short, aging man with a fringe of gray hair emerged from the heavy brush along the Cron River that he had been hiding in. He looked around, fearful someone was watching him, but the night was quiet.

He made his way by hidden paths through the brush until he came to the mouth of the river. There, hidden under a fallen tree, was a small canoe. He dragged it down to the surf and looked around again, but there was no one there. Few were bold enough to walk the shore after dark, especially with all that was happening now, but if he were seen, he would be lucky to escape with his life.

For he was a Sounder, the last of his kind in Qarath. One of the nearly-mythical folk with a strange affinity for the sea and its denizens. In the eyes of his fellow man he was an abomination, a figure from children's stories. He and his kind were said to take unwary children and feed them to the sea. None of which he, personally, had ever done, nor had the man who taught him the mysteries. All of which would make no difference at all to the frightened citizens of Qarath.

He paddled swiftly out to the dim shape floating a hundred yards from shore. Fluids leaked from the great beast and toothed fish had already been tearing at its corpse. Large pieces of its armored exoskeleton had been torn away, exposing the soft flesh underneath.

He leaned over and placed one hand on its side. It had not been evil. Normally it avoided all contact with people. It wasn't even a meat-eater; its claws were for defense against its predators. But it had been driven mad by the poison tainting the River and in its madness it had blindly lashed out.

He began to sing, a wordless song beyond the normal range of the human voice, filled with the crash and the roar of the sea. The song was both a dirge and a summoning.

The water around him began to churn and he paddled away from the creature. Tentacles emerged from the water and slipped around the creature's carcass. The tentacles tightened, and slowly the thing was drawn down into the depths.

CHAPTER 38

"I got a bad feeling about this," Tairus said.

Rome grunted his agreement. The two sat on their horses staring at a city set on top of a steep hill. The city was Veragin. The last city before the sea, and then they could turn around and head home.

Rome couldn't wait to get back to Qarath. Every day it seemed there was a new horror. From Quyloc he'd gotten a report about bands of men in the northwest who were burning people alive and something about a monster crawling out of the sea and attacking the city.

And now this, a whole city that seemed completely empty. Earlier that afternoon a scout had returned from patrol to say that something was wrong. He and the men in his squad had found no one on their forward patrols. Finally, they had advanced to within sight of the city itself. It appeared to be deserted. No one on the walls. No one moving around inside. No smoke rising. Rome had brought the army to a halt and ridden up here with Tairus to see for himself.

Was anything they were doing going to make any difference at all? How were they supposed to fight something like this?

"What do you know about Veragin?" he asked Tairus.

The stout man grunted. "Not much. But there must be some amongst our new recruits who do know." He turned and gestured to a soldier waiting behind him. "Tell the squad leaders to find someone who knows this city. Send him up here." The man hurried off.

"One of the gates is open slightly," Nicandro, Rome's aide, said.

Rome squinted, but it was too far away for him. "Why would everybody just leave?" he asked no one in particular.

"Maybe they didn't leave," Tairus replied. "Maybe they're all dead."

"If they're dead, how come there's no vultures or crows?"

"Because that would make sense," Tairus said, sudden heat in his voice. "And nothing makes any sense anymore."

Rome knew how he felt. Everything he thought he knew had been turned upside down. There was too much in the world that was impossible.

A few minutes later a soldier came hurrying up accompanied by an older man with a mustache growing gray and a limp in his walk. When the older man spoke, his words had a strange lilt, marking him as being from the city of Hen, which they had taken a few days before. "I've been to Veragin a number of times, traveling with my master." As if suddenly realizing who it was he was talking to, he took off his shapeless hat and crumpled it in his hands. Then he started to kneel.

"Stop that," Rome said. "Stand up and look me in the eye when you talk to me. You're a soldier, aren't you?"

"I am now," the man said, managing with some difficulty to look Rome in the eye. "I'm a soldier long as you say I am."

The man's clothes were simple and ragged and he carried no real weapon, only a knot of wood to serve as a club. He was one of the volunteers. It wasn't just soldiers who were joining the army; it was ordinary citizens as well. Rome had told Tairus to find a place for them in the army, give them something to do until they got back to Qarath and they could be properly outfitted and trained.

The man shifted, taking the weight off his bad leg, and Rome saw the scars around his ankle. A slave, then. Hen allowed slavery. Or it had. Rome had been happy to end that institution. No man should tie another with a chain and call his whole life for him. He reckoned a number of former slaves must have joined the army. "What's your name? I like to know who I'm talking to so if I have to yell at you later, I'll know who to curse."

The man blinked at him, surprised. "I've been called Clem so long as I can remember, but it seems to me I had another name once and it was Tover."

"Well, Tover. What can you tell me about Veragin?"

"They're a strange people," Tover said. "They worship the grim god Gorim. It's not just back of the hand worship either, but the real thing. Prayers four times a day, no matter what they're doing. Statues of the god everywhere. But they're fair. Strict, but fair. So long as you follow their laws and pray whefsn they do, they'll buy your goods and pay for 'em with silver." He peered at the city in the distance. "Seems kind of quiet right now, though."

"So they don't normally take a day of rest and all gather at some temple to worship for a day then?" Tairus asked.

"Never in the times I was there, master. I'm sorry I can't tell you more."

"No one's your master," Rome cut in. "You're a free man. Now you're a soldier. Go on back to your squad."

After the man had bowed and left, Rome turned back to Tairus. "Then there's nothing else to do but walk up and knock, is there?"

"It would be smarter to send more scouts first, until we know it's safe."

"Of course it would," Rome said, spurring his horse forward. Tairus followed with a curse.

⚔ ⚔ ⚔

"There's a foot sticking out," Tairus said. It was hidden in the shadows cast by the gate, almost like it was holding the gate open for them.

"So much for being at prayers. Unless they have a powerfully strange way to pray." Rome's attempt at humor felt flat in the still air.

They dismounted and proceeded cautiously, four soldiers and Nicandro following them with drawn weapons. They squeezed through the gate and walked into a scene from a nightmare. Bodies were everywhere. They littered the streets. They slumped from open windows. One lay halfway in a fountain. Men, women, and children. With dead hands they clutched their throats. Their faces were blackened and swollen.

"All dead," Rome said softly.

"Even the vultures," Tairus said, noticing a handful of feathered black carcasses littering the street. All lay close to bodies they had been feeding on. "That's why we didn't see any earlier."

"You know what's wrong here?" Rome said.

"You mean, besides all the dead bodies?" Tairus replied sourly.

"No. I'm talking about the flies. There aren't any. There should be flies everywhere." He bent to look closer at the body of a young boy, sprawled on his face. Around the body was a sprinkling of small black bodies. Flies.

"Don't touch anything. We need to get out of here. Right now," Tairus said. He'd seen plague before, and while this didn't look like any disease he'd ever heard of, it was still best to get far away from this place.

Rome stood and looked around. "I want to look around a little first. Maybe one of the wells was poisoned, and that was what caused this."

Tairus started to protest, but Rome was already walking away and all he could do was follow.

Everywhere they went it was the same. Dead bodies and a supernatural stillness that had the soldiers jumping at shadows, afraid to speak above a whisper, as if they might awaken something that slept in that stillness.

They walked up a broad avenue that led to a large plaza near the center of the city, carefully picking their way around the bodies. The plaza was encircled by statues, each twice the height of a man, and each depicting a snarling, horned figure.

"Those are statues of Gorim," Tairus said. He'd seen some smaller ones before that looked similar.

"They don't call him the grim god for nothing."

"Can we go now? You and I both know this wasn't caused by any poison well."

"Sure," Rome said, but he made no move to leave. Instead he stood there, looking at the palace in the distance.

Tairus sighed. What was wrong with Rome? "What is it?"

"Nothing, I just...this could be Qarath."

"What are you talking about?" Tairus looked at the soldiers accompanying them. It didn't look like any of them had heard.

"This could just as easy have happened to Qarath instead."

"Well, it didn't. Now let's go."

"We make all these plans, we build walls, we raise an army, we teach it how to fight—" He snapped his fingers. "—and it's all gone, just like that. None of it made any difference." He turned to Tairus and there was a fell look there that Tairus had never seen before. "What if we've already lost and we just don't know it?"

A chill ran down Tairus' spine when he said that. "Don't talk like that. You can't mean it."

Rome stared at him for a long moment while Tairus held his breath. Then a faint smile pulled at his mouth. "I'm just tired is all. I don't mean anything."

"Let's go back to Qarath," Tairus said. "It's time to go home."

287

They were a few blocks from the front gates when a voice called out from behind them.

"Wait for me! Don't leave me here!"

A man was hurrying towards them. He was short, nondescript, his hair mousy brown, his features forgettable. He wore brown trousers and a long, brown coat buttoned carefully to his throat with silver buttons. The soldiers took positions between him and their macht, their weapons at the ready. He slowed and held his hands up, palms outward.

"I'm harmless," he said. "My name's T'sim."

"What are you doing here?" Rome asked, his brows knit in a frown.

"I *was* a servant," he replied. "But now I don't think I'm doing anything at all."

"What he means is, why are you still alive?" Tairus said.

"Oh, that." T'sim looked at the bodies around him and his nose wrinkled as if he'd just smelled something bad. "I don't really know what happened. I came down to the market to fetch the copper smith for my master. I felt the needs of nature impose themselves on me and went into the public privy." He pointed back over his shoulder vaguely. "While I was…finishing up, I heard an outcry. When I peered out, people were dropping dead everywhere. Secretion, in this case, seemed the better part of valor, so I withdrew, re-bolted the door and waited."

"So you've been in the privy all this time?" Rome said, his tone clearly skeptical.

"It has not been so very long, I assure you," T'sim said hastily. "It occurred only this morning. It was over quickly. I am much less courageous than you may think."

Rome and Tairus exchanged looks. There was something really strange about this man, but Tairus couldn't have said what it was.

"I might have spent all night in there," T'sim added, "but I heard your voices and they drew me forth."

"What do you think?" Rome asked Tairus.

"We can question him once we get out of here. I don't want to stay another minute in this place."

"I couldn't agree more," T'sim said. "I've quite had enough of this place. Why I ever agreed to this contract is beyond me. I see I should have stayed home."

He accompanied them as they made their way for the gates and though he was short and he did not seem to hurry, still he made it there before the rest of them. He pulled one of the gates open further and stood there, holding it for them.

He stared down at the body lying in the gateway. "What did they see before they died, do you think?" His voice sounded almost wistful, like a child who has missed the party and wonders what went on without him. Tairus noticed that the hand holding the gate was almost absurdly small and delicate.

"Who cares what they saw?" Rome growled. "As long as we don't."

When Rome slept that night, he dreamed. Or perhaps it was more than a dream. He could not tell.

He walked through the sleeping camp and no one saw him. No one stirred. The camp was a giant painting and he was a shadow that flitted across it.

Now before him was the half-open gate to the city, though he had made no decision to come this way. A cold hand gripped his heart. He turned to go back to the camp—

And went up to the gate. The rising moon cast eerie shadows, turned the night ghostly gray and pooled the shadows. The dead lay where they had fallen, somehow more real than he was, than the ground he walked on. It was a dream, had to be, but he could feel the gate under his fingers, the rough grain of the wood.

He entered the city.

It was Qarath.

Rome awakened with a start. Outside, gray light was just leaking into the darkness. He was in his tent. It was only a dream. But when he stood his body was tired, as if he had walked all night.

He got up, pulled on his boots, left the tent and walked through the sleeping camp, which was just beginning to stir. He climbed a small hill and stared back at the ruins of the city.

He wasn't surprised when he heard the commotion. Three soldiers on the picket line, standing over something on the ground. Their voices came to him in the still air.

"What happened to him, do you think?"

"Is that Loil?"

Rome came up quietly and looked at the body for a long moment. It was a young man, with a thin beard the color of new straw. He lay on his side, in the fetal position. His eyes were wide with horror.

"What do any of you know of this?" Rome said, making the three jump.

"Nothing, Macht Rome," one of them said. He was heavy set and already sweating, though the morning was cool. "I just found him like this when I was heading out to relieve him on watch. Honest."

Rome hardly heard him. It was definitely time to go home.

CHAPTER 39

Rome rode through the gates of Qarath and everything was different. His people looked tired. They looked foreign. No one called out to him. No children ran behind his horse. He felt old and brittle. He felt like a stranger.

He tried to tell himself it was all in his mind, that he was just weary from the road, but he knew it was more than that. When he'd left, the coming war was just storm clouds on the horizon. Now they could feel the early winds, the first heavy flakes of snow, and they were hunkering down, frightened by what would happen.

"Do you feel it too?" he asked Tairus.

"I do."

"Maybe it was a mistake. Maybe I shouldn't have gone."

"Too late for that."

Rome looked over his shoulder at the army following him. It was easily five times as large as it had been. "That has to mean something," he told Tairus.

Tairus didn't turn to look. He'd been in a grim mood for days. "I guess we'll see."

They rode on in silence for a while, then Tairus spoke. "You see what they're wearing?"

Rome came out of his thoughts and looked at the people standing alongside the street, watching them pass. It took a moment, then he realized what Tairus was speaking of.

"They're all wearing Reminders." Not all of them, of course, but a great many had the many-pointed star inside the circle that was the Tenders' symbol from the days of the Empire. Some wore it in the form of a necklace. For others it was a patch sewn onto their clothing. One man had it tattooed on his cheek.

"The FirstMother didn't waste any time, did she?"

Rome just grunted. He had no idea what to say.

They rode through the palace gates and there was Quyloc, waiting on the steps of the palace. Rome looked at his old friend and all he could think was how happy he was to see him. Quyloc would make sense of everything. He always knew what was going on.

He got off his horse and handed the reins to a stable boy.

"The tower room?" Quyloc asked. He looked thinner than Rome remembered and there were dark smudges under his eyes.

"If you can do without me…" Tairus said.

Rome waved him off and he and Quyloc walked to the tower and started up the stairs. By the second landing he was thinking that there were too many stairs. He didn't remember the room being so high up before.

They got to the room and he walked across it to the big window that looked down over Qarath. He'd always loved this view, the way the whole city was spread out before him, but today it just looked flat.

He went to the table and sat down. "It's good to be home."

Rome rubbed his eyes and when he took his hands away he got a start. T'sim was standing there, just inside the door, a tray in his hands.

For a moment he was stunned. He didn't remember seeing the little man since this morning when they broke camp. He definitely had no memory of him following the two of them into the tower.

"T'sim!" he barked. "What in Bereth's seven hells are you doing here? Get out!"

"Only watching my chance to serve, Macht," T'sim said with a low bow. His voice was soft and calming as always. He glided forward smoothly and set the tray down before Rome. On it was a large mug of ale. A huge mug, really.

Rome picked up the mug and took a long drink. The ale was blessedly cool.

"Is it to your liking, sir?"

"Okay, well, I guess this time it's okay. But don't be sneaking around like that. It's hard on a man's heart."

"As you wish, sir," T'sim said, bowing. "Will there be anything else?"

"Not right now. Go talk to Opus. He'll find something for you."

T'sim bowed again. "As you wish," he said, backing out the door and drawing it closed behind him.

Rome stared after him. "There's something unreal about that guy," he said. "He's always hovering around, so quiet he's almost invisible. I keep forgetting he's there." He shook his head. "Still, he's good at it. Almost like he knows what I want before I do, and then damned good at getting a hold of it." He held up the mug of ale. "Where did he get this so fast?"

Quyloc was staring after T'sim. "There's something different about him."

"That's what I was just saying."

"I can't hear any Song radiating off him."

"What does that mean?"

"I don't know. That he's not alive?"

"You're joking."

Quyloc gave him a look. Rome put his head in his hands.

"Do we have a chance?" he asked.

"Sure, we have a chance," Quyloc said. "Just not much of a chance."

✗ ✗ ✗

Lowellin was waiting in the corridor when T'sim left Quyloc and Rome. He stepped away from the wall and blocked the small man's passage. T'sim looked up at him, as calm as ever.

"What are you doing here?" Lowellin demanded.

"I only came to watch. To know. I want to know what they see," T'sim said softly. The silver buttons on his jacket caught the light and reflected it in tiny stars.

"See that you do not cross my path," Lowellin replied. His ageless face was hard, his words cold. "I know how to deal with you."

T'sim bowed. "I have no concern for you and your schemes. I am only curious."

Lowellin stared at him for a long minute, his gray eyes boring into the smooth face. T'sim stared back at him, unblinking. "This must be torment for one such as you, the freedom you are used to," Lowellin said at last.

"It is…uncomfortable. I no longer care for it, I confess."

"You made a mistake then. The only one of your kind to cross over, into the new Circle."

T'sim lowered his head in acquiescence. "Perhaps a hasty decision on my part. I have had time to think on it."

"You will take no sides?"

"It is not the way of my kind."

"No. It's not." Lowellin stepped aside and motioned down the passageway. "So long as we are clear."

"This world would be more interesting," T'sim said as he moved by Lowellin, "if there were more like you." Once past he paused and looked back. "And like Melekath. I see why she had such difficulty choosing when it came to you two." He lifted his hand in what might have been a wave and disappeared down the stairs.

The story continues in *Guardians Watch*.

Before you go!

I'd like to thank you for reading *Landsend Plateau*. As much as I love writing, it takes readers to make the experience complete. A journey shared is a much more powerful experience.

You may not be aware of this, but reviews are vitally important to unknown authors like me. They give other potential readers an idea of what to expect. So, if you have the time to leave one, I'd very much appreciate it. If you're busy (and who isn't?) leave a short one. Even one sentence is enough!

Glossary

abyss—according to the Book of Xochitl, the place the Eight reached into to create Melekath's prison. Gulagh drew poison from the abyss and released it into the River, which is what is causing the strange diseases and mutations plaguing the land.

Achsiel—(AWK-see-el) lean man who leads the first group of raiders onto the Plateau, killing Meholah and bringing *ingerlings* to the Godstooth.

akirma—the luminous glow that surrounds every living thing. Contained within it is Selfsong. When it is torn, Selfsong escapes. It also acts as a sort of transformative filter, changing raw LifeSong, which is actually unusable by living things, into Selfsong.

Ankha del'Ath—ancestral home of the Takare. Empty since the slaughter at Wreckers Gate.

aranti—creatures that dwell in the wind, in the Sphere of Sky.

Asoken—the Firewalker for Bent Tree Shelter, killed by the outsiders.

Atria—(AY-tree-uh) name commonly used to refer to the landmass where the story takes place. It is a derivation of the name Kaetria, which was the name of the old Empire.

Azrael—(AZ-ray-el) the one the Takare call the Mistress, protector of wildlife on the Landsend Plateau. If a game animal is not killed cleanly by a hunter, it may cry out to her and she will bring violence on the one who killed it. She killed Erined, mate to Taka-slin.

Banishment—when the Eight sank the city of Durag'otal underground.

barren—area of bare stone on the Plateau. Nothing lives on the barrens except occasionally a tani or a poisonwood.

Bent Tree Shelter—village on the Plateau where Shakre lives.

Bereth—one of the Eight, who together with Xochitl laid siege to the city of Durag'otal.

beyond — also known as "in the mists," the inner place where Tenders can *see* Song.

Birna—woman of Bent Tree Shelter who recently gave birth. Wife of Pinlir, whose father was Asoken.

blinded ones—those people who have had their eyes burned out by Kasai. They gain the ability to use Kasai's gray fire and are in direct contact with the Guardian.

Bloodhound—one of Kasai's followers. He chased Netra up onto the sides of the Landsend Plateau and nearly caught her.

Bonnie—Rome's girlfriend, formerly a prostitute at the Grinning Pig tavern.

Book of Xochitl—the Tenders' sacred book.

Brelisha—old Tender at Rane Haven who teaches the young Tenders.

Caller—shortened form of Windcaller.

Cara—Netra's best friend.

chaos power—power from the abyss, also in the *Pente Akka.*

Children—the ones who followed Melekath to the city of Durag'otal and were Banished with him.

Dorn—Windcaller that Shakre had an affair with as a young woman. Netra's father.

Dreamwalker—the Dreamwalkers are those who are responsible for guiding the Takare in spiritual and supernatural matters.

Durag'otal—(DER-awg OH-tal) city founded by Melekath as a haven for his Children. It was sunk underground in the Banishment.

Eight—eight of the old gods, led by Xochitl, who created a prison around the city of Durag'otal and sank it underground.

elanti—tree-thing that lives in the middle of the poisonwood growth. Elihu believes they are protectors of Tu Sinar.

Elihu—(eh-LIE-who) the Plantwalker for Bent Tree Shelter and Shakre's closest friend.

Ergood—a noble who died under mysterious circumstances. His estate was then handed over to the Tenders for use as their headquarters.

Erined—mate of Taka-slin. She put several arrows in Azrael and gave Taka-slin the chance to regain his feet and take down Azrael.

Fanethrin—(FAIN-thrin) city to the northwest. Part of the old Empire.

feeder lines – the intermediate sized current of LifeSong, between the trunk lines, which come off the River directly, and the flows, which sustain individual creatures.

Firkath Mountains—mountains just to the north of Rane Haven. They reach nearly to the Landsend Plateau.

FirstMother—title of the leader of the Tenders.

flows – the smallest currents of LifeSong. One of these is attached to each living thing and acts as a conduit to constantly replenish the energy that radiates outward from the *akirma* and dissipates. If the flow attached to a living thing is severed, it will only live for at most a few hours longer.

Godstooth—a tall spire of white stone near the center of the Landsend Plateau. It marks the hiding place of the god Tu Sinar.

Golgath—one of the gods that stood with Xochitl at the siege of Durag'otal.

Gorim—one of the gods that stood with Xochitl at the siege of Durag'otal. Worshipped in Veragin, the dead city Rome found at the end of the summer campaign.

Gulagh—one of the three Guardians of the Children, also known as the Voice, in control of the city of Nelton. It has discovered a way to make a small opening into the abyss and when chaos power leaks out, use a living person to feed that power back up the flow of

LifeSong sustaining that person and ultimately into the River itself. It is this poison in the River which is causing the strange diseases and mutations plaguing the land.

Gur al Krin—desert that formed over the spot where Durag'otal was sunk underground. Means "sands of the angry god" in the Crodin language.

gromdin — according to Lowellin, a being who seeks to shred the Veil, thus allowing the *Pente Akka* to spill over into the normal world.

Heartglow—the denser glow of Selfsong in the center of a person's or animal's *akirma*. When it goes out, life ends.

Huntwalker—the Huntwalkers are those responsible for guiding the Takare in the hunt. Their primary concern is that game be killed cleanly, for otherwise it might call out to the Mistress, Azrael, who will then come and exact vengeance for its death.

Ilsith—Lowellin's staff. It takes the Tenders down to the River where they get their *sulbits*. Nothing is known of this creature or why it obeys Lowellin.

ingerlings—ravenous creatures of the abyss carried to Godstooth by Achsiel.

Intyr—Dreamwalker for Bent Tree Shelter.

Jehu (JAY-who)—young Takare who took the black mark from Achsiel rather than be burned alive.

Kaetria—(KAY-tree-uh) capital city of the Old Empire.

Karthije—(CAR-thidge) kingdom neighboring Qarath to the northwest.

Kasai—one of the three Guardians of Melekath, also known as the Eye. Kasai discovered a way to take the *ingerlings* from the abyss and use them against Tu Sinar.

Khanewal—one of the Eight, who together with Xochitl laid siege to the city of Durag'otal.

Landsend Plateau—place where the Takare live.

Lenda—a simpleminded Tender in Qarath. Something goes wrong when she takes her *sulbit*.

LifeSong – energy that flows from the River and to all living things. It turns into Selfsong after it passes through the *akirma*, which acts as a sort of filter to turn the raw energy of LifeSong into something usable by the living thing.

Lowellin—(low-EL-in) known by the Tenders as the Protector, he guides them to the *sulbits*.

macht—title from the old Empire meaning supreme military leader. Adopted by Rome for himself instead of king.

Meholah—Huntwalker for Bent Tree Shelter. He was killed by Achsiel for saying no to the question.

Melanine—FirstMother in Qarath when Lowellin arrives. She renounces her title and refuses him. Later murdered under mysterious circumstances.

melding—when a Tender allows her *sulbit* to join with her on a deep level. In order for a Tender to meld with her *sulbit* she has to lower her inner defenses and allow the creature into the deepest recesses of her being. Her will must be strong to keep it from taking over.

Melekath—the ancient god who was imprisoned along with his Children in the Banishment.

Musician—one of a highly secretive brotherhood who can manipulate LifeSong to create Music that transports the listener. Rumor has it that there is a pact between them and their god, Othen, which is where they get their power. Very little is known about this agreement beyond the fact that Musicians are required to play as long as the audience requests it, though none do so for fear of angering the Musicians.

nadu—the Takare believe that without the chants to guide them, the spirits of the newly dead drift off into the darkness and are swallowed by the *nadu*, ravenous shades that wait beyond the edges of the light.

Nalene—FirstMother in Qarath.

Nelton—small city a few days from Rane Haven where Netra and Siena were nearly caught by Gulagh.

Nicandro—aide to Wulf Rome.

nightbloom—a plant on the Plateau with purple flowers that causes catatonic sleep. Then the scurriers, insects that live symbiotically with it, devour the sleeping creature.

Oath—when the Takare first arrived on the Plateau, all life there turned against them and they were nearly all killed. Taka-slin, the legendary hero, traveled to the Godstooth and challenged Tu Sinar to come out and answer for his crimes. When the god did not answer, Taka-slin spoke the Oath, that the Takare would build no cities nor allow outsiders on the Plateau, and in exchange, Tu Sinar would call off his minions.

Oathspeaker—these are the elders among the Takare, usually Walkers, who make the annual trip to the Godstooth to renew the Oath first made by Taka-slin.

Othen's Pact—agreement made between the Musicians and the god Othen.

Pastwalker—the Pastwalkers are entrusted with remembering the past so that the Takare do not repeat the mistakes that led to the tragedy at Wreckers Gate. They can take others to actually relive past events from the history of the Takare.

Pente Akka—the shadow world that Lowellin shows Quyloc how to access.

Perganon—palace historian/librarian. He meets with Rome to read to him from the old histories. Also runs an informal network of informants.

Plains of Dem—where the Takare defeated the Sertithians.

PlantSong—the Song found within plants.

Plantwalker—the Plantwalkers are sensitive to the plants on the Plateau and can even communicate with them in a fashion.

poisonwood—an unusual, dense growth of tangled plants that grows around the *elanti* on the barrens on the Plateau.

Protaxes—one of the Eight, who together with Xochitl laid siege to the city of Durag'otal. Worshipped in Qarath by the nobility.

Rane Haven—where Netra grew up.

Rehobim—(reh-HOE-bim) when the outsiders first appeared on the Plateau, Rehobim was a member of the hunting party that they questioned.

Reminder—a many-pointed star enclosed in a circle, the holy symbol of the Tenders.

River—the fundamental source of all LifeSong, deep in the mists of *beyond.*

Seafast Square—place where Nalene defeated the creature that crawled out of the sea.

seeing—the act of perceiving with inner, extrasensory perception. It has nothing to do with the eyes yet what the mind perceives while *seeing* is interpreted by the brain as visual imagery.

Selfsong—when LifeSong passes through a person's *akirma* it becomes Selfsong, which is the energy of Life in a form that can be utilized by the body. It dissipates at death. It is continually replenished, yet retains a pattern that is unique to each individual.

Shakre—Netra's mother. She lives with the Takare, having been driven to the Plateau by the wind after being exiled from the Tenders.

shatren—animal similar to a cow, though smaller.

Shorn—powerful humanoid who crashed to earth near the Godstooth in a fireball.

Songquest—ritual that Tenders go through to acquire their *sonkrill.* They fast and wander the land until a spirit guide appears and leads them to their *sonkrill.*

sonkrill—talismans that the Tenders receive/discover at the end of their Songquest.

Sounder—one with an affinity for the Sea and its denizens. Due to the ancient wars between the Shapers of the Sea and those of the Stone, in which many people died and the seas and coastal areas abandoned, the people of Atria have a long history of fearing the Sea. As a result Sounders risk injury and death if they are found out.

spirit-walking—an ability that the Tenders of old had, a way of separating the spirit from the body, the spirit then leaving the body behind to travel on without it. A thin silver thread connects the spirit to the body. If the thread is broken, there is no way for the spirit to find its way back to the body.

sulbit—creatures that dwell in the River, living on pure LifeSong. In an effort to gain allies in the fight against Melekath, Lowellin gives them to the Tenders. At first the creatures feed on the Tenders' LifeSong, but then the Tenders learn to control them so that they only feed when allowed to, and then on animals. When a Tender melds with her *sulbit,* she gains the creature's natural affinity for Song and is able to take hold of flows of Song and bleed power off them.

T'sim—(TUH-sim) unusual man Rome finds in the dead city of Veragin. That he is more than an ordinary man is borne out by the fact that Lowellin knows him.

Tairus—(TEAR-us) General of the army.

Taka-slin—legendary hero of the Takare. He led them to the Plateau and destroyed Azrael when she attacked his people. After that he traveled to the Godstooth and made the Oath which allowed the Takare to remain on the Plateau.

Takare—(tuh-KAR-ee) the greatest warriors of the old Empire. After the battle at Wreckers Gate they renounced violence and migrated to the Landsend Plateau.

tani—(TA-nee) at its shoulder a tani is nearly as tall as a grown man, covered in thick yellow fur with one black stripe extending down each side. Incisors curve out of its mouth and down to its chin.

Tharn—one of the three Guardians of Melekath, also known as the Fist. It killed Gerath at Treeside.

Thrikyl—kingdom south of Qarath where Rome used the black axe to bring down the walls.

Truebane Mountains—mountains where Ankha del'Ath, the abandoned Takare capital, is.

trunk lines – the huge flows of LifeSong that branch directly off the River. From the trunk lines the feeder lines branch off, and off the feeder lines come the individual flows that directly sustain every living thing.

Tu Sinar—god of Landsend Plateau.

Veragin—dead city Rome's army finds at the end of the summer campaign. The people there worshipped Gorim.

Windcaller—men reputed to be able to call the wind and make it serve them. They are considered blasphemers by the Tenders.

Windfollower—name given by the Takare to Shakre.

Wreckers Gate—the name of the main gate at Ankha del'Ath, ancestral home of the Takare. According to the Takare, the wealth and acclaim they received as the Empire's greatest heroes blinded them. Eventually a rogue Takare led the Takare still living at Ankha del'Ath to rebel and the great gate was shut. The Takare legions returned home and slaughtered their kinsmen. When they realized what they had done, they threw down their weapons, forswore violence, and moved to the Landsend Plateau, where the affairs of the world could no longer tempt them.

Xochitl—(SO-sheel) also known as the Mother of Life, the deity followed by the Tenders.

Youlin—(YOU-lin) young Pastwalker from Mad River Shelter. She awakens the Takare warriors to their past lives.

ABOUT THE AUTHOR

Born in 1965, I grew up on a working cattle ranch in the desert thirty miles from Wickenburg, Arizona, which at that time was exactly the middle of nowhere. Work, cactus and heat were plentiful, forms of recreation were not. The TV got two channels when it wanted to, and only in the evening after someone hand cranked the balky diesel generator to life. All of which meant that my primary form of escape was reading.

At 18 I escaped to Tucson where I attended the University of Arizona. A number of fruitless attempts at productive majors followed, none of which stuck. Discovering I liked writing, I tried journalism two separate times, but had to drop it when I realized that I had no intention of conducting interviews with actual people but preferred simply making them up.

After graduating with a degree in Creative Writing in 1989, I backpacked Europe with a friend and caught the travel bug. With no meaningful job prospects, I hitchhiked around the U.S. for a while then went back to school to learn to be a high school English teacher. I got a teaching job right out of school in the middle of the year. The job lasted exactly one semester, or until I received my summer pay and realized I actually had money to continue backpacking.

The next stop was Australia, where I hoped to spend six months, working wherever I could, then a few months in New Zealand and the South Pacific Islands. However, my plans changed irrevocably when I met a lovely Swiss woman, Claudia, in Alice Springs. Undoubtedly swept away by my lack of a job or real future, she agreed to allow me to follow her back to Switzerland where, a few months later, she gave up her job to continue traveling with me. Over the next couple years we backpacked the U.S., Eastern Europe and Australia/New Zealand, before marrying and settling in the mountains of Colorado, in a small town called Salida.

In Colorado we started our own electronics business (because, you know, my Creative Writing background totally prepared me for installing home theater systems), and had a couple of sons, Dylan and Daniel. In 2005 we shut the business down and moved back to Tucson where we currently live.